ENVY

A SINFUL EMPIRE TRILOGY (BOOK 3)

EVA CHARLES

QUARRY ROAD PUBLISHING

Copyright © 2022 by Eva Charles

ALL RIGHTS RESERVED

No part of this book may be used or reproduced in any form whatsoever without express written permission from the author or publisher, except in the case of brief quotations embedded in critical articles and reviews.

This book is a work of fiction. Any references to historical events, real people, or real places are used fictitiously. All other names, characters, places, and incidents are products of the author's imagination. Any resemblance to actual events, places, organizations, or persons living or dead is entirely coincidental.

Murphy Rae, Cover Design

Dawn Alexander, Evident Ink, Content Editor

Nancy Smay, Evident Ink, Copy Editor

Faith Williams, The Atwater Group, Proofreader

Virginia Tesi Carey, Proofreader

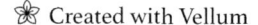

❦ Created with Vellum

A Sinful Empire Trilogy is dedicated to the three amigas, and the courageous women they represent. Women who knew that every successful revolution begins with the resistance.

Uneasy lies the head that wears a crown.

— WILLIAM SHAKESPEARE

NOTE TO READERS

Dear Reader,
    Welcome back to Porto! I trust you are here because you have read Greed and Lust. Envy is the final book in A Sinful Empire Trilogy. It is not a standalone.

Envy has two epilogues. There is one topic, in particular, that I believe readers will want fully addressed, but I couldn't do it justice in the story without slowing the pacing. I completed that circle in the first epilogue. The second epilogue is my gift to you for reading all three books. There is also a lengthy author's note, at the end, for anyone who likes a behind the scenes peek.

I do have a disclaimer: Redemption comes in all shapes and sizes, but Antonio is Antonio. While he does experience some continued character growth throughout the series, as does Daniela, he's still difficult and challenging. I believe the apt term is Alpha-hole. It would be disingenuous to turn him into a choir boy. Not only would it be a total personality change over the course of a year, but more importantly, it's just not who he is. If that's what you've been waiting for, I'm so sorry.

Finally, for those who experience emotional triggers, please know that **this is not a safe story.** In addition to the dark elements one would expect to find in a novel featuring a dangerous antihero, many of the difficult themes from Lust are revisited in Envy. Proceed cautiously, and feel free to contact me with any questions or concerns.

Thank you so much for reading Envy! I hope you love the conclusion to Daniela and Antonio's epic love story.

xoxo
Eva

PROLOGUE

Antonio

As I race toward the boat, Rafael's at the edge of the ramp, ahead, his tongue buried in a blonde's mouth.

I run straight toward them, and yank him off the startled woman. "We have a problem. It might be a bomb. Get to the pier as fast as you can. Now!" I roar, as he gapes at me, wide-eyed.

I don't wait to answer questions. I keep going, shouting for people to get off the ramp, even though I'm not absolutely certain where the danger lies. *But it's somewhere near the water. I'm sure of it.*

So many innocent people milling around. The race is over and my crew has family and friends on the boat. *Children.* But Valentina is all I think about—and Daniela. If something happens to that girl, her mother won't survive it. I have to get to her before it's too late.

"Go to the pier. Now!" I bark, at everyone I pass.

This part of the river is shallow along the bank, but it gets deep quickly. Valentina's not a strong swimmer. She's only had a couple weeks of formal lessons. If she's propelled any distance from the boat, even conscious, she's likely to panic—and drown.

"Abandon ship," I yell, before I even climb aboard. The boat's not sinking—not yet—but it signals the crew to get off the boat immediately.

I don't see Valentina—or Alexis. And where the hell are Santi and Mia? The blood pounds in my ears so hard, I can't think. "Where's Valentina?" I shout as people jump off the boat.

Lucas grabs me. "What the fuck is going on?"

"Danger from the water. We don't have time. Valentina? Where's Valentina?"

"Out there," Rafael says, pointing toward the river.

Santi has her, and they're swimming away from the boat. Mia's with them. I also spot Alexis, who is a strong swimmer, surrounded by guards not far behind them.

"What the fuck are you doing here?" I scream at Rafael, dragging him to the edge of the boat. "Swim as fast as you can toward Santi and Valentina. Stay with her."

"Go," Lucas shouts at me. "I'll make sure everyone's off."

This is my boat, my crew, and my responsibility. "I'm not going fucking anywhere until I know everyone's off this boat."

Lucas doesn't waste time or breath arguing. He scours one end of the boat for stragglers while I scour the other. When we're satisfied everyone's off, we dive into the river, away from the boat.

As we surface, we're showered with debris.

1

DANIELA

Rescue workers, along with several of Antonio's soldiers who were securing the pier, rush past me toward the river.

Thiago, Antonio's driver, grabs my arm before I get more than a few yards down the ramp. "*Senhora*, please don't go to the river. If you do, you'll take men away from the rescue. They'll need to protect you from whatever danger is down there."

I freeze. He's right. As much as I want to go to the riverbank, I don't want to take anyone's attention from the rescue. I need them to get to Valentina. And Alexis. And Antonio—and everyone else who's down there. I'd never forgive myself if anyone died because men were protecting me.

Thiago turns to Alvarez, who's scowling beside me. "Leave two men with me, another at the top of the ramp, and take everyone else to the river. I'll stay with her."

Alvarez's glare is stony, but he obeys without argument.

"I can't leave," I plead, peering into Thiago's eyes. "Everyone I love is down there." I'm not leaving without them. *I won't.*

"We'll stay put for now," he assures me. "There's too much

chaos between here and the car, and it's impossible to know what's happening on the river." Thiago pulls me to the railing, at the edge of the ramp farthest from the river, with a high stone barrier behind us. "This is the safest place for you right now."

Safety is the least of my concerns.

I cup my elbows, and bounce on tiptoe, trying to ward off the helplessness and despair as I search the river for any sign of life. The dense smoke makes it impossible to see anything.

The girls must be terrified.

"Antonio, where are you? Come back to me, dammit, and bring the girls with you. *Please.* Please," I beg, softly, over and over, while the emotion twists inside my heavy chest.

"He wrestled a far more dangerous river with a clear head," Thiago murmurs, with a hand on my shoulder. "He'll survive this, too, and he won't let anything happen to Valentina. You need to keep the faith."

Thiago was with him in the swollen river that day. Antonio's quick thinking saved both of their lives. I'm sure he wants to be down at the river searching for his boss right now, instead of guarding me. *I want him to be there, too.*

"Thiago," I grab his arm, "go to him. I'll be fine with the men who are here."

"No," he says adamantly, without considering it for a single second. "I'm exactly where he'd want me. If anything happens to you, he'll never be the same."

His voice drifts away, but I hear the words, although I don't process them—not then.

My energy is focused on the river, trying to locate the boat through the smoke. I still can't see it. "It's gone. The boat's gone," I sob. *They're gone.*

"No," he says gently, wiping the tears from my face with the edge of his sleeve. "The sails are gone, and the boat—at least part of it—is there." He points to an area off the bank.

I stare for a long while before I can make out the outline through the thinning smoke. One side of the boat appears to be submerged. *But it's there.*

A sense of hope surges inside, tamping down the despair. *Maybe. Just maybe.*

The blast didn't seem to have been as powerful as the one at Santa Ana's—not as loud, anyway. Still, no one survives an explosion. *I've been down this road before.*

Not unless they made it into the water.

I imagine Valentina gulping dirty water and gasping for breath while the river drags her to its muddy bottom. The thought consumes me, eviscerating the hope I had a moment before.

As the panic rises, my chest tightens until I'm having difficulty breathing. "Valentina can't swim." *Drowning is such an awful death. And terrifying.*

"She's not alone," Thiago replies calmly. "Antonio, Lucas, Santi, Mia—they're all strong swimmers. Lucas will protect Antonio above all else, but Santi and Mia are there strictly for Valentina." He clears his throat. "Antonio will protect her with his life. I'm certain of it."

I'm certain, too. "If he can get to her. It's a big if, Thiago. And it's not enough. I want them both back." *I'm not trading one person I love for another.*

"Faith, *senhora*. Even if you don't have faith in the Almighty, have faith in your husband. He's the man you'd want in the river with you."

No one knows this better than Thiago. Listen to him. I try. But it's hard to put my faith in God at times like this. He's let me down before. And regardless of what anyone believes, Antonio is human. Blood flows through his veins. His heart beats. I felt the steady flutter against my cheek, just last night, as I fell asleep on his chest. *He's not invincible.*

"Do you see them?" I ask, in a voice that sounds frightened and faithless. "Do you see anyone?"

He doesn't reply, but his gaze, like mine, is glued to the river.

Out of the corner of my eye, I spot two motor boats zipping through the water, and a third following. They're moving at such a high rate of speed the bows are out of the water. "Are those rescue boats?"

"That's the safety patrol, and the Huntsman support boat that's used during races in case there's an issue on the water."

Thank God. But what are they doing? They're going in the wrong direction. "Why are they headed away from the explosion?"

"Look over there," he says, pointing to the area where two of the boats have stopped.

There appear to be several heads bopping above the water, but they're so far away, I can't make out anyone. *If only I had the binoculars. They're in the tote bag, with my phone.*

I quickly scan the ramp for my bag. It's not here. I must have left it on the pier. Unlike my family, everything in it is replaceable. *I'll worry about it later—when they're safe. Please God, let them all be safe.*

"They're pulling people out of the water," Thiago says with the first sound of real optimism I've heard.

My heart leaps.

"Can you see who's out there?"

He shakes his head.

As the first boat pulls away, Thiago's phone rings. "Yes?"

The muscles in his face soften. "She's standing right here beside me. Not a hair on her head was harmed." Thiago's voice is thick. "The upper ramp. Certainly." He hands me the phone and nods with a gentle smile.

"I have her, *Princesa*. She's safe. Alexis, too."

At the sound of Antonio's raspy voice, the tears that have been threatening trickle down my cheeks. "And you?"

"It takes a lot to put down the devil."

I bring my hand to my mouth. "Is she hurt? What about you? Where's Rafael? Is everyone accounted for?" He already told me the girls are safe. And he's winded, but otherwise, he sounds okay, too. But I need to hear him say it again. *And again* —until I can see them with my own eyes.

"Valentina swallowed some water, but she's fine. Rafael is with the girls, Santi, and Mia in the support boat. They're on their way to Huntsman Lodge."

My heart stops. "You're not with them?"

"Not without you."

"Antonio—"

"You have my word that they're in good hands and that no harm will come to them."

I nod, although he can't see it. He wouldn't take a risk with the girls. Or Rafael. I know he wouldn't.

"Let me speak to Thiago," he says, brusquely.

I have so many more questions, but they'll have to wait. I reluctantly hand back the phone and watch carefully while Thiago speaks with Antonio. His expression is serious. Almost grim. "Yes," he replies. "Of course. You have my word."

As Thiago ends the call, Alvarez approaches from the lower ramp. He barely spares me a glance.

"Why don't you get the car," he tells Thiago. "I'll stay with her."

"No," Thiago replies gruffly, pulling out a gun. He doesn't point it at Alvarez—or at anyone. He just holds it near his thigh. "I have orders to stay with *Senhora* Daniela. The boss is on his way."

Alvarez nods, his eyes shifting from Thiago to me, then back. "It seems I'm not needed here. I'll go see where I can help." Despite what Alvarez says, he doesn't go toward the river. He jogs up the ramp to the pier.

I always assumed Thiago carried a weapon, but I've never seen him pull it out. I've also never seen him pull rank before, although he's well within his right. He has more seniority and clout than Alvarez. Before he became Antonio's driver, Thiago was his personal guard—a highly capable soldier. I glance at the white streaks peppering his dark hair. *But he's not so young anymore.*

Something happened with Alvarez. It could be just that Antonio's angry that he didn't stay with me on the ramp. *He is my personal guard.* But it feels like something more. "What's going on?" I ask Thiago.

"Antonio will be here shortly."

He doesn't say another word.

2

ANTONIO

I get a message from Lucas as the boat pulls ashore some distance from where the explosion happened. **Your phone has been populated from the backup. Safe to use.**

Anything on Cristiano?

Nothing.

I scroll through my contacts, and press Send when I get to the bastard's name. "You fucking sonofabitch," I shout into the phone.

"I told you I'd send your traitor on a silver platter. It's a figure of speech, not to be taken literally." Fedorov clucks. "I thought you were smarter than that."

"Do you realize how many people might have died because of your little stunt?"

"The timing was unfortunate, but I assure you the tardy messenger has been dealt with decisively. I understand no one died."

"Where's Cristiano?"

"Nikitin has him."

The oligarch. Fuck.

"Alvarez is the traitor?" I spit out, failing to keep my fury in check. *The bastard had access to my wife.*

"He is." Fedorov sighs deeply. "Always a punch to the gut when it's someone close."

Alvarez wouldn't be the worst punch to the gut. "Is Cristiano involved in any way?"

"Doubtful." He pauses. "Although I can't say for certain."

Fedorov's playing me. He wants to plant a kernel of doubt about Cristiano. *Or maybe he's telling the truth.* I push the thought away, but an uneasiness lingers.

"You're going to help me get him back, or you will never see another shipment move through Porto. I'll do everything in my power to destroy you."

"Calm down," he tuts, pissing me off even more than I already am.

"Don't tell me to fucking calm down. Who set off the bomb?"

"Unclear."

"What's your best guess?"

He sighs. "My best guess is that Alvarez planted the bomb on Nikitin's order. But if that's accurate, there was some sort of hiccup."

"What do you mean?"

"From what I've heard, neither you nor your wife were on the boat when it exploded. It seems like a lot of trouble to kill a couple of kids and your crew. Other than embarrassing you, it would serve little purpose. Unless…" His voice drifts off.

"Unless, what?"

"Unless the girl was the target."

My blood runs cold. He knows something about Valentina. Although, with Tomas dead, why is Valentina an issue? *Doesn't make sense.* I keep quiet and let him talk.

"Her father's powerful. He has more enemies than both of us combined."

He's not talking about Valentina. He's talking about Alexis.

"That's far-fetched."

"I suppose."

"I want Cristiano."

"I'm prepared to help return him to you, but I want one thing in exchange."

"What?"

"I want to have dinner with your lovely bride."

I want to have dinner with your lovely bride? He can't possibly have just said that.

"I'm getting off a boat. I missed the last thing you said."

"I want to have dinner with your lovely bride."

My blood begins to boil. Not a slow simmer. It's bubbling vigorously, about to spill over. "*No*," I growl. "What the fuck is wrong with you?"

"That's my price. Nonnegotiable."

"You'll need to come up with something else, because I was deadly serious about destroying you."

"There's nothing I want more than to meet the woman who's cast a spell on the king of a Port empire. You rule the region with an iron fist. Yet you've let this young thing under your skin—maybe even into your dark heart. Unwise, but entirely human, I might add. Nevertheless, I want to experience her magic firsthand."

"You fucking . . ."

"Not like that. Don't be a jackass. I want to have dinner with her. Just dinner. You can be there, of course. Maybe I'll even include Raisa, if that makes your *princesa* more comfortable."

"I'm done." He's lucky I can't get my hands on him right now, because the only people he'd be having dinner with are his ancestors.

"Think carefully before you hang up in a jealous rage." His tone has changed from doddering fool to sober *Pakhan*, on a dime. "You're asking for an enormous favor. You want me to betray my countrymen, perhaps even my president. There's no telling from how far up the order to abduct Cristiano came. I'm just asking for a couple of hours with some good food and better vodka."

And my wife. That's a deal breaker.

I don't respond. Fedorov might be an asshole, but he's right about one thing: I'm asking for a huge favor.

There's got to be another way to get Cristiano out of there.

"Think about my proposal, but don't take too long. There's no telling the circumstances under which your friend is being held."

I end the call without pleasantries and stride up the ramp to Daniela. When I make the final turn, she lunges toward me, but Thiago grabs her elbow and says something. She nods, and he releases her. His orders were to keep Daniela exactly where she was until I arrived, and to protect her with his life, if necessary. I also instructed him to shoot Alvarez if he got anywhere near her.

When I'm a few feet away, Daniela leaps into my arms. *I am so goddamn grateful that I didn't have to give her bad news.*

I hold her against my body and extend my hand to my driver. I've always prized loyalty, but after today, I have an even greater appreciation for it.

Thiago and several guards flank us, but they turn their backs to give us a private moment.

"You're hurt," Daniela murmurs, her brow furrowed as she examines my shoulder. "Your shirt's charred. That looks like a terrible burn."

The explosion occurred just as we surfaced, and I was hit by some smoldering debris. At the time, I was so hopped up on adrenaline that I didn't even feel it. Now my wet shirt's stuck to the lesion and it's burning like a sonofabitch.

"It's nothing. Just a few scratches." I hear the helicopter

landing on the pier. I'll breathe easier once she's on it, and we're in the air.

"You need to see a doctor. Do the girls need to be checked? Are you sure they're okay?"

I want to taste her, but if I do, I'll only want more, and there's no damn time for more. "I'm sure."

She sinks her teeth into her plump lip.

Fuck it. I slide my fingers into the hair at the nape of her neck and take her mouth roughly. The kiss is quick and demanding—and nowhere near enough.

"They'll see a doctor," I assure her, through a ragged breath. "It's already been arranged. But we need to get to the pier. The helicopter is waiting to take us back."

Daniela cradles my jaw in her hands. "Thank you for staying with her. For keeping her safe." Her eyes are glazed with unshed tears. "And for coming back to me in one piece."

I bring her fingers to my mouth. "I'll always keep her safe. And I'll always come back to you, *Princesa*. I'll find you wherever you are. Never doubt it."

I hold her against my side as we climb the short distance to the pier. She's soft and warm against my damp skin. She's also strong. It must have been hell for her as she waited for news. I would have done anything to spare her that heartache. She's had enough tragedy and upheaval in her life. She deserves peace. I need to find a way to give it to her.

I would have done anything for Cristiano. *Maybe I still would.* But I won't take a risk with Daniela. I'm not letting Fedorov anywhere near her. I don't trust him.

There has to be something else he wants.

3

DANIELA

Antonio tucks me under his arm and leads me up the ramp, his eyes scanning the pier as we approach.

"What's going on with Alvarez?" I ask, only half expecting an answer. "Thiago pulled out a gun when he approached us on the ramp."

Antonio doesn't respond.

"He didn't point it at him or anything." *Now I feel a bit silly for bringing it up.* "Maybe it was a coincidence."

"Only fools put stock in coincidences. Trust your instincts. Alvarez is a traitor."

There is no discernable emotion in his voice. *That's when Antonio is most treacherous.*

My heart falls into my stomach, as I grab his forearm. "What?"

"He's no longer your concern," he says, sharply, slamming the door on any further discussion.

Alvarez was my guard. Assigned to my protection by Antonio himself. He had access to my child. To our home. If he hasn't already, he's going to have a brutal end.

I have no sympathy for him. If he's a traitor, my family was at risk. As far as I'm concerned, his end can't be brutal enough.

Before I can push for more information about Alvarez, a tall, dark-haired guard who appears to be in his early thirties, approaches with my tote bag. I think his name is Duarte.

"You dropped this when the explosion occurred, *senhora*." He turns to my husband before handing me the bag. "It never left my sight."

Antonio nods.

"Thank you," I say, taking the tote. Everything inside might be replaceable, but I'm grateful not to have to wade through the bureaucracy.

"My pleasure, *senhora*."

As Antonio and I continue across the pier, I have so many questions spinning in my head—most of them about Valentina's condition. But he's told me all he knows, so I try something else.

"Did the explosion have anything to do with the package you received earlier?"

"The package was a heads-up."

What kind of heads-up? I want to ask, but we're climbing into the helicopter, and even I know now's not the time.

———

After we land, we go directly to a private elevator in Huntsman Lodge, where the girls are receiving medical care. "I know you're resourceful, but I'm still surprised you were able to get a doctor here so quickly."

"We've always had a staffed clinic here for emergencies, but after my accident we beefed it up. It's relatively small, but state-of-the-art and highly secure."

Because it's not safe to be in a hospital after someone tries to kill you. They're large and unwieldy, with people coming and going through too many entrances and exits. Hospitals can't be fully secured.

What kind of life have I brought Valentina into?

She was in danger from the moment the seed was planted. That had nothing to do with Antonio.

He lowers his face to the retinal scan and the doors open to a long hallway with gleaming floors, soft white walls, and bright overhead lighting. It's pristine. Antonio nods to the two guards flanking the inner doorway.

"The girls are safe here. As are you. But don't leave this wing—under any condition—without checking with me first."

"Somehow I doubt the guards will let me leave without your blessing."

"Not if they want to live to see the sun set."

God help anyone who crosses him today.

A woman dressed in scrubs greets us just inside. "*Boa tarde.* Valentina and Alexis are in room three, and Rafael's in room five." She smiles. "Although I'm not sure he's actually in the room."

Antonio mutters something under his breath about Rafael, and I thank the woman before following him down the hall.

"Has anyone been in touch with Alexis's parents?" I ask. *Her father's going to be furious. It took a lot of prodding before he allowed her to come back with us.*

"Alexis spoke with them briefly from the boat. They're on their way."

I hope Antonio's around to face them with me—especially Will.

The clinic might be more contained than a hospital, but it's larger than I expected, with several rooms off the main corridor. Perhaps a dozen. Even though we're moving at a good clip, it's taking us forever to get to the girls.

Although maybe the walk seems particularly long because there's a broody, preoccupied Antonio beside me.

He might be quiet, but it's not a peaceful silence. Someone

is going to pay with their life for what happened today. *As they should.*

While I'm feeling vengeful, I'm not as shaken up as I was after the explosion at Santa Ana's. Maybe it's because I know Valentina and Antonio are safe—that everyone's safe—and I need to remain calm for the girls. Or maybe it's because even though Antonio shares very little with me, I'm no longer firmly on the outside.

Two months ago, he would have never told me that Alvarez was a traitor, or that the package contained a warning. They're just crumbs, but a collection of crumbs can be the foundation for a satisfying meal.

I glance at his shoulder. It looks angry and painful. The wound is open, oozing through the charred fabric. The shirt fibers appear to be part of the wound. "Promise me you'll let a doctor treat that burn."

He nods. Although it's nothing more than a halfhearted attempt to pacify me.

"That's not a promise, Antonio. Open wounds get infected quickly. You can't threaten the germs away. They're not afraid of you, even when you're in a mood."

His mouth twitches as he pauses outside room three. "I'll have someone take a look at it."

"A doctor. Not Cristiano or Lucas."

He swallows hard. "Valentina and Alexis are inside. Go. I need to find out who blew up the boat."

"And you need to take care of your shoulder," I say, firmly, pushing open the door.

4

ANTONIO

My phone rings, and I duck into an empty treatment room to take Will's call. His shit is the last thing I need right now. But it's his kid, my explosion, and he's entitled.

"Yeah."

"Don't fucking 'yeah' me. I want to know how my daughter's faring."

He's a bigger pain in the ass than I am.

"The doctor's examining her, but it's just a precaution. The river's warm this time of year, and she didn't spend much time in it, anyway. You should be proud. Alexis is a strong swimmer, and she kept her wits about her in the midst of total chaos. Takes after her mother in that regard."

He snickers, and some of his anxiety seems to dissipate. "How's Valentina?"

"Okay. She's not much of a swimmer yet, but despite that, she remained calm enough to be rescued." No small thanks to Santi and Mia, who deserve a huge bonus and a month off. *They can have the former, but the latter is not happening.*

"It seems everywhere you go, Huntsman, an explosion follows. What the fuck is that all about?"

"Not entirely sure. The explosion at the church makes more sense than what happened today."

"How so?"

"The bomb caused a lot of havoc, but it was amateur. I don't know if the boat's salvageable, but it's mostly intact. The device had to be on the boat—not nearby, actually on board. I would have expected it to have been blown to smithereens."

"Bombs are incredibly finicky. Even in the hands of an expert."

"I know. But even the timing makes no sense whatsoever. The race was over. The boat was docked. Our boat usually wins. By usually, I mean every year. It's a running joke. If we'd won, no one would have been on the boat. We would have been headed to the winner's circle."

"It might have been a shot across the bow, so to speak. But I wouldn't put all my eggs in that basket."

Not putting all my eggs anywhere.

"Any chance this is blowback from the package I had delivered to you recently?"

"Possibly."

But not likely. Chernov left the country after he was summoned home. Lucas verified it. Other than him, I can't think of one person who would be interested in avenging Tomas's *disappearance.*

"I know this is far-fetched, but you and Samantha were at the church, and—"

"Alexis was on the boat." Will sighs. "I thought about it, too. Some fucker could be sending me a warning. Wouldn't be the first time. It's certainly easier to cause problems for me there than it is here. But it would have to be someone with inside information."

The bile rises in my throat.

"The wedding was one thing," he continues, "but I didn't give Alexis permission to travel until about ten minutes before they left for the airport. I did that on purpose to keep her whereabouts under the radar. And how would have anyone known she was going to be on the boat at precisely that time? It's a stretch."

"I agree. But I don't want to gloss over anything. That's not how I run an investigation."

"I'm putting together a team to assist."

I don't respond. I like Will, and he might be family, but there's no way he's barging in and taking over an investigation in my city.

"Your lead," he adds. "They move on your orders."

I can live with that. "The additional manpower will be helpful."

"They'll be on the ground before you lay your head on the pillow. I want a piece of the fuckers who forced my daughter into a river. What do you need?"

"Right now, extra hands would be the biggest help. I have men on the pier and along the bank searching for evidence, and divers combing the river for bomb components. We'll drag the whole damn thing if we have to. We also have feeds to sift through, but that will have to wait until we've swept and secured our equipment. We should be fully operational within the hour."

"You think you were infiltrated?"

Sooner or later, it happens in every organization. Still, it kills me to admit. But I don't hide behind my failures—I just make sure not to repeat them. "I know we were."

"I'm listening."

I fill him in on the Russians, Alvarez, Cristiano—and Fedorov's latest demand. I'm dispassionate and clear-headed as I lay out the cards. Rage and hatred account for a myriad of the world's poor decisions. I won't allow them to skew my calculations.

"I can't believe that sonofabitch involved your wife in a deal. Only the fucking Russians."

The cartels aren't above it either. But they're usually not interested in breaking bread.

"What are you going to do?" he asks, with rare empathy in his voice.

"I'm not sure I have a goddamn choice. If I make the deal, he wins. If I don't, he knows without a shadow of a doubt that I would make any sacrifice for her. That might be an even bigger win."

"Not might be. It would be a huge win for him. Right now, it's all supposition. But if you sacrifice your buddy to save Daniela from spending a few hours with that slimy asshole, he'll never wonder again. When Fedorov wants something big, he'll know just how to go about getting it."

It's all true, but it might not be just a few hours with a slimy asshole. I could be sending her into a trap. "It's only easy from where you sit."

"I never said it was easy. I said the alternative is untenable."

"There's got to be something else he wants."

"He's at the top of the food chain, fat and happy. My best guess is that he's not budging on this."

There's always another way. Always. We don't like to look there first, because it's often messy. I'd never touch his family, but I wouldn't hesitate to kill him with my bare hands and call it a good day's work.

"Hey," he says, pulling me out of my head. "Whatever you're thinking? Forget it. We're not talking about some two-bit Bratva soldier. He's the *Pakhan*. If you fail, everyone and everything you love will suffer. It'll be brutal for them. They'll keep you alive long enough to witness every atrocity."

"Then I won't fail."

"The consequences are likely to be the same if you succeed. It'll just be Fedorov's successor meting them out. We're talking dinner. You pick the time and the place. No one's more unreasonable than I am when it comes to my family, but you've got to put this in perspective."

"Dinner is bad enough. But you know as well as I do that it could be a setup. I don't believe for one second, that in my shoes, you'd expose Samantha to that kind of danger."

"You're wrong. I'm telling you, you're wrong. Would I need a mild sedative and a fifth of gin to make it through the evening without using my steak knife as a weapon? You bet your ass. But I would do it because it's the best option to ensure her long-term safety. For me, every decision comes down to that."

You're not alone. Since her father died, I've made few decisions where I didn't consider her safety paramount.

There's a knock on the door, and Lucas sticks his head in. I motion for him to come inside. It's a good excuse to get rid of Will. I've heard enough.

"Lucas is here. I need to see what he needs. I'll talk to you when you get here."

"We have a lead on Alvarez," Lucas says, as I toss my phone on the bed.

His name alone is enough to summon my demons. "Bring him to me alive."

"I figured you'd want to question him."

"Not me. That fucking traitor isn't getting one second of my attention."

Lucas nods. "I'll take care of it."

"No. You have enough on your plate. Mia's going to do it. We'll tell her what we want to know, and she'll be the one to encourage him to talk."

"Mia?"

Alvarez is old school, all the way. "There's nothing that will humiliate that asshole more than torture and death at the hands of a woman."

"Brilliant. Wish I'd thought of it."

"How long before the servers are good to go and all the passwords changed?"

"Forty minutes, give or take. Enough time to get that shoulder cleaned up."

"It's fine."

"You're not going to be able to get that shirt off without causing a shitload of problems for yourself. We're in a clinic, Antonio, and everything that can be done to track the sonofabitches is being done. Let me get a doctor."

"Do it," I mutter begrudgingly. He's right. "Anything to get you to stop nagging."

Lucas pauses as though he's going to say something, but then he hesitates. He knows about the recording, and about my call with Fedorov, but there's been no time to hash any of it out. I'm sure he's torn up about Cristiano. It's been the three of us for most of our lives.

"Say what's on your mind. Go ahead."

He peers at me from the doorway. "Cristiano isn't a traitor." His voice is thick with emotion. *He sounds a lot like I feel.*

"Get the doctor, and we'll talk while he fixes my shoulder."

5

DANIELA

Valentina and Alexis are together in a room, with a privacy screen between them. Mia is with them, as is one of Alexis's guards. I want to go straight to Valentina, but Alexis is in the bed closest to the door, and a doctor is with her. I go to her first, putting my hand on her arm and kissing the top of her head. "It's so good to see you, sweetheart."

I turn to the doctor. "How is she?"

"So far, everything looks great."

"I've been on a sailboat that's capsized," Alexis says, "so I was prepared. My father is probably popping an aneurysm, though."

Probably more than one. "They'll be here soon. I'm sure it helps him to know that you're okay."

"I doubt it." She grins as I make my way around the screen to my child.

"Lala," Valentina says softly. Like Alexis, she's wearing a hospital gown. Her hair is wet, and she looks a bit washed-out, but otherwise, she's perfect.

"*Querida.*" Somehow, I manage to keep the sob in my throat. I squeeze Mia's hand in gratitude, as I make my way around a nurse to the head of the bed, where I wrap my arms around my girl.

I press my lips to the top of her damp head. As I inhale the lingering stank of the river, it hits me like a wrecking ball. I squeeze my eyes tight. *I could have lost her—lost them both. If not for some quick thinking and a little luck—I would have lost everything. It all came down to seconds.*

This is not helpful, Daniela. Pull yourself together. Now.

"We're just about finished," the doctor announces, as I regain my composure. "Let's get rid of this screen so the girls can see each other while they chat."

"How is Valentina?" I ask with bated breath.

"We'll do a few blood tests and take some chest x-rays. Then we'll move the girls down the hall into a more comfortable room while we wait for the results. We'll monitor them for a few hours and if nothing changes, they can go home."

Chest x-rays? "Why a chest x-ray?"

"Just to be sure that water isn't anywhere it shouldn't be."

I nod, while I think about how to ask about water, and lungs, and amoebas in a way that won't alarm the girls.

"There's nothing to worry about," the doctor assures me. "Ordinarily I would recommend a watch-and-wait approach before ordering the x-ray, but *Senhor* Antonio isn't a big fan of watch and wait."

No surprise there.

"It's a non-invasive test," she continues, "and unlike in a hospital, cost isn't a consideration."

"Santi held onto me the whole time I was in the water," Valentina says, pulling my attention away from the matter of the x-ray. "And Mia told me what to do while we were swimming. She talked to me the whole time."

I smile at Mia, who hasn't changed out of her wet clothes.

"Then Antonio came, and the boats," Valentina adds. "As soon as I saw Antonio, I knew everything would be okay."

As soon as I saw Antonio, I knew everything would be okay. I find myself thinking that way sometimes, too—and I don't like it. Not for me, and not for her, and not for Antonio. It's unhealthy. Antonio's not our savior. He doesn't need that responsibility. And Valentina needs to believe that she can save herself. No man required.

"Mia, I'm here now, if you want to go change into dry clothes."

She shakes her head. "Santi is changing. When he gets back, I'll go. But thank you."

Mia is a woman in an overwhelmingly male profession. My father had no female soldiers, and Antonio has very few. Mia is the only one who is actually a guard. She's a good role model for Valentina.

"Rafael said that there was some type of malfunction with the sailboat," Alexis says, watching me with keen eyes. "It must have had a backup motor."

It seems like more than idle curiosity. *She's suspicious.* Alexis has been sheltered to some degree, but she's more worldly and sophisticated than Valentina.

"They haven't gotten to the bottom of it yet," I explain. "But they're working on it."

There's a quick rap on the door, and then it swings open to Rafael Huntsman dressed in blue scrubs. *No hospital gown for him.* Valentina's face lights up, and he has Alexis's attention, too.

When he enters the room, he holds out his arms. "What, a party, and you didn't invite me?"

The girls practically squeal in unison.

The doctor has both hands on her hips. "Have you been examined, *senhor*?"

She has Rafael's number.

"I'm good to go," he quips.

"We're not finished here, so you actually will have to go."

The doctor turns to me. "If you don't mind, it would be easier if you waited outside, too. We put both girls in here so they could stay together, but it's awfully crowded, and we need to get blood and x-rays."

When I don't respond, she keeps talking. "There's a waiting room down the hall. Someone will get you some coffee or tea. We'll set the girls up for a shower, and then get them to a homier room where they can watch a movie and have something to eat. As soon as they're settled, we'll come and get you. It won't be long."

I'm not ready to leave them just yet, but I don't want to make the staff's life any more difficult. I glance from Valentina to Alexis. "Will you girls be okay without me for a little while?"

"Yes," they say, like they're sixteen and I'm cramping their style.

I glance at Valentina.

"I'm not a baby, Daniela," she says dismissively. "You worry too much."

You have no idea.

"I'll walk you to the waiting room," Rafael murmurs, taking my elbow.

By the time we reach the doorway, the girls are giggling about something.

Maybe I'll take my worrying self down the hall to check on Antonio's shoulder.

6

DANIELA

"Has a doctor actually examined you?"

"I'm totally fine," Rafael replies, evading my question. "We weren't in the river long. I'm only here because Antonio insisted, and I've already pissed him off enough for one day."

He doesn't do it on purpose, but Rafael knows how to push Antonio's buttons better than anyone—except for me. I press my lips together, to hide my amusement. "What did you do?"

"Right before the explosion, he told me to get to the pier, and I followed him to the boat, instead." He wriggles his eyebrows.

Oh my God. "I'm sure he was upset that you walked right into the danger. He loves you."

Rafael shrugs. Love is one of those damning emotions that makes the Huntsman men uncomfortable. "I didn't do anything he wouldn't have done. But he's stubborn and refuses to see it."

Stubbornness, like evading questions, must be in the Huntsman genes, too.

"Have you seen Antonio?" I ask.

"Not since the boat. But a short while ago, Lucas was

looking for a doctor for him."

Good. "Do you think he's still in the clinic?"

"Probably. His shoulder's a mess. And he can't do business upstairs until they sweep everything. But you might want to stay clear of him. He's a bear right now."

I'm not afraid of bears. "You told the girls there was a malfunction on the boat?"

"More or less. I was vague. They were pestering Santi about it, and he won't lie to Valentina—and he shouldn't. Otherwise, trust will become an issue between them, and he'll be no good as her guard. I was just helping him out. They don't need to know every ugly detail."

"I agree with you—and Santi. Although I don't think Alexis bought it."

"Alexis isn't as innocent as Valentina. It's a shame," he laments, like an old soul. "Little girls shouldn't have to worry about things blowing up around them, and people dying left and right. It's no way to grow up. We should keep Valentina sheltered for as long as possible."

I sigh heavily. As much as I'd like to shelter her forever, Valentina needs to understand the world she lives in. At least some of it. But I don't argue. "Where's Cristiano? I haven't seen him at all today."

"He has the flu or something. Didn't make the boat. That's why we lost."

The flu? Hmmm. That's odd. Lara has the flu, too. Stop. You're becoming as suspicious as your husband.

I'd like to ask him about Alvarez, but I'm not sure what he knows, and I don't want to betray Antonio, so I keep my mouth shut.

"Valentina needs to learn to swim," Rafael says in a no-nonsense tone that is eerily similar to Antonio's.

He's right, though. We're surrounded by water, and swimming is more than a recreational pastime.

"She will."

"This is the waiting room." He cocks his head toward the arched doorway. "You'll be comfortable and safe here."

A guard I don't recognize appears out of nowhere and positions himself several feet from the door, with his back toward the wall. "I can see that."

"And in case you're a foolish woman who ignores sound advice, Antonio is in that room right there." He points to a door that we passed across the hall.

"Are you sure? I don't want to walk in on someone else."

"Someone else would be better." He shakes his head. "But you could always knock first." Rafael winks at me. "He's there. I asked Lucas where he was so I could stay far away. I'm no fool." He smirks down at me.

It must have been quite an experience for Antonio when Rafael came to live with him. But good for him, too. *Good for both of them.*

"Whoever did this today," Rafael says soberly, "they're going to pay. Antonio will hunt them down like dogs, and before he's done, they'll be begging to meet their God."

Chilling, but true.

"I'm going to see if I can find someone to sign me out. Do you need anything?"

"I'm all set." I stand on tiptoe and place a small kiss on his cheek. "Valentina's lucky to have you in her life."

"And we're all lucky to have you," he murmurs, giving me a squeeze before lumbering down the hall in search of freedom.

I don't bother to go into the waiting room, but I do ask the guard about a bathroom before I go bear hunting.

———

I'M ABOUT to knock on the door where Antonio is being treated, when I decide it might be better to surprise him. This way he has to tell me to go away to my face.

I slowly push open the door. It's barely cracked when I freeze.

"He wants me to exchange Daniela for Cristiano? Fuck him," Antonio snarls. "He can go straight to hell."

The flu, my ass.

Exchange Cristiano for Daniela. What? Cristiano's been abducted—or at least someone's holding him. *That's what.* And they want to make an exchange—*for me.*

Good Lord. What fresh hell is this?

"Daniela." Lucas's tone is almost accusatory, as he comes around the partition, blocking Antonio from view. His weapon is drawn.

I was careful not to make a sound, but they must have sensed my presence.

"I'm looking for my husband."

"I'll let him know," Lucas mutters, holstering the gun. "Where can he find you?"

Oh no. We're not playing that game. "I'll find him."

I march right into the room, and around Lucas, who doesn't make any attempt to stop me.

Before I step behind the partition, I take a breath. All of a sudden, barging in seems like a bad idea. *Too late now.*

Antonio's sitting on a stool, shirt off, while a doctor wearing headphones works on his shoulder.

He's beautiful, with his sun-kissed skin and hard muscle. But his gaze is sharp and biting. "Is there a problem?"

"Apparently there is. I'd like a private word with you."

His eyes narrow. "I don't have time for bullshit. Say what you came to say. But remember your place." His tone is so menacing that even Lucas flinches.

Remember your place. I have half a mind to grab the alcohol off the supply shelf and douse that ugly burn with the entire bottle.

7

ANTONIO

Daniela's eyes dart from me to the doctor and back. Whatever's on the tip of her tongue, she doesn't want it overheard. While I appreciate her discretion, she better not be here to stick her nose into my business.

Listening at the door is no different than spying. I don't care who you are. Lucas and I were having a private *business* discussion. Daniela knows eavesdropping isn't something I easily forgive. *Especially today.*

Someone put a bomb on my boat, my shoulder's fucked up, and I've had my fill of traitors. Daniela's not a traitor, but I'm sure she overheard something she shouldn't have, and now she wants to offer me her opinion. *Fuck that.*

I glower at her. "He can't hear you. Say what you came to say, or go back to the girls. I'm working."

She holds her head high and shoots me daggers. Normally she aims at least one that breaks the skin, but today, they all bounce off my chest. One after another. And she knows it.

"Someone has Cristiano and—"

I cut her off immediately. "Not your concern."

"Like hell it isn't my concern. I heard you talking when I came in. Someone wants to exchange Cristiano *for me.* How is that not my concern?"

Challenging me, listening at the door—it's all insubordination that I won't tolerate. I don't care if the doctor has no fucking clue. Lucas is here. She knows better.

I glare at her, before yanking the headphones off the doctor. "Get out."

Lucas, who has been staring at his shoes since Daniela first opened her mouth, is eyeing me warily. But no one breathes a word as the doctor scurries out.

When he's gone, I get up and cross the room to the built-in cabinet with a sink. I lean with my back against the countertop and fold my arms over my chest. I don't trust myself to have her within arm's reach. I'm edgy as hell, and she crossed a line.

"Sit down." I cock my chin toward the stool. She bristles at the command, and I'm sure she's tempted to tell me to go fuck myself, but wisely keeps her mouth shut and puts her gorgeous ass on the seat.

"What is it you think you overheard while you were spying on a private business meeting? *My* private business meeting," I hiss.

Undaunted, she peers directly into my eyes. Her self-preservation instincts leave something to be desired, but she has balls. Got to give her that.

"Someone has Cristiano, and they're willing to exchange him for me."

Not quite accurate, but eavesdroppers often miss the fine details.

"Let me guess. You have a suggestion."

She doesn't respond, but she doesn't lower her gaze, either.

"What is it you'd like me to do? Tie a big, pretty bow around your neck, and have a guard drop you off with the Russians?

Shall I send Lucas, or would you prefer Santi to deliver you to your death?"

She winces at the biting sarcasm, but it's well-deserved. The *princesa* needs to be put in her place, and I'm just the man for the job.

"Lucas, do you know how to make a bow? One of those big, fancy ones." My eyes don't leave hers, even as I speak to him. "Do we have red ribbon, anywhere?" Silence. "It's such a nice color for a *princesa*."

Daniela clasps her hands tightly in her lap before she speaks. "Please don't treat me like a child."

Despite the polite way she couches her words, her tone is demanding. *The woman doesn't know when to quit.* Normally I admire her tenacity, but my patience is thin right now and I've about had my fill, when she sticks out her chin and pulls her shoulders back.

"Cristiano is like a brother. To both of you," she says softly, glancing from me to Lucas, who I know admires her grit. "Surely there has to be a way you could make an exchange, or pretend to, while still ensuring my safety. My father would make those sorts of deals whenever thieves tried to blackmail him for grapes."

She's lost her fucking mind. *Does she really think I'd even consider a trade that involved her in that way?*

I'm done with this bullshit.

As I prowl toward her, Daniela's eyes widen, and she lists back on the stool. It's a slight movement, because there's really nowhere for her to go. But I saw it. She's afraid. *And she damn well should be.*

"I'm not your father," I growl, inches from her face. "And you're not a fucking grape."

I turn to Lucas. "Go see what's taking so long with the goddamn servers."

Lucas tips his head in a way that tells me he's concerned about leaving us alone. If I were him, I'd be concerned, too. But he doesn't question it, or ask to have a word outside, like Cristiano would do in this circumstance. Although the look he gives me as he leaves holds a plea for her safety.

8

DANIELA

"Challenging me and spying on my private conversations wasn't enough?" he sneers. "What gives you the right to storm in here and tell me how to conduct my business?"

I'm seated, and he's looming above me in a tirade. We've been here before, and I'm not backing down this time, either. I glance at the muscle pulsing in his jaw. *Although I do need to be smart.*

Not that he'd hurt me. I'm not worried about that. But when he's like this, he doesn't listen to anyone, or anything, and I need him to hear me out. If I overheard correctly, the stakes are enormous. Which is why he's in such a rage.

This is Antonio's way of not buckling under the pressure. It's predictable, but vile. *We'll discuss it another time.* For now, I need to help him see reason.

I peer into his stormy eyes and keep my voice low. "I'm your wife. The woman who loves you. The woman you sleep beside at night—unguarded. The woman who wants only the best for you—always. The woman you love. That's what gives me the right."

He's still seething, but I've taken some of the steam out of it. Hopefully enough so he'll listen.

"Who has Cristiano?" I ask as though we discuss this sort of thing all the time. "The Bratva or the oligarchs?"

Antonio glances at me from several feet away. The last question surprised him, but he recovers quickly. "What makes you think that either faction has him?"

"You asked if I wanted Lucas or Santi to deliver me to the Russians."

He averts his gaze, but he doesn't have the good grace to cringe, or God forbid, apologize.

"Once you brought them up, it wasn't hard to figure out. The Bratva and the oligarchs were causing problems even when my father was alive."

He swivels, fully facing me, with his head tipped to one side. "Did your father ever have a problem with either?"

My father didn't trust them, especially the oligarchs, but I don't remember any specific incident. "If he did, it's not something he shared with me. But I'm sure he would have mentioned it to you at some point."

"I would have thought so, too. But he left out other important details that would have been good to know," he grumbles under his breath.

Pesky details like that your father murdered my mother, and that I was raped by your cousin and had a child. I don't say any of it. There's no point. It's not going to help my cause, and Antonio doesn't need any more stress.

"Tell me what's going on. And before you say it doesn't concern me, remember that we're partners."

"We're not business partners," he replies curtly. "And this is a business matter."

"Not good enough, Antonio."

"I decide what's good enough. Not you."

"If you sacrifice Cristiano without doing everything in your power to save him, every time you look at me, you'll remember your friend with great sorrow. You'll wonder if you could have done something different. It'll eat away at you—at us—until there's nothing left."

"Cristiano might be a traitor."

I blink a few times before dismissing the allegation out of hand.

Antonio just leveled the gravest indictment without an ounce of *oomph*. I don't believe it, and the way he's gauging my reaction, neither does he. *But it certainly explains his mood.*

The impatience vibrates off him as he awaits my response. *My thoughts. My opinion. Something.* Ultimately, he might dismiss what I say without consideration, but he's interested in what I think. *Baby steps.*

I keep my body still and weigh my words carefully before I meet his gaze. "I don't know what happened with Alvarez, although I can buy that he's a traitor. But Cristiano?" I shake my head. "Not a chance. The evidence would have to be overwhelming and irrefutable to convince me otherwise. And it's not. If it were, you wouldn't have said he *might* be a traitor."

His focus is razor-sharp. He hasn't as much as blinked since I began talking.

"I don't believe it," I continue without hesitation. "And you don't believe it, either."

"I don't know what I believe," he murmurs, turning his back so I can't see his turmoil. His humanity.

My heart breaks for the man who is left with an unfathomable choice. *His wife or his brother.* The decision becomes easier if Cristiano is a traitor, but he knows it's not true.

I go to him—to where he's staring into the abyss—and rest my hand on his back.

"No," he shouts, jerking away like my palm is slathered in poison.

He rejects the attempt to soothe him—*rejects my love—*

with a visceral reaction that seems almost instinctive. It leaves my insides trembling. *A slap in the face would have stung far less.*

Without another word, I lower my arm and turn to leave.

"An oligarch has him," Antonio says quietly, as I reach the partition.

It's an olive branch. I don't move, in case there's more.

"The package at the dock was from Dimitri Fedorov, the *Pakhan* of the European Bratva. It contained a message from Cristiano that at face value made him out to be a traitor. But it turned out to be a cryptic warning. Fedorov can rescue Cristiano, but he wants to have dinner with you in exchange."

Fedorov can rescue Cristiano, but he wants to have dinner with you in exchange. What the hell, Antonio? You're so damn possessive, no one's allowed to see how I chew? I don't understand.

"Dinner? That's it? And you're not considering it?"

"It could be dinner. It could be a trap."

Of course. I didn't think of it. "Would you be there, too?"

He nods.

I realize there's some element of risk, but to do nothing is unconscionable. We can't just let Cristiano remain a prisoner—or worse. *He must realize this, too.*

"We have to do it." I step closer to him. "Antonio, you have to agree to it."

He doesn't say anything for a long moment. I'm not sure he even breathes. His expression tightens before he speaks.

"I intend to. It's eating me alive, but I'll agree to the terms. Because if I don't, Fedorov will know exactly how important you are to me. As my wife, you're always at some risk, but the risk will become infinitely greater. I have no fucking choice." With a swipe of his arm, he knocks over a metal cart, and the medical supplies scatter across the floor.

I have no fucking choice. Could there be a less tenable position for a man who craves control?

The most efficient way to destroy a man is to take his women. His mother, sisters, daughters—wife. Any one of them will do.

There's an element of possessiveness involved, and I have no empathy in that regard. But this is so much more. It's a challenge to his power, his honor, complete with the searing shame of not being able to protect me. *This is how they got to my father.*

Even if a simple dinner is where it begins and ends, Fedorov took one step toward the jugular. And like a cornered animal, Antonio is lashing out.

There must be something I can do to make this easier.

The chasm between us widens, as I stare at a wad of cotton near the exam table, while trying to come up with something helpful. Everything I think of seems patronizing or dismissive. I'm at a total loss when he, finally, speaks.

"You've weakened me."

The accusation twists in the blistering silence, the sharp edges slicing without mercy. My knees wobble, and I grab onto the nearest surface to steady myself.

As I absorb the pain, I close my eyes and brace for more. But there's nothing else. Maybe there doesn't have to be. The wound is already bloody and gaping. It might even be a deadly blow.

You've weakened me. I have.

I never wanted this. Yet I gave him my love and encouraged him to give me his in return. It was inevitable.

I gnaw on the inside of my cheek so that I don't cry. There's nothing more I can do or say right now that will change anything.

"I'm going to go see if the girls have moved into a new room. Let me know what you need from me regarding the dinner."

Antonio doesn't say anything. *Nothing.* I'm not surprised. *You've weakened me* stands on its own. He's going to push me away and bury the emotion, *the feelings,* until I'm nothing more than a responsibility, like feeding the vineyard workers during the harvest, or tithing the church.

As I walk around the partition to leave, Antonio grabs me from behind and pins me against the wall, with my hands above my head.

"Do you know how much I want to hurt you, *Princesa*?"

9

DANIELA

He's inches from my face. His eyes a black, soulless window into his corner of hell.

"I want to lay you over that table and beat you with my belt, until your skin is flayed open."

They're just words, Daniela. I swallow the fear creeping in. "But you won't."

His mouth crashes into mine, stealing my thoughts, my breath, and what's left of my composure.

"But I won't," he murmurs, when he pulls back. "Not today."

"Not ever," I whisper.

"I wouldn't take that bet if I were you."

He's wrestling with a demon, and I attempt to drag him away. "I'd take that bet anytime, anywhere. You won't hurt me."

When I lay out my unwavering faith in his love, he groans, as if in pain, and rests his forehead against mine. His breathing is ragged, and there's an intensity about him even in repose. The fight's not over. He's merely catching his breath.

I ache to wrap my arms around him, but he's holding my wrists securely in one hand. "Let me touch you," I plead, softly.

His grip tightens, as though the prospect of my touch threatens him in some way.

Antonio lifts his head and peers into my eyes while his free hand slides under my sundress. He isn't patient. There are no light caresses to my inner thighs to build my arousal. He goes straight to my panties. He wedges his feet between mine, pushing my legs apart, while his thumb skates over the gusset, working the silky fabric into my wet flesh.

"Someone might come in. And I need to get back to the girls."

"The nurses will find you when it's time." He nips my bottom lip. "But no one's coming in. Not even if you scream."

The devil is dancing in his eyes. I don't want to play with him when he's like this—not here, anyway. "This is a clinic." It's a halfhearted plea, and he knows it.

"You'd deny your husband? Even after his boat exploded?" His voice is low and raspy.

"You're manipulating."

"If I were manipulating, it would be much more subtle. You'd never see it coming. I'm just pointing out the facts."

He slips his hand inside my panties, and I close my eyes. "You're wet, *Princesa*. *Drenched*. My fingers are gliding over your pussy. Was it the kiss, or the thought of me fucking you in a public place?"

Antonio slides two fingers inside me, and before I'm ready, he adds a third, while his thumb works my clit. He knows exactly what I need to come, and he's going there with a vengeance.

There's no slow tease. No mercy. He's going to yank an orgasm from me in a way that leaves my mind reeling and my body shaking. The kind of orgasm that requires a respite in strong arms to feel grounded again.

My back arches off the wall, and I press my pussy into his fingers, as my lower belly tightens before release.

"You want to come all over my hand, don't you, *Princesa*?"

I don't answer, because I can't. Instead, I writhe against the wall, gasping for breath, my pelvic muscles fully coiled.

He pulls his hand away and brings his fingers to his mouth. "*Mmmm*. You're delicious."

I'm sucking air, mouth open. The throbbing between my legs is almost unbearable.

He frees my wrists and touches his nose to mine. "Does your greedy pussy need more attention?"

"Yes." I'm so aroused. I just need a little more. And I'm not embarrassed to admit it, or to rock my hips into his hard cock.

He steps back. "Then you should learn to stay out of my business."

I'm so worked up, and he's played me so expertly—so cruelly—that I begin to cry. It's an involuntary reaction. "This is how you're going to punish me? You're going to use intimacy like a weapon?"

"I'll punish you in any way that I choose. That shouldn't surprise you."

"You're despicable." I duck to get away from him, but he wraps his hand around my throat and holds me against the wall.

"This was just the beginning," he murmurs. "When you get home, you'll take out the black wand and edge for thirty minutes."

What is he talking about? "Edge?" *Fuck you. You can shove that black wand up your ass.*

"You'll take yourself right to the brink of orgasm, like I just did, but you'll pull back before you come. Don't stop until you're right at the edge. But don't you dare come."

He's insane. Arguing isn't the way to reason with him. *Maybe I don't want to reason with him. Maybe I want to play his sick games. Maybe I'm as insane as he is.*

"What if I can't help it?"

"If you disobey me, after the traitors have been dealt with, I'll tie you to the bed and spend twenty-four hours teaching you how to edge. You don't want that, *Princesa*. It will be torture, with you bound and begging for release. I'll know if you lie, because you're a terrible liar. So be a good girl, and edge for thirty minutes every night until this is over, and you'll be well rewarded."

He drops his hand from my throat, but my heart is still pounding.

"When will you be home?"

"When my work is finished. If you're lucky, that'll be tonight. Because when I do come home, I'm going to rock into that tight little pussy, while you come all over my cock. After being at the edge without any relief, it'll feel so good when it happens, *Princesa*. Tears will stream down your pretty pink cheeks while you tremble."

Antonio's phone pings, and he reaches for it.

"Will and Samantha will be here shortly," he says, eyes on the screen. "Valentina can go back to London with them until this is over."

Back to London? After today? No. "I want Valentina here with me."

He nods. "They'll take you both back to the house before they leave."

"Why can't we stay in the apartment upstairs?"

"I don't want Valentina at the apartment for any length of time."

So that's how it's going to be. "You're making me choose. I can send her to London and stay with you every night, or I can keep her with me in Porto, but I won't see you until this is all over. This is a new low, even for you."

"Listen to me." He cradles my face in his hands, tipping upward until our eyes meet. "I'm not asking you to choose. But if I were, the choice is simple. Mothers choose their children. Always. The end."

There's a knock on the door while I'm trying to come to grips with everything that's happened since I walked into this room.

"What?" Antonio snarls.

"I promised to let Mrs. Huntsman know when the girls were settled."

"Thank you," I say to the woman on the other side of the door.

"Thirty minutes." He slides his phone back into his pocket. "Text me when you touch the wand to your pussy, and again when you're through. I want to think about you panting and sweaty, aching with need."

"You're a pig."

"Is that so? Thirty-five minutes, *Princesa*. Not a second less." He smirks. It's more playful than mean-spirited. "It might not sound like it, but it'll be challenging. You'll see."

What an asshole.

The wand is hardly a punishment. Although being left aroused—*like right now*—is uncomfortable. But the complicated part is the power exchange. That's what this is all about. He's shoring up his power.

Some part of me wants to acquiesce quietly. While another part wants to scream *Red!*

There are times when I hand over control without a fuss. Usually it's in bed, where I prefer to let him lead—not that he'd have it any other way. But there are also times when I submit because he needs it for his peace of mind—or I need it for mine. As strange as it sounds, there's real freedom in submission.

The struggle for control will likely always be a *thing* between us, but as our trust has grown, it's become more subtle and nuanced. More civilized. Comfortable, even.

But there's nothing comfortable or subtle about what just happened. It's tinged with something I can't quite put my finger on. *Something ugly, maybe.* It feels almost as though he's dragging our relationship back in time, to somewhere I won't go.

I open my mouth to tell him that I need some time, but he doesn't give me the opportunity.

"Are you going to fight me on this? Because I can easily make it an hour."

I don't know how this is going to end, but it won't be settled here. That I'm sure of.

When I don't argue, he steps aside so I can leave.

10

ANTONIO

I allowed Daniela to weaken me. Did I just punish her for it? Was that what it was? *No.* I take full responsibility for my weaknesses.

The better question is, *What am I going to do about it?* But that's a problem to be tackled later. Right now, my plate's full.

In the meantime, I'm doing what I do best—distracting her. I'm taking away some of her self-determination. Forcing her to surrender some of her control to me. Do I crave her submission? *Yes.* Does she crave the opportunity to submit? *Also, yes.*

How are my demands, amped up with threats, different than what my father did, or Tomas? Was I coercive? It certainly sounded like it, even to my ears. But my conscience is clear.

Daniela has a safeword. It's what separates her dark prince from the devil he could easily become. Even though she seemed hesitant, even though the uncertainty was scrawled all over her gorgeous face, my *princesa* never used it today.

Red. That's all she had to say to change course. Is it fucked up? Maybe. But it's our favorite flavor of fucked up.

Although, I'll admit, today was different. The trust seemed

frayed at the edges—on both sides. I felt it then, and I still feel it now.

It's been a bastard of a day, and I overreacted to her prying. *No question.* But letting her creep into my world—into my business, with all its dark elements—only buys her more trouble. More anxiety. More worry. It's my burden, not hers. I won't allow it to weigh her down. Not while I'm still breathing.

But it's never easy with her. Every battle is hard fought, and I'm forced to earn almost every concession. We're both often bloodied before it's over.

Will she be uncomfortable from edging? So uncomfortable my cock is thickening at the thought of it. But nobody ever died because they didn't have an orgasm.

I take out my phone and toss it in the air a few times before I contact Fedorov. If there's a better solution, I don't see it.

The bitterness seeps in as I key in the message. But I'm not completely boxed in. He'll eat on my terms.

Dinner is on. I'll get back to you about the time and place. Cristiano is out of there today.

The phone rings seconds after I send the message.

"Huntsman," I answer, coolly.

"I'm not a big fan of texting." Fedorov *tsks*. "Too much typing."

Fuck you, asshole.

"Cristiano is currently in one of the guest houses on my property. I expected you to make a sound decision, and I took the liberty of having him brought here after we last spoke. I offered him medical treatment, as a precaution, but he refused. He'll be treated as a guest, so long as you uphold your end of the deal. He's all yours after our dinner. I'll await the details."

The old bastard ends the call before I can get in a word.

Medical treatment, as a precaution. What the fuck does that mean? Does Cristiano have a hangnail, or does the precaution have something to do with Fedorov's knowledge of old KGB tactics?

I fully expect my soldier to be returned to me in good health, I text. **Anything less will be treated as a punishable violation of the agreement.**

Duly noted, he replies.

Fedorov is a man of contradiction. Despite the *I'm an old man* bullshit he's always peddling, he's ruthless. Yet, he grabbed Cristiano before anyone had the opportunity to kill him.

Does he want to have dinner with Daniela so badly that he wasn't willing to take a chance with Cristiano's life? I'm sure getting him out of Nikitin's clutches took some doing. The oligarchs trust the Bratva as little as the Bratva trusts them. There's no love lost between the factions.

Something's not right. There's got to be more to it than a goddamn dinner. Now I'm even more concerned for Daniela's safety. *Sonofabitch.*

A knock on the door drags me from my horrific imaginings.

"Hey," Lucas mutters. "Anyone else here?"

"No."

"Alvarez is dead."

So much for interrogating him. Nothing has gone according to plan today. *Not a fucking thing.* "How?"

"A well-placed bullet to the back of the head. No signs of struggle. Looks like someone he trusted enough to turn his back on."

"Someone who didn't want him to talk."

"Probably on Nikitin's order."

"No assumptions. For all we know, Fedorov's behind it." Or someone else we haven't yet identified. "That end was easier than the bastard deserved."

Lucas grunts.

"Where did they find him?"

"In a boarded-up building near the train station. They're

sweeping the place for evidence. What do you want them to do with the body?"

"Leave it for the rats."

Lucas sticks his hands in his pockets. "Have you made a decision about dinner?"

I nod. "I just got off the phone with Fedorov. He has Cristiano. He's holding him as a *guest* until after the dinner tomorrow."

"What kind of condition is he in?" His expression tightens as he awaits my reply.

"I can't say for certain, but it didn't sound grim."

The muscles in Lucas's neck relax, much the same way mine did when I heard that Fedorov had Cristiano. It's not a perfect situation, but it's better.

"Wait," Lucas says. "He rescued him before you agreed to dinner?"

"There's something that doesn't feel right. But I can't put my finger on it."

"We have a little time to figure it out. Where's the dinner?"

"Here."

"Here? He agreed to that?"

"He will. Close the restaurant to the public—all day, so we can prepare. There's a separate entrance, so he won't have free access to the building. We'll need to allow a couple of his guards into the atrium, but the rest will have to wait outside. It gives us more control than we would have elsewhere."

"It's a solid plan. Although he's likely to be seen entering or leaving the restaurant."

Fraternizing with the Bratva isn't a great look for me, but most people who know me, know I'd never sell out the region to fill my coffers. *I'm not Tomas.*

"I can have dinner with whomever I want. What's going on with our computer equipment?"

"Fifteen minutes. They're working as quickly as they can. I

could probably push them harder, but we can't afford mistakes."

No, we can't, but we're left holding our dicks while the equipment is being checked. We need it to examine the feeds from the pier if we expect to ever figure out who put that bomb on the boat. "Fifteen minutes. That's it."

"Rafael asked about you. He also wanted to know if I thought Tomas's disappearance was in any way connected to the explosion on the boat."

Fuck. I've been dragging my feet on this. He needs to be told. I rub my palm along my jaw. "What did you say?"

"I told him it was too early to draw any conclusions. He knows Tomas is dead, Antonio. I could sense it."

I waited too damn long to tell him. Now he's holding it inside, letting it churn, until it gnaws a hole in his gut. *Goddammit.* "Is he still in the clinic?"

"I didn't give the okay for him to leave—so unless you did, he should be here. Although the kid's resourceful."

"Find him, and tell him to come see me."

Lucas has a hand on the door when I stop him. "When Cristiano arrives tomorrow, he'll be treated as any other man being returned to us. He'll need to be questioned, and he'll be treated as a threat until we know otherwise." *I never thought I'd ever say those words. Ever.*

"I don't believe he's been compromised. He'd take a bullet for you. Probably for me, too." Lucas swallows. "But I'll question him."

"No. I'll do it. But I want you with me."

11

ANTONIO

"Hey," Rafael says, carefully, as he enters the room. He knows I'm still pissed. "How's the shoulder?"

"My shoulder is not your problem. Were you seen by a doctor?"

He nods.

"And?"

"I'm fine."

He doesn't look any worse for the wear. The kid's at home in and on the water. He's like a fish. *A fish who never listens to a goddamn thing I say.*

"When I tell you to do something, it's not a suggestion. You knew damn well there was a problem. I recall using the word *bomb* when I ordered you to the pier."

"You weren't on your way to the pier. You were headed straight into danger." Rafael holds his head high. "There was no way I was going to let you do that alone."

"You weren't going to let me? I need your permission to come and go now?"

"You would have done the same thing if you were in my shoes. So I don't understand why you're so pissed off."

"You don't understand why I'm so pissed off? Fine. I'll tell you why. First, and most importantly, there was a goddamn bomb on the boat and you could have been killed. Second, don't tell me what I would have done at your age, in your shoes. A good leader is a good soldier first. Good soldiers follow orders. You keep talking about how you want to be an elite soldier in my inner circle, yet you can't follow a simple, clear order."

My ire is rising again—this time, it's aimed at me. I should have known he'd follow me. If anything had happened to him, I would never forgive myself.

The kid, who looks an awful lot like a man, leans back against the exam table across from me. "It was clear, but it wasn't simple. How was I going to walk away with you in danger? You act like it was so easy."

"We don't only follow orders that are easy. If that were the case, any asshole could be a soldier."

Rafael comes over to where I'm standing and squares his shoulders. "It would be my life's honor to be one of your soldiers. But if it means turning my back on you when you're in trouble, I'll have to learn to live without the honor. I will never turn my back on you, or leave you alone to fend off danger. Just like you didn't turn your back on me, or leave me alone with the monsters. Don't ask me to do the impossible."

I tamp down the swell of emotion. He's the young man I hoped he would be. Not because of his loyalty toward me, but because of his character, and his willingness to stand tall for what he believes in and to accept the consequences of that decision.

He's becoming a good man. But I'm not letting him off the hook. In part, he got to where he is because I held the bar high and set expectations. And I followed through when it would have been easier to sweep lapses under the rug. As much as I'd like to, I won't let this slide, either. He deserves better.

"I have a lot going on right now. But this discussion is not over. We'll revisit it as soon as I have time."

He crosses his arms over his chest. "What happened today?"

"We're still trying to figure it out. A lot of the evidence is submerged under water. It's going to be tough going, but we'll get to the bottom of it. In the meantime, keep your wits about you—and go nowhere, I mean *nowhere,* without guards."

He nods. "I never do."

With one exception, Rafael has had the same guards since he first came to live at the house. They respect his privacy, reporting virtually nothing to me. Would I like it to be different? Absolutely. But it's the only way it actually works. If he thought they were a pipeline of information, he'd be trying to lose them all the time. *That's what I did when I was his age.*

"Do you need anything else before I go?"

My stomach twists. I've thought a lot about what to tell him regarding Tomas. In the end, I fall back on some old advice from Dr. Lima. *"Rafael will let you know how much he's ready to hear. Watch for the signals. They're not always in words."*

"We should talk about your brother."

"Heard he was missing," he says flippantly. "I hope the end wasn't easy for him."

He knows me well enough to know I'd never let Tomas walk this earth after what he did to Daniela.

I give him a moment. Despite his bravado, and his hatred for Tomas, he was his brother.

"Did you learn anything about my mother?" he asks, softly.

Nothing good. I go over to where he's standing, with his shoulder propped against the wall.

I've had many difficult conversations with Rafael, but this news is akin to sticking a knife in his chest. "She's dead." I break the news with the utmost care and reverence, but it's not enough.

He pounds his fist against the wall, then squeezes his eyes

shut and lets his head hang. I stand beside him, quietly, giving him some time to grieve.

She's been gone for more than half his life—well more. But he's been clinging to a sliver of hope all these years. I just killed it, and it weighs heavier on me than any life I've ever taken.

His father had always accused my aunt of abandoning her children to be with a man. It was the ultimate way of shaming her. When Rafael was nine, he told me it didn't matter. *"I don't care what she did. I just want her to come back. I miss her so much."* It tore me up at the time. It's still hard to think about.

"Do you know where she's buried?" he asks, lifting his head.

"No. And I don't know how she died. Tomas confirmed her death. He overheard your father discussing it with mine. But he claimed not to know the details."

"Discussing it? Before or after they killed her?"

"Both."

"Son of a bitch. He didn't do anything to stop it? He could have at least fucking warned her. She was his mother."

I thought the very same thing. I put my hand on his shoulder. "Tomas wasn't like you. He was a coward."

"Do you think he might have been lying?"

This is the little boy in him talking.

"There's no way to know for sure. But I pushed him hard."

Rafael knows I questioned Tomas, and he knows his death was on my order. But he hasn't asked if I was the one to actually kill him. Maybe he doesn't want to know, or maybe he's grown beyond that. Boys always ask if you were the one to pull the trigger—or drop the bastard in a chemical bath, as was the case with Tomas. There's something alluring about it to them. Men never ask.

"Have you told your mother?"

"Not yet."

"She's going to take it hard. She's always held out hope that her baby sister was alive."

My mother's hope died years ago. But she kept the faith for Rafael. She's going to be sad, but not at all surprised.

"I'll find her body one day," he tells me earnestly, "and give her a proper burial."

There's something particularly awful about not being able to say goodbye, or to honor her in death. I'm sure his imagination has taken him to the most gruesome places—wondering if she suffered, or if she died afraid. I can't imagine how difficult it's been for him.

"Now's not the time, but you should talk to Lucas. We've been looking for her for years. There's no sense retracing our steps."

Before the words are completely out, Rafael embraces me. "Thank you for caring about her. Thank you." He repeats it over and over, until he finally pulls away.

His eyes are wet, but otherwise, he seems okay.

"Do you need anything else? I'd like to get out of this place and get some real food. I'm starving."

I chuckle. "One more thing. Daniela and I have an engagement tomorrow night. I want you to stay at the house with Valentina. Santi and Mia will be there, as well as Victor, but Daniela will feel better if you're there. So will I. Is that an order you can follow?"

He nods. "You don't need to give it another thought. I'll be there."

12

DANIELA

Security is tight as we head down to have dinner with Fedorov. Although that doesn't stop Antonio from scanning every corner of the private elevator before we step inside, as though someone might be hiding behind one of the gilded panels.

Hyperalert and edgy are a bad combination, especially on a man who has a gun holstered beneath his suit jacket, and another concealed at his ankle.

I rub my hand up and down his arm. The muscle is hard and tense—too tense for my liking. "I know how much you hate to be in this position, but we're doing the right thing. I have no doubt about it." *Although you are starting to make me anxious.*

I wasn't nervous until he showed up at the apartment to shower and change. That's when I learned that there are GPS trackers sewn—or welded—into most of my belongings, including the bracelet I'm wearing and my wedding ring. Apparently, it's been that way since I ran off. He tried to downplay it as a security measure that will never be activated unless it becomes necessary. It didn't make me feel any better.

Any other time, I would have told him exactly how I felt about being tracked without my knowledge and consent. But for tonight, I held my tongue.

Antonio turns toward me, his eyes raking over every inch of my body, in much the same way he examined the elevator before we got in. "I thought I told you to find some ugly rag to wear." He caresses my cheek with his fingers. "You're beautiful. Much too beautiful for your own good—or mine."

I adjust his tie. "You don't look so bad yourself for a hot-tempered, grumpy—"

He presses his fingers on my lips to shush me and flips a switch to stop the elevator. The alarm blares, and his phone rings immediately.

"We're fine. Just need a minute," he says gruffly into the phone, before dropping it back into his pocket.

Antonio's not above elevator sex. *And as I recently learned, I'm not, either.* But we're already late. *What's he doing?*

"We're hosting, and it's after eight. We should already be there."

"I don't give a flying fuck about etiquette. Your safety is my only concern. I want Fedorov seated first, so my men can have a few minutes to observe him and his guards before we arrive."

Everything has been orchestrated carefully. All the attention to detail should ease my anxiety, but it's having the opposite effect.

His dark eyes bore into mine. "This is a deadly serious meeting. I need you to be alert to danger at all times. Dimitri Fedorov is the *Pakhan* of the European Bratva."

This is the fourth time in the last thirty minutes that he reminds me.

"He likes you to believe he's a forgetful old man, harmless, but he's a ruthless monster. Do not let your guard down for a single second."

Antonio doesn't want me anywhere near the Russian, and

his list of instructions, including how I'm not to use the restroom unless absolutely necessary, are weighing on me. But I quietly go along with the plan, so as not to give him an excuse to scrap the dinner. It wouldn't take much. Besides, he knows this ugly business far, far better than I do, and every tiny detail was put in place to ensure my safety. I won't give him any reason to worry more than he is already.

I cup his jaw in my hand. "I understand the gravity of the situation. I don't have a death wish."

Without warning, he backs me into the corner of the elevator, caging me with his muscled frame, and crushes my mouth with his—no holds barred. The spicy scent of his cologne wafts into my nose, as he levels the toe-curling assault.

Rough. Demanding. Delicious. He takes no prisoners.

My husband is staking his claim—once again. His intensity sends a shiver through me, every nerve ending dancing in its wake. *More, please,* they whisper as they sway. It doesn't help that I edged last night with that evil wand, picturing him with his cock in hand while he thought about me wet and needy. I might have been following his instructions, but I felt the heady rush of power as I sent him the text that I was beginning.

"I am so pissed that you're burdened with this bullshit. When tonight's over," he murmurs, with his fingers still cradling the back of my head, "I'm going to fuck you until you've forgotten everything. Even your name."

My heart pounds as he steps back and flips the elevator switch.

He gazes at me from across the elevator. "No matter what happens, do not take off that bracelet. It has state-of-the-art technology inside."

"I won't." *I have a child to think of. She needs me—and so do you.*

When the elevator doors open, he takes my hand. "Valentina is safe tonight. Don't worry about her."

It's uncanny how he seems to always know what I'm thinking. I'm confident Valentina's safe. The president himself isn't as well-guarded as she is tonight.

"You're safe too," he adds, "as long as you follow the rules."

I lace my fingers through his as we step into the large atrium. We stop in front of the entrance to the restaurant, where Antonio hands Lucas the gun from under his jacket. It's a show for two of Fedorov's guards stationed nearby.

But that's all they get from him. Nothing more. Not a cursory glance, a perfunctory nod, or the weapon holstered at his ankle.

13

DANIELA

Dimitri Fedorov is utterly charming, with his snow-white hair and impeccable manners. He exudes a sense of wealth and refinement, but he's not in the least bit stuffy.

The man has lived a rich life, and between peppering me with seemingly innocuous questions about grapes, the perfume I'm wearing, and my favorite pastimes—the latter two are met with a stony glare from my husband—Dimitri regales us with his mesmerizing stories.

But through it all, I never forget that my own dark prince called him a ruthless monster.

By the time Port is served, even my husband has relaxed. Well, maybe he's not exactly relaxed, but I'm no longer concerned he's going to pull out that gun and threaten Fedorov within an inch of his life. *With Antonio, one needs to savor the small victories.*

"Since you've asked how I like to spend mine, what is it you enjoy in your free time?" I ask, smiling at Dimitri.

He stops with his dessert fork midair, searching my face. My question was a tiny bit cheeky, but not at all rude.

From the corner of my eye, I see Antonio reach below the

table. I hold my breath, but he doesn't actually go for the gun. *But he won't hesitate if it becomes necessary.*

"You're so much like your mother," Fedorov murmurs. "You even sound like her. If I close my eyes while you're talking, I can picture her sitting here instead of you."

My skin prickles. Not with fear, but with a kind of awareness that I don't understand. Isabel often said I reminded her so much of my mother. She would use the words he just used, or something similar. *If I close my eyes...* My father thought so, too. But how does Dimitri Fedorov know I sound like my mother? My parents had nothing to do with the Bratva. And I've never seen this man before tonight. I search his face, but he shows me nothing.

"You knew my mother?" It comes out with a bit of a squeak.

Antonio's hands are both on the table now, but his posture is rigid.

The Russian nods. "I was in love with her."

I gasp, and gawk at him with my mouth open.

"I don't care for any coffee," Antonio says, tossing his napkin on the table. "Dinner is over."

My heart drops into my stomach. I never knew my mother as an adult. When she died, I was a child. I'm always hungry for any little tidbit about her life—especially her life before she married my father. *Surely that's what he's talking about.*

I place my hand on Antonio's and weigh my words carefully, pleading with my eyes. "If you can spare a few more minutes, I would love a coffee."

I'm exceedingly polite and respectful of Antonio, although under the table, I lightly press my shoe into his. But I don't challenge him in front of Fedorov. I simply give him the opportunity to indulge his young wife. He can easily say, *I have to take a phone call. Let's have coffee at home*, or he can choose to humor me.

I hold my breath, waiting, and hoping. And waiting some more.

"I suppose I have a little time. But only enough for one short story about your mother." His lips twitch as he speaks. He just called out my manipulation about wanting coffee, not to embarrass me, but so our dinner guest would know he's fully aware of my hijinks. To be honest, I wouldn't have even cared if he had growled, *You're a fucking little manipulator, Princesa,* as long as I could hear more about my mother and this man.

Antonio turns to Fedorov with a scowl. "Remember that you're talking about my wife's mother. A woman who deserved respect not only in life, but in death."

Fedorov meets my gaze. "I would never disrespect your mother. I cared about her too much."

Whatever he has to say is more than just a tidbit. I can tell by his expression. "How did you meet her?" I ask impatiently, before Antonio changes his mind.

"I met Rosa when she was just a few years younger than you are now." He pauses for a moment, a cloud of sorrow descending over him.

I brace myself to hear some awful news about my mother.

"My oldest daughter, Arina, was abducted," he explains, with his hands steepled at his chin. "My family lived in Russia at the time. We searched and searched for her." He shakes his head. "The signs all pointed to Porto. A shipment of girls had come through the city on its way to Morocco, but the traffickers knew we were onto them—checking boats and train stations, even the airport. We had men stationed on both sides of the border. They couldn't leave the country. But we couldn't find them, either.

"At that point, I was desperate. Then I got a tip to contact a young woman who was involved with distributing birth control and smuggling abused women out of the country. She worked with two friends, and they had lots of contacts all over the country, but I was advised to speak directly to her."

"My mother?" I ask softly, butterflies swirling in my stomach.

He nods. "And yours," he says, glancing briefly at Antonio, who doesn't blink.

"It took us the better part of a month, but we found Arina. Your mother found her. Up north."

"Was your daughter harmed?" I ask, hoping that my mother saved the little girl before the worst happened. *She would have been crushed if they hadn't gotten to her in time. I know it.*

Fedorov's eyes flare dangerously. "Girls who are abducted are always harmed. It's just a question as to the extent. She hadn't reached the destination, where she'd be auctioned like a piece of meat. So I guess you could say the harm could have been worse."

"I'm so sorry."

"Don't apologize, darling. The men who hurt her paid dearly."

Antonio studies Fedorov closely, considering every word that comes out of his mouth. As awful as it is, I'm sure this kind of information gives him some leverage over the *Pakhan*—or it might one day. I use Antonio's newly found patience to probe about my mother, knowing full well the answers might tarnish my memory of her.

"You said you loved her. Was she married to my father at the time?"

He shakes his head. "She was betrothed to your father, and although she was resigned to her fate, she wasn't all that excited about it." He chuckles. "My love was unrequited. She never knew how I felt. Once I had my daughter, we went back to Russia. My family needed me, and your mother, who was more than a decade younger and about to be married, certainly did not."

I imagine my mother in the pictures taken right before she married my father. She was beautiful, with long, dark hair, and thick, inky lashes. *Spirited and full of fun.* She was like that all her life—her very short life.

I want to hear more. I'm hungry for every detail Fedorov's willing to share.

Antonio pours us more coffee. I'm sure he wants to know more, too, although not for the same reasons I do.

"Rosa was beautiful and strong-minded, and courageous. Like you. A woman a man meets only once in a lifetime. We went into some unsavory areas. I made it as easy for her as I could, but it was rough at times. She never complained."

"A young woman from an important family, betrothed. How was she allowed to go?" Antonio asks, tapping his fingers on the table.

"I was able to have her home nearly every night. Your grandmother," he says, gazing at me, "covered for her. At one time, she had also been part of the resistance."

"The resistance?"

He shrugs. "I don't have another word for it. That's what your mother called it."

I glance at Antonio, who has done much more listening than talking, which is fine by me. I have enough questions for both of us.

"When did you move to Porto?" I ask, sipping my coffee slowly so that Antonio doesn't get any ideas about leaving.

"Much later. After my wife and my youngest daughter died."

"I'm sorry. I can't imagine how painful it must have been for you."

"Your mother gave me a legacy. Although we didn't know it at the time. I would never have any more children. My middle daughter is unable to have children of her own—at least that's what she claims," he mutters. "But Arina has five daughters. They each sparkle more brightly than the sun."

I smile. I wonder if she told my father. Dimitri Fedorov ended up to be a very powerful man, and she'd rescued his daughter. Although my mother would have rescued anyone's daughter. Power and money meant nothing to her.

"Did my father ever know about any of this?"

He shrugs. "Not from my mouth. By the time I moved to Porto, her marriage—her reluctance to an arranged marriage—was in the past. Your father adored her, and she him. I owed her too much to ever interfere in her happiness. But I watched her from afar. She was an amazing woman."

"You never said another word to either of them?" Antonio asks, with the suspicion only thinly veiled.

He has a way of turning every question into an interrogation. It's especially irritating now.

"I had one or two business dealings with Daniela's father over the years. And once or twice a year, I would see Rosa at a social function, but we never spoke. I sent a basket to your family on Christmas each year," he tells me. "There's so much gift giving at that time of year that I'm sure it went unnoticed." This man, who my husband calls a *ruthless monster*, sounds almost wistful. "I made sure every basket included the nougat candy that I knew she loved."

"Dipped in chocolate," I say softly. Most of the baskets we received at the holidays went to charity. But there was one basket that my mother would always cut open—the one with the imported nougat. "I remember. She was always so excited about the candy." *Or maybe about her connection to the sender.*

For a moment, I forget he's the *Pakhan* of the European Bratva. He's just a man who loved a woman he could never have.

"I have a confession," Fedorov says, peering at Antonio.

"Tonight was a bit of a ruse. I knew what kind of magic your wife wielded that could bring a powerful man to his knees—I'd experienced it from a woman who was so much like her." He pauses for a beat. "But I wanted to see for myself that Daniela was safe. Here not as a prisoner, but of her own volition. I was fully prepared to rescue Rosa's daughter, just as she rescued mine."

My heart is melting, but when I glance at Antonio, I can almost see the steam coming out of his ears. *Some confessions are best left for the confessional.*

"Daniela," Antonio says between gritted teeth, "Lucas will escort you upstairs. I need a word alone with our guest."

I don't want to go. I want to hear more about my mother, but I do as I'm told, because we're here in exchange for Cristiano. I'm sure that's what Antonio wants to discuss.

When I stand, Dimitri stands. "It was an honor and a pleasure, *senhora*. Your mother would be so proud of you. While I'm quite certain your husband will take good care of you, I'm at your service should you ever require assistance of any kind."

"She won't be requiring your *assistance*," Antonio says pointedly.

Fedorov doesn't backtrack, and he doesn't blink. I have no doubt he doesn't give a damn what Antonio thinks—not on this matter.

While the two men engage in a standoff of sorts, something occurs to me.

"You leave roses at her grave." I don't ask. I know it's him.

"Only after your father died, and could no longer do it. I couldn't take care of her in life, but I can care for her in death."

My heart.

I want to throw my arms around him, but I don't dare. "Good night, Mr. Fedorov. I do hope we'll see each other again."

He leans in to give me a kiss on the cheek, but stops short and turns to my husband. "May I?"

Antonio's eyes flare dangerously. "No, you may not."

I'm mortified by the unnecessary rudeness, and I feel the color rise in my cheeks.

Fedorov winks at me. "I would never harm you. But your husband's right to be leery. I'm not a good man."

Lucas appears to take me up to the landing pad before I have a chance to respond.

14

ANTONIO

"I have a lot of questions. But let's start with this. Your romantic little *story* might have filled my wife's head with hearts and flowers, but I'm not so easily duped."

"Duped? You think it was all a lie?" He sighs heavily. "I only wish. Ask your mother about it, if you don't believe me. She helped cover for Rosa, too."

I plan on having a chat with my mother, although I'm not sure I want to know any more specifics about the danger she courted.

Fedorov likes to point a finger at the oligarchs, and while they're responsible for some of this mess, he's up to his neck in it, too. I can feel it.

I lean back in the chair and watch him carefully. "Did you have anything to do with Isabel's death?"

"Isabel? *No.* Her husband? That's another story. I hope you're not looking for an apology," he huffs. "That bastard came to me with a promise of 'useful information' about Daniela, just as I'm sure he contacted you, and your Uncle Abel."

"What did he tell you?"

"I arranged to have a man meet him with a bag of cash that

he wanted in exchange for the information. After that, Jorge had a lot to tell me."

"You spoke to him yourself?" That would be highly unusual, for the *Pakhan* to speak directly to some low-life weasel.

He nods. "In an encrypted video chat. I've already told you about my feelings for Daniela's mother. I was concerned, and I didn't trust him. So I questioned him myself. He told me about the girl."

Fuck. While this is less of a problem now that Tomas is dead, it's not nothing. Daniela still hasn't told Valentina. *That has to change.*

"I didn't believe him, at first," Fedorov continues. "What a despicable excuse for a man. No loyalty." He scratches his head. "My men grabbed a couple bags of trash from outside Daniela's apartment, and we had the DNA tested. It didn't give me all the answers, but it gave me enough."

He knew where she was living. He could have whisked her away, and I might never have seen her again. My blood runs cold. "You were monitoring my wife?"

"She wasn't your wife at the time. And I didn't know where she was until Jorge contacted me. But after? I kept an eye out. From a distance. I never interfered in her life the way you did."

"We were betrothed. She was my responsibility."

"So it seems."

I'd like to snap his fleshy neck. But I need to shore up the timeline. It's the only way to tell how much of this story is concocted. He's talking a lot—too much for someone as shrewd as Fedorov. It might all be a bullshit story he's using to probe for information he can use to harm Daniela—or me.

I'm not going to tell him a fucking thing. But I'm not done asking questions. "You had Jorge killed after you collected the garbage?"

He shakes his head. "After he spilled his guts, my man put a bullet in his head to shut him up. Jorge vehemently denied selling the information to anyone else, and I believed that part of his story. He was a lazy sonofabitch who wanted a free lunch, but he was too much of a pussy to try to play us against one another for the larger payoff. Besides, if your uncle had information about the child, he would have insisted Tomas seek custody of the girl immediately. He wouldn't have waited.

"May I?" he asks, with his hand on the Port bottle.

I nod. My uncle would have gone after Valentina the very second they lowered Daniela's father into the grave. Maybe sooner. No doubt about it.

"But I was wrong," he mutters, pouring himself a drink.

"About what, exactly?"

"About your uncle knowing." He tosses back the Port like a shot of cheap vodka, and pours another. "I had a traitor in my inner circle passing information to Chernov, who shared it with your uncle and Tomas. Abel had a stroke before he could act. That left the bumbling duo of Tomas and Chernov to make trouble."

"How does Nikitin fit into this?"

"I'm certain that both oligarchs had people close to them who were funneling information to the other camp."

"Certain?"

"How do you think I was able to get Cristiano out? I had men on the inside, too."

I'm not the one guzzling fortified wine, but I'm still having trouble keeping track of all the pieces. Given what we knew at the time, and now, most of what he's said makes sense—although I still don't trust him.

"From the way you were pulling the strings backstage," Fedorov adds, "I assumed you knew something about the girl." He eyes me, waiting for a reaction.

It'll be a cold day in hell before that happens. "Did Chernov give the order for Isabel's murder?"

"They wanted the child, at any cost. I'd look, first, to Chernov for Isabel's murder, but don't discount Nikitin. He's a fool, but he's the most capable of the two. You should know, my president has quietly called him home, but he's gone into hiding."

When the mothership calls you home, it's because they can cover up your death more easily on friendly soil. "You don't know where he is?"

Fedorov shakes his head. "No. But he's a vindictive sonofabitch, and until he's found, he poses a danger to your family. There will be more explosions."

It's all coming together. Everything he just told me might be true, or at least parts of it. But he's been blabbering like a teenage girl at a slumber party because he wants my help. *Until he's found, he poses a danger to your family. There will be more explosions.* The vindictive sonofabitch is also a threat to Fedorov. He wants me to find him.

"Who set the bomb at Santa Ana's?"

"I once thought it was on Chernov's order, but I've come to believe it was on Nikitin's."

"Why?"

"Because they were always undermining each other, like children currying favor. I've told you this. I suspect Nikitin wanted to cause trouble between Chernov and your cousin, so he could be the one to swoop in and help Tomas get custody of Valentina. Ultimately that would have helped him gain a foothold in Porto and made his president very happy."

It's plausible. Fedorov understands the relationship between the oligarchs and the Kremlin better than I ever will.

"I always assumed your father murdered Rosa," he says out of nowhere. "For that matter, the oligarchs thought so, too."

My guard has been on high alert all evening, but it just shot up further. "Why is that?"

"Because he died hours after her, and her husband was one

of the few people with a motive *and* the ability to cover up your father's murder." He looks straight at me. "Manuel beat me to it. If I had figured it out sooner, your father would have died a more painful death."

He might be probing. Or he suspects something, and is either giving me the nod, or he's sending a cryptic shot across the bow—more incentive for me to help him. If that's the case, he's out of luck. I don't give a shit who knows how my father died, or who they tell. I'm long past worrying about it. But I have one more question for this asshole.

"Did you pay the man who tried to kill me? The one who ran my car off the road, into the river?"

He looks me straight in the eye. "You're still alive, so the answer to that would be *no*."

That's a deflection, not an answer. On second thought—maybe it is.

"If you try to contact my wife, in any way—I don't give a shit if it's by carrier pigeon—I'll gut you."

"You move in a dangerous world," he cautions, his calculating eyes boring into mine. "If I were you, I would put away my pride and be grateful that there is someone else who has my wife's best interests at heart. Whether you believe it or not, I owe her mother a great debt, and that extends to her daughter."

I can take care of my own damn wife. I certainly don't need any help from the fucking Bratva.

"I want Cristiano. Now."

Fedorov stands. "My guest will be chauffeured to the rear entrance of the building as soon as I leave the property."

"Have a seat, *Pakhan*."

He glares at me through narrowed eyes.

"My wife is on her way to our home in the valley. You're not going anywhere until the helicopter lands and she's safely inside the house. Until then, you're *my* guest."

15

ANTONIO

When I get the call that a car has pulled up to the back entrance of Huntsman Lodge, I step onto the loading platform, flanked by guards, to accept the prisoner. *My best soldier. My oldest friend.*

Normally, I would never take delivery of a prisoner, but Cristiano isn't just anyone. Although he will be treated like any other soldier who might be compromised. No one gets a free pass—not for something of this magnitude. Only when I'm convinced he's not a threat will he get back his elite status. If I have any concerns, it will never happen.

My credibility as a leader is on the line. Every guard, every soldier, will know that even the highest-ranking lieutenant is subject to our rules. But by taking custody of Cristiano myself, I'm also showing him respect. That respect is what will allow him to continue to command men, when his name is cleared. *If it's cleared.*

A black SUV pulls up to the loading dock. When a tall man gets out and opens the rear door, I do something I never do. I pray. *Don't let him be compromised.* It's not much of a prayer, but it comes from the depths of my soul. I don't want to order his torture—or his death. *But you will, if necessary.* I will.

Cristiano's face is bruised, and I notice a slight limp as he's brought to me in handcuffs.

I search him for weapons. When I find nothing, I nod to Fedorov's man, who removes the cuffs.

While Cristiano rolls his shoulders, I hold out my hand to the guard beside me, and Lucas drops a pair of cuffs into my open palm. *I wonder if they felt as heavy in his hands as they do in mine.*

Cristiano doesn't make me force his arms behind him. He doesn't even make me ask. With a slow, controlled movement, he places his hands near his lower back, and I attach the cuffs. The click of the lock is almost crippling.

Boom! Boom! Boom! The platform rocks, as a ball of fire lights up the distant night sky. Even before I can process any of it, my guards push me down and toward the door.

"No," I bark, shaking them off. "I'll go when I'm ready." This is my fucking house, and I will not run and hide like a coward.

"Antonio," Lucas pleads. "You need to get inside."

"What's going on?" I ask Cristiano.

He shakes his head and looks me in the eye. "No idea. You should listen to Lucas and get inside."

Aside from a series of small pops, the explosion is over. The lodge is set on a high point, and I can see the smoldering fire. *Another small pop.* Whatever happened, a highly flammable substance was involved—like gasoline. A car bomb, maybe. It could be an innocent accident, but that's not ever my first guess, or even my fourth.

Once we're inside, I turn to Lucas, who already has his phone out. "Find out what happened."

He nods and with a somber glance at Cristiano, he goes to the elevator, and I call Santi, who's at the house in the valley. Normally I would call Daniela's guard, and although Duarte's trustworthy, he's new to the position, and he doesn't know the house as well as Santi and Mia.

"Any problems?"

"No, *senhor*. It's quiet here."

"Keep things buttoned up tight. No one in or out."

"Is there something we need to be concerned about?"

"You're guarding my family—you should always be concerned."

"Of course," Santi replies.

"There was an explosion nearby. It's still unclear if there are added concerns. Someone will be in touch."

Once we're deeper in the building, I dismiss the guards.

Cristiano and I walk silently. It's an ominous path for someone in handcuffs. The same path Daniela walked after she ran away. The same path Tomas took to meet his death. But when we reach the crossroads, we don't go to where my cousin was tortured. I lead Cristiano into the cave where I questioned Daniela.

Once we're in the center of the room, I pull up two chairs and set them about four feet apart. Before Cristiano sits down, I remove the handcuffs.

"You shouldn't do that," he mumbles, as I free him.

"I have a gun. I won't hesitate to shoot you, if necessary."

We sit facing each other in blistering silence. He doesn't hang his head, and I don't flinch—not even when a lifetime of memories passes before me. We might not have shared the same parents, but we grew up as brothers.

"Nikitin had you?"

He nods.

"How the fuck did that happen?"

"I left here early, the day before the race, to go down to the dock to check on the boat and make sure everything was set. On my way over, I saw a man chase a woman into an alley. She was screaming for him to get away. Without thinking," he says bitterly, "I went after them. It was a trap."

"I want to know everything. I mean everything. Don't leave out the time you stopped to take a piss."

He nods. "I want to know one thing, first. Do you believe I betrayed you?"

I don't want to believe it. "I'll answer your questions, once you've answered mine."

Footsteps approach, and I glance over my shoulder. Lucas holds up his phone so I can read the screen. **Fedorov's car hit a barrier wall and exploded.**

Jesus Christ. I don't bother to ask if it was an accident. We had dinner, Cristiano was safely returned, and his car blew up. I'm not a big believer in coincidences.

I peer at Lucas. He presses his mouth into a grim line and shakes his head. *No survivors.*

"Send men to the scene to gather everything they can. Call Santi and let him know. Tell him to touch base with Duarte."

"Already done," he mutters. "But the wreckage is still smoldering. They'll secure it, but no one's going to be able to comb through it for several hours."

"Pull up a chair," I tell him, with my entire focus on Cristiano.

"Talk to me."

16

ANTONIO

Cristiano draws a breath and blows it out with a weighty exhale. "A couple weeks ago when I got home from work, I suspected someone had been in my house. A drawer was partially open. Just a crack, but I didn't remember leaving it that way."

"Any chance it was one of your sisters?"

He shakes his head. "I'm very careful. For anyone watching from the outside, I vary my routine, but inside, everything stays the same. I don't take chances with my family. I've been crystal-clear with them about never entering my house without me. Just to be sure they don't get any ideas, I've never shared my alarm code with them. The alarm wasn't set off."

"Was anything else amiss?"

"No. I dusted for prints and examined footage from the security cameras. No prints besides mine, and there weren't any discernable gaps in the footage."

"And you never told us?"

"There was nothing to tell. I didn't find a damn thing."

This is such bullshit. Cristiano knows better than anyone that this isn't something you keep to yourself. He's warned guards countless times that this sort of thing needs to be reported and investigated. This is how organizations are infiltrated.

"Besides," he adds, "I'd been spooked for a while."

Spooked? "What the fuck does that mean?"

"All that stuff with your father and those two other fuckers—I couldn't stop thinking about it. My mother and sisters were at your house all the time. We lived on the property."

I know where this is headed, and my stomach burns as he continues, "I didn't have it in me to ask my mother, so I talked to my sister, Bianca. She denied that any of them ever touched her—or my other sisters." He pauses for a moment, looking at his feet. "Hugo cornered my mother a few times, but she got lucky. At least that's the story Bianca was peddling."

Alma works for me, but our relationship goes far deeper than that. For years, she was my mother's personal maid. She's still my mother's closest friend. She was the one who I found sitting at my mother's bedside, after Hugo beat her—for the last time.

If my father assaulted Alma, I can't do a damn thing to help her now. But I might be able to help her son find answers.

"You don't believe Bianca?"

"I don't think she lied to me. I think she told me what she knows. But there's no way my mother would have ever burdened us with that kind of truth." He shakes his head. "I don't know what to believe."

"Do you think my mother knows anything?" I don't even know why I ask, because if it happened, of course she knows. "I'll talk to her."

Even if Cristiano is compromised, I owe it to Alma.

He shakes his head. "According to Bianca, your mother and mine kept the girls and any woman with a pulse away from your father. Your mother took beatings over it. I don't know what the repercussions were for mine—if any. And I'm not sure it's worth dredging it all up. Hugo's dead. We can't kill him again."

It's a pity. There's great satisfaction in ending a reign of terror. I'd like to do it again. You can't undo the wrongs of the past, but you can ensure they're not repeated by the same culprits.

"Why did you send your family away right before the regatta?"

His mouth twists with uncertainty. "I wanted them gone while we were waging war. I didn't want to risk them ending up in the middle of something. I felt if they were safe, my head would be in a better place."

I feel the rage radiating off Lucas, who's an arm's length away. Alma lavished more love on him than his own mother.

While I'm furious that Hugo tried to force himself on her, for me, it's just one more assault my father levied against someone I care about. He terrorized my wife and my mother. Those are the deepest gashes. The ones that will haunt me for life. Everybody else is just one more painful slash.

Cristiano's not wrong. We don't have the right to demand answers from my mother and Alma, unearthing anguish that's not technically ours. There's not a fucking thing to be gained by it.

I need to stay focused on the task before me, as unpleasant as it is.

"What did Nikitin want from you?"

"Anything I could give him. He was desperate for something that would bring you down. So desperate that he was willing to believe that I'd actually help him. He was skating on thin ice with the Kremlin, and grasping at any lifeline. My initial reaction was to tell him to fuck off. It didn't get me much."

"Except for those bruises on your face."

He shrugs. "After his soldiers knocked me around, Nikitin's assistant, Mikhail, came to me, and advised me to play along.

He said there might be a bomb on our boat, but that if I played my cards right, I would be able to get a message to you before anyone got hurt. I didn't trust him, at first, but I couldn't come up with a better option."

Mikhail must be Fedorov's man inside.

"Nikitin was so anxious about his future, he bought my change of heart without much of a problem. It was nuts." He shakes his head.

Desperate people take desperate measures. It might be cliché, but it's true.

"Mikhail confirmed what we always suspected," Cristiano explains, looking from me to Lucas. "Those fuckers record everything."

"Why didn't you use the established SOS code?"

"I couldn't risk it. At that point, I was almost certain Alvarez was the leak. He was the only one who knew I'd left work early to go to the docks. I told him I was leaving my car at the lodge and walking over."

"I can't believe Nikitin fell for it so easily." It's the first thing Lucas has said the entire time. "Do you think it might have all been a setup?" He shakes his head. "Forget it. It doesn't make sense."

"It had me worried," Cristiano agrees. "But Nikitin knew he was a dead man if he couldn't get to you," he adds, cocking his chin at me.

"Chernov believed he could get a stronghold in the region by using Tomas's relationship to Valentina. He wanted Daniela dead. But with Tomas gone, Nikitin was going straight at you. If you're gone, the region is rudderless, at least for a while. That would give the Russians time to move in and stake a claim. It would also put Nikitin back in his boss's good graces."

"How do you know this?"

"Mikhail."

Fedorov's mole. Somehow everything swings back to him—although it seems like he's been neutered.

"I told a bunch of lies for the tape. But I worried that the message was too obtuse for you to quickly put together, so I leaned on our old code. We used that signal so often when we were kids, I knew you'd remember it."

Your back's against the well. It's code for: there's danger from the water.

It seemed so dumb at the time that Cristiano shoved Lucas for being the idiot who had come up with it. But somehow it stuck. If your back was against the well, it was also against the river. In our games, the greatest danger always came from the river.

"Who set the bomb on the boat?"

"Alvarez," he spits out with venom.

"He was working for Nikitin?" It's hard to believe. Alvarez was one of my best guards. I wouldn't have assigned him to Daniela's protection otherwise. But his ideas about honor were old school. I understand why he had issues with me, but it's hard to fathom why he'd turn on the region by working with the Russians. I don't get that part.

"Here's the thing," Cristiano says. "Mikhail denied it. But who else would Alvarez have been working for?"

No fucking clue. "How did you get out?"

"When Nikitin fled, he gave Mikhail the order to have me killed. But he didn't stick around to see it carried out. Once he was gone, everything fell into chaos. It gave Mikhail an opportunity to get me out and to Fedorov's place.

"What I want to know," Cristiano continues, "is why did Fedorov stick out his neck to save me?"

"We had a deal."

He cocks his head, waiting for me to say more, but I don't.

"What did it cost you?"

I ignore the question, for now. "To answer the question you asked earlier. Did I ever believe you were a traitor . . ."

We peer at each other. He expects the truth, and that's exactly what I intend on giving him. He can take it. As can our friendship. What it might not withstand is a lie.

"The evidence was staggering. In your own voice. I was torn between my responsibilities, and my loyalty to you—and the man I know you are. I promised myself that I wouldn't allow sentimentality to cloud my judgment, and I haven't, but it's cost me plenty." It's the truth. I would have done whatever was necessary, but it would have eaten at me until my final breath.

"He, on the other hand," I say, jerking my head toward Lucas, "was a staunch defender. As was Daniela," I add, almost under my breath.

"I would never betray you. Or you," he says to Lucas. "Never. Not because of the oath we took as soldiers, but because of the original pact."

The one we made when we were seven. We sat in a circle on the grass, between the river and my family's vineyards. With a pocketknife—the one I still carry—we drew blood from each of our wrists. We promised each other undying loyalty and brotherhood, as we held our oozing wrists in a triad, skin against skin, commingling our blood.

When the corner of Lucas's mouth twitches, I know he's remembering it, too.

Life isn't so simple anymore, and reminiscing is a luxury we don't have time for right now.

I rub my palms together. "Now that our periods are all synced, we have a problem."

17

ANTONIO

Cristiano's alert, waiting for me to fill him in. And I will. *Fully. He's not compromised. I'm certain. And I'm fucking relieved, too.*

"Daniela and I had dinner with Fedorov tonight."

"You and Daniela?" he asks, like I just told him the damn world was ending at the stroke of midnight.

"He wanted to have dinner with Daniela in exchange for your freedom."

Cristiano gapes at me, then at Lucas, his features tight. "You should have told him to go fuck himself."

I almost did. It would have been a huge mistake. An unforgiveable one.

"If you have a problem with my decisions," I growl, "take a goddamn number and get in line. But you won't like how I handle complaints. Just listen."

I lean back in my chair. "Fedorov left here minutes before you arrived. The explosion we heard was his car being blown to hell."

"*Jesus,*" Cristiano mutters.

"It takes a lot of doing to get to someone like Fedorov," Lucas adds. "It would be almost impossible, even for us."

"He knew he was vulnerable." Maybe I should have listened more closely. Although it's not that I didn't take him seriously. I just didn't give a damn.

"Fedorov gabbed tonight, like he was a housewife who didn't get out much. In hindsight, it was a soul-cleansing of sorts. Before he left, he asked for my help. Not directly. But there was no doubt in my mind he wanted me to help him find Nikitin."

I stand and grip the back of my chair. "Fedorov's gone, but we still need to find Nikitin. He poses a substantial risk."

They nod.

"I'm going to the valley for the night. Call me if anything comes up. *Anything.* On the way, I'm going to get in touch with the police chief. I want us to take the lead on that investigation. Get our ducks in order," I instruct Lucas. "No one you could even fathom might have ties to the Russians gets anywhere near any of the evidence. I want to know exactly what happened without those fuckers distorting it."

"You think the chief is going to hand the investigation over?"

"Once I tell him who was in the car? Fuck, yes. He'll send the file over with a thank-you note and a bottle of booze. They don't want to deal with the Bratva."

I glance at Cristiano. "You need to stay here, at least for tonight. Until we're certain there isn't a price on your head."

"Do you want me involved in the case?" he asks, carefully.

I see the glimmer of hope in his eyes.

"No. I want you sitting around with your dick in your hand, chugging bourbon. Yes, I want you on the case. Get your ass to the villa and help Lucas oversee the collection of evidence."

His features relax as the relief floods him.

"Do you have a sense of how close Mikhail was to Fedorov?"
"I'd say pretty close."
"Find him and bring him here. I want to talk to him."

18

DANIELA

I wake as Antonio curls his strong arms around me. *What time is it? Still dark. Good.*

When I got back from our dinner with Fedorov, I spent what felt like hours arguing with Valentina about whether she should be allowed to return to London with Alexis. By the time I collapsed into bed, I was so exhausted, I fell into a dreamless sleep.

I didn't feel the dip of the bed when Antonio climbed in. I didn't smell the warm, masculine scent that's uniquely his. *The one that's teasing me now.*

"Did Fedorov let Cristiano go?" I ask, sinking deeper into his embrace.

"*Mmhm*," he murmurs into my hair. "I'm here to make good on my promise."

The sleep melts away as his body envelops mine with a familiar heat that sends spires of energy through my languid limbs. I'm not sure what promise he's talking about, but I hope it involves that thick cock that's pressed against my ass.

"Did they hurt him?"

"Enough. I don't want to hear Cristiano's name from you, or Fedorov's, or the name of any other human with a dick, while you're in my bed. You want to say someone's name, say mine," he purrs, pushing his cock deep inside me, with a single brutal thrust.

My walls groan at the sudden fullness, stretching to accommodate him.

"Whimper it. Moan it. Cry it out while you come. But my name only." He pulls out, leaving me gasping.

"I promised I'd fuck you until you didn't know your name, and I'm going to do just that. But it's going to be slow torture, *Princesa*." He cups my sex gently, but provides no relief. If anything, it arouses me even more.

As the ache between my legs grows stronger, my hips sway of their own accord, grinding my pussy into his palm.

"*Uh-uh-uh*," he tuts, taking his hand away. "The path to bliss is going to be long and rocky—for you—and for me," he murmurs, gently pushing my hair off my neck and pressing his warm lips into the exposed skin. "I'm going to savor every frantic moan. Every shudder." He slides his mouth near my ear. "Every scream. Because you will scream for me before I'm through."

I'm fully awake now. The unremitting need pulses through me as he stakes his claim in a prelude of what's to come.

With razor-thin patience, Antonio rolls me onto my back, pawing at my nightgown, until it's in tatters. Until there's not a single thread covering me, and I'm fully bared to him.

He pulls back, and his eyes glitter dangerously as he admires his handiwork—or maybe he's admiring me. "You're beautiful. So beautiful. It's a crime to dirty you. But I'm going to do just that."

Searing heat radiates from him, while cool air dances on my bare skin, raising gooseflesh.

Every inch of my body burns for him.

Antonio draws a ragged breath as he nudges my legs apart and climbs between them. *I need him right here.* I snake my arms around him as he lowers his body onto mine.

I'm skin to skin in a sensuous feast with a dangerous man. *And I wouldn't change a thing.*

I feel the rumble in his chest as his mouth crushes mine, our tongues tangling in a way that sends my senses reeling.

When he pulls back, my fingertips find his face. They trace the elegant contours, dipping into a faded scar at the corner of his brow, before indulging in the prickle of an unshaven jaw. Classically handsome, with a dangerous edge. Although, he's *so* much more.

Silently, he captures my gaze, holding it steady, seeing everything I am. Showing me everything he is. The intimacy is almost too much to bear. But neither of us shies away.

We let the moment bathe us in an elixir so potent it could destroy us, if we're not careful. *If I'm not careful. Antonio knows no caution—especially tonight.*

The full moon shines through the drapes, providing just enough light for me to see the wolf baying in his eyes. It beckons me closer, even as it warns me away.

I choose to stay. To inch closer to the wild animal. I have no sense of self-preservation when it comes to this man. I want *everything* he has to give, even knowing it might leave me in pieces.

I make no apologies for what I want. I feel no shame. *He taught me to own my sexuality, and no matter what happens between us, I will always be grateful for that lesson.*

"*Princesa,*" Antonio mutters, in a strangled plea, sweeping the hair away from my face. His hand trembles with a barely controlled need that takes my breath away. "Keep your safeword close."

It's not a threat, but a warning, delivered in a rasp that amplifies his tenuous restraint. With the sand spilling from the only bag holding the dam, he's begging me to help him keep me safe.

19

DANIELA

"Always," I promise. "Always." Before my assurances are out, he lowers his head and sucks a nipple into his mouth. My back bows off the mattress, with no reprieve, until he pulls back to draw the other nipple in.

His mouth is hot as it teeters between gentle teasing and cruel nips that have my toes clinging to the sheets in a march toward surrender. It's a path I gladly walk, with the throb between my legs growing more impatient with each passing second.

I finger his hair roughly, matching his fervor. By some miracle, I remember to keep my hands away from his injured shoulder. Although, painful as it would surely be, I'm not sure he'd even notice.

When Antonio is like this, with a raw vulnerability cloaking the madness, it might seem as though I'm in danger. But in truth, it's when I'm at my most powerful.

"I need you," he whispers gruffly.

It's a staggering admission from a man who admits to needing no one and nothing.

"I need you, too," I confess humbly into the dark, without a scintilla of regret.

He grunts, almost painfully, and rests his forehead on my sternum, the intensity coiled tightly inside his powerful body.

I wonder who died at his hand tonight. And I wonder what kind of woman would welcome this man into her body like a prodigal son.

The woman I once was is slipping away. I hardly recognize her in the distance. In her place is a woman who finds the ultimate pleasure in the arms of a man with blood on his hands. A woman who believes vengeance is an acceptable form of justice. *Maybe this is all I ever was. All I was ever meant to be.*

"I'll be right back," he says, ravaging my mouth before getting out of bed. "Stroke that sweet pussy while I'm gone. Keep it nice and wet."

I do as instructed. I let my fingertips slide over the tender flesh, smearing the arousal into every fold. Imagining that it's his fingers, stroking me.

Antonio returns with the black wand and lays it on my belly. My eyes feel heavy and glazed. My skin is burning.

"Edge for me," he demands, sitting naked on a chair at the foot of the bed.

Too far away.

His large hands white-knuckle the chair's delicate arms. But it's his cock that captures my attention as it juts out from below the trail of dark hair, the skin pulled taut. It bobs under its own weight, proud and unapologetically male. *Like him.*

The room vibrates with rank sexual energy, but the intimacy from earlier has all but disappeared.

I rest a hand on the wand, worrying my bottom lip. "You seem so far away."

"Any closer, and your hair will be wrapped around my fist while I pound you into oblivion. That's for much later," he whispers into the room, like a blown kiss. "Much later."

I wasn't talking about the distance between us, but about

his sudden brooding. His body is here, but his mind is straddling two universes.

"Show me how you edge. Now," he adds, his patience beyond strained. "I've been thinking about it since yesterday."

Okay. I'll play. My fingers find a comfortable grip, and I ease the toy between my thighs. I'm so wet, I don't need lube. Even with the change in his demeanor, my body wants him. *I want him.*

With my eyes shut, I turn the wand on a low setting—it's how I always start. But even with a gentle buzz, my legs begin to tremble almost immediately.

"Faster," he instructs, his voice almost hypnotic.

As soon as I turn the setting up a few notches, a moan escapes into the room and my knees knock together. My skin is overstimulated.

"Open your eyes, *Princesa*. Let your husband enjoy your pleasure."

His husky voice curls around every nerve ending. I can't hold back any longer, and I push the wand away.

"Did I tell you to stop?" he demands, his tone laced with menace.

"You said edge," I choke out. "I was going to come, and I didn't think you'd like that." *Especially tonight.*

He gazes at me from the chair, features tight, stroking his cock from base to tip until it weeps—and every cell of my body aches for him.

I won't be denied.

Without permission, without a rational thought, or any thought at all, I crawl across the bed, and onto the floor, kneeling between his legs.

I hear the hiss. But he doesn't say a word, as his features twist into something I rarely see from him. *Uncertainty.*

As much as I want to know what has him like this, I don't ask, because now is not the time for talking. Now is the time for him to let go of whatever pains him. It's the time to lay down his burdens. *To forget.*

Now is the time to enjoy my dark prince.

I lower my head reverently and lap the salty bead from the slit in the swollen crown.

It's a small gesture that reaps a large reward. The guttural sound that rumbles from his chest is raw and salacious. *Dangerous.* A wolf snared by a morsel he can't resist.

I peek up at him through my lashes as I twist my hair into a knot to keep it off my face. He likes to watch while I suck his cock. *I like it, too.*

Without a word to break the spell, I wrap my hands around the base, swirling my tongue in small circles, until I reach the notch at the head. He shudders as I pleasure him, slapping his open palms on the arms of the chair while my pointed tongue laves the narrow groove.

I don't stop.

A calm energy descends over me, as I lick the ridge and meticulously attend to all the places I've learned drive him to the brink. He patiently taught me how to tease his cock, and now I'm using the knowledge against him. In the most carnal of ways, I use everything I know to send him catapulting off the edge, into a stretch of peace.

"*Princesa,*" he chants into the sultry air. "*Princesa.*"

His body tightens. First his stomach, and soon after his thighs. It's then, *right then,* that I suck him into my mouth and clamp my lips around the thick shaft, sliding deep.

He unleashes a string of expletives that makes my pussy gush.

"Not yet," he growls, as he pushes my head away.

But I don't go easily, not until he squeezes my cheeks together so I have no choice but to release him, and the heady control that I snatched from him for long, sensuous moments.

His eyes are coal black, as we gasp for breath. "I'm going to fuck your mouth, and then I'm going to fuck your pussy, right before I sink my big dick into your ass."

My heart pounds so hard that I fear it's going to burst through my chest.

He's taking no prisoners. It's going to be savage. The pain and pleasure will dance tonight, twining around us until it's impossible to tell them apart.

The pleasure will ultimately prevail. It always does, bursting like a ball of light in the night sky.

I wouldn't have it any other way.

20

ANTONIO

"Open," I demand, with my cock at her lips. She tips her head back and lets her jaw go slack.

"Such an obedient *princesa*." I stroke my thumb against her cheek, letting her experience the tenderness with the animal as I push my cock inside her pretty little mouth.

My throbbing shoulder is little more than a fleeting thought. Her mouth feels so goddamn good, my toes curl.

"Breathe through your nose," I remind her, because she always forgets to breathe.

When I'm satisfied she heard me, I hold her head between my hands and ruthlessly fuck that velvety mouth.

"Such a good girl," I coo, struggling to keep control. "Such a soft mouth for my cock. Touch your pussy. Light caresses. I don't want you to come. I just want you needy. For me."

She loves the dirty talk. So do I. But choppy sentences are all I can manage right now.

I thrust harder and deeper. She gags, and the tears stain her cheeks, until she remembers to swallow at just the right time. *Like I taught her.*

I'm a man possessed as I plunge into her throat. Consumed with chasing the demons away. Consumed with the fragility of life. Consumed with a pervasive need to possess every inch of her mind, body, and soul. There isn't a corner of real estate that I don't want to own. Even her heart—I might want that most.

When my spine begins to tingle, I pull out and drag her to the bed the way a predator drags his helpless prey to the lair. *There's no escape for her.*

She's still gasping for air, panting, as I hover over her to grab the plug I keep in the nightstand. We don't use it often during sex, but when we do, her orgasms—and mine—are earth-shattering.

My favorite use for the plug isn't when we're together, but when we're apart. When I'm away, I often have her insert it. *I demand it.* Not so much for pleasure, but to remind her she's mine. Every time she clenches her ass, she's newly reminded that she's not alone to face the world's problems. That I'm with her—always. And even when she can't see me, I'll always take care of her and keep her safe.

But tonight I promised to fuck her ass. And I will. But I don't trust myself to prepare her well enough to take me. I've managed to keep the demons at arm's length, but once I taste her, all bets are off.

I press the plug to her lips. "Warm it so that it feels good going in."

Her eyes flare with unbridled lust, and her mouth opens, like a little bird awaiting sustenance. As much as that sassy mouth arouses me, *and it does*, I enjoy her like this, too: subdued, wet, submitting to my every whim.

I tongue her nipples, blowing gently on each peak until it furls tighter for me. "You're such an obedient little whore. Maybe it's time to give you my cock. Would you like that?"

She nods, her face glowing with passion as she waits, patiently, for my instructions.

But I don't speak. Instead, I guide her knees to her chest and spread her open. My gaze lingers brazenly on her pussy before it moves to her face.

There's not a drop of shame there. *Not a single drop.* My dark, cold heart clenches. It wasn't that long ago that despite how much she wanted this, she would have been flooded with shame, with feelings that she couldn't explain pulling her under.

She let me guide her to a better mindset. It was a gift I wanted her to have. But it wasn't always easy—for either of us.

"Such a pretty cunt," I murmur, swiping my tongue across her wet, pink flesh a few times before easing the plug from her mouth.

It glistens, and I slide it through her slick folds while she whimpers. The strangled sounds go straight to my aching balls.

"Antonio," she pleads. "Please."

"What do you want, *Princesa*?" I ask, spreading lube on her pleated bud.

She swallows hard. "Your cock."

I brush my mouth across hers, as I insert the plug.

She groans at the intrusion, and my dick leaks.

"My beautiful *princesa*, my wife, my whore, my partner," I growl into her throat. "There's not a man alive who wouldn't kill to have you."

The words get lost as I sink into her pussy, sheathing myself fully inside her walls. Before she can catch her breath, I rear up and pull out, before diving back into the heat, my pubic bone catching her clit with each brutal thrust.

She's pinned under me, unable to squirm, unable to do anything but take what I give her. Every drop of her pleasure is my prerogative.

"I'm going to fuck your ass in this position, so I can see your face while I own that tight little hole." Her pussy clenches around my cock, and I nearly lose it. "That little bud is going to open for me, like it opens for the plug. It's going to welcome me inside, even though it knows I'm the devil."

I tweak her nipples until she cries out. "Come for me," I demand. "Come around my cock. Squeeze it until it hurts."

The orgasm is going to rip through her. For long moments, suspended in time, the pleasure and the pain will be indistinguishable. There won't be one without the other. Not tonight. She knows it, and it's holding her back.

I slide my hand between us. She doesn't need to give it up willingly, but I will have her orgasms—all of them—even if I have to yank them savagely from her.

"Come now, *Princesa*. Now," I demand, when I'm seconds away from emptying myself inside her.

My fingers are merciless. Finding the very places that drive her to the abyss. No let up. Nowhere to hide. *Nowhere*. "Don't think. Just let go."

With a scream that echoes in my veins, she gives it up, her body convulsing under me.

I don't soothe her. I don't fuck her through the orgasm. I wrench myself away, because I'm not done.

Without a modicum of restraint, I pull out the plug. Her eyes widen and she gasps for air. My savageness startles even me. I freeze for a second, before forcing myself to go slow, to check in with her, to lube my cock well—all while wrestling for elusive composure.

My hand strokes the swollen shaft, calming the fervor, as I summon control and decency.

When I find it, I move my cock to her back hole and breach each ring of muscle carefully. Every muscle in my body tightens as I struggle with the urge to sink balls-deep in a single thrust.

She's good. Precious. Don't hurt her. It's a chorus running through my head. *My better angels are near.*

I sink my teeth into her shoulder, and she cries out. It's fuel on a raging fire. "You shouldn't let me have your ass when I have so little control."

"You won't hurt me." The words tumble from her, with no hesitation. As if it's the truth.

But it's not. I could hurt her. *Some part of me wants to hurt her.* But her faith. Her trust. She's given them to me. *Her love.* All things I'm not worthy of receiving.

"I've told you not to take that bet," I grunt, sliding my hand between us, once more, rubbing my callused thumb in circles on her swollen nub. She's close to coming again, and I'm hanging on by the barest thread.

She closes her eyes as the waves of pleasure surge and crest.

A good man would let her have the moment to herself. But not me. I want it all.

"Open your eyes. Don't make me tell you again. I want to watch you come apart with my cock in your ass. I want to feel you shudder. I want to feel your tremors as you clench my cock like a dirty *princesa*. You're going to milk my dick, because it feels so good, doesn't it?"

"Yes," she whimpers, clinging to me.

And I'm done.

My movements get quick and jerky as she digs her nails into my back, drawing blood.

"What's your name?" I ask, remembering my earlier promise. *I'm going to fuck you until you don't know your name.*

"Daniela," she moans.

I rear up and plunge back inside, pinching her clit while she writhes under me.

"Antonio," she shrieks. "Antonio."

I don't let up. Not until her eyes glaze over, and I sense the drop.

"What's your name?" I repeat, through gritted teeth.

She doesn't respond.

Her legs twist around my waist, while her body shudders.

The sweat drips off me. I feel the final jerk of my hips and the primal thunder in my chest as I collapse on top of her, the demons at bay.

21

ANTONIO

I rest on her longer than I should. I'm so much bigger and heavier, I have to be a crushing weight. But I lost all sense of time—and I suspect she did, too.

She grimaces as I ease out of her slowly. I brush my mouth against hers. "I don't deserve you," I say humbly. "But I'm never letting you go. I'll destroy anything that dares come between us."

"*Te amo*," she whispers into my neck, wrapping her limbs tighter around me so that I stay close.

She cradles my jaw in her hand. "There's no room for anything to come between us. I won't allow it. That's why I drag you closer, every time you pull back. I won't allow the space to get large enough for anything to wedge between us. It can only happen if we allow it. My strength is different than yours. But it knows no bounds."

I roll over and pull her with me, until there's no daylight between us.

I've done nothing in my life that makes me worthy of this moment. Of her love. But I take it. Gobble it up like a starving man.

"Te amo, meu amor. Your goodness chases away my demons. When you're in my arms, I'm a better man."

As we lay quietly, the moon disappears behind the clouds. *Nothing lasts forever.*

She'll be fine without you.

It's true. Daniela's small, but she's not fragile. Her strength and resilience are something to behold. But I want more for her. I want her to have the peace I crave. *Something I'll never be able to give her. Not in my lifetime.*

"Come shower with me," I whisper into her skin. "Let me soap your gorgeous body and lather your hair. It's my turn to take care of you. Let me."

She deserves to be cherished and worshipped. But she hates even the thought of anyone fussing over her. It makes her feel weak, and she doesn't like to feel weak any more than I do.

"If you expect me to lower my walls for you," I say gently, "you need to work on lowering yours for me."

"I'm pretty sure I've done that."

I smile. "You have. But I want more. I always want more."

I feel her head bob against my chest.

"I'm not sure I can walk," she groans, stretching her legs.

"You don't need to walk. Not as long as I'm here to carry you, *Princesa.*" I press my lips to her head. "With any luck, that'll be for a long time."

But even as I say it, I hear the clock ticking.

22

ANTONIO

"Why do you have to be so unreasonable?" Valentina screeches. "It's ruining my life."

The joys of having a pre-teen in the house. Haven't missed this part. Although I've never heard Valentina like this.

I can't hear what Daniela is saying, because she's not shrieking at the top of her lungs. But my heart stops at Valentina's shrill response to whatever she said. "You're not my mother!"

I've heard enough.

Daniela will not be subject to this kind of abuse from a mouthy twelve-year-old. I don't give a shit if it's normal. I won't allow it.

While I storm toward Valentina's suite, my better sense takes over. I can't intervene in this. And it's not because she isn't my child. She's living under my roof and I'll do and say what I like, but this is their struggle.

Rafael and I had struggles, too. We persevered through them in our own dysfunctional way. If I swoop in and save the day, I diminish Daniela's authority. I've taken enough from her. I'm not doing that.

When I walk into the sitting room, the tension is palpable. Daniela's shoulders are hunched forward. She looks like she's been pummeled. Valentina is pouting on the other side of the room, with Lara comforting her. Someone's in the bedroom—the maid, I assume.

As soon as she spots me, Valentina rushes to my side. "Antonio, I'm so happy you're here. Alexis wants me to come to London and stay with her for a few weeks. I really want to go. Even Lara thinks it's a good idea for me to have time with my friend."

I glare at Lara, and she shrinks.

"Now is not a good time to go to London," Daniela says, with much more patience than I have on a good day.

"I don't have any friends here. And Rafael's leaving tonight. I'll be all alone, without anybody."

Daniela blanches. I don't think Valentina meant it to hurt her, but I feel the sting from here.

I turn to Lara. "This is a family matter that doesn't involve you. Leave us." It's harsher than it needs to be, but it's better than *Get the fuck out of my house*. She should have never insinuated herself in their struggle, and taking Valentina's side is inexcusable. Lara should be loyal to Daniela, above all else.

She gives me a brittle smile. "Of course."

Paula scurries out of the bedroom with towels in her arms, and leaves without a glance at anyone.

Valentina's eyes dart to Daniela as she inches away from me, like she's suddenly decided that I'm not an ally, after all. While I don't want her to be afraid of me, she dragged me into their squabble, and I don't put up with this kind of bullshit.

I quietly shut the door, before turning to her.

"I heard you screaming from down the hall. Girls who are old enough to travel are old enough to speak respectfully to adults." My voice is low, but firm.

She blinks several times, before staring at her feet.

"I'm always willing to hear what you have to say, as long as you speak calmly and respectfully. You can come to me about anything. I want you to come to me. But don't expect me to take your side over Daniela's. If she becomes a real ogre, or does something criminal, that's different. But until then, Daniela and I stand together. If you're looking to rant about how mean the adults are around here, and how it's ruining your life, I suggest you talk to Rafael. He'll have a sympathetic ear in that regard."

I glance at Daniela, who is standing up straight again, and then back to Valentina, who meets my eyes and nods.

"I'm sorry," she says, sincerely. "Please don't be mad at me."

She has that same desperation in her voice that Rafael would get when I corrected him, when he first came to live with me. It was hard to hear then, and it's hard to hear now.

"I'm not angry with you," I say gently. "And even if I was, so what? People who live together have disagreements. Sometimes those disagreements get loud and ugly. It doesn't change how we feel about one another. But I'm not the person to whom you owe an apology."

At first, I'm not sure she's going to apologize to Daniela. She definitely wouldn't even be considering it if I wasn't standing here. Not yet anyway. She's not ready.

"I'm sorry," she says softly in Daniela's direction. Valentina's chin is out, and she doesn't actually look at Daniela.

Not much remorse there.

But Daniela is kind-hearted and she doesn't demand more. It's the right call in this situation. Even an asshole like me knows it.

"I love you," Daniela replies. "I want you to be happy. And I certainly don't want to ruin your life. But I also want you to be safe. I'm trying my very best to juggle those things."

It's a sentiment I fully understand.

"May I be excused?" Valentina asks, giving me a sweet smile.

I point her toward Daniela, who nods.

She's a good kid. A *great* kid, and she's been through a hell of a lot. Daniela's first instinct is to shower her in kindness and look the other way at the transgressions. When Rafael came to live here, my natural instinct was to grab him by the throat and tell him to get in line when he got mouthy. I never did that, because he was a young boy who had been kicked around a lot. But I fell back on another of my instincts. I threw up my hands and disappeared. Fortunately for Rafael, that didn't last long. We had Dr. Lima, who wasn't afraid to critique my parenting style.

"What was that about?" I ask when I'm sure Valentina's out of hearing range.

Daniela blows out a big, noisy breath. "She wants to go to London."

"I got that part. But she's not normally so loud and obnoxious."

"I know." She straightens the cushion on the chair and returns some books to the shelf. "Valentina's been sassier since she got back from camp. Maybe even a little sneaky. She's testing me left and right. Some of it's hormonal. But I think she misses Isabel a lot, and she resents me *acting* like her mother."

There's real pain in her voice, and I know it's torture for her, maybe even more now that Isabel's gone. She could put an end to it by telling Valentina the truth, but even the prospect terrifies her.

"She's been through a lot in a very short time," I say, instead of *You need to tell her you're her mother, or I will.* "More than most kids have to deal with at her age. We need to have empathy, but don't let her make you the scapegoat for all her problems. It'll only get worse. And it certainly won't help her."

Daniela lowers herself to the arm of a chair and stares out the window. "I know. My feelings get in the way of my judgment. You don't seem to have that problem."

"You have to have feelings for them to cloud your judgment. I'm an unfeeling bastard."

She turns her head to smile at me. "Nice try, but I've seen those feelings."

She's talking about last night. Those moments after the sex is especially intense, when we show all our cards and the world bleeds away until it's just me and her, and a glut of emotion. Those are weak moments that I can't afford to indulge often, or ever, in the light of day.

"I live off those feelings," she adds, softly. "Your love strengthens me. I hope one day my love can do the same for you."

23

DANIELA

"It's easy to manage a fight when you're standing outside the ring," Antonio says, sidestepping my comments about feelings entirely.

God forbid anyone overhears us and learns that he actually has them.

"I had no plans to jump in the middle of that argument."

I'm not sure I believe that. He can't resist coming to my rescue. "She sees you as a hero," I say, a bit wistfully.

"And you don't like that."

Most people end their questions on an inflection, inviting the listener to respond. Not Antonio. Nearly everything comes out of his mouth sounding like gospel. I'm sure it's to signal the listener that he doesn't want a response.

But there's a touch of bitterness in his tone, too, because he always thinks the worst. I don't let it go. I want Valentina and Antonio, the two people I love most in this world, to be close.

"It's not that I don't like it." Not exactly. "I want her to be close to you. But the way she thinks about you feels a little maladaptive. Like she's scared, and counting on you to slay the dragons and make everything better. It's not healthy. What if something happens that's beyond even your ability to fix—the disappointment could be crushing. I don't want her to blame you."

He comes over and tips my chin up. "I have broad shoulders. I can take it."

"It's not just that. I don't want her to grow up to be the kind of woman who looks to men to save her. I want her to believe she can save herself."

Antonio gazes at me quietly for a moment. "She's not wrong, you know."

I swat his hand away. "About you being some kind of savior?"

He rolls his eyes. "About being stuck here without friends her own age."

I know she's right. It kills me that she left her friends behind in the US and has no friends to hang out with here—and she won't be going to school in the fall, unless something changes drastically. I know what it's like to be twelve and isolated from your peers. To have no one your own age to talk to, and laugh with, and be silly around.

"Antonio, when is this going to be over? I don't mean the run-of-the-mill we need to be careful stuff. I mean the increasing danger around us. When is life going to be normal for her?"

"No one wants it to be over more than I do. For all of us. But especially for you."

He gazes at me for a moment, then takes a step back, rubbing a palm over his jaw.

Something's bothering him.

"What is it?" I ask, getting to my feet.

He eases a section of hair behind my ear. "There's something I need to tell you."

More bad news. God, I hope not.

"Fedorov died last night after he left the lodge." He rubs his strong hands over my arms, but his voice is devoid of anything resembling sorrow or regret. He's more concerned with my feelings than he is that a man who we had dinner with last night is dead.

Maybe he wanted him dead. Maybe he's responsible.

I stagger back and find refuge behind a stuffed chair. But there's no escaping the pall in the room.

"Did—did you have anything to do with his death?" I don't expect an answer, but I watch for clues in his demeanor and tone.

"You know better than to ask me a question like that."

That's not a denial. It's chilling.

With my heart pounding, I back farther away, until I'm well out of his reach. I can't look at him.

"Not that it's any of your business," he says, prowling closer, "but I never kill anyone without good cause. Your world has a large gray center. My world is very black and white."

He pauses, scowling. "Fedorov's car hit a barrier. It didn't happen at my hand, or on my order."

He didn't kill him. The relief courses through me. Antonio is many things, but he's not a liar. Before I can respond, he turns to leave.

"Antonio."

He stops, but he doesn't turn around.

"Thank you. I realize I crossed a line in the sand, but I'm still trying to understand this life. The less I know, the more frightening it is."

He swivels to face me. "You grew up in this life. You were sheltered from a lot of it, but you're not a total innocent in that regard. What you're still trying to understand is me."

He's right, of course. I know what drives him. I know that beneath all the layers, hidden behind a concrete wall, there's a soft heart. But I'm still trying to understand the bounds of his depravity. Although recently, what I fear most is my growing tolerance for it.

"Can I ask another question?"

He snickers. "You already know that your last question was way out of bounds. But as long as we're alone, you can always ask. We've already agreed that it's your prerogative as my wife. But that doesn't entitle you to answers. You'll get them as I see fit—and even then, you might not like them."

I ignore everything he just said, except, *As long as we're alone, you can always ask.* The rest is his way of chiding me because I asked if he killed someone. Nothing more.

"Do you think the car crash was an accident?" *Please say yes. Give me a reason not to worry about you all day.*

"I need more facts before I think anything. Until I have that information, it wasn't an accident."

My heart sinks.

I want to know why someone would kill Fedorov, or if his death is connected to our dinner, but he's not in the mood to give me answers, so I don't ask.

"I need to go into the city. When I get home from work, we should talk about Lara."

"What about her?"

"You shouldn't have anyone on staff who undermines you with Valentina, or with anyone else. Get rid of her, or I will."

I can take or leave Lara, but Valentina likes her, and there's been so much upheaval in her life. "No more changes right now. Lara's not perfect, but I can deal with her. I could bring in someone else who's worse."

"Think about it."

I have. Long before today, but I keep coming to the same conclusion. "When will you be back?"

"Why? Is that pussy in need of more attention already?" There's a glimmer of playfulness in his eyes that wasn't there a minute ago.

I feel my cheeks pinkening. "I think everywhere in that region has had plenty of attention. Thank you very much."

I close the space between us. "Be careful. There's something in the air. I can feel it."

He presses his lips to the top of my head. "Think about letting Valentina go to London," he says softly. "Not today, or tomorrow, because she shouldn't be rewarded for shouting at you. But think about it. She'll be safe at Will and Samantha's."

I don't know. It feels like I'm expanding the distance between us. Although there's no reason—except for selfish ones—for me not to let her go.

"I realize it's a short flight on a private jet, but I'm not ready to send her alone."

"You could go with her. Spend a couple days with Samantha, and then come home. We can go together to pick her up in a week or two."

I'm running out of reasons to have her stay. Or at least the reasons I keep coming up with are more about me missing her than about anything else.

"The harvest will be early this year," Antonio says, shifting the conversation. "We're maybe six weeks away, possibly seven. Some things were put in place months ago, but there's a lot of preparation still to be done. I host several events, including a gala, and some smaller ones to benefit local charities. I normally hire a party planner who organizes the events. But this year, maybe you can oversee the planning."

I smile. The harvest and the activities surrounding it are such an important part of our way of life. It's been years and years since I participated. "I would love to organize some events. I'd also like Valentina to be part of it."

"Absolutely. But she doesn't need to be here for all the preparation. While she's in London, you can use the time to get up to speed on what's been done and what still needs to be done."

I nod while a million ideas pop into my head. This isn't the same as tracking down missing girls, like my mother did, but I can do some good things for the community.

"I have something else for you to think about."

"Something good, I hope."

"What if we set up a school on the property for Valentina?"

"A school just for Valentina?" He really is insane.

"No. We could find a few other girls her age to participate. It's just a thought I had while she was complaining about not having friends."

His phone vibrates, and he pulls it out. His expression is neutral—a practiced neutrality.

"I have to go. Let me think about it some more, and we can talk about it later. I wouldn't mention anything to her yet."

With everything the man has to worry about, he's thinking of creating a school for my daughter. It's hard not to love him. I stand on tiptoe and press a kiss to his cheek. "It's bad luck to leave without kissing your wife goodbye."

"The problem is that once my mouth is on my wife, there's never any rush to leave. But I don't want to buy any bad luck. I tempt fate often enough."

Too often. Much too often.

24

ANTONIO

I reread the text I received a few moments ago from Lucas. **We have Mikhail. How do you want to proceed?**

I call, instead of texting back. "That was fast."

"We put out feelers, and he showed up. He needs friends. Where should we put him?"

He risked his life to help Cristiano, albeit on Fedorov's order. But I have no reason to trust him. Even less now that Fedorov's gone. I don't trust anyone who comes in voluntarily any more than I trust someone who comes in kicking and screaming. *Maybe less.*

"The small conference room adjacent to my office. I'll contact Cecelia and have her clear my schedule. Bring him in through the back. Put him on a service elevator. Tight security. He's not a prisoner—yet. But don't take your eyes off him for a second."

"He's been on the run. Could use a shower. We'd all be happier in that conference room."

"It's going to have to wait. Anything on the accident?"

"It's tough going. That car was blown to bits. Our guys are finding debris blocks away. This was a professional job."

"Make sure you run DNA tests on any body parts you find." *I want to know who was in that car.*

"If we find anything worth testing. You can take a look at the photos from the scene. This was nothing like the explosion on the boat. They made sure there was no fuck-up this time."

"Do we have anything that ties the explosions together?"

"Nada."

"Keep looking. There has to be some connection."

Although, sometimes it feels like separate and distinct entities are causing havoc. Each running their own shop to bring me down. But that's unlikely.

Tomas is dead, and no one else would bring in the Russians. I have plenty of enemies, but outside of Nikitin, I can't think of anyone who would risk so many innocents to get rid of me—especially with Fedorov gone.

25

ANTONIO

Cristiano, Lucas, and our guest are in the conference room when I arrive.

Mikhail appears to be in his late thirties, maybe forty, five or six years older than me. Although he looks like he hasn't been anywhere near a comb, a razor, or soap and water for some time, so it's difficult to tell.

"So we're clear," I say, pulling out a chair across from him, "I appreciate everything you did for Cristiano, but that was yesterday, and today is a new day. Where's your boss?"

He folds his hands on the table in front of him and sits back, eyeing me like I'm every bit the arrogant bastard I am.

"You're as personable and charming as they say."

I glare at him. "From the way you smell, I'm thinking you're living on the street instead of high on the hog in an oligarch's mansion. If you hope to improve your lot, I suggest you skip the editorializing. Where's your boss?"

"I assume you mean Nikitin, although he wasn't my boss."

That's exactly who I mean. I nod.

"I don't know where the bastard is. He fled with a handful of his best guards, but I'm sure once they learn that he's been summoned home, they'll either disappear or turn him over. Their loyalty to him will only go so far."

"You don't have any idea where he might have gone?"

"None. If he made arrangements, it wasn't through me. His jet is in the hangar, and his yacht is docked in Porto. A logical guess would be that he left the country. Crossed into Spain over land."

"But you don't believe that."

"I don't think he'd leave without at least making an effort to bring you down."

Fedorov said he was vengeful. "Why is that?"

"The Russian government wants a stronger foothold here. It would serve their interests well."

"So Chernov and Nikitin got their marching orders from the Kremlin?"

"Possibly. But I wouldn't go that far. Their fortunes were tied to the Kremlin. I believe that they wanted you gone as a gift to their boss. The Bratva exists as a parallel entity to the government—although in theory, it's subject to its laws. The oligarchs hold their power at the behest of the president. You'd make a lovely gift."

This guy has a lot of balls for someone who's stinking up the room. I can respect that. "You said their fortunes *were* tied?"

"Chernov's dead. And Nikitin won't see another cent from the Russian coffers. They might not have been acting on orders to bring you down, but once they made an attempt, there would be an expectation that it was executed properly."

There certainly have been a lot of missteps, and more than one event that should have killed me, or someone I care about, but I'm still standing.

What I want to know is why Mikhail came in so willingly, and what his connection is to Fedorov, and if he's here on Bratva business.

"Who killed Fedorov?"

"Nikitin was responsible, I'm sure. Although it's possible that the order could have come from somewhere higher. But I don't think so. Nikitin was small and petty. A vindictive son of a bitch. He would have wanted to punish Fedorov for rescuing Cristiano."

"Fedorov had a lot of enemies. But he was killed by someone who got close enough to tamper with his car. So it wasn't just some bloke down the street who he forgot to tip."

"That's why I came the moment I heard you were looking for me. I assume you want Nikitin. Even though I don't know his whereabouts, I know him. I might be able to help."

Mikhail is Bratva. They wouldn't help an old lady out of a ditch, if there wasn't something to be gained for them.

"What's in it for you?"

"Revenge. Fedorov was my uncle."

"Your uncle? That's interesting, because he told me he had no successor."

"He does not. I'm not his successor."

"But you're blood. He trusted you enough to put you in Nikitin's house. And you cared enough about him that you're looking for revenge. I don't get it."

He eyes me for a moment. "My mother was Dimitri's youngest sister. Like all good Bratva princesses, she was betrothed to a man from a like-minded family. But before she got married, she met the love of her life and got pregnant. My grandfather turned over his youngest daughter, just seventeen, to her betrothed's family. But she never made it. Somewhere along the journey, she disappeared."

Bratva princesses don't just disappear. *Neither do wine princesses, like my Aunt Vera.* But Mikhail's mother got lucky. Her betrothed's family would have killed her and paraded her body through the streets to teach every young girl a lesson.

"Dimitri was able to get her to the US," Mikhail continues,

"and set her up with a new identity. He wired money regularly, and made sure we never wanted for anything. He would visit me when I was in college, and later—but he never saw her again." He shrugs. "Not because he didn't want to, but because it would have put her life in danger. Bad men have long memories."

We do. And we pass along a list of grievances from generation to generation.

"Is she still alive?"

He peers into my eyes. "I've said all I'm going to say about my mother."

Fair enough.

"How did you end up with Nikitin?"

"My uncle put out the word that he was interviewing a Russian American Ivy League graduate as an assistant. Nikitin hired me out from under him."

He smiles.

"The oligarchs are different from the Bratva. They're not trained in our ways. Many of them don't have useful skills other than schmoozing, and they're motivated by money."

"We're all motivated by money, Mikhail."

"Not solely by money. Some of us take an oath to something larger than ourselves. Certainly, larger than money. Not the oligarchs. They're in it for themselves."

"Fedorov was the leader of the European Bratva. Is there any other arm that would want him dead?"

"With regard to the rest of the Bratva, he was revered and trusted."

"Do you have a family?"

"No."

"You'll stay with us until this is over."

His brow furrows. "I'm a prisoner?"

"No. Not yet. If you want to keep it that way, I strongly

suggest that you don't do anything that even gives me pause. That would be unwise," I advise, pointedly. "We'll protect you. But you're not to go anywhere without a guard. I mean *anywhere*. We'll keep your weapon, your phone, and any other electronics you have with you. Lucas will set you up with everything you need."

I don't think this guy is lying, but I don't trust him, either.

When they leave, I turn to Cristiano. "Are you up for this? He just saved your life. I'm grateful, but that doesn't mean I won't kill him if he turns out to be a liar."

Cristiano looks straight at me. "I already sent his DNA to be tested against what we got from Fedorov's dinnerware."

I nod.

"I'm grateful to him, too. And I'll be even more grateful if he can help us find Nikitin so we can toss his lifeless body in the ocean. As far as I'm concerned, we're at war."

Unfortunately, that's true.

"But are you comfortable with me working closely with Mikhail?"

I get up to leave. "You wouldn't be working with him, if I wasn't."

"Thank you," he says before I reach the door.

I turn around. "For what?"

"For the other night. For treating me like any other person of suspicion. Every guard, every soldier who works for you understands the weight of the oath they took, better today. Everyone is held to the same standard."

"Don't read too much into it."

"I know it cost you—all of it, from the recording, to the pat down, right down to the cuffs."

I don't say anything as I open the door.

"I know you, Antonio. You do what's required, even as it eats at your soul."

"I'm glad you're back," I say with one hand on the doorframe. "Lucas is the absolute worst sailor I've ever run into. Did you hear we lost the damn race?"

My friend's mouth twitches at the corners. "Next year. We'll win big."

Next year. It seems so far away.

26

DANIELA

Samantha and I are having a cold drink in the shade of an ancient sycamore, waiting for Antonio's mother to arrive. The girls are sunbathing near the pool, with the music turned up loud enough to be enjoyed by the neighbors—if there were any actual neighbors.

"Like Will, Antonio is—" Samantha pauses for a moment, as if searching for the right words to describe her relationship with my husband. "Not someone I'd want to cross. But he has a soft spot for people he cares about, and he's always been there for me. I would never hesitate to go to him for anything."

She glances over my shoulder. "Look who's here."

I turn around to see Lydia, followed by a man and a woman, who appear to be waitstaff, and two guards carrying tiered trays.

"She wanted to take us all to tea, but Will and Antonio shot that idea right down. So it looks like she brought tea to us. From Claridge's, no less. I adore her. But she's nuts," Samantha whispers.

Lydia gushes over Samantha and me, before giving us each

a big hug. While I'm wrapped in her embrace, I can't help but think of my mother. She would have loved an afternoon with the girls. *Three generations of us.*

Although, if she were here, I wouldn't have Valentina, and I certainly wouldn't be married to Antonio. It's a bittersweet moment for me, but I won't allow the melancholy to spoil the afternoon.

"I suspect if I follow the music, I'll find my girls." Lydia chuckles, reaching for a tote bag at her feet. "I brought wide-brimmed hats and some other trinkets for them. What's a tea party without a little flair?"

Samantha winks at me. The girls are twelve, yearning to be older and more sophisticated. I doubt they'll want to play dress up. Hopefully they won't hurt her feelings.

―――

WE WERE SO WRONG. The girls strutted around in bikinis with the floppy hats and long strands of faux pearls that Lydia brought, sticking out their budding breasts, until Samantha decided that we'd had enough of a "titty show," and made them put on cover-ups before they sat down to tea.

For two hours, maybe longer, we have a tea party. We chat and laugh a lot. Lydia tells stories about my mother, and Vera, and Antonio, which Valentina, and even Alexis, eat up. She also listens intently to every word that comes out of the girls' mouths, as though they're dropping little gems, instead of tidbits of pop culture.

I don't remember either of my grandmothers. They passed when I was very young. I'm so happy that Valentina has Lydia —a *grandmother* who loves her for simply existing.

When the girls eventually have enough, they excuse themselves and disappear in the direction of the house.

"I'm going to take the rest of the pastries inside," Samantha says, "and peek on the budding chorus girls to make sure they're not sneaking cigarettes and gin."

Cigarettes and gin?

"I'm kidding," she assures me, when my jaw hits the ground.

Sneaking contraband and experimenting with friends. I missed out on that phase of life.

"Is my son good to you?" Lydia asks, after Samantha gathers the leftovers and takes them inside.

I nod and take a sip of water. "He's good to me, and to Valentina."

The muscles in her face unfurl with my assurances.

"He's always been complicated. Even as a child, he had a maturity well beyond his years. He saw too much. Took on too much responsibility too soon. He still had some fun in him, though. But the years, and the ever-growing responsibilities, have made him so serious. So stern. Sometimes I struggle to find the boy who beamed when he handed me a flower he picked from the garden. He rarely laughs anymore. I hope you can help him find the joy in life again."

My heart clenches. "I'm trying. He's a work in progress, but we'll get there." At least, most days I think so.

"He adores you," she says softly. "It's the one thing that gives me solace. I love my son with all my heart, but I'm still having a hard time forgiving him for forcing you to honor the betrothal contract."

Her face is lined with sorrow. For most of her life, she worked to make things easier for Portuguese women who were caught between a ruthless dictator and a society that was slow to evolve. Antonio's behavior must feel like the worst kind of betrayal.

"I'm so sorry, *meu amor*," she says. "I tried my best with him.

I pleaded with him to do better, but it seems it fell on deaf ears."

We've been through this before, and I'm sure she's let Antonio know how she feels. Lydia is no shrinking violet. *It must have been hell for her, married to Hugo.* She's going to apologize to me for as long as she lives.

I place my hand on hers. "I hate that I wasn't given a choice about the marriage. And I won't stand for it with Valentina. But I have a choice now. I could leave. It wouldn't be easy, but Antonio wouldn't hold me against my wishes. Not at this point." *Not now that he knows what his father did.*

Skepticism has replaced the sorrow on her face. She doesn't believe it. But I believe it. Every word. It would be ugly, but he wouldn't hold me as a prisoner.

"I choose to stay," I tell my mother-in-law, my mother's best friend. "And I choose him."

Lydia squeezes her eyes shut, but a few tears trickle out. "He's lucky to have you. Strong men need strong women."

She sips some water.

"Hugo wasn't strong. He was just loud, and mean to the bone. Evil personified."

"Antonio's nothing like him," I say, emphatically.

"No." She shakes her head. "But he needs someone to pull him back when he starts in that direction. I was never able to do that for my husband. Hugo, and Abel, too, were not men you could reason with." She sighs. "I won't be around forever. I'm counting on you, my dear, to help Antonio grow into the good man I know is inside. He has the ability to put an end to some of the old ways that are harmful." Lydia squeezes my hand. "A lot rides on your success. I have great faith in you."

There's something about her words, her tone—the entire conversation, really. It's been wistful, almost resigned, and ominous.

For a moment, it feels as though she's passed me the mantle. Welcomed me to the resistance that she, and Vera, and my mother, and even my grandmother, revered.

I'm honored, and I hope I'm worthy.

27

ANTONIO

"Where are we with Nikitin?" I ask the three men around the table in a cramped office inside one of the Port caves. Now that Mikhail has joined the search for Nikitin, we can't convene in the villa as often as we used to. That space is still sacrosanct, and only Cristiano, Lucas, and I have access.

"He's been sighted in Morocco and Algeria," Lucas says.

Every criminal on the lam is sighted in Morocco and Algeria at some point. It's usually bullshit. Someone trying to cash in on a reward.

I turn to Mikhail. "How likely is it that he would be in either of those places?"

Mikhail shakes his head. "Morocco, maybe. Algeria? I don't see it."

I don't either. And the border between them is dangerous as hell.

"Although, he has to be desperate," Mikhail adds. "From what I've heard, all but one of his guards has abandoned him. And it's easy to get lost in either of those places."

"If you can survive," Cristiano mutters.

Mikhail nods. "Nikitin is an oligarch. A billionaire. He's used to a cushy life and a platoon of guards protecting him."

"A cushy life is out the window when you're on the run—especially when your primary bank accounts have been frozen by your government."

I slam my fist on the table. "If he's in such a world of hurt, why can't we locate him?"

"He's not exactly poverty-stricken," Mikhail reasons. "He does have cash with him."

"That disappears quickly."

"We can put out feelers everywhere, but we're not going to capture him without boots on the ground." Mikhail has been hankering to go to Africa and search.

It's true, but I can't send men off to scour the world without some sense of where he's hiding. "We need credible information before we send out a search party."

"I want to go," Mikhail says, catching my eye. He's not asking for my permission, and he doesn't have to—we've given him safe harbor, and in return he's helped piece some things together, but he doesn't work for me.

"I can start in the Canary Islands, because despite what our sources tell us, I think he's more likely to be there than anywhere else. Then I'll move to Morocco, and Algeria, if all else fails. In the meantime, we'll keep searching the web for clues, and checking in regularly with our contacts. I can't stand to be here waiting to get on with my life, and I refuse to do that until my uncle's murder is avenged."

He's impatient. I get that. I want Nikitin, too, and before the harvest, which is getting closer by the day. "You realize that he could be anywhere, and what you're planning might be futile."

He nods. "Our best chance is with me on the ground, and all of you doing the things that can only be done from here with sophisticated equipment."

"I agree. Although, I can't afford to send men on a wild-goose chase. Not right now. We're getting ready for the harvest with all it entails, and I need every soldier I have here. But I can fund your trip. I'll outfit you with whatever you need and cover whatever expenses you have."

"I can find a few men to take with me, and while I appreciate the offer, I can fund my own trip. The Fedorov fortune is vast, and some of it has found its way to me. I can think of no better way to use it than to find Dimitri's killer. What I do need from you is safe passage out of the country. Off the continent would be even better."

"Done," I say without hesitating. "Let's stay in regular contact. We'll share our information, and you'll share yours. If you change your mind about funds, you know how to reach me."

28

DANIELA

Antonio promised to get home early enough that we could have a quiet dinner. I haven't seen him in three days, and I've missed him. Even his growly, possessive nature that makes me want to push back hard. Honestly? Maybe I've missed that the most.

"Duarte, I'm going to stop by to say hello to Antonio before I go up to the apartment." He might not be there, but it's worth a try.

"Is he expecting you?" my new guard asks.

It's a fair question, I suppose. God forbid someone should drop in on the king without a proper invitation.

"No. I'm going to surprise him."

He gives me a small smile, not a hey-it's-your-funeral kind of smile, but an *ah, newlyweds* kind.

"Do you mind taking my bag up to the apartment?"

"It would be my pleasure, but *Senhor* Antonio would not be happy if I let you roam around this building alone. The public has access to the main floors. I'll accompany you to his office, and then I'll take the bag upstairs."

Duarte is a breath of fresh air compared to Alvarez, who

was not only a traitor, but a grumpy bastard. "I don't want you to get in trouble."

"I don't want to get in trouble either. Your husband won't forgive me as easily as he'll forgive you."

That's probably true, although I wouldn't be forgiven so easily for traipsing around without a guard. Security has been tighter than ever since Cristiano was abducted off the street.

Duarte holds the elevator door for me, and I pick up the phone outside the suite to call Cecilia to let me in.

"*Senhora*," she says, pushing open the heavy French door, "it's so nice to see you."

Now that I'm in a secure area, Duarte quietly slips away. "It's good to see you, too. Is Antonio in his office?"

"He is. I'll let him know you've arrived." She stops for a moment, on our way down the hall. "He is expecting you, correct?"

That would be a resounding *no*. I hate to do this, but I really don't want her to announce me. "I came directly from the airport, and I'm so thirsty. You know how dry the air is on a plane. Would you mind getting me some water, please?"

"Of course," she chirps. "I'll be right back."

As soon as she's out of sight, I knock on Antonio's door.

"What?" he growls like a rabid dog.

I don't know how Cecelia puts up with this nonsense. *Maybe she's like me, and loves dogs—rabies and all.*

I turn the knob and push open the door. "It's your midday dose of good cheer, *senhor*," I announce with a big grin.

He leans back in his chair, his eyes glittering, trying hard not to grin back. "I thought I told you that I don't like unexpected visitors."

"And I thought I told you that the rules on visitors don't apply to your wife."

With two fingers, he beckons me closer. "Come here."

"*Senhor*, I'm so sorry," Cecelia cries from the doorway. She turns to me. "I didn't realize you were going to come in."

Poor woman.

"Don't worry," I mouth, taking the water from her. "He's happy to see me."

Antonio's wolfish gaze is fixed on me, as he barks orders to his assistant. "Go home. Transfer your calls, and take them from there. Make sure all the doors to the suite are locked before you leave. Even the inside staircase."

"Should I come in tomorrow?"

His eyes are brazenly raking over my body. "I don't know, Cecelia. Do you still want your job?"

She nods. "Yes."

"Then I would definitely come in if I were you."

God, he's insufferable.

"Where were we?" he asks when she shuts the door behind her.

"I was about to make myself comfortable in your lap."

He continues to undress me with his eyes as I saunter toward him. "Is that so?"

When I'm within arm's reach, he swivels his chair and pulls me into his lap. My hip grazes his erection as I find a comfortable position, and his eyes flare.

"I've missed you, *Princesa*," he murmurs, cupping the nape of my neck to bring my mouth closer to where he can devour it.

Any doubt I might have had about why he sent Cecelia home is long gone.

"Valentina was having a fabulous time when I left," I pant when we come up for air. "Your mother looks great, Samantha sends her best, and my flight was uneventful. Thank you for asking."

He sinks his teeth into my bottom lip.

"*Ahhh*," I cry.

"Wench. I would have gotten to all that, but not before I say hello to your pussy. You know how needy it gets when it's ignored." He slides his fingers under my skirt. "Next time you come to my office, leave your panties at home."

"Does that mean I'm welcome to stop by any time?" I manage on a moan.

"As long as you're prepared for what you'll get when you arrive." He nips my earlobe, as he shoves the silky gusset aside. "Oh, *Princesa*. I think you are prepared. So prepared," he whispers, sliding his fingertips over my wet flesh.

29

ANTONIO

I have a ton of work to do, but I sent my assistant home so I could play with my wife for the rest of the afternoon. *I'm insane.* This woman drives me beyond all reason, and has since the morning I visited her, after her father died.

Daniela whimpers into my neck as I stroke her pussy and slide two fingers inside. Every time her walls clench around them, my dick gets harder. This isn't going to last long, and considering we're in my goddamn office, it probably shouldn't.

"I'm going to put you on your feet, and you're going to undress. Take everything off—every single stitch of clothing, and be quick about it, because if I have to help, you're not going to have anything but threads to cover your gorgeous body when you leave here."

I find the rough patch on her walls and curl my fingers against it before sliding them out. Her desperate little moans fill the sultry air between us. "Don't worry, *meu amor*. I'm going to take good care of you. Anything you don't get now, you'll get tonight. Over, and over, and over, until you beg me to stop."

She teeters a bit, before she finds her footing.

"Keep your shoes on." *It'll narrow the height difference and make it easier for me to fuck you against those windows.*

Daniela saunters across the room to lock the door. I don't say a word about it.

She decides two things any time we have sex: whether to lock the door, and whether to use her safeword. All other decisions are mine, unless I decide to hand her a bit of control. Although I rarely do, because even though she thinks she wants it, in the end she doesn't enjoy the sex anywhere near as much—and as a consequence, neither do I.

After the lock is secure, she comes and stands a few feet away from me, her eyes burning with unfiltered passion as she slips out of her jacket and little dress.

I'm torn between watching her strip and ripping off my own clothes so we don't waste a damn minute once she's naked. But I can't take my eyes off her.

Despite my warning, she's moving at a leisurely pace. Entertaining me. Teasing me.

I stand and unbuckle my belt. When I pull it off, her eyes widen, and my little *princesa* sticks out her chin, daring me to strike her.

But I don't have the patience that kind of play requires. Not right now. *Maybe tonight.*

"Don't tempt me. I'm hanging on by a single thread."

She's wearing a pale-lavender thong. There's an innocence about the color that makes my dick thicker and harder. And despite what I told her a few minutes ago, those panties are mine.

"I changed my mind. Leave the thong for me."

The little hellion smirks. My belt might be off the table, but my palm is itching to slap that gorgeous ass of hers.

Once her clothes are off, she watches me make quick work of my own. Her eyes slide all over my body—like she owns it. *And right now, she does.*

Without a word, I prowl toward her, my hand stroking my swollen cock. She's riveted by every jerk of my wrist.

I back her toward the floor-to-ceiling windows that overlook the old city. "Turn around. Face the outside, with your hands on the glass." I stand behind her, my cock pressing into her graceful back, and I gaze over the city. *Our city.*

"What do you see?"

"I see home," she murmurs. "I see all the people who came before us, and everyone who will come after. I see the river of gold that brings life and prosperity to the region. And I see promise. So much promise."

I see those things, too. Every time I look out these windows, I see them, too.

"Tell me what else you see, *Princesa*." I run my hands over her flawless skin, lowering myself to the ground, so I can eat that delicious cunt I've been craving since she left. "Talk to me, Daniela," I murmur, spreading her legs, and rimming her little hole before running my tongue to her pussy.

"*Mmmm.*" She sways forward, and I steady her.

"I love when you lick my pussy," she whispers. "It feels so good."

"As good as having my cock inside you?"

"No." She gasps as I suck her clit into my mouth. "Nothing feels as good as that."

I lick, and suck, and nibble, until her legs are trembling in my hands.

"Press yourself into the glass," I demand, sliding up, and pinning her against the window with my body. "Let the cold glass make your nipples hard. So hard, they'll etch your pleasure into the window so I can admire it every day."

I place one hand on her belly and the other on her throat, and I sink balls-deep into her.

I feel the muffled scream leave her throat, as I watch her reflection in the glass. Her eyes are closed, and her mouth is open. She gasps, and I feel her pulse quicken as my thrusts become deeper and more erratic.

"Open your eyes, *Princesa*. Gaze over your city while I fuck you."

Her fingertips curl on the glass as she gets closer to release. I let my hand find its way between her legs, as I keep up the punishing rhythm. She's squirming madly, like she can't decide if she wants my cock or my hand more.

She'll have both. I tighten the grip on her throat, ever so slightly.

"Antonio," she whimpers. "Antonio."

My vision is spotty as I gaze at her reflection. Mouth open, eyes filled with lust.

I loosen my hold on her throat and press my palm to the window, bracing myself so that I don't pound her right through the glass.

"Come for me, *Princesa*. Come all over my cock."

When her muscles contract, I lower my head and sink my teeth into her neck. My *princesa* loves a bite of pain with her pleasure.

"*Ahhhhh.*" Her body bucks as the orgasm tears through her.

I'm done.

I pound my fist on the window as my balls tighten, and I empty myself inside her.

30

ANTONIO

The closer we get to the harvest, the fuller my schedule is and the more irritable I become. I'm being pulled in a hundred different directions all at once, with not nearly enough time to enjoy my beautiful wife.

Daniela's fully immersed in the harvest, too, and with the final preparations for the "little school" we created. That's what Valentina christened it, because there are only five students—all girls. She's ecstatic about meeting some kids her own age.

I'm happy for her, and for her mother who's excited about Valentina's life becoming more normal. They both deserve some normalcy, and I know I could use some, but I'm not holding my breath.

No matter how busy I am, my attention never wavers far from that bastard Nikitin, who wants to shorten the time I have left on earth.

Lucas turned up several good leads, and Mikhail and his men have gotten close, but the disgraced oligarch has managed to stay out of our clutches. I'm not so concerned with my personal safety, but Nikitin's not a soldier who understands the importance of patience. The longer he's out there, the more desperate he'll become. This puts everyone I care about at substantial risk.

Which is why I have to make an unpleasant call to my mother. I've put it off too long as it is.

"Hello," Lydia Huntsman Taft says in a voice that resounds with happiness—happiness that I'm about to put a damper on.

"Good morning. How are you?"

"Any day that begins with a phone call from my son is a good day."

I call often enough, usually on my way to work in the morning, that she's not suspicious.

"And you, *querido*?"

My mother is the only human being on earth who refers to me as *dear*. It makes me smile every time she says it.

"Busy."

"Busy is good. It will keep you out of trouble."

Hope springs eternal.

"How are my girls?"

"You see more of Valentina these days than I do. From what I understand, you've been making yourself at home at Samantha's."

She chuckles.

"And Daniela—" I start to say she's busy with the harvest, but that would be unwise given what I'm about to say to my mother. "It's nice to have her to myself." *And it is. More than nice. Much more.*

"That's what a mother wants most for her children. That they're healthy, and happy, and loved, and they have someone to love them back." She sighs. "You make your mother so proud when you speak lovingly of your wife. Because what a mother doesn't want is for her daughters to be forced into a loveless marriage, or for her sons to be so callous they don't care."

I don't reply because I'm tired of the discussion. She's made it abundantly clear how she feels about arranged marriages.

Given her own, and her baby sister's, she has every right to be wary. But my marriage is not her concern.

"Do you know anything about Dimitri Fedorov?" I begin with the subject that will give her the least amount of heartburn.

"The Russian gangster?"

"Yeah."

"He's the head of the European Bratva, although I heard he recently died in a car accident. Are you having some issues with the Bratva? You don't want to get involved with them, Antonio," she warns, like I'm a boy who's thinking about hanging out with the rough kids down the street.

"No issues. Tell me what else you know about Fedorov."

"Do you have a list of people that you're going to ask me about? Because I don't have all day. As a matter of fact, I have an appointment to get a pedicure. And then I'm spending the afternoon at the pool with my granddaughters. I'd like to take them to a show or shopping, and then to lunch, but their fathers are such spoilsports."

Their fathers. I adore Valentina, but I never think of her as my child. *Not exactly.* Although, I would be honored if one day she decided I was a good enough man to be her father.

I've just fallen into my mother's trap. She's doing what she always does when she doesn't want to discuss something—obfuscating.

"I'm not a five-year-old you can distract with a lollipop." *Although for a moment, you did.*

"You were never a child to be distracted with a lollipop. You were stubborn and persistent. And you haven't changed."

"Did you know him? Or better yet, did Maria Rosa know him?"

"Mind your business, Antonio." She uses an acerbic tone to shut down the line of questioning.

I'm sure it works with some people, but it only makes me more determined.

"From your tenor, I assume they were well acquainted."

"What's this all about?"

"Daniela and I had dinner with Fedorov the night of his accident. He told a story about how Maria Rosa helped get his daughter back. He said she had a good friend who could corroborate—and suggested I ask my mother about it."

"*Pfft*. It's not your business."

"Daniela is my business. That makes her mother my business. And I don't think anyone would argue that you're my business, too."

She huffs. "It's true. But don't ask for the details, because you won't like what you hear."

I know enough about the escapades of the *three amigas* to know that what I hear will give me nightmares.

"Was he in love with her?" I ask, probing to see how much of his story was true.

"I don't know anything about that. But if you're insinuating—don't you dare sully her memory. Not to me, and not to Daniela."

"I don't intend to sully anyone. Fedorov actually said that she wasn't aware of his feelings."

"That, I believe. Everyone loved her. Rosa was beautiful and good. She was special. Her daughter and her granddaughter inherited those qualities."

I won't argue with that.

"Is there anything else you want to tell me about him? Let me rephrase. Is there anything else I should know about him?"

"Is that why you called this morning, right before the harvest, when there isn't enough time in a day to eat, let alone chat about dead Russians?"

If only it were that simple.

"I called to say hello, as always, and to tell you that I don't want you in Porto for the harvest."

She doesn't utter a single word for what seems like an eternity. But I sense her fury. The seas from here to London are tumultuous with angry swells. *I wish it could be different. Not this year.*

I don't want to have to worry about her and my wife all week with Nikitin still walking the earth. It's bad enough Daniela will be at risk, but at least she occasionally listens to reason. My mother, however, doesn't give a shit what I say. She does as she damn well pleases.

"It seems you have your wires crossed, *meu amor*. It doesn't matter how old you are, I'm still the parent. I don't take orders from you."

No, she doesn't take orders from anyone. *Not anymore.* Most days that pleases me to no end. *But not today.* I should have been smarter about how I broached the subject.

"I didn't mean to issue an order." I don't want to worry her unnecessarily, but I need her to listen, and do as I ask. "Things are unsettled here. I know you're looking forward to the harvest activities, and I was looking forward to having you here, but the heightened security is going to have us stretched thinner than usual. It would be better if you didn't come this year."

"Better for whom? For you? Because it certainly wouldn't be better for me. Why don't we cut right to the chase, Antonio? I'm going to the harvest. I went from my father's house to my husband's. Your grandfather wasn't the tyrant your father was, but neither Vera nor I did a thing that wasn't sanctioned by him. In these last twelve years, for the first time in my life, I've made my own decisions. I live my life on my own terms. It's been more freeing than I ever imagined. And no man, not even my son who I love dearly, will order me about again."

She pauses for a breath. "You lay out the terms that you would prefer for the visit—details that will make you more comfortable about my safety—and I'll tell you which ones I can accept."

My blood pressure is through the roof, but I won't argue with her, because it's futile. I could make her stay in London, but I don't spend more than a second entertaining the idea. For decades, she lived under the thumb of a monster, and my grandfather was no picnic, either. I won't become another bastard who sucks the joy out of her life.

It's not a sound decision on my part—no decision borne of weakness ever is. I won't kid myself. That's what this is—me being soft.

"We don't need to stay at my house in the valley," she adds, to sweeten the pot. "We can stay at your house, if you prefer."

I don't prefer. But it will make protecting her easier, and it'll save us some manpower.

"Staying with us is a good idea. We'll have more time to spend together." I pause for a beat, trying to decide how to phrase my *request*.

"I'll respect your right to self-determination, and you'll respect my authority while you're in Porto. I can't have you questioning me at every turn. Especially publicly. It diminishes my power in the region."

"You don't need to worry in that regard. I've been playing the game my entire life. I defer to your authority more often than you know, Antonio. Why do you think I've never asked you about Tomas's disappearance?"

I assumed you were saving that for the face-to-face conversation I won't be having.

31

DANIELA

Paula, Lara, and I are at a table in the corner of the ballroom that I've turned into a command center for the harvest activities I'm overseeing. The room is so large it takes up almost an entire wing of the house, although we won't be holding any events inside, weather permitting.

Lara is making an effort—I think—although she's made it abundantly clear that she doesn't believe Paula should be involved in the preparations at this level.

But I want Paula to be heavily involved. I want her to learn everything there is about entertaining on this scale. The harvest happens every year, and eventually, I'd like her to be my personal assistant, and shift Lara to a more administrative role.

Paula doesn't talk just to hear herself, and unlike Lara, she knows her place. *That's harsh.* I sound like Antonio. I don't mean to be a bitch. It's just that Paula supports me at every turn, while sometimes it feels as though Lara supports only herself.

I open my tabbed notebook. "Let's go over everything, one more time." I read off the bullet points, one by one. "Valentina and I will handle all the planning for the children's party—including the activities. But we'll need all hands on deck during the event."

My mother always had a big party for the kids, who don't see much of their parents during the harvest. But this is the first year Huntsman Port is holding a children's event. Antonio was all for it, when I told him, and Valentina is so excited about the event.

"Maybe we should cap the number of children," Lara suggests. "If it's rainy and windy, and they end up inside, it could be a catastrophe."

"I don't want to leave anyone out. If their parents work for us, they're invited. We'll have enough activities and enough supervision to make sure there isn't a catastrophe.

"Lara," I say, moving on, "you continue to keep track of the RSVPs as they come in, organizing them by event. And please start working on the seating arrangements for the formal event, so that we're not doing it all at the last minute."

This is where Lara excels. She knows who should be seated at the same table, and who should be seated on opposite ends of the tent.

"Also, don't forget the favors need to be wrapped, and the baskets for the ladies' and men's rooms assembled."

"Of course. Have we decided who will be in charge of the table settings and the flowers?"

I purse my lips, but keep my eyes on my notebook. We've been through this several times, but she just won't let it go. I address my response, not to Lara, but to Paula. "You'll take care of the table linens, the dish and glassware, the utensils, and the flowers. Victor and I will help."

"I'll have some time," Lara says. "I can help, too."

The table settings and flowers are sexier, and in general, more fun than seating arrangements. I get it, but Lara really does have plenty on her plate.

"We need to stay flexible," I explain, "because at any given point, something could go wrong and we'll need to adjust. But for now, I'd like us to focus on the tasks we've been assigned. It's the best way to ensure that nothing falls through the cracks."

Paula nods, but Lara sticks her nose back in the laptop without acknowledging me.

"Paula, starting this week, I want you to leave your work in the house to Johanna until the harvest and all the activities that follow are done." She's been training a young maid who will pick up the slack when she's unavailable.

"Is she ready?" Lara asks, frowning at Paula.

Maybe Antonio's right about her undermining me.

"Johanna's ready enough," I reply. "If the bathroom sinks aren't wiped out every day and the towels replaced, we'll survive." I don't mean to be glib, but it will do everyone some good, myself included, to clean up after ourselves for a few weeks.

"What about *Senhor* Antonio? He's more particular."

What she means is that *Senhor* Antonio is more refined than his wife. *If only she knew the half of it.*

I flash her a stiff smile. "Leave my husband to me."

After reviewing my notes one last time, it looks like we've covered everything. "That's all I have, ladies. Unless either of you have anything, let's meet again on Wednesday. In the meantime, please don't make any final decisions." I say this for Lara's benefit, because Paula doesn't have the confidence to make independent decisions.

As Paula gets up to leave, Lara turns to me. "May I have a word with you?"

Oh, God. "Of course."

She starts the moment Paula is out the door. "I didn't want to say too much in front of her. But she's a simpleton. The flowers and the table settings are important. They say a lot about *who you are. Who your husband is.* Leaving those decisions to someone who has been raised as she has will surely bring disaster."

Good Lord. Could she be any more pretentious? If we wanted to say something about who my husband is, we'd give out sex toys that growl as party favors.

I draw a breath and try to find the patience to have this discussion.

"No one wants this to go well more than I do. But I think it's a bit dramatic to say that somehow the wrong shade of camellias will create a disaster. There's more of a chance for disaster if you sit the president with the prime minister."

It's tongue in cheek, because they've been at each other's throats for weeks, but she's so hell-bent on co-opting me to her position that it goes right over her head.

"It's just—"

I hold up my hand. "Paula will be fine. Victor and I will make sure of it." She doesn't say anything, but I can see that I haven't changed her mind. "Paula hasn't been exposed to the world in the same way that you and I have been, so she hasn't had many opportunities to learn. That doesn't make her a simpleton. I would appreciate it if you don't refer to her, or anyone else in this household, that way."

"I apologize," she gushes. "It was inelegant phrasing. You're right. She just hasn't had the experience."

I nod. "I'm sorry, but I need to go. Victor's expecting me."

We leave without another word about floral catastrophes. But I have a feeling I haven't heard the last of it.

32

DANIELA

When I get to the kitchen, Victor is putting together a mid-morning snack for the vineyard workers.

"How was your meeting?" he asks, carefully wrapping *Bolo Levedo*, sweet flat muffins, that smell delicious.

"Fine," I mutter. "Let me wash my hands, and I can wrap while you do something else. I want to be in a good position to sneak one."

He chuckles. "Help yourself. There are plenty.

"It's so quiet here without Valentina," he murmurs, turning his attention to preparing coffee. "I don't like it."

"I don't like it either. But I video-chatted with her last night, and she's having a wonderful time. Lydia is spoiling both girls rotten."

"I'm sure she is, and why not?" Victor beams. "I'm looking forward to seeing *Senhora* Lydia. She's such a lovely woman."

"Always has been."

"Tell me about your *fine* meeting."

I glance at him, and he smiles. Victor knows it was anything but fine.

"Do you think it's a mistake to involve Paula in the party preparations? Is it too much for her?"

"I've changed my mind about Paula. She's quite anxious when faced with a new task. But once she gets comfortable, she's very capable. If you have the time and patience to teach her, you'll have someone who will assist you for years."

"That's what I think, too."

"And unlike Lara, who came well-versed on *everything*," he says in an exaggerated tone, "Paula will learn your tastes. It's a trade-off, but one that will serve you well in the long run."

"You're not a fan of Lara?" I ask, gauging his reaction.

"It doesn't matter if I'm a fan of Lara. What matters is whether you're a fan. Don't let anyone get too close who doesn't have your best interests at heart."

"Anything in particular I need to be concerned about?"

"No," he shoots back. "But you're a young woman without a lot of experience running a large household alone. Your assistant needs to be someone you can trust implicitly." He pauses. "I hope I haven't overstepped."

"Never. And you're right. After my mother died, I was in charge, but I always had Isabel at my side. She was very experienced at running the house." *She learned at my mother's hand.*

"Do you imagine that you'll ever be able to trust Lara as much as you trusted Isabel?"

Well, no, but that's hardly a fair comparison.

"Trust your instincts, *senhora*. Always trust your instincts. I'm certain your husband would tell you the same thing."

33

ANTONIO

Lucas, Cristiano, and Tavares, the head guard who is in charge of day-to-day security, are waiting for me in the vineyard behind my house. We're going to walk the property and go over the security details for the upcoming events.

While security is always tight here, these kinds of events pose enormous risks because delivery people are in and out, not to mention the caterers and musicians, and all sorts of guests, some less savory than others.

Plus, Nikitin is still out there somewhere, with a boatload of cash that can buy a lot of things. He's been staying one step ahead of Mikhail, and our efforts to track him from here have fallen flat.

"Let's go, gentlemen. We have a lot of ground to cover."

"I don't know how much time you have, but the plan has a lot of detail. Would you prefer just the highlights?" Tavares asks.

I stop and turn to him. "No, I would not prefer just the highlights," I say pointedly. "I want to know how you're going to protect my family, our guests, and everyone who works here. Every detail." And I want Cristiano and Lucas to hear it too, so we can be certain that everything possible is being done to avoid a problem.

"What's the process for entering the premises?" I ask. Might as well start at the beginning.

"While security will be heightened, the process for visitors is similar to what we normally use," Tavares explains. "It's sound, and everyone's familiar with it, which is a plus. I'll be given a running list of names of anyone needing access."

"Who is permitted to add to the list?" Cristiano asks.

"The three of you, of course. *Senhora* Daniela, and her staff."

"Which staff, specifically?"

He nods and checks his notes. "Victor, Paula, and Lara.

"*Menina* Valentina," he adds, "must go through Santi or Mia to add anyone to the list, as usual."

"What about my mother?" I ask.

"That's up to you, *senhor*."

I'm not crazy about giving my mother carte blanche to have a bunch of old biddies in and out, but she's going to want to visit with her friends while she's in Porto, and it's better if they do it here.

"She can add visitors. But every one of them has to abide by the rules. No one gets a pass. Regardless of who they claim to be."

"I assure you there are no passes. We've done background checks on every supplier, as well as their employees. Any individuals we had concerns about were taken off the list and the company notified. Everyone will need to show identification at the gate."

That's all fine and good, but this is the same damn thing we do every day.

"I realize there's an upside to staying close to our normal protocols, but there will be thousands more people coming through during the week. The last I heard, we'll have over seven hundred and fifty guests here the night of the gala. That's besides all the help. You better tell me you have something more, Tavares."

He's seems taken aback by my brusque manner, but the stakes are higher than usual this year. If he's looking for someone to stroke his ego and tell him he's beautiful, he should talk to his wife. Those are not my strengths.

"We have many more security measures that will be in place once the harvest activities begin. The number of guards will be quadrupled—at least. We'll pull some from other locations, and everyone knows that if they call in sick, they better be on their deathbed. Along with uniformed personnel, we'll have guards in plain clothes circulating through the individual events, and with Lucas's help, we're planning to install cameras in and around the tents."

I glance at Lucas.

"My people will assist in monitoring the feeds," he says. "And they'll check the equipment throughout the day and evening to make sure it's all working properly."

Lucas's people are well-trained and disciplined, as are Tavares's guards, but they have better technological skills.

"Everyone will walk through a metal detector upon entering," Tavares continues. "In addition, suppliers, like the catering staff, will be patted down, trucks gone over with metal-detecting devices, and we'll have a couple of bomb-sniffing dogs for the week."

"There will be a children's event," I say. "What's the plan for that?"

Tavares nods. "Much the same. Although the parents all work for Huntsman, in some form or other, so I'm not overly concerned."

I glare at him. "You get paid to be overly concerned."

"That's not what I—"

I hold up my hand to shut him up. "Figure out a way to keep

security tight without scaring the kids half to death. It's supposed to be fun for them."

"We want it to be fun for everyone," Tavares assures me. "And we've been working long hours to make that happen in a secure environment. My goal is that once people enter through the main gate, no one will notice the enhanced measures."

Public events are always a huge security clusterfuck for everyone, but especially for Tavares, who bears the brunt of the responsibility. He's a pro, and I've probably been harder on him than need be.

"I appreciate all the time and effort that's gone into this. I'm sure you've had some sleepless nights."

He chuckles. "Not yet. But they're coming."

I glance from Cristiano to Lucas. "Anything else?"

Lucas shakes his head.

"No," Cristiano replies, "but we should meet again the day before the first event, to touch base."

"I agree. You're satisfied, Tavares?"

"Never," he says. "But I'm pleased with what we've put together."

"I am, too. But the truth is that no matter what we do, there are no guarantees." *It's what keeps me awake at night.*

"Indeed," he says, soberly. "We're minimizing the risk. We'll get it low, but it's impossible to get it to zero. The only way to do that is to cancel the events and lock down the place."

Don't tempt me.

34

DANIELA

I sip coffee while I rifle through my makeup bag for under-eye concealer. With all the last-minute details for the gala tomorrow night, I've hardly slept in the last two days. I'm running on nervous energy and caffeine. *Lots and lots of caffeine.*

For us, the harvest celebration actually began late yesterday afternoon when Antonio ferried Valentina, Rafael, Lydia, her husband Edward, and me into a helicopter, to one of his vineyards in the northernmost part of the valley.

At first, he didn't tell us where we were going, just to dress casually. Lydia and Rafael clearly had some inkling, but no matter how many questions Valentina asked, they weren't talking.

When we arrived at the winery on the property, where some Huntsman Port is made, I began to have an inkling, too.

We were here for the *corte*, the first stage in the treading process, where the newly harvested grapes are placed in *lagares*, granite troughs, and the treaders link arms, shoulder to shoulder, and stomp, crushing the juicy grapes gently to extract the sweet pulp from the skins.

While they tread, an accordionist plays and everyone sings.

It's a centuries-old tradition, and even Port houses that have turned to modern methods of crushing grapes still participate in some form of the *corte*. It's an integral part of the storied history of Port wine and our region.

Although we were vintners, and not wine makers, my family was always invited to participate in the *corte* by at least one of the Port houses. Even my normally dignified father would step, barefoot, into the wide, thigh-high vessels and tread. But in a million years, I never expected Antonio Huntsman to roll up his pants and link arms.

As we follow the accordion music, I catch Antonio's eye and grin like a child awaiting Santa Claus. My husband, my beautiful husband, who has once again surprised me, glances at Valentina, and flashes me a conspiratorial wink. He wants to surprise her. And he does.

After we watch the treaders work for a while, a middle-aged woman beckons us to join them in the *lagar*. I gaze at Valentina, who seems unsure, unlike me, who's wanted to climb in from the minute we arrived.

"Come in with me," I urge, laughing. "It's so much fun."

In a fit of giggles, Valentina steps into the *lagar* behind me, and links arms with Antonio and Rafael, first, and later with Lydia and me. Every time she laughs, my heart fills with joy.

While I'd participated in the *corte*, even after she was born, Valentina never did. It wasn't simply that she was a bit young, but she was my maid's daughter, and wasn't invited to attend with me. When I was sixteen, it hit me hard, that this was the way it would always be.

As they tread arm in arm, Rafael whispers something to her that I can't hear, and the laughter bubbles from her chest. I cling to the moment, letting the happiness envelop me, because I've learned that life is fleeting, and you have to savor these moments as they happen.

Some of the treaders would work all night, but we left after rinsing our feet and enjoying a hearty supper with them, which involved more singing and merrymaking. I'm pretty sure I still had a smile on my face when I fell asleep. *Or maybe the smile was from the devilish treats Antonio had for me when we were alone in our bed.*

I'm finishing my makeup when Antonio comes into the bedroom. *Speak of the devil.*

"It's so odd to have you home at this hour of the morning, in the middle of the week."

"That's a very modest outfit, in a very innocent color," he observes, stalking toward me. "If I hadn't heard you whimpering for my cock last night, I might even think you were a chaste little thing."

"You don't like my suit?" I ask, a little concerned that I'd chosen the wrong outfit for the luncheon.

"It's perfect," he murmurs, with one hand on my hip, and the other fingering the ends of my hair. "Like you. Pink is almost as beautiful as red on you." His eyes sparkle with the kind of mischief we don't have time for.

Pity.

"Where's Valentina?" he asks, as his growing erection grazes my hip.

"She and her friends are organizing the prizes and materials for face painting tomorrow." I smile as I say *her friends*. Antonio's *little school* idea took a lot of doing, but it changed her life overnight.

"We don't need to leave until ten forty-five. Maybe we should take advantage of the hour we have before we leave," he says, pinning me against the bedpost.

We don't have time for this, but that doesn't stop the pulsing between my legs.

"As much as I'd like a repeat of last night, there won't be time to shower, and I don't want to walk into the luncheon reeking of sex."

"Why not?"

"Because I heard they're giving out prizes, and announcing a vintage year."

"Really?" His eyes twinkle madly.

I nod. "A Huntsman Port made exclusively from grapes grown at Quinta Rosa do Vale is getting one. The top one," I whisper. "I'm surprised you haven't heard."

"No one tells me anything." He smirks. "But unless one of those pompous bastards on the committee has been whispering in your ear, don't get ahead of yourself."

I'm not getting ahead of myself, and he knows it. "This is your moment."

"This is our moment," he says, with his hard cock wedged between us. "We should celebrate. Right here and now."

"I thought we shouldn't get too far ahead of ourselves?" I ask, much too cheeky.

"Are you denying me?"

A zing of pleasure rumbas through me as Antonio tugs on my hair the way he does before he wraps it around his hand.

"Never." I shake my head. "But I have to be downstairs when they deliver the china for the gala tonight."

"When I asked you to oversee the events, I didn't mean for you to manage every detail yourself. You should have delegated more."

For a second, I feel a twinge of sadness. Nelia, who planned our wedding, and died in the bride's parlor at Santa Ana's, is the one who oversaw the harvest events for Antonio in the past. I worked from the meticulous notes she kept, wishing all the while that she was here to help me. We would have had such a great time doing it together.

"I delegated plenty," I assure him, straightening his tie. "And once we get on that helicopter in an hour to go to the luncheon, I'm done. From then on, it's all in the hands of party organizers and the caterer. But I've loved every minute of the planning. It's been a great joy for me, Antonio."

"I know," he says, dragging his thumb over my cheek. "I love the things you added. The greater focus on charity, especially. It makes me proud to have the Huntsman label sponsoring those events."

I'm proud too, not because the flowers and the linens we chose are perfect together, but because every meal we serve this week, and there will be thousands and thousands, the local food kitchens will also serve. Same food, prepared by the same chefs. It's in honor of my mother, who believed it was our collective responsibility to feed the poor.

When I ran it past Antonio, he said, "*I think it's a great idea, and I don't care about the expense, but everyone doesn't need to know our business. The donation should be made anonymously.*"

What I've noticed, especially since I got involved with the harvest, is that in addition to what the Huntsman company does to support charitable organizations, Antonio donates generously to myriad causes—always anonymously.

"I'm proud of you, too." I press my hand to his heart. "I'm certain that your young Port is going to take a prize—probably first place—but I know you would trade it in a heartbeat for a vintage year for the valley. You're a good man, and a great leader. My father was so right about that. Enjoy your moment."

"Our moment," he reminds me, again, in a husky voice. "Go do what you need to do, because you're far too tempting. If you don't leave now, not only will there not be anyone to approve the place settings, but we won't make it to any of the festivities."

I cup his jaw. Even recently shaven, it prickles my skin. "Promise me you'll enjoy this week. That any time you're feeling irritable, or like you want to kill someone, you'll tap into this moment."

He nods. "I'll come find you when it's time to go."

"I'll be in the tent."

35

DANIELA

As I look around the tent, I have a small panic attack. Tonight, we're hosting seven hundred and sixty people for dinner and dancing, and the tent is still in complete disarray. Although there are dozens of people scurrying about.

This is, by far, the largest event of the week, with the most dignitaries in attendance. *High maintenance hell.* After tonight, it's all downhill from here.

"Look at you!" Victor cries. "You look lovely."

"Thank you." I smile at the man who has been my biggest source of support since the moment I arrived—seven months ago. It's hard to believe it's been that long. "Is the china here yet? I'd love to see how it looks with the linens and flowers."

"Everything's here. The caterer will have a fit," he whispers. "She gave specific instructions that no one is to go into the staging tent until she arrives at noon, but by then you'll be at your luncheon. Let me see if I can sneak into the tent and grab a few things so we can set a table."

The very last thing I need is for the caterer to be in a snit. "Maybe we shouldn't rock the boat. She's so persnickety."

"I'm just going to look. If I come across the dinnerware,

without disrupting her setup, she'll never be the wiser. That way you'll know that everything's perfect before you leave. It'll be one less thing for you to worry about."

I don't normally ask a lot of him, but Victor believes that one of his missions in life is to make me happy. I do love that about him. "Only if you can do it easily. Don't get into trouble because of me."

He winks. "I don't get into nearly enough trouble for a man of my age. I'll be right back."

Victor must be in his mid-fifties, maybe a bit older, but he moves with the ease of a much younger man.

After he disappears, I wander around, looking for something to do. The dance floor is being assembled at one end of the enormous tent, gold ballroom chairs with thick cushions are being placed around the tables, and young women are decorating the posts with small twinkling lights. At this point, there really is nothing for me to do but get out of the way. It's an odd feeling after being so involved for weeks.

When Antonio enters from the back of the tent, my heart stops. He's wearing a deep-navy suit, tailored to within an inch. It's a modern cut, with classic details. The inky fabric is rich and luxurious. *The man looks good enough to eat, and tonight, after everyone has gone home, I'm going to do just that.*

"I see you changed."

"Don't want to be upstaged by my date." His gaze rakes over me, top to bottom. "But there's no way around that."

As he admires me lewdly, I feel myself blushing, like a teenager, and divert his attention to the tent. "What do you think?"

"It's chaos," he says, shaking his head as he looks around.

"Controlled chaos. I'm glad you saw it now. Wait until you see how it looks tonight."

"I have no doubt it'll be perfect. My beautiful, talented wife was heavily involved in the planning." His brow furrows as he regards me. "You okay, *Princesa*? You seem restless."

"I'm a little nervous," I confess. "I wasn't until I came out here and realized, *it's happening*. We're having an intimate dinner party for hundreds of our *friends* this evening. I've never done anything like this before. I guess it's a little late to mention that," I say sheepishly, even though he's fully aware.

Antonio takes hold of my chin and tips it up until I'm staring into those sultry dark eyes. "Don't spend a second worrying about tonight. Many of our *friends* are insufferable bastards, like me," he quips. "If a waiter drops a tray of drinks on someone, or if the caterer forgets forks and we need to eat with our fingers, it'll serve them right."

Antonio squeezes my hand, and my anxiety lessens, some.

"We need to go in about ten minutes," he says, reaching for his phone. "I need to take one more call before we board the helicopter."

I'm excited about the luncheon. I want to watch Antonio's face as his young wine walks away with everything. It will be a financial boon, but he doesn't need the money. He does need more things that make him smile, though.

"I need to find Victor. He has something to show me, and then I'm ready."

"Ten minutes, Daniela. Ready or not."

Don't get your panties in a twist. Although, if Victor is right, I need to be more concerned with pissing off the caterer than Antonio.

"I'm just going to the staging tent, a few yards from here."

"Huntsman," he says into the phone, walking away.

I'm not even sure he heard me.

I hike my purse onto my shoulder and go in search of Victor. There won't be time to see a fully set table, but I'll have a good idea of how it's going to look once I see a dinner plate near the cloths.

I approach the staging tent gingerly, holding my breath,

hoping that no one from the catering staff sees me skulking around were I don't belong, and rats me out to their boss.

As soon as I step into the canopy, I hear a woman crying. I take a hesitant step closer.

"Please don't hurt us," she sobs.

Victor's kneeling beside a young woman who was setting up fairy lights. Their hands are behind their heads. A man, with his back toward me, appears to be holding them at gunpoint.

Oh my God. My heart pounds in my ears. But he hasn't spotted me, yet.

Shaking, I crouch behind the stacked crates of bar glasses near the entrance. I'm not sure if I can get out without him seeing me.

"I told you to shut the fuck up," he hisses.

The crying stops abruptly.

"What have you done?" Victor barks.

I find a narrow opening between the crates. When my eyes adjust, I see the woman lying on the ground.

The gunman scans the area around him, before going over to her.

Do I scream? *No.* But I'm not sure I can go for help without him noticing me leave. *What if he sees me and kills Victor?*

I feel my purse at my hip.

I have a phone. And a pistol. "Go nowhere without it," Antonio warned me, just a few days ago. And I haven't.

The man drags the lifeless woman behind some boxes at the edge of the tent and throws a tablecloth over her. He keeps his gun on Victor the whole time.

I reach into my purse for my phone. The mints I tucked in earlier rustle, and I freeze. The gunman is striding toward Victor, and he doesn't flinch at the sound.

I shudder when my fingers graze the gun barrel as I pull out the phone.

Without wasting another second, I send Antonio, Duarte,

Cristiano, and Lucas the same text: **Gunman has Victor. Staging tent.**

"You're next," he snarls, grabbing Victor by the neck. He lets out a muffled cry.

"Please don't kill me," Victor pleads, in a voice I barely recognize.

If I wait for someone to save us, Victor's not going to make it. You have to do something!

I place my phone on the ground and pull out the small pistol with trembling fingers. *Quiet. Quiet. Don't spook him*, I admonish myself, all the while, praying for help to arrive before I have to use the gun.

What if I miss?

I hear Santi's reassuring voice in my head: *You won't, senhora.*

As soon as the gunman turns his back, I stand, cock the pistol, and aim.

POP! POP! POP!

36

ANTONIO

After getting off three clean shots, I step behind Daniela, lower her arm, and take the weapon from her trembling hand.

Jesus Christ.

The tent is teeming with guards, knocking over crates as they search for more trouble, but the fucker I'm most interested in is at Daniela's side, like he should have been the entire time. I glower at Duarte, Daniela's personal guard, before dragging her to my chest.

"Are you okay?" I whisper into her hair.

"Yes. Victor?" she whimpers.

He's alive. I didn't hit him, but I'm not sure if he's injured, and I won't lie about it. "I want to know exactly what happened, but first, let me see about Victor."

"There's a woman under a tablecloth," Daniela says, "over there." She points to a corner where a couple of soldiers are on their knees. *They must have found her.* "She might be—she's hurt."

I don't want to leave her, but I need to know how this

happened, and if there's more to come. Given the number of guards surrounding us right now, this is probably the safest place for Daniela.

I turn to Duarte. "You and I need to talk. But right now, she doesn't move from this spot. And don't take your fucking eyes off her. Not for a goddamn second," I bark, before striding across the tent to Victor.

"What about Valentina?" Daniela's voice is twisting with terror.

The kind of terror that makes me want to go on a murderous rampage. This was supposed to be a wonderful day for her—for us.

I stop and turn to face her, and my stomach burns. Daniela's pale, and her features are drawn tight. *I am so pissed at Tavares for letting this happen under his watch.*

"Santi and Mia know. Valentina's in good hands." I don't say *she's safe*, as much as I want to. Because I don't know. But I'm confident Lucas sent out an alert the second he got Daniela's text. "Call Santi or Mia if you want to check for yourself."

Her head bobs a few times.

Lucas intercepts me on the way to Victor. "Your mother's fine. She's getting her hair done for tonight. She hasn't heard a thing about this shitshow."

"Let's keep it that way."

Victor is shaken up, but appears uninjured. The gunman is dead.

It would have been helpful to have him alive so we could interrogate him, but when I took the shots, my main concern was for Victor's life. I don't regret that.

"You need to see a doctor."

"I'm fine," he huffs.

"Not a request."

He nods. "I came into the tent to get something, and noticed him loitering—it almost looked like he was hiding. No one was supposed to be in this tent, and he didn't look familiar. When I asked to see his credentials, he drew a gun and grabbed the young woman who followed me in."

Loitering and looked like he was hiding. Those are not the marks of a highly experienced individual. We should have been able to prevent it.

Tavares strides over. "The woman is unconscious, but alive."

"He hit her in the head with the butt of the gun," Victor explains. "She was bleeding when he moved her."

"What the fuck happened here?" I ask Tavares, as Lucas hands me the badge that was around the gunman's neck.

"I don't have answers for you yet." He looks me squarely in the eye. "But I will."

I grab him by the throat. "I'll be gone a few hours, and when I get back, I expect to know why my wife, the person behind you, wearing makeup and a pink skirt, had to pull out a gun, while this fucking property is overrun with trained soldiers under your control."

I release him, before my fingers dig too deep into his carotid arteries. "I want to know his name. How he got in. Who hired him. And the last place he stuck his dick. *Everything.* Or the next person I put a bullet in will be you."

To his credit, Tavares doesn't flinch.

I shove the identification badge at him. "Somehow, I don't think he's with the catering company."

"Take care of this fucking mess," I growl to no one in particular, before I go back to Daniela.

I take her hand and let my thumb find her pulse. It's still racing. I don't know how she's going to make it through the day once the adrenaline shuts off.

"Where was Duarte when this happened?" I could ask Duarte, himself, because he's standing right here. But I won't show him that kind of respect.

"Antonio," she presses her hand to my chest, "please calm down."

"Don't tell me to calm down. You could have been killed. That gun you carry should be merely a precaution for a doomsday scenario. It's not meant for you to have to protect yourself in our home." I say it as much for her guard as for her.

"Duarte was stationed at the front entrance of the tent, watching everyone who came in and out."

Why the fuck wasn't he watching you? She needs two guards on her at all times, like Valentina. Now I'm not just pissed at him. I'm pissed at myself, too.

"Why didn't you follow *your* protectee, *my* wife, when she left the main tent?" I ask Duarte.

"I have no excuse," he says, in a clear voice. "I apologize. It won't happen again, but I understand if you want to relieve me of my duty."

"I forgot to tell him," Daniela says softly.

"You forgot?" I ask, my tone a mixture of disbelief and more anger.

She nods, but it's possible she's protecting him. Daniela's first instinct is always to protect everyone around her. I have no doubt she'd cover for him, even if it meant taking the blame herself.

I stare straight into Duarte's eyes. "Did she tell you she was leaving?"

He doesn't answer, and that tells me everything I need to know about what happened, and about him. Duarte has been with me for long enough to know that I don't fuck around with this kind of thing. He wouldn't be relieved of his duties. He'd be dead before the sun set. Yet, he chose to remain silent in order to protect her. I won't fault him for protecting my wife, even from me.

"I realize it wasn't in the original plan, but you'll be coming to the luncheon with us. The venue is secure, but in light of what just happened, I want extra security. Give me a moment with my wife."

He nods. "Certainly, *senhor*."

After he leaves, I call Santi. It'll buy me some time to let the rage lessen before I deal with Daniela.

Before he says hello, I lay into him. "I don't know what kind of instruction you're giving my wife, but she pulled out a gun today, and she hesitated. That will never happen again. After this week is over, I want her on the range every day, until she won't even hesitate to shoot you." I glare at Daniela while I speak, because my order is meant for them both.

I end the call before he can get in a word. Santi knows exactly what my beef is. If you aim a gun at an armed man, you better not hesitate a millisecond before you fire.

I'm struggling to control my anger, but I won't embarrass Daniela in public, and I won't allow her to take the brunt of my fear—because that's what this really is: fear disguised as rage. Daniela in a room with a gunman—it's bloodcurdling. I can't sweep this under the rug.

"You forgot?"

"I have a lot on my plate, and I'm used to moving around our home—and the property surrounding the house—without a shadow. I was in a hurry to find Victor and it didn't even occur to me to tell Duarte." She touches my arm. "Please don't do this. Not today."

I gaze into her warm brown eyes, pleading for me to move on, and I do what she asked of me earlier. I tap into the intimate moment we shared this morning in the bedroom. Her joy. Her cheekiness. Her goodness. And my heart, that's so filled with love for her that I can no longer even pretend that it isn't there. The longer I gaze at her, the more docile the beast raging inside becomes.

"Are you sure you're up for the luncheon? I'm happy to make your excuses. You could rest for a couple of hours."

She holds both my hands, lacing our fingers together. "I wouldn't miss it for the world."

For a few seconds, while I bask in the glow of her face, admiring her steely backbone, I forget that someone is trying to kill us.

37

DANIELA

The luncheon is something I've always known about, but it's a private affair that only involves the Port houses. *A grand private affair.*

We were thirty minutes late, but they held the lunch for us, because Antonio personally notified them that there was a malfunction with the helicopter. I guess that's what we're calling dead gunmen these days. He doesn't usually lie—he doesn't have to—but with the gala at our house tonight, it seemed wiser to keep the details under wrap.

It's been kept so quiet that even Valentina doesn't know. Or at least she didn't mention it when I spoke to her on the way to the luncheon. *Hopefully she doesn't know.* I'd hate to think that my sweet girl is so jaded that an intruder with a gun isn't worth mentioning.

Premier, the Port house that Abel Huntsman owns, had no one in attendance. They're apparently in disarray, mired in legal woes, because Antonio is insisting that with Tomas *missing,* and Abel incapacitated, the company belongs to Rafael. Not everyone agrees.

The young Huntsman Port walked away with *all* the important prizes. I was positively giddy, but Antonio entered the end zone, cool as a cucumber, like he'd been there before. I suppose he has—although never like this.

What took me by surprise is that each time Huntsman Port was called to the podium to collect a ribbon or a trophy, Antonio took my hand, eyes shining with pride, and pulled me to the stage with him. It sent a clear message to everyone in the room: I was not just his wife. I was his partner. No one appreciated that message more than my heart.

The helicopter descends, circling Quinta Rosa do Vale before it lands on the west side of the property. I haven't been here in more than six years, and I'm flooded with emotion. But I'm prepared for the onslaught. I expected a wide range of feelings. After all, this is where I grew up, where my parents died, where I first learned to be a mother, and what I abandoned when it became too dangerous for my little cobbled-together family. Those are just the highlights. Millions of memories are sandwiched in between.

Antonio takes my hands and presses a small kiss to each knuckle while we wait for the blades to stop. "We can stop at the house before we leave, but we won't have much time to spend there."

I shake my head. "I'd prefer to come back when there's more time." *And no one to witness my emotions spilling out all over the place.* I want to see the house. I want to wander through the rooms and soak up the memories while I have a good cry. But I've waited this long. I can wait a while longer. *Today isn't the day.*

An armored SUV takes us to a covered picnic area in the vineyards where Antonio will congratulate the workers and tell them that the Port they made won the big trophy and a dozen ribbons. He'll hold them up, one by one, and they'll cheer.

The results from the luncheon are always kept closely guarded, until everyone has had an opportunity to go back and share the news, sometimes good, sometimes not so good, with the workers who had a hand in production. It's a respected tradition.

We pass the winery on the far end of the property that was built while I was in the US. Wine was never made here until Antonio took over the property. This winery is where the prize-winning Port was made from grapes harvested from the D'Sousa southern vineyards. *My mother's vineyards.*

When the car stops, Antonio gets out, and helps me out, too. He holds my hand tight as we duck into the covered pavilion, to raucous applause.

My head is whirling. I've been present for moments like this for much of my life. Winning Port is rarely made without D'Sousa grapes.

Some of the faces I see are new, and others are old friends, who recognize me and wave madly. I wave back, feeling inside like a little girl with braids who skipped through the vineyard with her dollies, and later her friends.

I feel my parents. I see them in the faces of many of the workers. It's a poignant moment, but there's a pure joy that overcomes the wistfulness.

Antonio climbs three steps to a raised platform. I stand nearby, feet firmly on the ground, wrestling with emotions that are bubbling precariously close to the surface.

"You don't fool me," he says, playing to the crowd. "I know your cheers are for the friend I brought along."

More applause. Whistles. Laughter.

My cheeks are warm, but I grin from ear to ear.

"I want to thank each of you for all the hard work you do, day after day, to keep the vines healthy and lush, the grapes juicy and sweet, and the Port stellar. Without you, our Port would be just another bottle of wine."

More applause. Almost deafening. I clap, too. The crowd is respectful, but not reserved, even in the face of Antonio Huntsman, who has a well-earned reputation of being ruthless. But he treated them all fairly when he took over after I left. He honored contracts, gave everyone a raise, and made enhancements to the property. He earned their loyalty.

"I know you're waiting to learn the results from today's luncheon," he teases. "I'm going to let someone special tell you about it."

Antonio steps off the platform and puts his hand out so I'll go up. We didn't plan this—at least I didn't. I must look like I'm about to faint, because he leans down and whispers, "This is your moment, *Princesa*. Enjoy the hell out of it."

The crowd begins to chant *D'Sousa, D'Sousa*, as I climb the steps to the microphone, with my head spinning like a top.

I compose myself while they chant and cheer, and by the time they're quiet, I know exactly where to begin.

"It's my great honor to be here today, on behalf of my parents, and representing Huntsman Port. I've missed you so much." That last part wasn't rehearsed inside my head. It just came gushing out of my heart.

"We missed you, too!" Several people shout back, to more whooping.

My entire being smiles, as I put out my arms. "You did it!" I cry, practically doing a little dance on that mini-stage. "Huntsman Port, made exclusively with Rosa do Vale grapes, won everything! You did it!"

"We did it!" a man shouts from the back, as people leap to their feet, hugging each other.

This isn't just a windfall for a company. This is a point of pride for every single person in this room. They didn't just create an outstanding Port; they're celebrating their part in the rich history of the Douro Valley. Vintage years live forever.

"*Te amo*," I mouth as Antonio tries to hand me the prizes and trophies, but I don't take them. Instead, I take his arm and tug him toward the stage, begging with my eyes for him to join me. And he does.

We hold every ribbon in the air, every trophy, then display it on a table for people to admire close up as they leave.

"Before we go, and leave you to get on with your day," Antonio tells the crowd when we're done, "I have one more announcement." He nods to a man in the corner, who brings a standing easel, draped with a velvet cloth, to the stage. He places it at the edge, where everyone can see.

"Do you want to unveil the masterpiece?" Antonio asks me, before turning toward the room, his eyes glittering. "She doesn't know what this is, either," he says in a stage whisper to the crowd, who are eating out of his hand.

This is the boy I fell in love with as a child. In charge, always, but not afraid to be playful. I don't see this side of him often enough.

"These good people don't have all day, woman. Get on with it."

I laugh with everyone else while I carefully remove the cloth.

I gasp, clenching the velvet to my chest, while I step back to admire a rendering of the Huntsman and Rosa do Vale logos, melded together to create something new. When I glance at Antonio, the dam breaks, and my tears and smiles twirl joyously.

"The Port that garnered so many of this year's awards will be released under a brand-new, exclusive label. The new label will only feature special vintages. It celebrates the partnership between Huntsman and D'Sousa. This is the first new label that Huntsman has put out in a century."

I can barely breathe as I leap into my husband's arms like no one is watching.

38

ANTONIO

I glance down at Daniela, who's fallen asleep in the car, with her head on my lap. She's out cold. The excitement of the day—good and bad—has taken its toll. I brush a few strands of hair off her angelic face.

She proved beyond a shadow of a doubt today that she can withstand the tempest that is my world. *Our world*.

An hour after pulling out a pistol to confront a gunman, she was sipping an aperitif and smiling sweetly while a bunch of assholes fell over one another to impress her. She's tough. *Tougher than she should need to be.*

But I still haven't figured out a way to create a life where she doesn't have to be so tough. Where she can be safe, and string together long stretches of peace. It's the greatest failing of my life.

I scroll through my phone for new information. Lucas and Cristiano have been sending updates since we left this morning. They're both at the property, and I need to talk to them, even if it means waking her.

I text them: **Go to my office. Call when you're set up on speaker.**

Daniela stirs, but she doesn't open her eyes.

If I had a single misgiving about the woman I lured across the Atlantic and held against her will, it was gone when Daniela got up on that stage today and squealed, "You did it!" to the adoring crowd. She actually danced a little jig as she beamed.

The woman born to be queen of the valley, *my queen*, took her rightful place today. She cast a light so bright that even I didn't seem like an ogre standing next to her. If some fucker hadn't gotten onto my property with a gun earlier, it would have been the perfect day.

Even if it takes my life, I will keep you safe. I'll find a way. You have my word, I promise her silently.

The phone vibrates, and I answer immediately. "Where are we?" I ask my most trusted advisors.

"Every corner of this place has been searched, inside and out," Cristiano says. "All clear. He acted alone."

I'm going to need more evidence before I'm convinced he acted alone. "Do we know who *he* is?"

"Claude Sorento, a hitman from Algeria."

He might have been there alone, but he wasn't acting alone. Hitmen are paid mercenaries. They don't kill merely for sport.

"Not the best in the business," Lucas adds. "Lucky for us, you get what you pay for."

"Any ties to Nikitin?"

"Money was wired to him from offshore. We're tracing it. I won't be surprised if it leads back to Nikitin."

Nikitin has lost his loyal guards, but he has access to a boatload of money. The Russian government seized some of his accounts, but those were the ones they knew about. Billionaires always have accounts stashed for a rainy day. *I know I do.*

"Anything from Mikhail?"

"They're still chasing their tails. Nikitin has managed to stay a few steps ahead of them. Mikhail denies it, but I think the oligarch knows he's on his trail."

"Do we have enough men for tonight?"

"We can always use more. But we're satisfied with our numbers and capability. I'm not making excuses for Tavares," Cristiano says, quietly, "but I don't see how he could have kept Sorento out. He killed the delivery man, and had forged credentials already in place. An excellent forgery, by the way. The guards swept the truck when it arrived, but along with all the dishes, there were thousands of utensils, plus pots and pans, and serving pieces that kept setting off the metal detectors. We think the gun was hidden in the bottom of a metal box holding forks. It was lined in satin, which helped obscure the false bottom."

This is a goddamn nightmare. Next year we're having a fucking picnic with paper plates and plastic forks. "He have help from the inside?"

"Nothing we've been able to pinpoint. We did question Paula, Daniela's maid, who had given his name to the guards to put on the approved list of suppliers."

"And?"

"She set off some alarm bells," Lucas continues, "but it might have been because she was so damn nervous. She was sweating and crying. We're holding her, and we'll question her again later. If she has anything, I doubt it's going to be earth-shattering."

Canceling tonight is out of the question. If I can't secure my own damn property, how can I be trusted to keep everyone else's secure? Besides, it goes against everything I believe in, everything I am, to run and hide. The party's happening. *Although, I do wish we had another day to investigate more thoroughly.*

"So to recap, we're having a huge fucking gala tonight, and

we have shit. We're essentially as vulnerable as we were this morning."

"No," they say in unison.

"The entire place will be locked down at four thirty," Cristiano explains. "No one on or off the premises until the guests arrive at eight. If any more help is coming, they have to be here before four thirty. If they're leaving, they need to be gone by then. No exceptions, except for you and Daniela. That gives us three and a half hours to sweep everything one more time."

I glance down at Daniela, who's stirring again. "My family will all be there tonight." *Everyone who's important to me.* "Warn every guard and every soldier you run into today. There will be no mistakes."

39

DANIELA

"Where's Paula?" I ask, as Antonio takes his tux out of the suit bag.

I don't want to have an argument with him right before our guests arrive, but Victor told me that a guard took Paula to be questioned, like everyone else, but that unlike everyone else, she never came back.

"She's been detained for questioning. But from your tone, I suspect you already knew that."

"You're torturing her?"

Antonio glares at me over his shoulder. "Did I say that?" He rummages through a drawer until he finds a pair of thin black socks. "But it's none of your business, *Princesa*. Stay out of it."

"Detained for questioning" is a loaded term that can mean many different things, depending on who's doing the questioning. *Cristiano?* Not too bad. *Lucas?* Not good. *Tavares?* Hell. "Who's questioning her?"

"Did you not understand me?" He scowls.

Oh, I understood you. "She's a member of my personal staff."

"Who provided the name of a hitman to the guards so that he would have access to our home. *To you.*"

A hitman? No way. "She would never do what you're suggesting."

He steps closer to me, so close I can smell mint on his breath. His nostrils are flaring, and suddenly the closet seems too small.

"Listen carefully. You're welcome to plead for her life, if it should come to that. And I am welcome to indulge you, or to slit her throat, if that's where the facts lead. I've been abundantly clear that I will not allow anyone who attempts to hurt you to go unpunished."

When he's like this, there's no winning with him. I quietly go over to my side and pull out shoes for tonight before leaving the closet. I'm worried about Paula. Even if she's safe, she's going to be a nervous wreck. I could have warned her about what to expect, or at least shown her some kind of support, if I'd known.

"Next time you detain someone from my personal staff, I would appreciate a heads-up," I tell him, when he comes into the bedroom.

Antonio walks across the room and stops when he's well inside my personal space. He slides a finger from my throat into the deep V of my silk robe.

"Lucas questioned her," he says softly.

He doesn't want to fight. Neither do I.

"She's fine for now. Let's just get through tonight."

Using his big body, he nudges me closer to the bed.

"Not now," I mumble, pushing him away. I'm still annoyed with him.

"You've already denied me once today. Denied yourself. It's not happening a second time."

He runs his nose along my jaw, while he unties the robe and eases it over my shoulders. Without even a small kiss, he lowers himself to his haunches and spreads my legs. I could stop him, but it's been a hell of a day, and my body is aching for his tongue. *I want the release.*

His fingers caress my inner thighs. "Touch your pretty cunt, *Princesa*," he murmurs.

I almost whine, *No! You touch it. I want your magic.* But that will not get me the orgasm I'm craving.

I slide my hand over my freshly waxed pussy and go straight for my clit, rubbing the swollen nub until I'm swaying. That's when he swats my hand away.

"I want your orgasm to be mine." His voice is raspy, as he plunges two fingers inside me and begins to flick his tongue over the tight bundle of nerves. When I grind my pussy into his hand, he slides in a third finger.

Ahhhhh! I cry, my legs trembling. I tug on his hair to keep myself upright.

His fingers curl inside me, as he sucks my clit into his hungry mouth.

I hear myself moan as my belly tightens. It's right *there*. I'm right *there*.

"Come for me, *Princesa*. Come all over my fingers." He sucks harder, and I latch onto his head and let the release drown me in giant waves.

"I'm going to shower," he says, while I'm still panting. "We don't have a ton of time before we need to be downstairs. If you don't want your hair to be soaking wet, join me at your own peril."

He's incorrigible. *Plain and simple.*

Although, I'll admit, it's hard to resist that thick cock, bobbing proudly with every stride he takes. But I don't want my hair dripping wet, *and it will be*, so I'll just have to satisfy myself with an extra-long look at his gorgeous ass.

When he disappears, I pick up my robe and throw on a sundress before going to see if Valentina needs any help getting ready.

I try not to think about Paula being held, God knows where, or the gunman from this morning, and I push away any concerns that I have about tonight. I'm not worried about the food or the flowers. I'm worried that the gunman has a friend who slips in with the guests.

40

DANIELA

When I get to Valentina's room, she's not there. Santi and Mia have been glued to her all day, but I go downstairs to see for myself.

Duarte is at the bottom of the stairs in a black tux with a red bow tie.

"You look very handsome. I didn't get a chance earlier to thank you for not telling Antonio that I left the main tent without informing you." My thoughtlessness put him in a really bad position, and I still feel terrible about it.

He nods. "When I was assigned to your protection detail, your husband told me I had one job, and that was to protect you. To do my job well, I need you to trust me. While I can't promise, I will always do my best to never betray your trust." He's earnest, and he means every word.

The difference between Duarte and Alvarez is night and day. But protecting me from Antonio's wrath is too much to ask of him. Plus, I don't really need that kind of protection.

"I appreciate your loyalty, but please don't feel you have to cover for me with my husband. I know it puts you in a terrible position. Believe it or not, I can handle him quite well. But that's our little secret."

Duarte pretends to zip his lips.

"Is that what you're wearing?" Lara asks, aghast, interrupting the sweet moment with my guard.

"Yes," I say brightly. "Do you like it?"

Her mouth is open. "Uh—"

"You can relax. I'm not wearing a sundress to a black-tie event. I'm looking for Valentina."

"Her little friends just arrived, and she's introducing them to *Senhora* Lydia."

Duarte nods, indicating that this is correct. I've known him for less time, but I trust him more than I trust Lara.

"Is she dressed?"

Lara smiles. "To the nines. She looks beautiful. The color of her gown brings out the purple in her eyes."

My heart drops into my stomach. *Relax, Daniela. Tomas is dead. Most people here won't remember Vera as a child. And if they do, they can think what they want. No one would ever say a word to her.*

"Paula won't be with us this evening, so there's no one to do a last-minute check of the tent. Would you mind doing it before you change?" I ask Lara.

"I don't mind at all." She tips her head to the side. "Is she okay?"

"I believe so."

"Are you okay? You look a bit wan."

Thanks. "Nothing a bit more blush can't cure. It's been a long day."

"Can I talk to you for a moment?"

"Sure," I force myself to say. I'm not in the mood for a private *chat* with Lara. "But let's not go far. We both need to get dressed."

We move a few feet away from Duarte, although I'm certain he can hear us.

"Did Paula have something to do with what happened in the staging tent?" Lara probes shamelessly.

I don't know how to reply, so I take a page out of my husband's book. "Why do you ask?"

She shrugs. "A guard took her to be questioned, and I haven't seen her since. Everyone else who was questioned has been released."

"I'm sure Paula didn't have anything to do with what happened." Lara is always so unkind when it comes to Paula that I feel the need to defend her.

"Paula has always had a reputation as a sneak. Even when she worked in the caves. She would spy on people and then turn them in to Jacinto to curry favor. That's how she got the job as your personal maid. She certainly wasn't qualified." Lara huffs. "She looks out for herself. It's only one step further to accept money to get a bad man inside."

After this week is over, Lara needs to be fired. She can go back to Jacinto, but I don't want her on my staff. "Do you know that she did that?"

"Well, no. But—"

"No buts, Lara. It can irreparably damage someone's reputation to spread rumors. I don't like it."

"I would never spread rumors. I'm just making you aware. If there's nothing else, I'll go and do a last-minute check of the tent."

What if Paula is an issue? I can't let my feelings about Lara influence how I feel about Paula, one way or another. I need to keep them separate.

"Hey," Cristiano says, coming up behind me as Lara leaves.

I smile at my husband's handsome friend. "This place is swarming with hot guys in tuxes."

He chuckles.

"Let me ask you something."

He shuts one eye. "Save me, Duarte." He groans.

Duarte puts up both his hands. "You're on your own, brother."

"Ask. I'll try to answer."

Sure you will. "Do you remember the day I snuck off the property? A few weeks after I got here."

He raises his brow. "I don't think anyone who was around Antonio while you were on the run will ever forget it."

I doubt I'll ever forget it, either.

"Who told you I left?"

He pauses to think. "The guards told us. Lucas, actually. But I don't remember who alerted them. I can check. Is there a problem?"

"No. I just wondered if it was Paula."

"What makes you think that?"

"I didn't tell her, but she had to suspect something was up. To be honest, I never gave it much thought, but Lara just said something, and it got me thinking."

"What did she say?" he asks in that disarming way he uses to get people to spill their guts before they realize they said too much.

"She said—" I stop, because Paula is under a lot of scrutiny, and if I tell Cristiano what Lara said, it will likely become worse. It's true she sneaked around with her boyfriend in a way that would have gotten them in trouble—or at least him in trouble—but it's a huge leap from sneaking to have lunch with your boyfriend to assisting a hitman.

This is exactly what Lara was hoping to accomplish.

"It's nothing. Lara's always putting down Paula, and she was spreading gossip."

He nods. "I supported Lara for the assistant position. I thought she'd make a good companion for you. But the more I'm around her, the less enamored I am with her."

If Cristiano doesn't like you, there's probably something about you that's not worth liking. "What's changed your mind?"

He slips his hand in his trouser pocket. "Not sure."

"Not sure, or not sharing?"

The corners of his mouth curl slightly. "I'll try to find out who ratted you out," he says with a wink.

41

ANTONIO

When the evening's over, after we've sent the last of the fucking dawdlers home, I take off my jacket, ditch the tie, and roll up my sleeves on the way to ask the band to play one more song. I want to dance with my wife.

Not the polite practiced dancing we did earlier, but the kind of slow dancing that high school kids do: arms around each other and hormone-laden bodies pressed together without a smidgeon of light between them.

Dancing is not my favorite activity, but Daniela loves it. She and Valentina are always singing and dancing. Although I can get down with the kind of dancing I'm thinking about.

"What do you want to hear?" the vocalist asks.

"Something with a slow tempo made for dancing with a beautiful woman."

"My specialty," he says, with a knowing smile.

I find my wife, who has slipped off her shoes, and is walking around the tent, thanking the help. She has on a red dress that's skimming the floor now, like it skims her curves. It's backless, and I took every opportunity tonight to rest my hand on her silky skin.

Daniela spots me and sashays in my direction with a sexy smile and shimmering eyes. She wore her hair down tonight, and it makes her look even younger than her twenty-four years. *She is gorgeous.*

That damn dress, though. It shows a bit of cleavage—too damn much as far as I'm concerned. During dinner, the prime minister, who was seated beside her, kept glancing at her tits. That son of a bitch is damn lucky I didn't stab him in the eye with my fork. But I will not be supporting him in next year's election. Take it to the bank.

Although now that everyone's gone, I'm going to appreciate the hell out of those tits.

"They're playing our song."

"We have a song?" she asks softly, with that touch of sassiness that my cock loves.

"Dance with me."

"You don't have to ask twice. Although that really wasn't a question. You know, the whole inflection thing at the end of the sentence really works. You should try it sometime."

"Keep it up," I say softly, as I take her into my arms. "And I'll fuck you right here in the middle of the dance floor."

She wraps her arms around my neck. "Ah, my charming date has given way to my dark prince."

I cradle the back of her neck with one hand and slide the other to her ass. "A dirty *princesa* needs a dark prince to satisfy her."

"It's true," she whispers into my neck. "Tonight was like a fairy tale. Something I'd always dreamed about, but thought I'd left behind when I went to the US."

I pull her closer, until there's no daylight between us. "This is who you are. Who you were born to be. If I have one regret, it's that I didn't understand that when I let you go to the US. I wish I would have known sooner how perfect you are for me. If I had, there's no way you would have left the country. If I had made a better decision, I could have loved you longer."

Earnest and humble. It's the kind of confession a powerful man only makes to a beautiful woman he can't live without. And even then, only once in a blue moon.

The band plays on and on, and everyone and everything bleeds away—except for her. I inhale her scent like the greedy bastard I am, and let her goodness seep into every pore, until the need to devour her becomes overwhelming.

"I need to meet with Tavares and the rest of the team before I leave. Go upstairs and wait for me," I murmur, brushing my mouth against hers.

"Don't be long," she whispers, gazing at me with so much unfettered lust in her eyes, I almost bag the meeting.

But I can't.

———

THERE WERE NO SURPRISES TONIGHT, but even so, the morning's events make the discussion with my men longer than I hoped. When I get upstairs, the light is dim, and my *princesa* is asleep, snoring softly.

I don't turn on the light, but I make a fair amount of noise as I change, hoping to wake her and finish what we started on that dance floor. But even when I slip into bed behind her, she doesn't stir.

"*Mmmm*," she murmurs, when I curl my naked body around hers. But she's not awake.

Even though my cock is aching for her, I don't wake her—or attempt to take her. She's had a huge day. And it's only the first day of the celebration. Two hundred children are coming tomorrow for lunch and a carnival, courtesy of Daniela and Valentina.

It's been a hell of a day for me too, and I could use some

sleep. I inhale the sweet scent of orange blossom and shut my eyes, hoping for a little peace.

The gunman's face appears the minute they're closed.

I pull her closer, tighter, shielding her with my body.

I can't lose her.

42

ANTONIO

"Are you sure my granddaughter can't come to London with me for a few days of shopping and spoiling?" my mother asks, for what must be the tenth time today. She's too much.

It's been wonderful having her here for the last ten days, but now that the festivities are over, it's time for her to go home.

I'm not opposed to her taking Valentina with her either, so Daniela can have a few days to herself, and we can have some long, glorious nights without worrying if the bedroom door's locked or whether we're making too much noise. *Not that I actually worry about any of those things.* But it's Daniela's call.

"Not this time," Daniela replies, again. "She's already missed so much school because of the harvest."

"The next long weekend then. Promise me."

"I promise."

"It was an amazing week," my mother says. "Everything was perfect."

Other than the first day. But we managed to keep it so quiet, even Lydia Huntsman didn't get a whiff of it. Everyone from the outside who worked the events signed non-disclosure agreements, although the biggest deterrent from talking too much was not the threat of being sued, but the concern for their lives. And no one on my payroll would dare breathe a word.

"Your mother would have been so proud of you," she murmurs to Daniela. "You did your parents proud, and your husband. I'm so proud of you—of you both," she gushes, taking my hands.

My mother is five two on a good day, but she's tough, and as much as it drives me crazy, at times, I'm happy that she lives life on her own terms.

"Antonio, I don't always agree with your ways. They're not befitting a modern leader. Daniela can enlighten you. You need to listen to her more." She touches my cheek. "But even with that, I'm so proud of the man you've become, and the way you've shouldered immense responsibility. Although sometimes I worry the burdens are too much. That they keep you awake too many nights and rob you of all serenity."

"I sleep just fine," I assure her. *Especially when my wife is in my arms.*

"And don't be so serious all the time. You're so handsome when you smile."

She turns to Daniela. "Make sure he finds time to play."

"Heavy hangs the head that wears the crown," she whispers when I bend over to kiss her cheek. "Don't be afraid to take it off from time to time—or forever, if that's what your heart requires. *Te amo, meu amor.*"

"*Cuidad*," I say to her. "Be careful. No unnecessary risks."

I shake hands with her husband, Edward. "Take good care of her. She's a handful. It's not an easy job, but you're the man for it."

He smiles, putting his arm around my mother.

"Don't be afraid to get in touch with me if she doesn't cooperate."

My mother starts to chastise me, when Rafael saunters into

the foyer with a leather duffel bag. "I'm ready," he announces to the room.

"Where are you going?" I ask, knowing full well.

"Back to London. I'm on break until my internship begins, and I intend to make the most of it." He flashes Daniela a grin.

"You're not going to London."

"No?"

"We have a discussion to finish. You know, the one about following orders."

My mother and Daniela glance at each other; Daniela winks and my mother rolls her eyes. Those two are trouble when they're together, conspiring against me.

"This won't take long," Rafael says to Edward. "Is it possible to wait a few minutes? I have plans tonight in London. Besides, I rarely get to fly on Will's plane. He has a flight attendant, Jana, who gives unbelievable—" He pales when he looks at my mother and Daniela, whose eyes are narrowed. "Foot rubs. She gives unbelievable foot rubs. Do you mind?"

"That won't be necessary," I tell Edward, before turning to Rafael. "Your plans will have to wait."

"Oh, for God's sake, Antonio," my mother grouses. "Don't be too hard on the boy. As I recall, you weren't much for following orders, either."

I raise my brow, to remind her not to undermine me with Rafael. She gets the message immediately, and doesn't say another word.

After we say goodbye to my mother and Edward, I kiss Daniela on the cheek. "I'll meet you upstairs when we're through. We have a lot of catching up to do."

"I hear you," Rafael mutters. "And I understand coded language."

For a moment he sounds like a sullen teenager, but it's to be expected. He's not much more than a teenager, and I did abruptly change his plans.

Daniela turns toward the stairs. "By the way, that's not a foot Jana's rubbing," she whispers loudly to Rafa on her way past. "Have Antonio tell you about the birds and the bees."

We've already had that talk. But I'll add it to the list of uncomfortable things we're going to chat about now.

43

ANTONIO

"There are a lot of hoops to jump through, but I'm trying to put some things in place with regard to Premier," I explain to Rafael once we're in my office with the door closed. "As far as I'm concerned, the company belongs to you."

He puts up both hands. "Not interested. If you want it, be my guest."

I'm not going to argue with him. He's going to cut his teeth on it, during his internship, and if it's not for him, fine. But he's a kid and he's not throwing it away to avoid painful memories of his family that he hasn't fully worked through.

"I'll oversee the transition until you've had time to think about it," I tell him. "But I want you involved in some of the decision-making during your internship."

He peers at me, eyes wide. "You're kidding."

"Have you ever known me to be a big kidder?"

He shrugs.

"No. You haven't, because I'm not. If you don't want the company, I'll buy it from you. No one's asking you to dedicate your life to Port. But you don't make any decisions now. Not until some time has passed. You just learned about your mom's death," I add gently. "It's not the time to make a big decision."

"I'm not going to change my mind," he replies, like the stubborn jackass he can be.

It runs in the family.

"I'm not changing my mind, either. About any of it. Premier will be part of your portfolio during the internship." I don't give him an inch of wiggle room.

He throws up his hands. "You're the boss. I'll be working for you."

"When you show up for your first day of internship, I highly recommend you bring a better attitude. Otherwise, it's going to be a long, painful experience for you. Don't think I'm above giving you a failing grade."

He glances up at me. A failing grade on his internship means he doesn't graduate with his class. Rafael knows from experience I rarely issue a threat I won't make good on. It would kill me, but I'd do it if I thought it was the right thing for him.

"Are we done?" he asks, standing.

"We're just getting started. Put your ass back in the chair."

He sits, reluctantly, but he does it. Rafael wants to please me. I'm always humbled by that, even during tense discussions like this one. "You disobeyed a direct order after the regatta."

Rafael sighs. "We've been over this." He doesn't apologize, which is just as well, because he's not sorry.

"There were a handful of young soldiers who left the pier where they were ordered to protect Daniela, to come to my rescue, like you did. There will be consequences for all of you."

He sticks his chin out. "What exactly do these consequences entail?"

"They entail spending the next month up north, reviewing some basic training and helping to winterize one of our vineyards. The training will be familiar to the soldiers, because they've already had it. While you've also had a fair amount of training, it wasn't like this."

Rafa drums his fingers on the arm of the chair. He's nervous. Despite his bravado and carefree attitude, Rafael's not a huge risk taker. He's great with people, but he has dyslexia, which can sometimes pose challenges. What I have planned for him is not anything he can't handle in that regard, but there will be a lot of time for reflection, and that might be the most challenging aspect for him.

"I had plans for the time before my internship. Plans that don't just involve me."

"You might have to disappoint some people."

I can see the anger building.

"You're making me go to some remote area up north for a month to get my ass kicked every day, instead of a little R and R that I worked hard for?"

I shake my head. "I'm not making you do anything. This is your choice, son. You can't make a man be a good soldier, or a good leader. You can only give him opportunities to grow and develop."

He snatches a paperweight off my desk and tosses it from one hand to the other. "And that's what this is? An opportunity?"

"Men who lead need to learn to follow first. Men who follow need to know that their leader earned his way, and that he's deserving of their loyalty. Leaders ask others to make sacrifices. Good leaders understand what those sacrifices cost. I'm not talking about giving up a few weeks at the beach, chasing pussy. I'm talking about real sacrifice. So yes, this is an opportunity."

He puts the paperweight back. "Forget me for a minute. Soldiers went to your rescue, and you're punishing them? Are they good soldiers—or are they just expendable, so you don't care about dumping them up north for a month?"

"Soldiers aren't expendable, Rafael. These are good men, capable, but young and not as disciplined as they need to be, for their own safety as well as for those around them. They're also getting an opportunity. If I didn't think they had the highest potential, I wouldn't bother."

He swallows hard and nods.

I might have actually gotten through to him. But before he can respond, there's a knock at the door.

Bad timing. "What is it?"

"We have some news on our missing oligarch," Cristiano says from the doorway.

"Rafael and I are almost finished. I'll text you when we're through, and we can meet in here."

"Oligarchs?" Rafael asks. "Anything to do with the hitman?"

I don't tell him to mind his business, because this is his business.

"We're looking for a connection."

He nods.

"The helicopter leaves in an hour, if you're going."

"That doesn't exactly leave much time to pack."

"You're not going to war…you don't need to get your affairs in order. Everything you need will be provided for you—right down to your underwear. All you need to bring is a change of clothing for the return trip."

"I don't suppose I can take electronics?"

Maybe I was wrong before. This might be the most challenging part of the month. "Not even your phone."

He blows out a breath.

"It's your choice, Rafael. It won't change anything between us."

"You know damn well I don't like it, but I'm going, Antonio."

I never had a moment's doubt he'd go, but that doesn't mean that I'm not proud of him. "Listen, I know this isn't what you expected. But I won't be around forever. You're next in line."

He peers at me with a straight face, but I see the surprise in his eyes.

"There's no better man I know to take the reins than you. I have complete faith in you, Rafael. But you're young, and impulsive, and headstrong—those qualities can get you into trouble. I know from my own experience."

"This conversation is taking a turn I don't care for. I'm happy to go to camp for a month in the middle of fucking nowhere, but you better not be going anywhere, old man, because I'm not ready to take any reins. I have a lot more foot rubs in my future before that happens."

I massage my temples. This is Rafael's way of dealing with his fear of abandonment. His father did a number on him before he came to live here. I blame his brother, too. I hope the devil prepared a special place in hell for them.

"Why are you still here?" I ask. "Get going. Your ride leaves in an hour. Find me before you leave," I tell him as he strolls out of my office.

44

DANIELA

Antonio knocks once on the door and barges right in. "You do realize it's customary to wait until someone says *come in* before you enter, right?"

"*Pfft,*" he replies, shedding his clothes. "I heard the water sloshing around. I knew you were in the tub."

"What has that got to do with it? What if I was in here, enjoying a private moment with myself?"

He dims the lights and turns on some moody jazz. "If that's what I thought, I wouldn't have bothered to knock."

My eyes feast on him, as he hovers above me, motioning for me to move forward so he can get in behind me. His muscle is lean and sculpted, and everything about him, including that fine cock, is mouthwatering.

"You're a brazen *princesa*. Like what you see?"

"Every inch."

The corner of his mouth tugs into a little smirk.

"This tub is huge—why don't you sit across from me so I can look at you while we talk?"

"I don't want to talk. I want to feel you," he murmurs, climbing in behind me and wrapping his arms around me, pulling me against him. He gently presses a kiss to the back of my head.

Mmmm. He can be so tender and sweet, but it rarely lasts long, although I'm seeing more and more of it.

"What took so long? I hope you weren't too hard on Rafael."

"Have you been waiting for me all this time?" He snatches my hand out of the water, and turns it over to see if my fingers are shriveled.

"Four hours? In your dreams."

He tweaks my nipple.

"Ouch!" I yelp, slapping his hand. "Valentina and I took the horses around the corral, and then we reheated some leftovers. Now she's in bed. School is going to come as a shock after a week of play. Tell me what happened with Rafael."

"He's not happy," Antonio mutters, settling deeper into the warm bath.

"What did you do?"

"I gave him an opportunity to be a leader in much the same way your father gave me an opportunity. I'm trying to teach him to be a responsible and disciplined man. Your father did that for me, and I'll always be grateful. I'm sure I was as much of a pain in the ass as Rafael is—maybe more."

My father. I'm not as angry as I was with him when I first learned about what he did, but my feelings are still in a twist. *He should have told me.*

"So you taught Rafael how to execute a betrothal contract?" Antonio pinches my ass, and I squirm, spilling some water over the side. "What exactly does an opportunity to be a leader entail?"

"Ask Rafael when you see him. Right now, all I want to do is play with your pussy." He hooks his legs around mine and spreads them apart, letting the warm water lap against the sensitive flesh.

It feels heavenly—but I want more.

"What are you waiting for?" I wiggle my ass against his hard cock.

"You're asking for trouble."

"Begging for it."

He slides one hand across my chest, holding me firmly against him, and the other under the water, until he finds my throbbing pussy. While his fingers leisurely circle my warm folds, I lay my head back against his shoulder and close my eyes, moaning gratefully as his skilled hand works me into a frenzy.

"You're my life," he murmurs. "My queen."

When he unveiled the new Huntsman and Rosa do Vale logo, I knew then that I was his queen, but I don't think I'll ever get tired of hearing him say it.

"Antonio!" Cristiano shouts, pounding on the bathroom door, startling me. My relaxed husband tenses at the voice. "I need a word with you. It can't wait."

I hear the urgency in his tone. Antonio must too, because he gets right out and grabs a towel.

"*Fuck,*" Antonio grumbles. "Give me a minute."

My stomach flutters uncomfortably, as Antonio dries himself quickly and slings the towel around his waist.

"I'll be right back. Don't go anywhere. And don't get any ideas. I want to be the one to make you come. This better be fucking important," he mutters, shutting the door behind him.

Other than a handful of select staff, no one besides family is allowed on this floor. Cristiano would certainly be given more leeway than anyone, but he would never disturb us in our bedroom—not unless something terrible happened.

I get out of the tub and dry myself, too. *He won't be right back.*

45

ANTONIO

Cristiano is pacing my bedroom when I open the door. He's gray. His eyes filled with pain. Sorrow. Apprehension.

"What happened?" I ask, knowing whatever it is, it's bad. *Very bad.*

He doesn't say a word for several seconds. The crippling silence is veiled in doom, echoing off the walls. If it goes on any longer, I'm going to shake him.

"What happened?" I demand, forcefully this time, even though I really don't want to know. I just want to go back and sink into the bath and get lost in Daniela.

The knot in his throat bobs. "Your mother's plane never landed in London. Air traffic control lost contact with them somewhere over the Atlantic."

The words are tangled in a thick, viscous muck, and it takes me…I don't know how long…to process them.

Your mother's plane never landed in London. They lost contact with air traffic control over the Atlantic.

No.

My mind reels. Ghastly images stumble over one another. I

open my mouth, gasping for air, but there doesn't seem to be any in the room.

"I'm sorry," Cristiano says somberly. His mouth is still moving, and words are coming out, but all I hear is *They lost contact with air traffic control over the Atlantic.*

My mother. The woman who stood between me and my father, weathering his fists so that I wouldn't have to suffer. The woman who was finally, finally happy.

Instead of sorrow, rage consumes me. It's a venomous hate snaking through my body, sucking up brain cells as it slithers.

Stop! Just fucking stop.

I can't allow myself to get mired in emotion. Not if I'm going to do her any good.

I draw a breath. And then another, until I can speak. "What do you know?"

Cristiano cracks his knuckles. "Nothing more than I just told you."

"Anything from Will?"

"That's how we heard about the plane. He tried to call you."

I pick up my phone from the dresser. A half-dozen missed calls, and messages. While I lounged in a bubble bath, fingering my wife, my mother was killed. *Maybe murdered.*

Not now. Later. Plenty of time for self-loathing later.

"I'm going to get dressed, and I want to go to the site of the crash." I glance at him. "Immediately. Make it happen."

"We don't know that there was a crash."

Bullshit. He doesn't believe that any more than I do.

"Planes don't disappear into thin air over the Atlantic. This isn't a sci-fi movie. Pinpoint the location where the plane was last heard from, and figure out how to get me there."

Cristiano has something to say, but he wisely nods instead.

The bathroom door creaks, and Daniela peeks her head out. Her face barely registers.

"Go," I tell him, as she slips into the room wrapped in a robe. "I'll be down in five minutes."

Cristiano nods and leaves without another word.

"What's wrong?" Daniela asks, following me into the closet.

I can't with the questions—even from her. I just want to be left alone so I can think.

"Air traffic control lost contact with my mother's plane." My mouth is bone-dry, and I struggle to get the words out.

"What does that mean?" she asks, like she's having trouble processing the news, too.

I can't help her. I'm still trying to wrap my own head around it.

"Antonio," she murmurs, reaching out to me.

"Not now." I jerk away. "I'm in a hurry." *And I need to stay focused on locating that plane.*

And you'll encourage me to find refuge in your arms. I can't do that right now, no matter how much I want it. "If you want to help, leave me to do what I need to do."

The phone rings. "One minute," I growl, answering.

I turn to Daniela. "You are not to leave this house without permission from either Cristiano, Lucas, or me. No one else gets a say in the matter. If you chose to ignore this order, I will hold your guard personally responsible for the transgression, and you'll be the one to break the news to his wife and children that he's never coming home."

I have no fucking idea what happened with that plane, and until I know, this place is on lockdown. I will *not* lose her, too.

Daniela pulls her robe tighter, but she's become so accustomed to my mercurial moods, she's not fazed. Although there's pity in her eyes that I can't bear to look at.

"Antonio," she says softly as I storm out of the closet.

I don't stop for her, because I don't have time to spare.

"I love you," she says in a clear voice, wrapped in warmth and goodness.

The words hit me squarely in the chest, leaving a raw, tortured wound. "It might be better for you if you didn't."

46

ANTONIO

"What the fuck happened?" I bark at Will on my way downstairs. "That plane came from London today. It was supposed to be under your control."

"I'm sorry," he says, quietly. "So sorry."

You fucker. "That's it? I'm sorry?"

"Samantha's father was on that plane too," he bites back, "so don't insinuate that I didn't take every necessary precaution."

Samantha.

I blow out a breath. "I'm not insinuating anything. I'm trying to figure out what the hell happened." *And I'm fighting a murderous rage.* "Was there a mayday call?"

"No warning. It's too early to know what happened."

No mayday call means the plane exploded.

Exploded right out of the sky. Maybe it's better if they didn't see it coming.

I stop on the bottom step to pull myself together before I have to face anyone.

"We have rescue crews headed to where we last heard from them," Will continues.

"Double whatever you have going out there. Send me a

complete manifest. I want to know everything about everyone who was on that plane, and anyone who had access to it. And send me the coordinates. I'm on my way to the site."

"There is no actual site, Antonio. Not yet. We don't have enough information."

"Don't care. I'm not sitting around stroking my dick, praying for good news."

"I would tell you not to come, but I'm the last person to give that advice." He pauses for a beat. "Antonio, I'm going to tell you what I told my wife. Brace yourself for bad news. It doesn't look good."

That's the last thing I want to hear. And I don't want anyone else to hear it either. Once people think it's a recovery mission, rather than a rescue, the urgency wanes.

"I don't give a shit how it looks. Save the prophecies for your wife. We keep our foot on the gas, and we don't let up until we find them."

"Agreed."

Cristiano and Thiago are waiting for me out front with the car.

"You know, Will, you keep dumping this shit on me, but explosions seem to be following you around, too."

"Oh, this was personal. A message to both of us."

"Why, though? We don't share the same enemies."

"No. But we help each other out from time to time. Not that long ago, I delivered a package to you. Some might say a package with a lot of value."

"You'd be surprised how little he's been missed." I know I've been.

"But he was in the Kremlin's pocket, and they're pissed—all the way up."

"They're not happy. But the Russian government isn't coming after me because of some chump I disposed of. Nikitin only wants me in an attempt to get back into his president's good graces, to save his ass—and maybe for some revenge. There's no way his behavior is sanctioned from high up. Not at this point. I just don't believe it."

"I don't either. But I keep going back to something you said the other day. The reason it's so hard to identify the enemy is because the attacks seem to be coming from more than one direction."

It's true. Maybe truer today than when I originally said it.

I climb into the back of the SUV. I'm done navel-gazing. I want solid answers, not speculation. "I've gotta go. Keep me updated. And get me those coordinates."

47

DANIELA

On the bench at the foot of the bed is a tray with snacks, and some wine. Victor's off for a few days, and this tray is certainly not his work anyway. It looks like it was thrown together by a teenage boy, or a man who isn't used to preparing snacks.

I pick up the decanter of Port and bring it to my nose. It's the one that will be released under the new label. Was that just a week ago that we stood side by side celebrating?

Lost contact with the plane. I don't have the strength to think about what that means.

After I get dressed, I go downstairs to make a pot of coffee. Duarte and Mia are on the first landing, flanking the bottom of the upper staircase. Normally, it's just one of them at this time of the evening, stationed at the bottom of the stairs.

They nod when they see me.

"It's going to be a long night. I'm going to make some coffee. Please help yourself to anything in the kitchen."

"Thank you."

I brew two pots of coffee and make sandwiches. Antonio

and Cristiano are going to need sustenance. *Or maybe I just need something to do.*

I put one pot and a few sandwiches on a small cart Victor keeps in the kitchen, and add some cookies and water.

As I wheel the food to Antonio's office, I pass two guards in the back foyer, who are normally stationed outside the house. *Antonio doesn't believe whatever happened with the plane was an accident.* That's what the added security is about.

When I reach the office, I knock. There's light under the door, but no one answers.

I turn the knob quietly and crack the door. "Antonio?" *Nothing.* "Cristiano?" *Still nothing.*

I push open the door, to find an empty room. *Did he leave? That doesn't make sense. Why go to his office in the city at this hour? What could he possibly do there that he can't do here?*

I leave the cart and search the house for him, even though I know there's nowhere else he'd be. But there's a gnawing inside me. *I need to find him.*

"Have you seen Antonio?" I ask Duarte and Mia.

"Not since he passed us on the stairs," Mia replies.

"Did he say anything about where he was going?"

They shake their heads. "He was on the phone."

I don't call Antonio, because I know he won't answer. I call Cristiano instead, but my call goes directly to voicemail.

"It's Daniela. I'm worried about Antonio. Call me."

I go to the guards at the front door. "Have you seen Antonio?"

"*Senhor* Antonio left with Cristiano."

Nervous energy is bouncing inside me now.

"Do you know where they went?"

"No."

Not that you'd tell me even if you knew.

I call the guard house next. "Did Antonio leave the premises?"

"I'm not at liberty to discuss *Senhor* Antonio's whereabouts."
Of course not.
"What about Cristiano? Surely you can tell me if he's still on the premises?"
"He's not here."
They're together. That makes me feel a little better.
I try Cristiano again.
"Not a good time, Daniela. We're about to board a plane."
At least he answered.
A plane? What if what happened to Lydia's plane wasn't an accident? What if Antonio's plane is compromised, too?
"Are you going to London?"
"We're not going to London. We're meeting rescue workers at the site of last contact."
"Do you think that's a good idea?"
"It's the plan." It's impossible to tell if Cristiano thinks it's a good plan, or if he's just following a tortured Antonio into hell.
"Where exactly are you going?"
"Atlantic Ocean—somewhere between Porto and London."
"Do you think the plane might have veered off course?"
"Anything's possible."
But not realistic. He doesn't have to say it. I hear it in his tone.
I lower myself to the bottom riser of the stairs. The loss of a parent you love, who loves you, makes a bigger hole in your heart than you're prepared to handle. The grief sneaks in at unexpected times, in unexpected ways. Antonio doesn't operate well under those circumstances.
"Cristiano, is he okay?"
"He's in full control mode. You can talk to Victor, but don't tell anyone else that the plane is missing, or where Antonio is. Lucas is your go-to person. We will be able to communicate some from our location, but it will be sporadic and impossible at times."

"Cristiano, don't let him do anything foolish. I need him to come back to me. And don't leave his side."

"I don't intend to."

48

ANTONIO

My heart stills when I spot the debris field from the helicopter.

The plane either exploded midair, or when it hit the water. Experts will know.

I want to know too. I want to know every goddamn thing there is to know about how this happened.

As the helicopter descends, I scour the ocean for *any* sign of life.

I watch in disbelief, as the surface is spotlighted and the divers are lowered into the icy, cavernous hole that is the Atlantic.

Reluctantly, anger leaves my soul, making room for a staggering grief, moving at warp speed as it takes up every corner, banging against the periphery and testing my humanity beyond reason.

I'm cold and numb, as I comb the violent sea for any hope.

"*You're not more powerful than I,*" she taunts, the evidence of her might bobbing on the surface.

Seat cushions.

A suitcase.
Flotation devices.
Scraps of metal that made up the plane.
And thousands of objects I can't identify from this distance.
But not a single sign of life.

49

DANIELA

It's day ten when I receive the message from Cristiano: **He needs you. Call Lucas for details.**

I haven't heard a peep from Antonio in ten days.

The time hasn't passed quickly. It's inched forward second by second. On day one, I comforted a grief-stricken Samantha. On day two, I broke the news to Valentina, who sobbed in my arms. On days five, six, and seven, I demanded Lucas answer every goddamn question I asked.

But there hasn't been a single day where I haven't been wallowing in sorrow as I waited for news. Not a single hour that I haven't mourned Antonio's absence. Not a moment where I haven't longed to ease his pain. Every tick of the clock makes me more frantic for him.

Imagine how dire things must be for Cristiano to ask you to come? I give myself only a moment to dwell on Antonio's emotional state before I call Lucas.

"I received a message from Cristiano asking me to come. He said to contact you."

"Yeah."

One small word, laden with misgivings. That's all it takes for me to know he doesn't agree with Cristiano.

"Lucas, I'm just going to say this once. Antonio needs me, and I'm going. Today. I need you to tell me how that's going to happen."

He huffs. "First, I want you to know what you're up against. They're on a no-frills barge in the middle of the ocean. A storm has been forecast. Antonio's not in a good frame of mind. Every time they find a body that's not Lydia's, he sinks deeper into the dark. He refuses to come home without her body." He draws a shaky breath and blows it out. "My best guess is that he won't be happy to see you."

That would be my best guess, too. I shut my eyes tight. *Oh, Antonio.*

"I get the picture. How soon can I leave?"

"An hour. The plane is being fueled. It'll take you to a helicopter that will take you out to the barge. Pack light, dress warm, wear rubber-soled shoes. Bring an extra pair, if you have them, and rain gear."

A storm has been forecast. He needs you. Two simple sentences, each loaded with emotion that pits my love for Valentina against my love for Antonio. *A mother always chooses her child. Always.* Not this time.

I knew this moment was coming. I've been waiting for a signal from Cristiano. "Lucas?"

"What?"

"I don't expect a problem, but I prepared a custody agreement in case something should happen to Antonio and me. It's informal, but it's been notarized and signed. Victor witnessed it. I've left it in our closet in the lockbox. If anything should happen, Rafael is to have custody of Valentina."

He's quiet for a moment. "Does Rafael know?"

"I've never talked with him about it, and he's still up north and unreachable. Although I'm saying it again—I don't agree with not telling him about the plane crash. He was very close to Lydia."

"That's not our decision to make." He pauses for a beat. "You don't need to do this, Daniela. When Antonio's finished licking his wounds, he'll come home. He'll leave on his own timeline, whether you're there or not."

"I have to go, Lucas. I know how to reach him in the dark, but at some point, he might sink so deep it'll be impossible to drag him out. I won't let that happen. I'm going, and I will bring him back with me."

"We'll do everything in our power to keep both you and Antonio from harm. But if something unexpected happens, your wishes regarding Valentina will be carried out. I'll see to it myself."

50

DANIELA

I'm on a transport helicopter, being secured into a sling to be lowered onto the barge where Antonio has been holed up for ten days.

My stomach is queasy, and I'm happy I didn't eat on the plane.

"Remember, you don't need to do anything—just hold on, stay calm, and enjoy the short trip," a charming man reminds me as he checks to be sure I'm tethered properly. "The wind has picked up a few notches. If you start to get blown around, just take deep breaths and remain calm. You're wearing a life jacket and you'll be connected to the chopper by this cord until you're safely on the boat."

He keeps telling me to stay calm, like it'll be so easy while I'm suspended midair, being blown around over the cold ocean.

We've been over this several times. I nod and pull my lips into something that resembles a smile. The truth is, I'm scared to death.

The helicopter begins to hover, and when it's as low and steady as it can be, someone opens the door and a great whoosh of cold air slaps me in the face. My heart thunders as I leave the safety of the helicopter. If it weren't Antonio in trouble, I wouldn't go through with this.

The descent happens in slow motion, and as instructed, I don't look down. I close my eyes and I count backward, like I do to distract myself when I'm anxious. But Mother Nature is so noisy that it's hard to concentrate.

Before the howling wind has me completely panicked, someone on the barge has my ankles and is pulling me to safety.

My heart is still hammering while they help me out of the protective suit and helmet. Cristiano is on the deck, waiting for me. He's disheveled and wan, and he looks exhausted. I don't see Antonio.

"Where is he?" I ask Cristiano, who takes my backpack.

"He's on the other side of the deck. Behind the stack."

"Does he know I'm here?"

"No. I'm sure he assumes the chopper was dropping supplies, or fresh divers. Do you need a minute before you see him?"

I shake my head. "I'm sure he'll be angry I came. Let's just get it over with."

Cristiano pauses, as though he's weighing some news, or maybe considering his words. "You should know that he's long past feeling emotions like anger. He's turned inside in a way that I've never seen. Not from him."

"He just lost his mother. I'm sure he's blaming himself for her death."

"It's more than that. Bigger."

Grief is bigger than you think. Bigger than you can imagine, until you've wrestled with it yourself.

The light mist and fog, along with the stench of brackish water, haunts me as we cross the expansive deck.

I'm on a barge in the middle of an unforgiving ocean. No land in sight. I'm a strong swimmer, but still. Before the thoughts consume me, I shove them away and keep walking. *Antonio needs me.*

The ship is clean, but austere. At least up here. They've been living on this thing without a creature comfort—at least it appears that way. *I should have come to get him sooner.*

When we go around the middle stack to the other end of the barge, Antonio's gripping the outside rail as he stares into the choppy water, with his shoulders hunched forward. The fog and the mist combine to paint him as a tragic figure.

I swallow a sob and brace myself for—I'm not sure what. Rage? Sadness? Indifference? *I don't know.*

He doesn't turn around as we approach.

"It's probably best if we have this conversation in private," I whisper to Cristiano.

"I'm not leaving you yet."

Dealing with Antonio under these conditions is a bit like tossing the dice. It might have been better to warn him that I was on my way so he'd have a chance to get used to the idea before I arrived. But if Cristiano had breathed a word about it, Antonio would have insisted—no, *demanded*—I not come.

"Hey," I say softly, resting my hand on his back.

He stiffens, before turning to face me. "What the hell are you doing here?" His voice is hoarse, the vocal cords strained. He looks bone-tired and haggard, and my heart aches.

"I've come to bring you home."

"I'm not going anywhere while the search is ongoing."

"Then I'll wait with you."

He glares at Cristiano. "You allowed this?"

"I asked her to come."

"Get out of my sight." He waves us away. "Both of you."

"I'm not going anywhere," I say quietly. "You'll have to toss me in the ocean if you want me gone."

He glowers at me, his face gaunt, his eyes sunken shells rimmed in black.

I step closer and wrap my arms around him, resting my head on his chest. "I loved her, too," I murmur.

For what feels like an eternity, he doesn't move a muscle, not even to push me away. Eventually, his arms find their way around me. It's only then that Cristiano slips away.

Antonio and I cling to one another for long moments. Neither of us speaks. We just breathe.

51

ANTONIO

It's been days since I've given my company any thought. Other than locating my mother's remains, I haven't thought about a goddamn thing—except Daniela.

When all hope of finding anyone alive evaporated, I allowed my mind to wander to thoughts of her. When the pain and guilt ate at me, I found comfort, imagining my body curled around hers, in a peaceful sleep.

As much as I don't want her here, it feels so damn good to hold her. It's the first time I've felt anything in days. Orange blossom and goodness drowns the smell of weathered planks and seawater. I shovel it in, like a starving man.

She's shivering. I pull her away from the edge of the barge, to a bench where I sit when I'm tired of standing. It's protected from the wind.

She looks small and vulnerable, and even though she came to take care of me, I have an overwhelming urge to take care of her. I take off my jacket and wrap it around her shoulders before I sit beside her.

"How's Valentina?" I ask, not that I have the gumption to

care about much right now, but because it's what a decent human being would do.

"She's busy with school. But she misses you, and asked me to give you a big hug and a kiss with warm lips."

I miss her, too, but I don't say it. "Valentina and Rafael could have easily been on that plane." It's been clawing at me since I boarded the aircraft in Porto. When I think about it, I can barely breathe.

She sighs deeply and takes my hand. I'm sure she's thought a lot about it in the last ten days, too.

"But they weren't."

"This time."

I feel the familiar rumble of fury, as it barrels its way in. It's not helpful, but it's such an improvement over despair.

"Your mother loved you. You were a wonderful son. You did everything in your power to protect her."

"That's a lie!" I spit out, foaming at the mouth. "She did everything in her power to protect me. That's the goddamn truth."

"Antonio." Daniela doesn't shrink. She lays her head on my shoulder and slips her arm through mine. "I know it's a lot to ask right now, but don't judge yourself so harshly. No one blames you for what happened. Please don't blame yourself."

I don't give a shit what other people think. This was *my* fault. I think back to the day I visited my uncle after his stroke. How sanctimonious I was with Tomas. Belittling him for allowing the monsters to murder his mother.

"It was your fucking job to protect her," I barked. *"There's a special place in hell for men like you. Men who fail to protect the women who are important to them. She gave you life. I don't know how you live with yourself."*

The rage is swirling, knocking away any remnants of numbness. *My mother didn't just give me life. She protected me with her own life. I should have protected her with mine.*

"Instead of talking to the voices in your head, talk to me," Daniela urges.

"I highly doubt you want to hear my thoughts." The stark reality of who I am, and what I'm capable of, will only create a fissure between us. Even if it heals, there will be an ugly scar.

But maybe it's better if she learns the truth. She should know exactly who she's dealing with so she doesn't end up on the bottom of the ocean, too.

"When I was away at school, I got a call from Victor. It was almost thirteen years ago, now. He never called. But he was worried because my father was spinning more and more out of control, and Victor was afraid he was going to kill my mother."

I fist my hand into a tight ball, but Daniela pries my hand open and laces her fingers tightly through mine.

I don't deserve this woman. Maybe when I'm done, she'll know it, too.

"I took the next flight out, and when I arrived home, my mother was in bed. Contusions all over. Cracked ribs. A broken arm. A fractured jaw. You name it. The doctor had given her pain medicine at the hospital, and she was asleep. Alma sat by her bed. Watching over her in case Hugo came back for another round."

I remember the day like it was yesterday. My mother's motionless body, the scent of lavender room spray that Alma spritzed to mask the medicinal smell of bandages and antiseptic creams—and the dried blood that hides for days before you notice it.

"I was in a blinding fury. Furious with my father for what he'd done, and furious at my mother for going back to him. I'd begged her to stay with your family until I came home after the semester. But she didn't."

I squeeze Daniela's hand so tight she winces. "Do you know why?"

She shakes her head. "Tell me."

"Because the sonofabitch threatened to kill me if she didn't come home. I was her weakness." *From the moment I was born.* "She never said a word about it to me. She never confided it in anyone but Alma."

I pause for a moment, deciding whether to tell her the rest and risk any hope we have for a future.

Don't hold back. Let her see you for what you are. Maybe she'll walk away. She'll be safer without you. If she doesn't do it on her own, you'll have to send her away. You know that. But maybe you're no better than Tomas in that regard. Do you have the balls to do what it takes to protect her?

I do. I would do anything for her.

"In a rage," I continue, "I searched for my father. I found him in his office in the vineyards, with a bottle of moonshine. It was his favorite spot to go after he delivered a beating."

I can still taste the hatred. Still see his smug face, as though beating the shit out of a defenseless woman, *his wife*, was some great accomplishment.

"We didn't exchange words. I lunged at him, grabbed him by the throat, and squeezed until he turned purple, eyes bulging." Occasionally, I remember his face before he went limp. *But never with regret.* "I didn't heed his pleas. I reveled in his gasps for air."

Except for drawing a shaky breath, Daniela doesn't react.

Not yet. She's fiercely loyal, and protective of me. I'm going to have to do something reprehensible if I want to push her away. I can't think about it now. It'll have to wait until we're home.

I drape my arm around her shoulder and bring her closer. *I need her closer.*

"What happened?" she urges.

"Your father came in while I had my hands around Hugo's neck. He pulled me away, but it was too late."

She draws back, as though sensing this is connected to her story, too. And in a way, it is.

"Why was my father there?" she asks. But she knows the answer. Even if Daniela hasn't put together all the pieces, she's shrewd, and she knows how it works in our world.

"At the time, I didn't know why your father was there—and I didn't think much of it. Later, I assumed he came to tell my mother that Maria Rosa had died. That's what I believed—until recently. Until you told me about what happened in the meadow—how my family tortured you and your mother. Since then, my thinking has changed."

"How so?" she asks warily, searching my face as I try to piece together the events for her.

"According to what you've said, Manuel believed—rightfully so—that Hugo was the ringleader. I'm sure he came to kill my father for what he'd done."

Daniela wraps my jacket tighter. She's quiet, but I feel her mind churning.

"Within an hour of Hugo's death, your father made a couple of phone calls and had me on a private plane out of Porto. 'Do not tell anyone you were here,' he cautioned. Although several people who worked for my parents had seen me, including Victor and Alma."

This is a lot to process, and I see the uneasiness in her face.

"Your father, with all that he was dealing with, cleaned up my mess that day. Hugo had a lot of enemies, but he had a lot of power, too. Some unethical but important people benefited from his corruption. If not for your father, I would have spent the rest of my life in prison. If not worse. I owed him my life."

"That's why you agreed to marry me."

The emotion vibrates from every syllable. It's not a question, but it begs a response. *I won't lie to her.*

"Yes. It's why I agreed initially, and why I would have agreed even if I knew what my family had done. Your father knew what I owed him—that's why I still don't understand why he didn't tell me everything. It would have saved a lot of heartache —for you."

Daniela's shoulders are hunched and her head down, as she clasps her hands in her lap.

"I'm not leaving without my mother's remains. I want to take her back to Porto and bury her in a beautiful spot, under a flowering tree. It's the best I can do for her now."

I slam my fist on the bench. "She's gone, Daniela, and you're next. This is how they're going to destroy me."

"I've always known that our marriage wasn't made on love," she says softly, after long moments pass. "But I love you now, and I believe with all my heart that you love me."

She latches onto my shirt front with both hands. "Do you really want to protect me? Because out here, like this, you're no good to anyone."

I believe that I still have something to offer my employees, and the people of the valley who depend on me to lead them to prosperity. But I'm not sure anymore that I have anything to offer her that outweighs the danger I bring to her life.

"You're safer without me."

"I don't believe that. Neither do you. And even if it were true, I'd take my chances."

You're a fool, Princesa. There is no fairy tale. It's all smoke and mirrors, and then you die.

52

ANTONIO

I hold Daniela's hair back while she vomits for the fourth time tonight.

The storm is getting closer, and the boat's listing. She's been quiet since I told her that I murdered my father. I thought she'd finally had enough of me. But it turns out she's seasick, and nothing seems to be helping.

The crew is planning to batten down tomorrow afternoon to wait out the storm. The search will be suspended for at least a day. *There's no choice.*

I hand her a wet cloth to wipe her mouth. When she's through, I bring a bottle of water to her lips.

She pushes it away. "I can't. I'll be sick again."

"You've lost a lot of fluids. You need to at least take a few sips." The last thing she needs is to get dehydrated out here in the middle of the ocean.

"I can't."

"First thing in the morning, you're getting on a chopper and going home before the storm gets bad."

She shakes her head. "Not without you."

"You have a daughter."

"We have a daughter who adores you. And we have Rafael to think about, too. He doesn't even know about the crash. I don't care if he's doing some important training. It's not right."

She's angry. In full mother-bear mode. But she's not entirely correct about Rafael. While it might not be right to keep him in the dark, it's necessary for him to complete his training like any other soldier.

I pride myself on doing what's necessary above all else. And now something else might be necessary.

I've spent ten days ferrying between helicopters and boats. At first, on tenterhooks, waiting for some sign of life that never materialized. It didn't matter how loud I yelled, or how much money I threw at the search. At one point there were so many rescue teams, they were getting in each other's way.

The ocean is a beast, and we might never find my mother's remains. I've always known it, but I'm stubborn.

Now I need to get Daniela off this goddamn boat before the storm. That has to be my priority. I could force her onto a helicopter, but she'd be back. She's stubborn, too, and resourceful. It's one thing to punish myself, but I'm not going to punish her.

I gaze at her pale, clammy face. She's curled into a tight ball, shivering under layers of blankets.

It's time to go home.

It's what's necessary.

AFTER DANIELA FALLS asleep in my bunk, I find Cristiano on the hull.

"How is she?"

I shake my head. "Get a transport here first thing. I want to be off the boat before the storm hits."

I see the stark relief in his face. "Good idea. Do you want me to stay and oversee the search?"

"You're coming with us. I want the security fortified at Quinta Rosa do Vale. Erect towers around the perimeter, like at my place in the valley. Tighten the boundaries between the house and the vineyards. I want that property to be the most secure location on the planet. And I want it done within a week."

Cristiano tips his head.

"Just do it."

I take one last look over the side of the boat, into the belly of the beast. It continues to mock my powerlessness without mercy.

I've always loved the ocean. But I'll never feel the same way about it again. In my mind, it will forever be a watery grave.

53

DANIELA

A few days after we get home, we board the flight to London for Edward's funeral. We have Valentina with us, and several guards, with dozens more on a plane that left Porto two hours before us.

The plane has been swept from top to bottom several times, not only by some of Antonio's men, but by an independent team that sweeps the president and prime minister's planes. I have complete confidence that this flight will make it safely to London. *We wouldn't be going, otherwise.*

Cristiano and Lucas are on the plane, too, and I invited Alma, Victor, and Sonia to come with us. They were all close to Lydia, and mourn her death like family.

The morning we left the barge—and the search—was painful.

Antonio was the last person on to the helicopter. Cristiano and I were already aboard, caught up in our own grief. Leaving was the right thing to do—for all of us. But that didn't make it easier.

My heart wept as Antonio peered over his shoulder to the ocean below, before they shut the helicopter doors behind him.

I'll never forget the resigned sorrow that marred his handsome face. If I live to be a hundred, I hope to never see it again.

Edward's funeral might be the closest thing we get to closure. Antonio won't discuss holding a memorial service for his mother, and I won't push him.

He glares at Sonia when she boards the plane, and then at me.

"She's my guest," I say firmly. He doesn't argue, but a few minutes later he takes his dour self and goes to the back of the plane with Cristiano and Lucas, who are more inclined to ask permission and obey orders.

The one thing I'm sick about is that Rafael isn't here. He still doesn't know about Lydia. No matter how much I pleaded, Antonio wouldn't budge on it. I considered trying to reach him myself, but I would be furious if it were Valentina and he completely disregarded my wishes.

We'll return to Porto early this evening. Alma will be staying an extra day or two to go through Lydia's things. I wanted to stay to help so she wouldn't have to do it alone, but Antonio refused to spend a second longer in London than necessary. I could have stayed without him, but despite outward appearances, he has a long way to go before he heals, and I want to be there for those difficult moments. *And there will be difficult moments.*

Everyone manages grief differently, but no one is immune to its whims. Not even Antonio Huntsman.

WHEN WE ARRIVE at the church, Antonio goes immediately to Samantha and wraps his arms around her. "I'm so sorry," he murmurs, the sorrow palpable, twisted around every tortured word. "I should have taken better precautions."

"Wasn't your job," Will mutters, without missing a beat. "It was mine."

Antonio straightens, head high, shoulders back. "My family. My responsibility," he replies, in that tone he uses daring anyone to challenge him.

But Will is no shrinking violet, and he's blaming himself, too. It was his plane. His flight crew. And the plane had been housed in a hangar in London, under his protection. It wasn't on the ground in Porto long enough for the bomb to be planted then.

Samantha steps in to prevent what could easily dissolve into a pissing match about who owns the tragedy.

"They loved each other madly," she says softly, with one hand on Will and the other on Antonio. "They died together. As difficult as that is for us, I have to believe it's what they would have wanted."

Samantha watched her father suffer in the aftermath of her mother's death, like I watched mine. In some perverse way, it almost feels that it is better this way.

I glance at Alexis and Valentina huddled together, tissues balled in their hands. And I wonder at what point all the death and loss becomes too much for Valentina. It's crushing me, and I'm an adult.

Something has to change.

54

ANTONIO

When we get back to the house after Edward's funeral, I go directly to my office to plan my next move with Cristiano and Lucas, and Daniela spends the rest of the evening helping Valentina with a school project.

By the time I climb into bed, she's almost asleep. But I reach for her, like I do most nights. Although tonight, there's a greater urgency.

I sweep the hair of her neck and trail kisses over the smooth skin.

While she moans, softly, I hook a finger into a flimsy nightgown strap. "If you'd like to wear this again, you better take it off quickly." It's not so much a suggestion as a warning. My patience for anything that blocks me from her is razor-thin tonight.

She rolls onto her back and cradles my jaw, searching my eyes for demons to be exorcised.

They're there, Princesa. Do you see them? They've come to play tonight.

I tug at her nightgown, and she swats my hands away.

"It's my favorite. Don't tear it," she chides, sliding the thin fabric over her head, exposing her gorgeous tits to me.

I grab the nightgown from her hands and toss it in the direction of the bench at the foot of the bed.

"I want you right here," I murmur, pulling her with me as I roll onto my back.

She squirms on my hard cock seated between us.

"I love you," she whispers, with her fingertips pressed to my unshaven jaw.

"I don't deserve your love, *Princesa*. You could do so much better than a man like me."

She hates when I say it, and squirms on my dick again to distract me from my worst impulses. This time I don't let her get away with it.

Ouch! She jerks, when my palm comes down on her ass.

"Stop squirming, unless you want more." Her eyes glitter at the threat, but it's not what I want tonight.

I slide my hand through the silky hair at her nape, cupping her head, and own her mouth. My tongue explores roughly, rooting into every corner, tasting her sweetness, until I've stolen all her breath.

"You're mine," I claim, without apology. "It doesn't matter what happens. The whole fucking world can come tumbling down, and you'll still be mine. *Always*."

I tug her hair back, forcing her eyes to meet mine.

"Say it," I demand. "I want to hear you say it."

She gazes at me, eyes wide, gauging my mood. Something about it scares her. *It scares me, too.*

"Say it, *Princesa*."

"I'm yours. *Always*. And you're mine. *Always*," she vows, without flinching. "Even if the world comes tumbling down."

It's a promise I will hold her to.

I find her mouth again, rougher than the last time. I delve

deeper, sealing the promise with an intensity that no one would dare challenge. *She's mine.*

When she can't breathe, she pulls back. "What has you like this?"

"You. You have me like this." *And I can't make it stop.*

I grasp her thighs, pulling her up, until she's astride my hips, on her knees. "Ride me. Ride me until you ache."

Before she can move, I wrench myself into a seated position and ease her legs around my hips. I slide my mouth over her throat. She shudders as I sample her sweet skin.

When I can't wait another goddamn second to have her, I slip my hand between us to check if she's ready—although I already know. *I smell her arousal. It wafts around us, scenting the air like a priceless perfume.*

"Get on my cock, *Princesa*. Don't make me wait."

Daniela tips her chin, and with sultry eyes, she lifts her hips carefully and notches my eager cock at her entrance. Her movement is slow and deliberate, and she taunts me with her tits as she obeys.

What little patience I had evaporates.

"You're teasing me. You need to be taught a lesson," I rasp, digging my fingers into her hips and sheathing myself with her wet cunt. It's a long, brutal slide, and she cries out at the intrusion.

I force myself to still, pulling her to my pounding heart.

"I want to ride you."

"Oh, you will, *Princesa*. You're going to ride me so long and so hard you'll remember it for a week. But first, let me enjoy you, like this," I whisper in her hair. "I want to feel your snug walls hug my cock."

She clenches her pelvis, and my cock jerks. She does it again. And again. Until I'm struggling to control myself.

"Take what you want. Go ahead," I urge, holding her hips

firmly and guiding her movements so that it's a slow, steady climb to pleasure.

I feed off her mouth as she rocks her hips.

Normally we devour each other, but not tonight. Tonight, I'm consuming her. Bit by bit. Every kiss, every thrust, every zing of her pleasure is my obsession.

I pin her wrists at the base of her spine, forcing an arch in her back. She moans as I draw a nipple into my mouth, and as I suck, her movements become jerkier, desperate.

She's riding me hard. But I'm in complete control. I take, and take, and take, wrenching one orgasm from her after another.

Before the night's over, there is no inch of her body that I haven't enjoyed.

My limbs ache and my body protests, but I demand one last orgasm from her. *From me.*

She cries as she shatters. The sheer intensity of our fucking bleeds its way out in tears. For long moments, I catch the droplets on my tongue, because like her, they belong to me.

"You're the best thing that's ever happened to me," I tell her while I hold her against my chest. "In the short time we've had together, you've given me more than I ever dreamed possible."

She presses her fingertip to my lips. "Don't talk like that. We're young. We have so much time left to love each other."

I hold her while she falls asleep. But I can't sleep. My conscience is screaming. *You're a selfish monster.* I am.

I demanded everything from her tonight. I allowed intimacy to drift in and shroud us in its warm, comfortable arms. I took all she had to give—mind, body, heart, and soul—knowing full well that it would make tomorrow harder for her —*and for me.*

Because when the sun peeks over the horizon, it will be a new day.

55

DANIELA

The next morning, I wake to Antonio fully dressed, sitting in a chair in the corner of the room. He's not reading a paper or scrolling through his tablet. He's watching me sleep.

"Good morning," I murmur, stretching. "I'm surprised you're still home. But I like it."

"I want you out of my house before the end of the day. Take Valentina with you."

What? I bolt upright in bed. "What are you talking about?"

"I thought I made it pretty clear. But maybe I was wrong. Get out of my house. Take your daughter. I want you both gone before the sun sets. Is that better?"

My brain is still addled from sleep, and although I hear the words, I can't wrap my head around any of this.

Last night was amazing. Not just the sex—that's always pretty amazing. But the intimacy that swirled, in and around us, made the physical act magic. We've never been closer. *What could have possibly happened since then to make him like this?*

"What's gotten into you?" I ask softly. "I don't understand."

"Life's too short to spend it stuck in a marriage that neither of us wanted." He says it matter-of-factly, like one might say,

Life's short—buy the shoes and eat the cake. "You know exactly why I married you, and you married me because I didn't give you a choice."

This is such bullshit. He's pushing me away. Either for my own safety, or to protect himself from any more tragedy. That's what this is: Antonio being Antonio.

I won't indulge it.

"If you don't want to live here with me, stay at your apartment at the lodge. I'm not going anywhere."

"This is not a fight you're going to win," he says, striding to the door.

"Where do you expect me to go?"

"Quinta Rosa do Vale."

He's sending me home. The bastard is sending me home. But I have news for him. This is now my home. And my daughter's.

"Up until now, my parents' house hasn't been safe enough for me to visit, but all of a sudden it's ready for me to move in with Valentina? Antonio, what's this really about?"

"In balance, you're more trouble than your worth."

Asshole. Liar. "So—everything—last night was a lie?"

"You have a sweet little cunt that can persuade even a powerful man to follow you anywhere. And I get distracted by the tight squeeze, like last night. But once the afterglow fades, it's still just another cunt."

He's full of shit, and his disgusting words bounce off me without landing a blow. I don't dignify his filth with a response.

"I've signed some paperwork," Antonio says from the door. "I'll deposit a monthly sum into a bank account for you. It'll be more than enough for you and Valentina to live well, but you'll also get the proceeds from any income derived from Quinta Rosa do Vale. Although I'll keep the property. I earned it."

"You earned it?" I snarl. "Fuck you. I'm not going anywhere."

"We'll see."

"I'm tired of listening to this little fantasy you've concocted, because that's all it is. You won't convince me differently. But I'm done," I say, throwing up my hands. "Get out."

He's quiet for a moment, considering my reaction to his nonsense. *That's what it is.*

I didn't cry or plead. I'm sure that's what he was expecting. But I shut it down, using a page from the Antonio Huntsman playbook. Not intentionally. It just came out.

He taps his hand on the doorframe. "We can do this the easy way or the hard way, *Princesa*. But you're the one who will be getting out."

I might have surprised him, but it was a fleeting victory.

"I don't believe last night, or anything we've created together, has anything to do with my irresistible pussy. You don't believe it either. But it was one of the meanest things you've ever said to me, and there have been plenty. I expect an apology. Our fate is entwined. It always has been. You've said so yourself."

He gazes at me from the doorway.

There's something in his expression. Empathy? Sadness? Regret? *I'm not sure.*

"I don't want to hurt you." It's almost a heartfelt plea. "Don't make this any harder than it needs to be."

He leaves without another word, which is fine by me. I've heard more than enough.

I have a twelve-year-old who handles grief better than this man. While I don't believe for a minute he was being sincere about it being over between us, I am worried about his state of mind. *Dr. Jekyll and Mr. Hyde had nothing on him.*

Antonio spoke to me in a clipped tone, with a veiled threat or two sprinkled in. But he didn't raise his voice. There was no snarl, no anger in his tone—or his expression. He was *completely* in control—as though it was rehearsed. I can't decide if that's good or bad.

But this wasn't the end of him pushing me away. That I am sure about.

Bring it on, my dark prince. Do your worst.

56

DANIELA

I'm lying in bed, trying to sleep, but all I can think about is that bizarre *conversation* this morning with Antonio. Even after thinking about it all day, it still makes no sense.

He'd moved past the cold, calculating, mean-spiritedness as a way to gain control—at least with me. But the minute things got too hard, that's the first place he sought refuge.

It's what he knows.

No excuse.

I haven't heard a word from him since he left, nor have I tried to contact him. I'm willing to work through whatever this is, but I won't beg him to lie beside me.

The outer door to the suite clicks while I'm flipping my pillow for the tenth time, so the cool side will be against my cheek.

I hear voices in the sitting room, before the bedroom door opens, and the overhead light comes on. My hand flies to my face, shielding my eyes from the sudden brightness in the room.

When my eyes adjust, I look up to Antonio and an attractive redhead in the room—maybe six feet from the bed.

I sit up, pulling the covers around me. "What's going on?"

"I have a friend with me," my husband says, like we're in the garden in the middle of the day and he invited someone for a cup of tea. "Lisbet, this is Daniela. Daniela, Lisbet."

The redhead clings to his arm, even as I glower at her.

"Where are your manners? Aren't you going to say hello to my beautiful friend?"

There is something so awful about this that's impossible to describe with words. But I don't shrink from the moment. *I won't.*

"Get out of my house, *right now*," I warn *Lisbet*. My voice is shrill, and my blood pressure is skyrocketing.

"I thought you said she liked to watch?" she whispers to Antonio.

"I thought so. I mean, she's still here, even after I warned her I was done with her. What did she expect?"

I get out of bed and plant my feet firmly on the floor. "What I expect is that you'll be a man about it, and not drag every whore who offers you a blowjob into our bedroom."

"I'm not a whore," the whore says, indignantly.

A part of me recognizes this isn't her fault. It's his. Although she's not off the hook. She wasn't at all surprised to find me here.

"My daughter is asleep in this house. If you don't leave immediately, I'll consider you an intruder and I'll blow off your empty little head." I move toward the gun safe.

"Wait in the car," Antonio tells his *friend*, without a glance in her direction. "I'll join you shortly."

To her credit, Lisbet leaves without a fuss.

"What are you doing?" I stomp toward him and beat furiously on his chest, until he catches my wrists.

"I gave you a choice: the easy way or the hard way. If you're still here tomorrow, I'll tie you to this bed, and make you watch as I fuck whoever catches my attention for the night. It's over between us."

I wrest my hand free and slap him in the face so hard it leaves a red imprint on his cheek. My hand stings, too—*almost as much as my heart.*

Antonio doesn't say a word. There are no threats. There's no angry flare in his eyes. *He's happy I slapped him. He deserves it, and he knows it.*

"You are a heartless son of a bitch. But I'm not a fool." I swipe the back of my hand over his lifeless cock. "You get hard at the mere thought of me taking off my clothes. Yet you wanted her so bad you were willing to rub my face in it, but your dick is soft? You're going to have to do better than that if you expect me to buy your bullshit."

Maybe I'm imagining it, but I swear there's a glimmer of pride in his eyes, as he strides toward the door.

You're not going anywhere, before you hear me out.

"I don't give a damn where you lay your head tonight, but you will not sleep in my bed, again, until I have a sincere apology, and your word that you will never pull this kind of disgusting stunt again."

"An apology?" he snickers, not bothering to turn around. "I'm just getting started."

After he leaves, I pace the room until I'm exhausted. Then I climb back into the bed that smells like him—*like us*—and cry myself to sleep.

I don't cry because of some bimbo with striking red hair. She's nothing. I cry because he might be too far gone for me to reach. It might really be over for us.

Whether it is, or isn't, I won't allow him to disrespect me this way. I don't care how much he's hurting. And I sure as hell won't allow Valentina to witness any of it.

I'm going to have to fight this battle from Quinta Rosa do Vale. That much is clear.

57

ANTONIO

When Santi calls, I'm at my desk in the villa with Cristiano and Lucas.

"We're on our way to Quinta Rosa do Vale."

He's deferential and he'll follow orders, but he respects Daniela and adores Valentina, and I'm sure he doesn't like how this has gone down. *I'm not crazy about it either.*

"Anything else?" I ask.

"No. Just letting you know, like you asked."

"Santi, it goes without saying that security needs to be tight. I've spoken to Duarte, as well, but no matter how hard Daniela pushes, take no chances, even if the risk seems small. Get me involved right away if she becomes a problem you can't handle."

"I understand, and so does everyone else. You made it pretty clear the other day."

I end the call and glance from Lucas to Cristiano. "Showtime."

The room is deadly quiet. They hate my plan with a vengeance. All of it. I hate it, too, more than they do, especially what happened last night. I'd rather plunge a knife into my soul than repeat it.

I declared war last night—on my wife. It was one of the most difficult things I've ever done. Daniela is tough, and she fights for us with everything she's got. I don't have time to push her away slowly, to wage small battles until I wear her down. In the long run, I'm not sure that's a better approach, anyway. *Bleeding out, slowly, is a painful way to die.*

"Pay off the redhead," I instruct Cristiano. "Tell her that her services are no longer needed."

I'm not sure Daniela bought it, anyway. Although who knows? As much as I admired her grit last night, it could have been nothing more than bravado—a way to save face, or to shame me.

When she whipped her hand over my cock to see if it was hard, and then called me out on it—*fuck*—I wanted to toss her on the bed and worship her body until the sun came up.

"Is there a change to the plan we should know about?" Cristiano asks, warily.

"I have someone else who can fill in as the flavor of the week."

"Why the change?" Lucas can't stand change in a carefully constructed plan. Even if it's a plan he despises.

Because I can't stop thinking about the horror on Daniela's face when I brought another woman into our bedroom. The sense of betrayal in her eyes leveled me. I would never betray her in that way—*never*. But I need her out, and I need it to feel real to everyone, including her.

"I've decided that there is a better option." He's waiting for more, but that's all he's getting. I hate explaining myself even more than Lucas hates change.

58

DANIELA

I've been up since four this morning, packing things we'll need and trying to come up with a way to explain the inexplicable to Valentina.

What I'm most angry about is that he's not here to say goodbye to her. I'm an adult and I can handle his moods, but she's a child who's had so much loss. She deserves more from him, and he damn well knows it.

"He doesn't love us anymore?" Valentina asks when I tell her we need to stay at Quinta Rosa do Vale for a little while. Although I'm grateful she doesn't press, because I'm not sure what *a little while* means. "I can be good. Tell Antonio I'll be better. I won't argue with you anymore. I know he doesn't like it."

I'm so angry at him, I'm practically shaking. I put my arms around Valentina and pull her to my breast, willing myself to stay calm for her. "Of course he still loves you. This has nothing to do with you, *menina*. Nothing at all. And it has nothing to do with me. Antonio's hurting, and he holds everything inside. He needs some time alone to work through his sadness."

I say it, knowing it's only half true. Yes, he needs to mourn, but he's pushing me away—and it's different this time. Something feels different. It does. *Why?* I'm still stuck on that.

"Do we need to pack everything?" she asks, a bit calmer.

"No. Pack as if we're going on vacation for a week. Maybe two." I force a smile.

"Can we bring the horses?"

Good question.

"Let me check with Silvio. Why don't you start by laying things out on the bed you want to take?"

Before I contact Silvio about the horses, I text my husband. He won't respond, but he'll read the text. *I'm sure of it.* Antonio's going to know exactly how he made Valentina feel.

My hand trembles as I key in the message: **"He doesn't love us anymore?" That's the first thing Valentina said when I told her you asked us to leave. "I can be good," she promised. "Tell him I'll be good."**

Congratulations, Antonio. This time you actually did it. You are the monster you believe you are.

It's vengeful and mean, but he deserves it. Every word.

I press Send before I change my mind.

―――

WE SAY a quick goodbye to Victor, who has tears in his eyes that he wipes away before Valentina can see them. "One day, later this week, I'll bring lunch," he tells Valentina. "And maybe we can bake a cake."

She nods. "A chocolate cake. It's Antonio's favorite. Maybe you can bring a piece back to cheer him up."

"You have a kind soul, *menina*. He's going to miss you." Victor turns to me. "And you. More than he thinks."

I don't say goodbye to anyone else. Almost anything I say will invite speculation about my marriage. Victor can make the excuses.

This morning, I sent an email to Lara telling her to take a few days off. No explanations. This might be a good opportunity to sever ties with her. I would take Paula with me, but she's been fired, and I don't know how to reach her.

Santi, Mia, and Duarte ride with us, and there's a car in front and one behind, carrying soldiers.

"What about school?" Valentina asks, eyes wide. "Will I still go to school?"

It crossed my mind last night while I was dragging a suitcase from the closet. But like so many others, the thought floated in and out.

"There's a building in the vineyards that will make a good school," Santi explains. "No one uses it much at this time of year."

My father's old office—I'm sure.

"What about my friends?"

"It's a bit farther to travel, but we'll send a car for them," he replies, easily. Unlike me, he knows the details.

She smiles and nods.

"Has the building been made suitable for the girls?" It was an ample space and comfortable. I'm not worried about its suitability. I want to know how long this plan has been in the works.

Santi nods, sheepishly. *He knew that we'd be moving before I did.*

It's another betrayal. Not by Santi—not really. I'm sure Antonio read him the riot act. Duarte and Mia, too.

There are no flowers blooming at this time of year, and the vines have already been cut back. But the first thing I notice when we pull in are the high guard towers ringing the property, like at our—like at Antonio's house. They weren't here when we came during the harvest. We weren't here long, but I would have noticed them.

But they didn't pop up overnight, either. Antonio knew long before yesterday that he was kicking us out.

How could I have not picked up on anything? How?

"Look," Valentina cries, pointing to a duck pond. "I remember feeding the ducks with you and my mom. Do you remember, Lala?"

"I do." Like it was yesterday. "You loved to toddle right up to the edge, and Isabel was always so afraid one day you were going to fall in." *I'm so sorry that I haven't shielded Valentina better, Isabel. You were a better mother to her than I can ever hope to be. To me, too.*

When the car stops in front of the house, I draw a breath and gaze out the window. In addition to everything else, I'm going to have to contend with all the memories buried inside.

One hour at a time, Daniela. That's all that's required to get you and Valentina through the next few days. You've dealt with far worse.

The front door opens, and a woman comes out to greet us.

"It's Cristiano's mom!" Valentina cries, bouncing out of the car. "She's so nice."

Alma? Alma works at Antonio's apartment in Huntsman Lodge. *Why is she here?*

"Alma, this is a nice surprise," I say, standing behind Valentina, who is embracing her.

"Can I go inside?" Valentina asks.

Santi is already inside, and Mia is with Valentina. "Sure."

Alma smiles softly. "This house is beautiful, but it needs a little life."

"Did Cristiano ask you to come?"

She shakes her head. "Antonio." She sighs. "He wanted me to help here, until you're able to hire someone to run the house. I hope you don't mind. This is your house."

I take her hand. "I'm so happy you're here." *And I am.* "But it's so far to go back and forth every day. Would you like to stay with us, at least during the week?"

"My room is already set up."

I chuckle.

Alma squeezes my fingers. "It's not my business, but I've known Antonio since he was in diapers," she waves her arm in the air, "and I have some thoughts about all this."

"That gives you a leg up on me, because I'm having trouble putting the pieces together. Although in my heart, I think this is tied to Lydia's death."

She tips her head from side to side. "Yes and no. You make him a better man. He knows this right down to the marrow. I was talking to Lydia last night."

Wait. "You were talking to Lydia, Antonio's mother? Last night?"

She smiles. "I was doing all the talking, but she was with me. I felt her presence."

I feel my mother's presence sometimes, too.

"Antonio's power was challenged," Alma explains, "and not in a small way. He needs time, my love. He needs your patience while he regroups. And he needs to be sure that his fortress is so strong that no one will touch you. That's what this is about. Not his mother, who he loved, but you, who he can't live without."

I'd like to believe it. But my heart is already in tatters, and I can't afford to tell myself any more lies.

59

ANTONIO

"*Bom dia*," I say quietly from the doorway in Sonia's office. She lifts her eyes from the computer screen and gapes at me from across the desk. It's been a long time since I showed up here unannounced. Up until yesterday, I couldn't imagine ever darkening her doorway again.

"Do you have a meeting with the president? I don't remember seeing your name on his schedule."

"I came to see you."

She shuts her eyes. "I've been waiting for this."

Cristiano and Lucas have been handling our joint venture for me, since the day she allowed those pictures to be printed. I didn't shut down the operation, but I have no doubt she's been waiting for me to cut her loose.

"It's not what you think. Come take a walk with me. I'll buy you a coffee."

"A walk?"

In the past, she would have said, "*You just show up in the middle of the workday, and expect me to jump?*" But she'd always come.

"Fifteen minutes. That's all I need."

She grabs a coat, has a few words with her secretary, and we head outside toward a coffee shop on the grounds of the presidential palace.

"How's Daniela?"

Given the text I got this morning from her, I'd say she's fit to be tied. *And she should be.* I considered Valentina when I made the plan. I took care of the concrete things—she'd have school, her friends, her horses—but I didn't spend enough time considering her feelings. I'll make up for it at some point, but for now, there's nothing I can do.

"I don't know how she is. She moved out."

Sonia stops abruptly and turns toward me. "I didn't have anything to do with that, if that's why you're here."

"Relax."

"It's hard to relax around you these days, Antonio, even under the best of circumstances. What happened?"

Not your business. "I'm here to ask a favor."

She doesn't hesitate or hedge. I knew she wouldn't. "What do you need?"

She's asked for plenty of favors over the years, and I'm sure she thinks I'm calling one in. I'm not. I granted her the favors because I wanted to, not because I thought there would be a *quid pro quo.*

"Some companionship."

She gawks at me with her jaw on the ground.

"One week, if all goes well. Two weeks at most."

"You want me to find you a—a—a *companion*?"

I shake my head. "No," I say with so much indignance, that her brow unfurls.

"You're going to be my companion. I have dinner plans, tickets to the theatre, and all sorts of other fun stuff planned. You're going to help me forget about Daniela. And I expect to see our pictures plastered all over the internet."

"Forget it. If you want to be a huge dick, have at it. But I won't be involved." She turns on her heel and heads back toward her office.

She and Daniela have clearly come to some sort of understanding that doesn't involve me. They're not friends, but Daniela invited her to come to London with us, and Sonia's decided that she won't play games with Daniela. *Good for them. But I still need the favor.*

I grab Sonia's arm. "Why not? It's not that different from what you did last time."

"Last time was a mistake. I can't do it. Besides, what will it possibly accomplish? She knows we have absolutely no interest in each other. You made it pretty clear the moment you outed me."

"I hope you're not expecting an apology."

She lifts her chin and glares.

"The fact that she knows is precisely why I'm asking *you* to help me." Sonia is a bright woman. She's trying to figure out what my game is, and I'd tell her, but I can't. Not the details. "Look. This isn't me trying to punish Daniela. And I certainly don't require a jealous wife to make my dick hard. Those are the only two things I can tell you."

"I don't know. I don't like it. Can't you find someone else to do it?"

My heartburn is back, full force. "I do have someone else. But it's going to be more painful for Daniela if I go that route." *I want to avoid that at all costs. I was even willing to come to you.*

"Is this about avenging your mother's death?" she asks gently.

"It's about protecting my family, Sonia. Giving my wife the peace she deserves. The vengeance will be mighty tasty, but this is about a lot more than that."

She gazes into my eyes and smiles softly. "I never thought I'd live to see the day a woman stole your dark heart. It's got me all gooey."

I roll my eyes, even though she's not wrong. "Are you in?"

"Maybe."

"What do you need to make it a yes?"

She pauses for a moment. "I'm still upset about the way you treated me in your office that day. But I would have done anything for your mother, Antonio. She held my hand during some of the darkest moments of my life. I realize I did a bad thing with those photos, but you were brutal to me. I expected more of a pass after all these years."

"You might not appreciate it, but you did get a pass. If it had been anyone else who leaked those photographs to hurt my wife, they wouldn't have lived to see the next sunrise."

Sonia pulls her mouth into a grim line and nods. She knows it's true.

"I'll do it. But if at any point I feel as though your motives are ugly, and that this is just some sick mind game you're playing with Daniela, I'm out."

60

DANIELA

Three days after we arrive at Quinta Rosa do Vale, I wake up to a picture of my husband and Sonia leaving the theatre. The photo includes the caption: *Trouble in Paradise?*

Antonio is pressing his lips to Sonia's forehead. It's intimate. If I didn't know better, I'd vomit all over the laptop.

Maybe I don't know better. Maybe that day in his office was all a lie to cover up their relationship. *No. I don't see it.* While Antonio's capable of anything, Sonia couldn't possibly be that good of an actress. *Could she?*

The truth is, I don't know what to believe these days.

After stewing about Sonia's sexual identity for much too long, I borrow Alma's phone to call Cristiano. It's been days since he's answered a call from my phone.

"*Mãe*," Cristiano answers with a smile in his voice, thinking it's his mother.

"It's Daniela," I say quietly.

"Daniela," he repeats, clearly taken aback. "Antonio isn't—"

"Maybe he is, maybe he isn't, but I didn't call to speak to my husband. You don't need to lie to cover for him."

"What can I do for you?" He's all business now.

"You can tell me why Antonio and Sonia have decided to embarrass me in such a public way. It's bad enough they would do that to me, but what about Valentina? Those pictures are everywhere. It's as though he made no attempt to keep them out of the media. What in God's name is going on?"

"I'm not in a position to discuss Antonio's personal life. You'll need to speak directly to him about your marriage. I'll let him know you called."

"I expected better from you, Cristiano." My voice wavers, and I want to kick myself for it, but I manage to say my piece. "Your behavior is almost as much of a knife in my back as Antonio's. I deserve to be treated better than this—by both of you."

He's quiet on the other end. At first, I think he ended the call, but I hear him breathing.

"Maybe more than anyone," he says with an apologetic gentleness, "you know the heart of the man you married. If you allow yourself to think about this with an open mind, you'll find that none of it should come as any surprise."

"You're saying that I shouldn't be surprised he betrayed me?"

"I'm not saying that at all. That's a fool's interpretation. You're smarter than that."

It's an obtuse response typical of Cristiano: respond to the question, but provide no clear answer.

But it's all I'm getting, because he ends the call before I can ask anything more.

61

ANTONIO

Cristiano, Lucas, and I are in the villa, tying up last-minute details for my trip to Morocco and trying to predict the unforeseen circumstances, because of course, there will be some.

Nikitin is spending his last days on earth. That's the only thing I'm one hundred percent sure about.

The Russian government had already seized all his known assets. But Lucas tracked down every offshore bank account that belonged to the billionaire, and rerouted the account information to Russia. Before the day was over, they'd sucked up every cent more efficiently than a fancy vacuum cleaner.

He's without resources to open doors. It also means that the number of men he can hire, and the quality of those men, is severely limited. It's better to have no men than men who are disloyal. He's desperate in every regard.

His former lavish lifestyle is a thing of the past. Powerless oligarchs with dwindling bank accounts are not in high demand, especially on the party circuit. Although, we are planning a big bash for him. I guess you could call it a farewell party.

"Maybe you should confirm with Jake one more time before we leave," Lucas suggests. He doesn't like the idea of drawing an outsider into a plan with such high stakes.

Normally I would agree with him, but Jake's not an outsider to me. I've known him since college. Along with Gray, Jake and I were close, and although we certainly don't share everything, we've kept the relationship tight all these years.

Jake's a stand-up guy who's loyal to the bone. He didn't blink when we asked to use his island when we needed a safe place outside the US to meet Valentina after Isabel was killed.

"Just don't leave a mess," he drawled, "or I'm grabbin' my shotgun and comin' for you."

"There are plenty of things to worry about, but Jake isn't one of them," I grumble, while scrolling through my phone. "But I'll touch base with him, if it means you'll stop nagging like a fishwife."

"Hey, you fucked-up *sumabitch*," Jake drawls. "I hear it's hunting season in Morocco. I'm thinking about bagging me a blonde and a brunette. Although redheads are mighty tasty, too. *Mmhm.* Can't decide. Think three pussies in one hunt is too much for an old man like me?"

I'm glad the phone isn't on speaker, because Lucas would be in heart failure.

Jake had a rough start in life and spent some time in prison when he was a kid, before the tide turned. Now he's a Harvard-educated businessman who made a killing on Wall Street and owns a bourbon distillery that's quickly becoming a household name. But he likes to pretend he's a good ole boy—dumb as fuck. It's served him incredibly well up until now. Although it's not the image we need him to project if we want our plan to work.

"We're there to hunt Russians, not pussy."

We rented a mansion in Morocco, in Jake's name, and he's throwing a big party. Beautiful women, excellent booze, and high rollers who sweat power and money. All things billionaire oligarchs can't resist—especially those on the outs. Not to mention, I'll be there. When Nikitin learns that, he's going to be so excited for an opportunity to kill me, his tiny dick's going to stand up straight.

"Always a killjoy, Huntsman. You used to be a hell of a lot more fun before you handed over your balls to a woman," Jake grouses. "I'll be in the country as planned, but if you don't mind, I'm going to skip the big bash."

"Don't mind at all. I'm surprised, though. I know how much you love big parties."

He snickers. "Especially those with self-important buffoons hanging around the buffet."

The plan had always been for Jake to quietly slip away long before the party. If things go sideways, I don't want it to blow back on him. Besides, he exports a lot of expensive bourbon to Russia, and there's no reason to rock that boat.

With any luck, we'll lure out Nikitin early enough that I'll be long gone before the first guest arrives, too. I would rather not have a gunfight in the middle of a party that's not in a place where I control the authorities.

"Just remember the deal we made, Huntsman."

Aside from lending his name to the party, he's going to show up with me at some upscale places, where we can spread a lot of cash around. In exchange for his help, he gets my matured Port barrels to age his bourbon, no charge, for as long as he wants them. It's a fair deal as far as I'm concerned.

"I appreciate your help. The barrels are yours, as many as I have, for as long as your dark heart desires."

"All kidding aside, I'm happy to help. It's the most trouble I've gotten into in a long time."

"I doubt that."

He chuckles. "And those barrels—" Jake continues.

"You don't want them?"

"Oh, I want them. But I know what those honey barrels are worth, and I'm more than willing to pay top dollar for them babies." He pauses. "Whatever you're up to is clearly important. That's why you called. I'm glad you did, by the way, and I'm honored to help. You've certainly saved my sorry ass plenty of times, and I'm sure there will be plenty more times when it needs saving. Buy me a drink in Morocco and we'll call it even."

"It is important. I'm trying to save my family." *Something that Jake understands well.* "But the drink and the barrels are on me. And I'm happy to save your sorry ass any time."

62

DANIELA

The phone vibrates on what was once my father's desk, and I turn it over, foolishly hoping it's Antonio calling to apologize. *There must be something wrong with me.*

I'm still clinging to the fairy tale of the dark prince and the dirty *princesa* who overcome all the obstacles trying to tear them apart and live happily ever after. *There's definitely something wrong with me.*

Lara flashes on the screen. Not exactly the evil queen. That's Sonia. Lara's more of a mean stepsister. And I must be a glutton for punishment, because I take the call.

"Hello."

"Daniela. It's *so* good to hear your voice."

"It's nice to hear yours, too." And, in a strange way, it is nice to hear from her. That's how it is with familiar things. We gravitate toward them, even when we know we shouldn't.

"I know you don't have much use for an assistant right now."

That's a loaded remark. And exactly why I'm so wary of her.

"But I'm still working at *Senhor* Antonio's house," she

continues, "and I'd love to drop over some mail that's addressed to you."

I let the *Senhor Antonio's house* remark roll off my back.

"Mail?" *Of course I'm still getting mail there. I hadn't really thought about it.*

"I didn't open anything that looked personal. But I suspect there are condolences for *Senhor* Antonio's mother's death, and congratulations are still coming in from the harvest events."

I'm not sure I want to deal with the mail, or Lara for that matter.

"I can respond to the condolences on behalf of *Senhor* Antonio, so you don't have to be bothered."

I don't think so, dear. Senhor Antonio is still my husband.

"Are you free on Friday morning to bring the mail?"

"If I'm not, I'll make myself free. Will Valentina be home? I'd love to see her."

I don't want her here while Valentina's home. I have no idea what kind of little bomb she'll drop.

"I'm sorry. She'll be at school."

"Another time, then. Would you like me to bring the rest of your things?"

She wants to know if I'm coming back. I'm not telling her a damn thing. She can ask *Senhor* Antonio, if she wants to know. *He'd love that.*

"I have everything I need," I say brightly, before we hang up.

This probably isn't fair, but I've always felt like Lara enjoys others' pain. Some people are like that. Maybe it's because of what happened to her husband and young son. Misery loves company, and all that. Or maybe she's just a shit-stirrer.

"Excuse me," Alma calls, sticking her head in the door. Her arms are full, and I rush to help her.

"What do you have?" I ask, looking at the shallow plastic tub.

"After you went to visit your aunt in Canada"—*oh, God, that story certainly has had a long life*—"Antonio had me come here and pack away anything of importance." She takes the cover off the tub. "This was from a drawer in your father's bedroom."

The container holds my mother's cashmere shawls, all neatly folded, in a rainbow of colors. Paper-thin but warm, she had one near her all the time. After she died, I took the red one to remind me of her. I still have it.

"Did you know your father kept a drawer with a few of her things?"

I shrug. "I didn't know." I left so soon after he died that we never went through all his things.

"Maybe he kept the drawer for you," she says, holding up a small Bible.

It's the one my great-great-grandmother carried on her wedding day, and since then, every bride in the family has carried it, too. *Except me.* When Antonio and I got married, I chose not to sully it. *Turns out it was a good decision.*

I take the small white book and open the cover gingerly, so as not to break the fragile binding. Inside is the signature of every bride who carried it, with her wedding date. I lightly trace my mother's neat handwriting, getting lost in the swirly font.

"There's this, too," Alma says, pulling out the larger, family Bible, from the bottom. It wasn't so much used for prayer, but to memorialize important dates, for future generations—births, baptisms, marriages, deaths, and the like.

There was so much to do after he died, so that we could leave quickly, that I never recorded my father's death, and certainly not my marriage. And of course, there's no mention of Valentina—it's as though she doesn't exist.

You need to tell her so she can take her place in the family history, a small voice inside me says. *It's her legacy, too.*

I tamp down the voice, until I can't hear it anymore.

Alma holds out the family Bible to me. "There's comfort in prayer." She shrugs. "At least I've always thought so."

I nod, not because I agree, but because although she hasn't asked me outright, by now she must have seen photos of Antonio out on the town, partying like a man with a new lease on life.

This morning, a photo of him was splashed everywhere. He's apparently spending a week with friends in Morocco. *He wasn't wearing his wedding ring.* That bothered me more than the redhead.

Although neither the photo nor the caption crushed me as much as I might have thought. But it made me sad for him—for us. Every day, there's some new insult. He's drifting further away, and instead of being an anchor, I'm the distant shore.

I gaze at Alma. "You've seen the pictures?"

"Garbage," she replies. "I threw the newspaper right into the trash this morning, where it belongs. But from the look on your face, you saw the article."

I know Antonio's acting out, but there's something about the very public way he's doing it that's especially nasty. Although as long as Valentina doesn't see it, I don't care all that much what people think. Anyone worth caring about will recognize him as the problem.

"I didn't see the paper, but I read the piece online."

She pushes the Bible in my direction, but I shake my head. "It's a little late to be praying for my marriage."

"Not for your marriage, *querida*. For you. You need clarity and the strength to do what's best for you and for that beautiful girl who has your good heart."

For a moment, I almost expect her to say *And Vera Huntsman's eyes*—but she doesn't. Although I'm sure Alma has wondered about it.

"Shall I take the box to your room?" she asks, before going about her business.

"No. Just leave it here."

When she's gone, I carefully take out a cheery pink shawl

and bring it to my nose to see if I can pick up any hint of my mother. I'm not sure it smells like anything, but I convince myself that there's lingering perfume—*her perfume.* I close my eyes and inhale the scent, and for a moment, I feel her love.

For the rest of the day, I wrap myself in the delicate shawl, hoping it will give me the willpower to stay away from any more Google searches of Antonio.

63

ANTONIO

Lucas breezes into the conference room adjacent to my office in the lodge. "Plane's fueled. Everything's in place."

In addition to my men, Will has also sent a small cadre, and Mikhail and his men will be in Morocco as well, although they're strictly behind the scenes, monitoring Nikitin's movements.

We've been dropping resources in for the last two weeks. Including funneling men and women into Morocco through Algeria, the Canary Islands, and from all over Europe and Africa, by air, land, and sea.

We didn't want a sudden influx so that there wouldn't be anything to tip off Nikitin and draw him back into hiding. The only way we'll need all the security is if we're forced to take him down at the party. Hopefully it won't come to that, but we need to be prepared.

I miss Daniela more than I'd ever admit to anyone, *including myself*. I want this over, so I can sink my cock into her warm body every day for the rest of my life. *If she'll have you.* I don't spend too much time on that thought. This is almost over. *It has to be.*

I'm not leaving Africa until we've put the sonofabitch in the ground.

"All right." I glance from Cristiano to Lucas. "We're ready."

I turn to Lucas. "Take the rest of the afternoon off, and do whatever it is you need to do before we leave. Water your plants. Get your dick wet. Whatever. I don't want to see you again until we board that plane tonight."

Cristiano puts out his hand to Lucas. "You need anything, you know how to reach me, day or night."

Lucas nods. "Don't worry. I'm not afraid to wake your lazy ass up."

"For the record," Lucas says to me on his way out, "we could do this without you actually being there. He'll show up if he even *thinks* you're going to be there."

"Maybe. But if he hears I'm there with beautiful women on my arm, throwing around money, it'll piss him off to no end. Remember, he likes revenge."

"Me too," Lucas quips, before he disappears.

"Nikitin isn't the only one who's been seeing you with beautiful women on your arm," Cristiano reminds me, tweaking my conscience, like it hasn't been bothering me enough.

"I'm well aware. Trust me."

"You don't have to do this," he continues, catching my eye. "I want the bastard, too. His fucking people abducted me off the street and held me prisoner. Nothing ever goes according to plan. We can find another way to get him. A way that isn't going to risk your life."

I need this to be over. If I die wiping him off the face of the earth, at least she'll be safe. She has no value to him, except as a vehicle to get to me.

"I'm done looking over my shoulder. I'm done having people I care about blown out of the sky and abducted from alleys in broad daylight. But more than anything, I'm done living with the fear that Daniela is next. If Nikitin gets his filthy hands on her—" I suck in a long breath. "It will be a blessing if he kills her immediately. We both know it. She's already been through hell. I'm not sure she can go through it again. She deserves better, even if I don't."

"I get it. I don't like it, but I get it. But I want to go with you. I have skills that can be useful. I'm begging you to reconsider."

I peer at him and shake my head. "No."

"Is this because of—"

I hold out my hand to stop him. "It's because Lucas is the right man to take with me. He has better technological skills than either you or me—or anyone else. And you're the right man to leave here."

He drums his fingers on the desk, impatiently, or maybe impertinently. Either way, he's pissed to be left behind. Yes, it would be more than a little helpful to have him with us. But I need him here, more than I need him there.

"If anything happens to me, you have the ability to oversee Huntsman operations. You can transition Rafael, making sure he has all the support he needs to take over successfully. It will be a lot for him." I pause to let some of this register with him. "And you'll make sure Daniela and Valentina stay out of harm's way, and that they have everything they need to make them happy. Lucas can do some of it, but you're better at the emotional pieces. You have a kind of humanity that neither Lucas nor I have."

He does. If I have to leave Daniela and Rafael in someone's care, I want it to be his.

"You better fucking come back. Because I'm not cleaning up the shit you leave behind." His words are tough, but it's a cover for his voice that's thick with emotion.

"You're antsy because you're staying behind. We have a solid plan."

"I know," Cristiano replies. "And I'm glad Lucas is with you. He's meticulous. It's just—this is bigger than what we normally get involved in. Other than lending Will a hand from time to time, and our little offensive in the US with Daniela, we operate in our little corner of Europe. We're local thugs."

Local thugs. I chuckle. "I plan on coming back and cleaning up my own shit. But I need to remain focused, and in order to do that, I need to leave someone behind who I'm confident can carry on if the plan goes off the rails."

"I know you want this over, but don't take any unnecessary risks. Nikitin is dangerous because he has nothing to lose. If he kills you, his luck could change overnight."

"I don't have a death wish."

But I have everything to lose as long as that bastard is breathing.

64

DANIELA

The family Bible has been glaring at me from the desk for days, silently badgering me to add my father's date of death, and maybe my wedding date. As much as I'd like to ink *Valentina Rosa* on the yellowed pages, I can't, not until she knows.

When I finally capitulate, I take a black pen from the desk that won't smudge, and open the leather-bound cover.

There's a sealed envelope right at the front. It's yellowed, although not as badly as the book itself.

Daniela it says, across the front, in my father's scrawl. The back has a wax seal with the Rosa do Vale logo to discourage anyone else from opening it.

My heart beats a little faster as I imagine all the possible scenarios. An apology for arranging my marriage? A father's declaration of love? A message for Valentina?

They all seem too fanciful as they flit through my mind. My father was a practical man. I'm sure the letter reiterates information about the property or his business that he wanted to be certain I remembered.

If that's all it is, why are you hesitant to open it?

I stare at the envelope for what feels like an eternity, before I slide a letter opener under the flap, leaving the seal intact.

My hands have been trembling since I saw the letter but as I read, my stomach shakes, too.

Daniela, meu amor,

You're reading this because you are recording the date of my death, or perhaps your marriage to Antonio. I love you with all my heart and soul, but right now, I'm quite sure my affection isn't returned.

You must be angry and confused. You have every right to be.

When you were a little girl, I was your hero. You believed that there was nothing I couldn't do. But by the time you were twelve, you learned that I couldn't do what was most important in this life: protect you and your mother.

What happened in the meadow was my worst fear realized, my most tragic failing, and greatest shame. What kind of man doesn't protect the women he loves?

I have a confession, meu amor. I was never a hero. I was a coward. This was true long before your mother's death. I was always too soft with her. I let her do as she pleased, even when I knew it was dangerous. I always gave in to her, because I could deny her nothing. I loved her too much.

I started to make that mistake with you, too, but unlike your mother, I changed course before it was too late.

You wanted me to avenge your mother's death. I heard your pleas, and even after you stopped asking, I saw it in your eyes. I wanted revenge too. But I couldn't take it. Not because I didn't love her, but because I loved you too much. Killing Abel and Tomas would have meant war. War that would have put you and Valentina at too great a risk—a risk I wasn't willing to take. I swallowed my thirst for revenge every day of my life.

But that's not why you're angry with me today. You're angry because I arranged your marriage to Antonio. Although I believe, in my very soul, that he's the right man for you, and that you are the right woman for him, I would have never disrespected your mother by choosing your husband. She would have been angrier at me about that than you are now.

But I don't care about angering either of you. I won't be soft about this. I won't fail you again.

Antonio is the one man I trust to protect you and Valentina. The one man with the power and fortitude to stand up against his family. Because if either Abel or Tomas ever make the connection, they will come for you, and for your child. This is their path to Quinta Rosa do Vale.

Antonio is a strong man who needs a strong woman. And you are a strong woman who needs a strong man. Together you will leave a mark on the valley like none other, and more importantly, you'll have beautiful babies who I would give my soul to hold in my arms.

I did not share the news of Valentina with Antonio. It's your secret to divulge when you're ready. Although, I prevail upon you to do it as soon as possible. He will stand by you. I'm as sure of it as I'm sure my health is failing quickly.

I should have told you about the betrothal agreement, but I'm too selfish. We have so little time left, and I don't want to spend it arguing, or take my last breath with your disappointment in me reflected in your beautiful face. I hope you can one day find it in your heart to forgive me.

All my love to you, and to my sweet Valentina,
Papai

I TAKE a couple of tissues from the box on the desk, wipe my eyes, and blow my nose. But my body is still wracked with sobs.

He assumed I'd read the letter shortly after he died. Under ordinary circumstances, that would have been true, but I was too busy putting plans in place to escape, because I knew that with my father gone, they would eventually come for Valentina.

I rest my head in my arms, on the desk, and I cry, and I cry, and I cry—until there's nothing left.

When I'm cried out, I'm still angry at him for not telling me about the arrangement. But it's tempered, because I understand the overwhelming need to keep secrets from a child you love so you don't destroy their spirit with the truth—*so they don't hate you.*

It's why I haven't told Valentina that I'm her mother. Although this letter makes me more determined to tell her the truth—even though it terrifies me. I don't want her to read it in a letter after I die, when I won't be there to hold her, or to answer her many questions, or to help her work through the anger of betrayal. *It's not fair.*

I reread the letter, pausing when I reach these lines:

I couldn't protect you or your mother. It was my worst fear realized, my most tragic failing, and my greatest shame. What kind of man doesn't protect the women he loves?

I don't give a damn how many beautiful women are on my husband's arm—fake dates, like Sonia. That's all they are. I don't care if he's running around from Marrakesh to Casablanca, partying until dawn. I don't care how many photos capture his every illicit move. And I don't care how many stories are written.

I don't pretend to know what's going on behind the scenes. But I do know he loves me. No one, and nothing, will convince me differently.

He loves me.

And I love him, too.

His mother's death was devastating, but more than that, it brought him face-to-face with his worst fear, what would be his most tragic failing, and greatest shame: that I will be next, and there's not a damn thing he can do about it.

What kind of man doesn't protect the women he loves?

The kind of man that Antonio Huntsman can't bear to be.

65

ANTONIO

We haven't been able to smoke out Nikitin. Jake and I gave him plenty of opportunities to believe he could get to me in Marrakesh, and later, in Casablanca. We were all over social media, broadcasting our whereabouts, but he never even tried.

Now we're left with the damn party that I hoped to avoid.

Will's team isn't convinced he'll actually show his face, and they might be right. But we all believe he has something planned. No one believes it more than me. I feel it in my bones.

"I can't believe he's going to wait for the party," Lucas mutters. "It's a riskier plan for him than it is for us."

Lucas and I are on a conference call with Cristiano, checking in like we do every day to keep him in the loop and run details by him. The distance gives him perspective that we don't have.

"The actual party is risky for everyone," Cristiano says soberly. "Although you'll have a lot of people on the ground. But I wouldn't be at all surprised if Nikitin makes a move before the event, like he did during the harvest."

I wouldn't be at all surprised either. We know he hired the hitman I shot in the tent. Lucas traced the payment to one of Nikitin's offshore accounts.

"It's what he knows," Cristiano adds. "Don't forget, he's an oligarch, not Bratva. Without funds and his government's backing, he doesn't have what it takes to be original."

Lucas's phone buzzes, and he gets up. "I need to check on something. I'll be right back."

"Go. I think we're done, anyway."

"Have you heard anything from Daniela?" I ask Cristiano before we end the call, because I'm a fucking pussy.

"She's holding up—like she always does for Valentina. I haven't spoken with her. I only know what I hear through Duarte, Santi, and Mia. My mother is pissed at you about the photos, so she's not speaking to me."

"I'll talk to Alma when I get back."

"My mother will get over it. But—" He pauses.

"Say it. Whatever it is, just say it."

"You're not going to like it."

I'm well aware. "Just fucking tell me what's on your mind."

"If you don't get Nikitin, or even if you do and for some reason it's not over, you need to stop for a breath and take care of your relationship with Daniela. Relationships are like people. They can only take a certain amount of battering before they're dead. It doesn't matter if the beating comes from a well-intentioned place or a sworn enemy. Trauma is trauma. Not everything can be revived—or forgiven. Before you left town, you did some serious damage."

He didn't say one thing that I haven't mulled over—and over. Daniela might not forgive me. Deep down, I know I'm her destiny, just as she's mine. *But fated lovers often find tragic endings.*

Forgiveness? *I'm not sure.* I knew it was a huge risk when I hatched the plan. I don't want to lose her. *I'll suffer her loss until the day I die.*

But I made two decisions as I sat watching her sleep the morning I told her to get out: her long-term safety and peace of mind was more important than having her beside me, and that I wouldn't hold her against her wishes, ever again. I stand by those decisions. *And I will stand by them if it fucking kills me.*

Lucas storms in, before I can respond. "There are two men at the gate from an HVAC company. They're here to repair the air conditioning."

"Air conditioning repair?" I ask, suspicion curling around each word. "It seems to be working fine to me."

"I think so, too," Lucas adds. "It was so cold last night I thought my balls were going to freeze and fall off."

"Any chance one of them is Nikitin?" I'd love to get that bastard today, so I can go home and start trying to put things right with my wife. The longer it goes on, the worse it will be.

"No." Lucas shakes his head. "That we know. Will's people are running their pictures through facial recognition software, but it could take awhile."

"Call me back," Cristiano says, concern in his voice. "This needs your full attention."

"Who contacted them?" I ask, ending the call.

"They claim the owner of the house phoned them when we rented it. The system has been on the fritz, and she thought that we'd need it fully functioning before the party."

When the house was rented, we made a big deal with the rental agent about the place being lavish and in pristine condition, because we were going to throw an A-list party while we were here. But this is suspicious as fuck. "Has anyone confirmed with the owner or the HVAC company?"

"Can't reach the owner. The woman from the company wasn't sure who had contacted them. She confirmed the identity of one of the repairmen. She suggested the other could be an apprentice. I didn't speak with her, but from what I was told, she sounds like someone who doesn't pay close attention to details."

"Are they still at the gate?"

Lucas nods. "They have no weapons or explosives, and they appear to have equipment that would be used by an HVAC company. The consensus is we should let them in and see what they're up to. It could be nothing."

It's not nothing.

"Let them in. The sooner the better, before they change their minds."

"There are feeds all over this place," Lucas continues, "but we don't know their game. I agree we need to let them in, but I don't like it. You should leave the property."

"I'm not going fucking anywhere."

66

ANTONIO

We're monitoring the feeds near the AC units, as is Will's team in London.

The house is twenty-five thousand square feet and runs on fifteen separate units confined to the cellar and attic. The men are working together, which seems strange since this is a big job. *I don't believe for one second the middle-aged guy is an apprentice.*

My eyes are glued to the feeds, but it's like waiting for mold to grow. I don't have the patience for this type of activity. I prefer to assume it's mold and douse the son of a bitch with bleach before the spores appear.

"That looks like it could be a small canister," someone from the London team says.

Lucas enlarges the image. The object is tiny, and I would have never recognized it as a canister.

"That's not a component that should be part of that unit," a woman remarks.

"A bomb?" a man behind me asks.

"Aerosolized poison," Lucas replies. "The Russians love poison."

"Maybe," the woman from London replies. "It would be my first guess. You need to proceed as though it's a highly lethal toxin." Someone says something to her that I can't understand. "Remember the terrorist threat on the Japanese transit system?" she continues. "This could be a similar nerve gas. I suspect the cooling unit is the conductor, and it will release the toxin when it's turned back on. Get everybody out of that damn house."

We have people who can defuse a bomb on site, as well as a team to manage chemical agents, and testing capability. All thanks to Will, who is involved in sketchy shit and almost as invested in this outcome as I am.

"Grab those two bastards and take them out back. Secure the canisters using an abundance of caution. Test whatever's inside so we know exactly what we're dealing with," I order. "Everybody else, away from the house."

―――――

ONE OF THE *repair*men is a career criminal who has served time for armed robbery, and the other is an actual HVAC guy looking to pick up some extra cash on the side. He has a clean record.

Neither of them is a mastermind, but they know something.

"Who gave you the canisters?" I ask the two idiots tied to a trellis out back.

"Don't say a fucking thing," the one with the prior criminal record hisses. "He'll kill you."

I pull out my knife and tap the blade against my palm. "If by he, you mean me, I will kill you if you don't answer my questions truthfully." I run my blade against the throat of the real repairman, who has already pissed his pants. He's the most likely to turn quickly, although he might not know as much. "Where did you get the canisters?"

"A Russian," he sputters.

"What's his name?"

He shakes his head. "I don't know."

"What about you? You know?" I ask his friend, making sure he sees the blade in my hand.

"Some oligarch. Never told us his name."

"Really?" I ask, sticking the knifepoint into his bicep.

"*Fuck*," he shouts. "I don't know his name."

"What's in the canisters?"

"Freon."

"Freon my ass." I plunge the knife into his thigh. *More screams.* It's not anywhere near as satisfying as it will be to hear Nikitin's screams, but it'll suffice for now.

"It's some chemical," the repairman says quickly. The guy is shitting his pants.

"What kind of chemical?"

"We don't know the details. We were just told to be very careful, and not to open them. He told us to put one into the coolest part of each condenser and turn the system on high before we left. He said we should tell you that the system had to be kept on high overnight."

"Where do you meet him?" I ask the criminal, holding my knife to his throat for incentive.

Every muscle in his body contracts. "A speakeasy. In Marrakesh."

Mikhail and his men are in Marrakesh. "I want a name and an exact location."

Lucas holds up his phone: **Sarin**

Nerve gas. Jesus Christ.

"We told you everything we know," the criminal groans. "We want our money."

"Your money?" I want to slit his throat, and I will, but I might still need him.

"Before we discuss money, this is what we're going to do," I say to the repairman. "You're going to call the man who hired you. You have a way to reach him, right?"

He nods.

"Tell him that you're having trouble getting some of the condensers open. Ask him which ones he wants you to work on. Keep him on the phone for as long as you can. Don't say anything that will tip him off, or I'll kill you and everyone you love."

Some men might choose to let the repairman live since he's giving up useful information, but not me. But I'll make his end quick and relatively painless. The other asshole, though, he's going to bleed out slowly.

"Somebody give him a script and set him up to make the contact." I turn to Lucas. "Alert Mikhail. We'll track the call to a precise location, and Mikhail can grab him and bring him to us."

67

DANIELA

"Good luck with your history test," I tell Valentina as she leaves for school.

"Easy peasy," she says, flashing me a confident grin. "Since it's the weekend, can we make popcorn and watch a movie tonight?"

"I would love that."

"Do you think I could invite someone from school to sleep over? You promised that I could."

Santi shakes his head.

"I did promise. But I never said anything about tonight. Let me think about it. There are only five of you, and I don't want anyone's feelings to be hurt." *Or yours.*

Which is why I need to buy a little time.

"Oh," she says, frowning. "I didn't think about that. I don't want to hurt anyone's feelings, either. Can we invite everyone?"

I smile, and hand her a raincoat and an umbrella. "That might be better. With a little more notice, they could bring their things with them to school and stay when it's over. They don't exactly live around the corner. Let's plan for next weekend," I promise, eyeing Santi, who doesn't blink.

"I love you, Lala," Valentina cries, throwing her arms around me.

It's been so long since we've had a moment like this. I feel like all we ever do is argue. I squeeze her tight and inhale the fruity scent of her shampoo. "I love you, too, baby. I'll get some face masks and some polish, and we can have a spa night while we watch our movie."

She's still smiling when she strolls out the door with Santi and Mia.

Maybe I'll make some cookies or cupcakes for tonight, too.

"I'd like to go to the store at some point today," I tell Duarte, as I pour us each a cup of coffee.

"For polish and masks?" he says, with a tiny smirk.

I nod.

"I'm sorry, *senhora*," he says sincerely. "But you can't leave the property. Someone will get what you need."

"Alma isn't here, and I haven't hired any staff. So I'm not sure who'll be visiting the beauty aisle for me. Unless you plan on it?"

He shakes his head. "I would be happy to pick you up whatever you need, but I don't go anywhere without you, and you don't go anywhere. Make a list, and one of the guards will get everything. And maybe some nice tea with sugar cubes. My wife and daughters always have lemon tea with lavender sugar cubes when they have a spa day."

Duarte has a charming way of lessening any blow. I knew he had a wife and children, but I don't know anything about them. But before I can ask him about his family, his phone rings.

"You can let her come," he says before hanging up.

"Lara's here," Duarte tells me. The guards at the gate have checked her vehicle, and she's been cleared.

With mail. I suppress a groan. I should have told her not to come. Although maybe she won't mind going out for face masks and nail polish. Whatever she gets will be better than what one of the guards buys.

"Did you trade in your cute little car for a van?" Duarte asks, when he opens the door.

"God no. That's my neighbor's van. He let me borrow it because I had so much mail to bring, not to mention the packages. Plus, Victor sent some things for Valentina. My car's just a two-seater, and the trunk leaks like a sieve when it rains. Not very useful on a day like today," she mutters. "Where should I park so that everything doesn't get wet when we carry it in?"

"The garage," Duarte instructs. "I'll open the door for you. Park in the bay closest to the house."

A van full of mail. *Lucky me.*

68

ANTONIO

The nerve gas has been disposed of, as have the two assholes doing the dirty work.

Nikitin is here, and the devil is dancing inside me, impatient to get his chance with that fucker.

I let Will's people take a turn with him, and then Mikhail. Lucas is softening him up for me now.

I'm packing, because as soon as I have what I want from that bastard, I'm out of here.

A bolt of lightning pitches the dim room into a scathing light. I glance out the window. A hurricane is forecast to make landfall in the next few hours. But right now, it's pouring, with an occasional roar of thunder that I imagine as whooping and clapping from the demons gathered in hell, awaiting their favorite son. *He'll be joining them soon.*

Lucas comes into the living room as I toss my duffel bag near the door. "He copped to the hitman, to abducting Cristiano, and to the gas, but that's it. He's not ready for you. But the weather's deteriorating quickly and if you want to get out, you're going to have to leave soon."

If the meteorologists are to be believed, the hurricane could keep me here for another week. Seven more days away from Daniela. Seven days for whatever wounds I've caused to fester.

I check the weather app on my phone. *No change.* My time is running out faster than Nikitin's.

If Lucas says he's not ready, he's not ready. We haven't had him long enough, and time is everything when torturing a man for information. *Everything.*

I glance at Lucas. There's nothing I can get out of Nikitin that a determined Lucas can't. Or Mikhail, who is Bratva to the core. They want him almost as much as I do.

But I want revenge on my terms. I want the end to be brutal. I want to revel in his screams. I want his blood to rain over me. I want memories of the death stench to lull me to sleep tonight.

The wind howls, battering the shutters. The lights flicker, but they don't go out.

"Let me take a whack at him."

I stride through the house, to the room where the prisoner is being held. When I get there, I grab a chair and straddle the back.

Nikitin's been bloodied. His left eye is swollen shut and his bottom lip is split. The prisoner's hanging from a rafter, with his toes grazing the floor.

It's taking everything I have to remain seated. I've waited so long for this moment, and I want my justice *now*.

But that's not how it works.

"I see you've been served an appetizer to welcome you."

"I can help you, Huntsman. I have information. I have money. We can make a deal."

Sure we can. What a stupid fucker. "What kind of information?"

"About the Bratva."

"I don't give a shit about the Bratva. Tell me about the plane that blew up over the Atlantic. The one carrying my mother. Then maybe we can deal."

"I had nothing to do with killing your mother. Nothing," he cries.

He's not ready to give up anything of consequence. I can already tell. He needs time to think about his plight. He needs to be hanging higher off the floor so that his arms feel like they're going to fall off. It's going to take time. *It always does.*

Thunder rocks the foundation, and a bolt of lightning illuminates the room. The lights go out, and seconds later, the generator kicks on.

I have a decision to make. I can torture this man, and after he tells me everything he knows, I can take my revenge for my mother's death. Or I can leave while I can still get out, and go to my wife to ask for forgiveness. If I choose Daniela, someone else will have to finish this. *I can't have everything. Not today.*

Either way he'll be dead, justice will be served, and Daniela and Valentina will have a more normal life. *So will I.*

Thunder booms, and the lightning strike follows immediately. *The window is closing.*

I pause to listen to my churning gut. In this moment, the pull to Daniela is far greater than even the revenge.

With unwavering resolve, I get up and go to my prisoner. The one I've hunted for weeks. "You're not worth another moment of my time." I plunge the knife into his side, careful not to nick anything that would kill him too soon.

He screams like a little girl. It's an addictive sound, feeding a craving that's been gnawing at my soul.

I want more.

But I step back, until he's out of reach.

"Find out everything. Then end him. Make it slow and painful. I want confirmation of death."

I hand Lucas my knife and walk away.

69

DANIELA

"I have something to show you," Lara says, with a forced smile, when she returns to my father's office after making us tea.

"What is it?"

"I think it's better if I show you."

"Is something wrong?"

"Oh no, it's nothing like that." Her eyes light up. "It's just a small surprise I have for you."

A surprise, for me? I really don't want anything from Lara—it'll only make it harder to let her go. But I follow her to the kitchen and into the pantry while she chatters about some new maid at the house.

I gasp when I enter the pantry. Duarte is on the floor. He's not moving. I rush to him. "Duarte," I cry from my knees. He doesn't open his eyes. "Duarte!" I shout louder. *He's unconscious.*

"Call security," I instruct Lara. "Have them send an ambulance. Hurry!

"Did you see what happened?" I ask, placing my fingers on his throat. His breathing is shallow, but he has a pulse. There's some foaming near his lips. And blisters popping up on his arm.

Why isn't she calling?

"Lara, call—" When I look up, she has a gun pointed at me. It takes me seconds to process.

There was no surprise. She did this.

My heart hammers, as I slowly feel for Duarte's weapon. "What happened to him?" I ask. "He must have had an accident," I muse, even though I know it wasn't. "No one will blame you. But we need to get him help before he dies."

I can't find his gun.

Lara's grinning, like she won a damn prize. "You're such a stupid woman. And you're not even that pretty. I have no idea what someone like Antonio Huntsman sees in you."

She's bitter. She wants Antonio. Is that what this is about?

My chest tightens as I scan the pantry for something I can use as a weapon, but she's standing so close. I can't reach anything.

I glance at Duarte's arm. *More blisters.* "What did you do to him? He needs medical attention."

"If you listen carefully and cooperate, he can have the help he needs."

I'm panting, struggling to stay calm. "What do you want?"

"You're going to come with me. And you're not going to give me any trouble. Otherwise, I'll kill you and take your precious Valentina with me instead. The little brat will go in your place."

I can't breathe.

She can't get to Valentina without going through Santi and Mia first. I glance down at Duarte. He's very capable, and she got to him. *I didn't even hear a sound.*

"I have men stationed outside the school."

She has men? Who is this woman?

Lara holds out her phone so I can see the screen. *It's*

Valentina. She pulls it away quickly, but not before I can see the whiteboard behind her. *She's at school.*

"What do you want?"

"Change into these clothes." She kicks a tote bag at me.

I grab the bag and stand. "I'll be right back," I assure her, taking a step toward the door. Although I have no intention of coming back. But I'll call or text Santi to warn him.

"You'll change here," she snarls, shoving me further into the pantry. "You know I loved Antonio, right? I deserved him. And I would have made a better wife than you."

Oh my God.

I need to find a way out or Duarte's going to die. *And me, too.* I eye a quart of tomato sauce on the shelf. It could work—if I can distract her for even a few seconds.

"Can you turn your back while I change? Please."

"No!" she barks, chambering the gun. "Don't pretend you're so modest and good. You let Tomas fuck you. He told me you begged him."

I can't breathe. It's hot. *So hot.* Black dots cloud my vision. *Small breaths. Stay here. You can do this.*

I hang onto a shelf. "I was twelve. I didn't let Tomas do anything. He raped me."

"Liar!" she shouts. "He told me."

"He lied to you, Lara. I didn't let him do anything."

"He loved me. He would never lie to me. Tomas was going to marry me and we were going to live here, with Valentina."

I feel myself heave and hold my stomach. *Small breaths. You can do this. You've been through worse. You can do this. Stay alert for an opportunity. She'll make a mistake.*

"Get dressed. We're going to see an old friend. Take off everything. There's underwear in the bag."

The bag contains lacy lingerie—it's expensive—and a designer dress with matching shoes.

"What friend?"

"It's another surprise," she gushes. "If you don't come, he said he'd love to see Valentina. She's so pretty."

I hang my head and vomit. Some of it lands on Duarte's shoes. He doesn't move an inch. I'm not sure he's still breathing.

"You're disgusting," she sneers, tossing my sweater over the vomit.

"The guards will see me leave, and they'll call Antonio." *He won't let you get away with this.*

"Haven't you been following the news?" she taunts. "Antonio's not in Porto. He doesn't love you. Just like he didn't love me."

"Lara," I plead, "you don't have to do this. It doesn't matter whether Antonio loves us. We don't need him. We can figure something out. Just me and you."

"Tomas didn't love you, either," she continues, without responding. "But he loved me. And then Antonio took him." She gapes into my face. Her eyes are narrow and the irises black, as if the pupils have taken over. "Antonio needs to be punished."

She's unstable. Be careful.

"I'm not worried about the guards. They already checked the van. There was just mail and packages, and the equipment my neighbor uses to provide physical therapy. I'm your trusted personal assistant. They're not going to check the vehicle on the way out."

She's right.

"You're going to get into the back of the van and hide, just like you climbed into the back of the pickup truck. Remember?" she mocks, like I'm a piece of trash. "Alvarez hated you. He told me how you snuck out of Antonio's house and went to the dock like a whore."

"Lara, you don't have to do this. I can help you. Please let me. They'll listen to me. We can say that Duarte had an accident. That he fell and knocked his head."

She doesn't acknowledge my suggestion. "Put all your clothes and shoes in the bag. Your phone, too."

When I take too long, she holds up another image of Valentina at her desk.

"You better hope I get away with it, because if I don't call in fifteen minutes to say that we've left, your daughter's guards will be dead—like him." She cocks her chin at Duarte. "And Valentina will be on the way to make an old man's dreams come true."

70

ANTONIO

The flight from Marrakesh to Porto took less than two hours. The weather was a bear, and we only got out by some miracle. I have a quick stop to make at the lodge and then I'm going to Quinta Rosa do Vale to make things right with Daniela.

I'll beg if I have to, but I won't force her to come home with me. If she needs time, I'll give it to her. If she says no, I'll respect her decision. *No.* I won't do that, but I will work day and night to get her back. No matter the cost. She's mine. *Like I'm hers.*

Will calls while I'm in the elevator. "Hey," I say, answering. "Thanks for your help."

"I didn't call for your thanks," he replies, brushing me off. "This was my problem, too. I called because Nikitin finally copped to planting the bomb on the plane, but I'm not convinced."

My jaw tightens. "Why not?"

"He wanted it over. But he couldn't provide enough information to satisfy my people that he did it."

"He probably didn't actually plant the bomb. We never thought that. He paid off someone."

"That's what he claimed. Pointed to a British national who I've had some *disagreements* with from time to time."

I feel the stress leave my shoulders.

The bomb appears to have been Will's problem. My mother was collateral damage. It doesn't make me feel any better. She's still dead.

"That's why it always felt like there was more than one bad actor," I muse aloud.

"We haven't checked out that theory yet. It could be the bullshit of a man being tortured."

It's always a risk, but Nikitin was involved in a lot of the shit that's happened. We know that for certain.

"Let me know what you find," I mutter, hanging up. Until I know more, I'm not letting Will's conjecture ruin my plans with Daniela.

When I enter the villa, Cristiano's on the phone, and from his expression, it's something serious. *I can never catch a fucking break.*

He's ashen, as he holds the phone out to me. "It's Tavares. Daniela's been abducted."

"What?" I bark, grabbing him by the shoulders and shaking him while my entire reason for being implodes. It would hurt less if someone yanked my beating heart out of my chest.

But there's no time to writhe in pain. Not with Daniela in danger.

71

ANTONIO

"Where the hell is my wife?" I roar at Tavares through the phone. "And where is Duarte?"

"I'm sorry—"

"Don't fucking sorry me." I want to choke him. "Who has her?"

"We don't know. Lara was visiting, and she's gone as well. They found Duarte unconscious in the pantry. It looks like contact poison."

The Russians. This could have been something Nikitin set up to go down long before we grabbed him. He knew I was in Morocco.

No speculation. I need hard facts.

"How long has she been missing?"

"When Valentina returned home from school, she wasn't there. Mia found Duarte's body in the pantry."

Jesus Christ.

"Is he alive?"

"Barely. They used a blistering agent. It's touch and go."

I can't worry about Duarte right now. "Do we know how long she's been gone?" I demand, again.

"No. Lara left the house at ten thirty. We assume *Senhora* Daniela has been gone since then."

Six hours.

Fuck. Six hours is an eternity. She could be anywhere by now. In any condition. We need to find her.

"What about the camera feeds?"

"We're working on it. The camera in the garage might have been hacked. But it's just speculation right now."

"Do you have any other information?"

"It's too early—"

I end the call, before he finishes.

"Are the tracking devices on Daniela's belongings activated?"

"As soon as Tavares called. Several of them are pinging," he says, pointing to a screen on the wall. "It's like she packed a bag."

No. It's like they wanted us to find her.

"Where is she?"

"I'm trying to figure that out. It looks like Abel's. But that doesn't make sense."

Abel's? "I sealed Tomas in a chemical bath myself. He did not come back to get his revenge."

"Lucas is so much better at this," Cristiano gripes, frustrated.

"Then get him on the fucking phone."

"I'm already here," Lucas replies. "The pings are coming from Abel's. They're not even being rerouted."

They want me. "I'm going right now."

"We'll round up a team. It won't take long."

"Not waiting. Meet me there." I grab my keys off the desk.

"It's a trap, Antonio."

"I don't give a shit. My wife's life is in danger. Round up your goddamn team and meet me at my uncle's house. She's not going to be alone for one second more."

"She might not even be there. It could just be her belongings."

"She's somewhere." I don't let myself think about the horrible things that could have happened to her in six hours. If I did, I wouldn't be able to function at the level I need to be functioning. If Daniela's not at the house, there will be something there to help us. *Even if it's a trap.*

"That's our only clue to her. Get in touch with Rafael and get a layout of that house before you go charging in. I haven't been inside in more than a decade. Rafael hasn't either, but he might remember it better than I do. Do not, I repeat, *do not* go inside that house without a cogent plan. That's how hostages get killed. She's not dying because we were idiots."

"Antonio," he shouts. "You can't go in without a plan either. They might have already killed her, and they're waiting for you."

I'll take that risk.

"She's not dead." *I would know if she was dead. But she needs me.* "If they want me, they're going to hold off killing her until they have me."

"That's even more reason to wait."

I shake my head. "Once I'm there, I can bargain. I have lots of bargaining chips at my disposal." *She has nothing.* "They want me. We all know it. But while they're waiting for me to show up, they might be torturing her. I will not wait. If they kill her, it's because it was always the plan. But at least she won't die alone." *I can't let that happen.*

"What if they kill you?"

I stop and admit something that I've known for a long time but I've never said to anyone. But I want them to understand the stakes for me. "I have little reason to live without her." The words, the truth—*my truth*—springs from my chest into the somber silence.

Lucas clears his throat. "You need to wear some kind of listening device."

"They'll find it and take it out on her. I can't risk it."

"Not this one," Cristiano says, handing me a small device that's about the size of a SIM card.

"It's the one we've been trying out," Lucas explains. "The battery life is too short to be effective as a plant, but it will serve us for a few hours. Put it under your belt buckle."

Once it's secure, I peer into Cristiano's eyes.

"Instruct every man you take with you that Daniela's life is worth a hundred of mine. Convey this order: They save her first. At any cost."

72

DANIELA

I'm in the back of a van that Lara forced me into, stuffed inside a long, narrow container used to store therapy equipment. It's coffin-like, with a few holes along the perimeter, too small to allow much air flow. I feel like I'm suffocating, and I try to keep my breathing slow and shallow to conserve oxygen.

I've been trying to keep calm by counting backward. It works for a short time, but I don't get very far before I'm thinking about Valentina.

Santi and Mia will keep her safe. *Duarte couldn't keep you safe. He was only one person.*

Stop, Daniela. You're sucking up too much air.

79, 78, 77, 76…

As soon as Antonio learns I'm gone, he'll increase her security and look for me. My wedding ring has a tracker. They'll activate it, if they haven't already, and he'll find me. I know he will.

75, 74, 73…

The van swerves and comes to a stop. When the rear door opens, there are muffled voices.

What if they find me? I can't let them. Lara's men at the school will grab my baby.

"Valentina will be on the way to make an old man's dreams come true."

No! No! No! I will not let that happen.

I hold my breath until the door slams shut.

We're moving again, although slower. That must have been some sort of security check. *Maybe we've reached where she's taking me.*

The van inches over a small bump before it comes to a complete stop. Lara cuts the engine. *I think she's driving, but I don't know.*

I hear voices as the back door is pulled open. *Men's voices.* I don't recognize them. And Lara. I hear Lara.

The lid is removed from the container where I'm hiding. "Get out," Lara hisses.

My eyes adjust to the light as I climb out. But my limbs are so stiff and unstable from being folded into that box that I stumble out of the van.

A strong arm grabs me roughly before I fall.

"You're so clumsy," she chides.

I glance at the man beside her, and then at the younger one still holding me by the arm. They look to be guards. They each have a rifle slung over their shoulder, and the older of the two is holding a handgun.

"Where am I?" I ask the younger guard, who doesn't look quite as menacing as the older one.

He doesn't answer.

"She's a stupid whore," Lara says, with all the superiority that she usually reserves for Paula. "But she gave me no trouble."

"You did good," the older guard says before lifting his gun and shooting Lara point-blank in the head.

I jump at the *bang*.

Lara crumples to the dirty floor. Lifeless eyes stare into nothing as a halo of blood expands around her head.

It's the sort of thing nightmares are born of, but I keep my eyes fixed on the horror because I'm afraid to look at the man who pulled the trigger.

"I hope you're smarter than she is," the guard taunts, holstering his weapon, "because there's no stupider whore than her."

The younger guard pulls me through the garage into a house I don't recognize.

It's in pristine condition. Neat as a pin, with expensive furnishings and artwork. *It smells of lemon oil.*

There are photographs clustered on a table in a room we pass, but I'm too far away and moving too quickly to be able to identify anyone in the photos.

The place is enormous, but I don't see another human being who might help me.

No one here is going to help you. Pay attention to your surroundings so you can help yourself.

We move silently until we reach a wing in what seems like the farthest end of the house. The guards take me through a few locked doors before we stop. I hold my breath as the older guard knocks a couple of times.

A gray-haired man in a costly suit opens the door. He looks vaguely familiar, but I can't place him.

He steps aside without a word and the guard shoves me into a room, where terror seizes me. I take a step back, and then another, until I bang into a chair.

Abel Huntsman is propped in a wheelchair, the Premier logo hanging on the wall behind him.

My skin crawls.

He's old and his skin is shriveled like a rotten fig. But even feeble, he terrifies me.

I look from one man to the other. I'm not sure who's in

charge. *Maybe the man in the suit?* "Why am I here?" I mutter at him, when I can speak.

"Sit down and shut up," the older guard warns, slapping me hard across the face.

"No, no, no," the man in the suit tuts. "*Senhora* Daniela is our guest."

"You're here as bait, dear," the man explains. "Just like you came when your daughter was threatened, your husband will come for you."

I begin to sob. Lara was right. I'm a stupid woman. But what choice did I have? Antonio's going to follow the tracker in my ring. And they're going to kill him. It's too late. *Maybe not.* Maybe they don't know I'm gone yet.

Abel blinks several times at the older man.

"Bind her securely to the chair," he tells the guards.

I need to get rid of this ring. Maybe flush it down the toilet.

"May I use the bathroom first, please?"

"No," the older guard barks, pushing me into a chair.

It's okay. Antonio will know it's a trap. He'll bring soldiers with guns. Cristiano and Lucas won't let him walk into an ambush. It's true. I just need to bide my time until they get here.

I shudder when the guard places his rough hands near my breasts, but I don't fight. My goal is to stay alive until Antonio and his men get here. He'll know it's a trap. They'll plan for it. *I know they will.*

Abel doesn't speak, but his eyes track my every movement, as though he's alert. It's eerie. Like a photograph in a horror movie. But this isn't a movie. *This is real-life horror.*

"We'll leave you to relax," the man in the suit says. The guards snicker as they leave.

It's just Abel and me in the room.

The panic rises, and I can't seem to control it. I plant my feet on the floor firmly and wiggle my toes to ground myself.

I scan the room, noticing details I don't give a damn about.

It's an office of some kind. There's a heavy wooden desk. And floor-to-ceiling windows, mostly covered by heavy drapes. There are two doors. The one we came in, and another behind Abel. They're made of the same dark wood.

After a few minutes, my heart stops pounding quite as hard. I can't look at Abel. But I don't dare shut my eyes. I'm afraid to even blink.

Eventually I drift into a state of limbo. My body remains alert and my eyes keen, but I'm somewhere else, thinking about Valentina.

"It's so nice to see you again, my dear," a man's voice says. "It's been such a long time."

I scream and jerk, nearly tipping the chair over. A few drops of urine leak into my underpants.

I—I was—under the impression that he didn't speak. That he wasn't alert at all. My heart is thundering again, and I clench my hands into fists to try to regain some control.

But I say nothing.

"Were you surprised to see me?"

His voice is weaker, but I would know it anywhere.

I open my mouth, but I can't make any words come out.

He presses a button on the chair, and it moves until he's just a few feet from me. "I don't like to repeat myself, Daniela, especially to a woman. Were you surprised to see me?"

I pull in a breath. But I still can't talk. *Move your head up and down. Up and down. You can do that. Up and down.*

I don't feel my head move, but it must have, because he smiles at me with a mouth full of graying teeth. "Good. I love surprises. I hope you do too, because I have so many planned."

73

RAFAEL

I wave at the cook who's on his way to the parking lot at the camp where I've been training for the last month.

Antonio said I'd be here four to six weeks. Three weeks ago, maybe even two, I would have been ecstatic to leave. In the interim, I've learned a lot about myself, and I'm not sure I'm ready to go.

But I've been summoned to the office, and I suspect my time here has come to an end.

"Captain," I say to the instructor in charge who's been kicking my ass for four weeks and rubbing my face in the dirt when I'm down. "You wanted to see me."

"Cristiano is on the phone. You can take the call in there," he says, pointing to a smaller office in the back.

"Do you know what it's about?"

He shakes his head, but he doesn't seem concerned. "If you stand there all afternoon, you'll never find out."

What a ballbuster. I go into the office, pick up the landline, and press the blinking key. I'm surprised I even know how to work one of these dinosaurs. "Hey."

"Rafael, it's Cristiano. Lucas is on the call, too."

Cristiano *and* Lucas calling. That has *never* happened. *Something's wrong.* "What's going on?"

"We need the layout of your father's house. Can you help us with that?"

"Yeah. Of course. Why?"

"We don't have a lot of time for discussion," Lucas says, sidestepping the question.

This has something to do with Antonio. "Is Antonio there?"

"No," Cristiano grunts.

This is bullshit. "What the hell is going on?"

"We need your help," Lucas says testily. "Antonio needs your help."

"Then tell Antonio to call me himself."

There's nothing but silence for what feels like fucking forever. *I knew it. Antonio's in trouble.*

"This is complicated," Cristiano says, carefully.

I'm not letting these fuckers play me like I'm a kid who needs to be protected. "I love complicated."

Lucas huffs. I'm close to both of them, but Lucas has far less patience for me. Our childhoods were not that different. And I'm the annoying little brother he never had.

"It appears Daniela was lured to your father's house. We're not sure why, but we believe she's being used as bait to get Antonio there. It worked. The minute he learned she was there, he headed straight over."

With every word, my head spins faster and faster until everything's a jumble.

"Wait a minute. Tomas is dead. My father is little more than a vegetable. Who lured them there?"

"We don't know. Antonio is outfitted with a listening device, but we won't know anything until he gets inside. The house is huge. We need a layout so we can form a plan to rescue them."

Not without me. *A família primeiro. Sempre.* "I'll give you what you want, but I'm going, too. They're my family."

"That's not happening," Lucas says, like he's a goddamn king.

Like fuck it's not happening.

"Look, I have a lot of respect for you both. I've always looked up to you. But this is how it is. If Antonio is incapacitated, I'm in charge. I'm going. You can come, too, or you can blow me off and go off on your own, but that's insubordination." My heart pounds as I lay out the facts for Antonio's top men.

"Nobody said Antonio was incapacitated. And you've never been in this type of situation before," Lucas responds pointedly.

"It doesn't sound like either of you know what the deal is with Antonio. I haven't been in a situation like this, but I know that house, and I know those guards better than anyone else you're bringing in with you. I can handle a weapon. You both know that."

They don't say a goddamn word. I'm sure they're plotting a way around it.

"You should know before you put yourself at risk," Cristiano explains, "that Daniela recently named you Valentina's guardian if anything should happen to her and Antonio."

Nice try, Cristiano. Although it does give me pause. What would happen to her if— That's what they want you to think. It might not even be true.

"That's just more incentive for me to go in and drag their asses out of there. I'm not ready to be anyone's guardian."

"Fine. Be an asshole," Lucas mutters. "But send us the goddamn layout so we can start working on a plan."

"Rafael." Cristiano's tone is sober. "I shouldn't be the one to tell you, but once you leave the camp, you're liable to hear. I don't want you to be blindsided." He takes a deep breath. "Your Aunt Lydia was killed in a plane crash."

My knees buckle, and I grab the edge of the desk to steady myself. "When?"

"On her way back to London after the harvest."

On the plane I was supposed to be on.

"And not one of you fuckers had the decency to tell me before you buried her?"

"No burial. Her body hasn't been recovered. There hasn't been any kind of service."

Jesus Christ. I can't form the words. She was my only real connection to my mother. Antonio must be devastated. *Everyone's gone. Or in danger.* My chest hurts. *How could this have happened?*

"If you're going into that house, you need to put your head on straight," Lucas chides.

He's right. Man up, Rafael. This is no time to be a pussy. "Don't worry about me. Where's Valentina?"

"With Santi, and Mia, and my mother. They're at the apartment in the lodge."

"We need the sketch."

I grab a sheet of paper out of the printer and sit down to draw. "I'm working on it."

Because of my dyslexia, reading's never been easy, but I can calculate complex math problems in my head, and everything becomes clearer when I draw it out. As I sketch the interior of the house, it occurs to me that there's another way in.

"I want to talk to Ruiz," I tell them. "He was my mother's guard, and he tried his best to protect me after she was gone." *He was the only one on the inside who stuck his neck out for me.* "Up until he retired, he was the head guard at the house, in charge of security. The younger guards all respected him. They always listened to him. He could help get us inside."

"It's too risky," Lucas says before he even considers it. "What if he sells you out?"

"He would never do that. Besides, Antonio and Daniela are

being held prisoner, and you think the guards are going to be surprised to see Antonio's men show up? No one needs to sell me out for that. Let me talk to him. He might not be willing to help, but if he's not, he won't say anything. You can work on a plan while I go to see him. We have nothing to lose."

"We have to try," Cristiano mumbles.

"Do it," Lucas adds, resignedly.

74

ANTONIO

As soon as I pull up to the gate outside my uncle's house, a welcoming party surrounds the car with their guns pointed at me.

Stupid fuckers.

I don't make any sudden moves, and I keep my hands where they can see them.

"I'm getting out," I tell them, with my hands behind my head. I can't afford to be killed now, but if I have to surrender, I'll do it on my own terms.

No one asks my name, or my business for being here. *They know.*

One soldier pats me down, and two others check the car. They'll find nothing. Not my phone, or wallet, or any weapons. No contraband that they can use as an excuse to hurt Daniela. *Not that they need an excuse.*

They handcuff my hands behind my back and shove me into the back of a Jeep. Other than the handcuffs, I'm not secured. I've come of my own accord, and they know I'm not going anywhere until I have what I came for. But it's arrogant. Almost insulting.

"Is my wife here?" I ask the two guards in the Jeep with me. Neither of them says a word. *Truthfully, I'd have been more surprised if they replied.*

When we get to the house, three men are waiting for me. All familiar faces. The most outwardly menacing is Gustavo, who took Ruiz's place as head of security, the youngest of the trio was Tomas's personal guard, and the third is Costa, Abel's right-hand man—*when he needed a right-hand man.* That sonofabitch worked for my father before he came to work here. Costa was a trusted advisor, who I summarily fired before my father's body was cold.

When this is over, I'm putting all three of these fuckers in the ground.

"So good to see you, Antonio," Costa murmurs, the slime oozing off him.

If he's waiting for some show of respect, he's going to be disappointed. "Take me to my wife."

The younger guard, who was Tomas's shadow, takes a swing that lands squarely on my jaw, sending my head careening to the side.

"You're done giving orders, Antonio. Your arrogance was your downfall. I always knew it would be," Costa says smugly.

I have Daniela to consider, so I don't say everything I want to say. But I won't cower before them either. That's likely to be just as dangerous when dealing with these kinds of assholes. Every time they take a whack at me, or they think about hurting Daniela, I want them to remember that I'm powerful, and that I'm not done. If nothing else, it'll at least give them a moment of pause.

"Either kill me or take me to my wife."

I brace myself for another blow, but it doesn't come.

75

RAFAEL

When I got off the helicopter, Thiago was waiting. I had him drop me a couple of blocks from the house so as not to put Ruiz or his family in danger.

"Ruiz," I greet the tall man who opens the door. He has less hair than I remember, but he still holds himself proudly.

"Rafael." He embraces me. "Look at you. You're a man. Tall. Broad shoulders."

I chuckle.

"I think about your mother all the time," he says with sadness. "If I had been there." Ruiz shakes his head.

My mother disappeared the day of his daughter's wedding, when he was off. He was always a good man, and he adored my mother. I'm hoping to take advantage of some of that adoration.

"Not your fault, Ruiz. You were loyal to her to the end. It's good to see you."

"It's been a long time. You're always welcome at my house, but I'm not sure why you're here today."

"I need your help."

"Come in," he says, motioning me inside.

I'm comfortable sharing some of this with Ruiz—all of it,

really—but his sons still work at the house, as does his nephew. I look around to see if anyone else is home as we enter.

"We're alone. You sounded upset when you called, so I sent my wife to my daughter's so we could talk freely."

Coming here is not without some risk, but he's sincere. I know he won't betray me.

"I don't have much time, so I'll get straight to the point. Antonio and his wife are being held prisoners at my father's house. Do you know who would do that?"

He thinks for a moment. "Tomas?"

Tomas? "Tomas is dead. He's been dead for almost two months."

His forehead crinkles. "No," he says, shaking his head. "Your brother went into hiding because Antonio was trying to kill him, so he could take over Premier. Tomas's been gone, but he's still in charge. He's been sending orders through Gustavo, who replaced me as the head of security when I retired."

Antonio would have never have told me Tomas was dead if he wasn't. I don't spend a second wondering about it.

"No, Ruiz. I don't know who's in charge, but my brother's dead. You have my word."

He puts his hand on my shoulder. "I know you weren't close, but I'm so sorry. What is it you need from me?"

"I need you to talk to the guards at the house. They trust you more than anyone. I'm not asking them to betray their oath by actively helping me. I just need them to let us inside so we can get Daniela and Antonio out."

As I talk, the magnitude of the favor begins to sink in. I'm asking Ruiz to risk his life, and the lives of his family. But there's no choice. Even with a sketch of the interior, we're not getting in there without taking massive casualties, and even then, there's no guarantee that we'll get either Antonio or Daniela out alive.

He lifts his chin, and I expect him to turn me down.

"Rafael, what you're asking might not be a direct betrayal, but I've sent men to their deaths for less."

I have no doubt it's true. I'm fully aware of what I'm asking of him. And I know it's not fair, but I press on.

"If you don't want to do it for me, or for my mother..."

Daniela, forgive me, but I have to do this. I'm sorry. I pull up a picture of Valentina on my phone. "Do it for her."

I hand him my phone, and his eyes narrow as he gazes at the picture. I chose one with a clear resemblance to my mother.

"Her name is Valentina," I explain. "My mother is her grandmother. Her mother is Daniela D'Sousa, Maria Rosa and Manuel's daughter," I remind him. "My brother raped her when she was twelve." The bile rises in my throat as I spit out the revolting truth. "My father set it up." I give it a moment to sink in. "Vera's granddaughter needs your help. Don't let her down."

It's a cheap shot, because I know he believes he let my mother down, but I'm desperate, and right about now I'd sell my soul for his help.

He stares at the picture for some time before handing back my phone. After what feels like a lifetime, he nods. "But if we're going to do this, we need to do it right."

My hand is shaking while I text Cristiano.

It's a go. Meet us at my father's. Stay well back from the property until you hear from me.

76

ANTONIO

The bastards lead me through a door in a wing of the house I've never been in. When we were kids, Abel did business here, and there was always a guard posted at the entrance. But not today.

We go through a maze before we stop. Costa opens the door, and a guard shoves me inside. I see Abel in my periphery, but my eyes go immediately to the woman tied to the chair.

She's alive. She's alive. She's alive.

My heart is about to explode, as the relief courses through my veins.

I kept telling myself she would be alive when I found her, because I needed to believe it. But the goddamn truth is that I wasn't sure.

Daniela's eyes widen when she sees me, and a gasp tumbles out as a sob. This must be terrifying for her—especially before I arrived. *I'm going to tear these fuckers limb from limb.*

Her face is swollen on one side, but otherwise she looks unhurt. But that doesn't temper the rage inside me. I can't stop thinking about how afraid she must have been to be dragged here and locked in a room with this monster.

I need to stay in control so that I can live long enough to send these assholes straight to hell.

I glance at my uncle. His eyes dart from Daniela to me and back, like he's enjoying the spectacle. Although I doubt he's capable of enjoying anything.

"Who's the mastermind? You?" I ask Costa.

He doesn't respond.

"Let her go, and I'll have a large sum of money deposited into your account." He's always been motivated by money. "Surely we can come to an agreement on a suitable amount."

He still doesn't say anything.

"What do you want? D'Sousa grapes? A share of Huntsman Port?" I look from one bastard to the other. No one utters a word.

Gustavo is an arrogant fucker, who isn't anywhere near the man his predecessor was, and Tomas's old guard is nothing more than a punk. There's no chance either of them is running this show. Costa's the only capable one here, but now that we're in this room, he's no longer the big man he was when I arrived.

"Who's in charge?" I demand, my patience something of the past.

"That would be me," a not-so-feeble voice says from the wheelchair.

What the fuck? I side-eye Daniela while I try to come to grips with what's happening. But I pivot quickly, so Abel doesn't have the upper hand for too long.

"Good afternoon, *Tio*," I say cordially. "It appears you've made quite a recovery."

He chuckles, but his movement is halting. If I had to guess, I'd say he's not getting up any time soon. Although Abel has always been clever and dangerous. Not as dangerous as my father, but more dangerous than Tomas or these three pinheads.

"Secure him to a chair," he instructs the guards.

I gaze at Daniela while they're cuffing me to a chair about four feet from her. Her eyes are washed-out, like she's been crying, and it cuts me to the quick. I need to get her out of here. *But how?*

My uncle doesn't need money. *But he wants something.* I have to figure out what that is if I'm going to negotiate Daniela's release.

Abel studies me, shrewdly, waiting for me to blink. I mull over the possibilities, but I keep coming back to the same thing. *He wants me.*

"Whatever this is about, it has nothing to do with Daniela." I keep my tone firm but even. "You have me now. Isn't that what you really want?" It's just a guess, but I'd be willing to bet a large sum on it.

"Don't tell me what I really want, *boy*. You took both my sons from me." He's angry, and I have no doubt he would strike me if he could.

"And you took my life," he continues. "I've been forced to pretend I never recovered my faculties from the stroke just so you wouldn't kill me after you found out about Tomas's child."

Daniela jerks at *Tomas's child*, and her chair shifts a few inches. The guards are alert but they don't move toward her.

Tomas's child. I should have killed you even when I thought you were incapacitated. That was a mistake. I don't say it, because unlike these other three, Abel doesn't care about my power. He's got nothing to lose, and he's likely to take out any disrespect I show him on Daniela.

He's slumped in the wheelchair now. That angry outburst cost him.

"You have me. Let's settle this between men. We don't need a woman to be part of the discussion."

Abel is looking far less alert than he did when I first entered. He appears almost sluggish. It's a two-headed coin. He could fade and I'd be back dealing with Costa, which isn't ideal but preferable, or he could end this before he's too tired to do anything. And by end, I mean he could kill us.

"You want revenge. Take it from me. Real revenge is never satisfying when it's exacted from a woman or a child."

Appealing to his sense of honor is futile. He has none. But I can't leave any stone unturned—not when it comes to her safety.

"I'll take my revenge against you," he snarls. "In good time. But I want revenge from her as well."

"She never did a thing to you."

"Her father killed my brother."

I shake my head. "I killed him." *Just like I'm going to kill you.* "With my bare hands." Abel's top lip curls. I want him to know I'm the responsible party, not Daniela's father. It'll help take some of the heat off her. But I can't provoke him too much. Cristiano needs time to get here.

In the meantime, I want all his attention, all his pent-up fury, focused on me. I just need to figure out how to best make it happen.

I could pretend not to give a shit about what happens to Daniela. It might make him less interested in her—or he might have the guards slap her around to test my resolve. I'm not taking that risk.

Begging is my only option. Although it isn't something I know well.

It will also remind them she's my greatest weakness, and that puts the attention squarely back on her. It's a fine line to walk. *But I have to try.*

"Let her go," I plead with the devil. "She's an innocent."

"She kept my granddaughter from me for all these years." His speech is garbled. "Didn't you, dear?" he asks, like he's some sweet old man.

Daniela glares at him, but she doesn't respond.

"What did I say about asking twice?" The kind old man act is gone. He found a second wind.

It must be the prospect of threatening a helpless woman. *Fucking coward.*

The guard steps toward her with a raised hand, and I tug at my cuffs. *I can't move. Sonofabitch.*

"No!" Abel cries. "Don't mar her face again before the party."

As soon as Cristiano gets here, that's where I'm starting with these fuckers. I'm going to slice off their noses, and shove them into their mouths, and then I'm digging their eyeballs out.

"Just a small dinner party," Abel mumbles, like he's talking to himself. "It'll be just the five of us. But first, I need a short nap to restore my energy."

Costa peers at him like he's crazy. *And he is. Or arrogant.*

It's a mistake to let too much time pass before either moving us to a more secure location, or dealing with us decisively. My men could come storming in at any moment. *Unless he knows something that I don't.*

"Don't worry," he assures Costa. "They're not going anywhere."

77

ANTONIO

After Abel and Costa leave, the two guards check our bindings and go, too. Even from several feet away, I see Daniela's relief when the door shuts behind them.

There have to be listening devices and cameras in this room. My guess is that the guards left us alone to see if they could learn anything about my men and the plan, as if I'm stupid enough to say anything to tip them off.

I could mislead them, but since I don't know anything about what Cristiano and Lucas are planning, it's wiser to keep my mouth shut.

When I gaze at my wife, with her swollen face, bound to a chair but still holding her head up—the angel who has given me so much more than I deserve—I vow to use this time well. Not to waste it in a tirade of vitriol at our jailors, but sharing an intimacy that I never knew before her.

"I've missed you," I tell my beautiful *princesa*. "Although I had a different plan for our reunion."

"I never doubted you'd come," she whispers. "Did you see Valentina?"

"She's safe, and where no one can get to her. I promise."

Daniela gives me a small smile that warms my cold heart.

I don't know what's in store for us, or if Cristiano and Lucas can devise a plan to get us out in time—although I have great faith in them. But if this is the end for me—or God forbid, for Daniela—I want her to know how much I love her. I don't want to die with a single word unspoken.

I don't give a damn who's listening. Certainly not Cristiano or Lucas. I already told them how I feel. And not these fuckers, either. They know she's important to me. That's why they brought her here. I don't care what Abel says about exacting revenge from her. That's just a bonus.

"I'm sorry about what happened at the house before you left. I never meant to hurt you. That woman—"

"Meant nothing," she says, gazing at me with understanding and forgiveness that I haven't done a goddamn thing to earn. "I know. I always knew. But it was extreme—even for you. I worried that you were so far gone, in such despair about your mother's death, that I would never be able to reach you."

"My mother's death leveled me. You're right. But my behavior that night was calculated. I was trying to smoke out an oligarch who we believed posed the greatest danger to you. I wanted to give you the normalcy that you desperately want for Valentina, and above all else, I wanted you to be safe. We believed he was behind everything. Obviously, that's not true."

She nods as the tears roll down her cheeks. "I love you, Antonio. I've always loved you—even when I hated you. When I was a little girl, I would scribble *Daniela + Antonio* in my notebooks, and draw hearts around our names with red ink."

My gut aches as I smile. I had so many opportunities to do well by her, and I let most of them slip away. We were on a solid footing before the plane exploded, but I took too goddamn long to wake up.

"You told me something not too long ago, *Princesa*, that

stayed with me. You said, *I don't know if I would have chosen you then. But I choose you now.*"

"I remember," she says so softly I can barely hear.

"When I signed the betrothal contract with your father, if I had a choice, I wouldn't have chosen you then. You'd always been a little girl in my mind. I never thought of you as a woman, or a partner of any kind. But that morning in your father's office, before you fled the country, I chose you. And I've chosen you every day since. And I will choose you every day for the rest of my life."

Her shoulders shake, as her body is wracked with sobs. The most difficult thing about this moment is that I can't hold her—or even touch her.

"I didn't have anywhere near long enough to love you or Valentina," she says, gazing at me. "But I cherish every second we had together. I'm grateful for the way you pushed me and made me stronger. You gave me an opportunity to be the woman I would have become if that day in the meadow had never happened."

Oh, baby. Emotion is a jagged blade slicing through me—rage, regret, sorrow—only tempered by my overwhelming love for her.

"I did what I know. But it was selfish. I was selfish. I should have done so much better by you."

"We were destined to be together," she replies, wistfully. "I know you don't believe in an afterlife, but I do. My faith is strong enough for both of us. Nothing that tears us apart in this world will keep us apart in the next. I promise." The tears are streaming, but she's smiling.

She's losing faith that we'll be rescued. I want her to believe—for as long as she can—that we're going to get out of here.

"Hey. Chin up. The fat lady hasn't sung." I say the American idiom in English. The men listening won't understand, even if they know the words. But I'm betting Daniela will.

She flashes me a knowing look, but doesn't give anything away.

I just gave her a sliver of hope, although it could turn out to be an empty gift.

When I got back from Morocco, I went to the lodge to get something from my desk. I had planned to ask Daniela to marry me—again. Although last time, I didn't ask. I shoved a piece of paper in her face and demanded she get with the program.

I've been contemplating asking her now—in case I don't make it out. But it seems too self-serving at this moment. Too contrived.

I'm a realist, but I believe my men will get here in time to save her. *Maybe to save us.*

I don't have faith in God, but I do have faith in them.

78

DANIELA

I'm just shy of twenty-five, and this is the fifth time I've been sure I'm going to die. The day I was raped and they killed my mother, when I was in labor with Valentina, on the ship when I fled Antonio's house, and after, in the cave while I waited to be punished. And now. There seems to be something grossly unfair about it.

Somehow this time seems easier. I don't feel quite so alone.

I don't want to die. I've got a daughter to raise and a husband to grow old with.

I'm relieved I never told Valentina that I was her mother. Maybe I'm wrong. I don't know. But I can't help feeling it might be easier for her this way. If I die, and she doesn't know, maybe the loss won't feel as acute.

I glance at Antonio. Someone took a swing at him, and his jaw is beginning to bruise. He's still the most beautiful man I've ever laid eyes on. Inside and out. The outward beauty is there for everyone to see, but he keeps what's inside heavily guarded, under lock and key.

Antonio didn't fall into a trap today. He knowingly risked

his life *to save mine*. He courageously entered the enemy's quarters to make the trade—his life for mine.

It's the greatest gift that one person can give another. There is nothing comparable.

I squeeze my eyes shut to fend off the tears. The fat lady might not have finished, but she's singing the last verse, regardless of what he wants me to believe.

I hope they kill me first. I can't bear to watch him die.

When the lock turns, I sniff loudly to stop the tears before the death squad arrives. The four of them are creepy, and their lecherous looks make my skin crawl as they enter.

They're going to rape me before they kill either of us. *Antonio knows it, too.* They're going to make him watch the way they made me watch while Hugo raped my mother, and then made my mother watch while Tomas raped me. That's their calling card. They don't just destroy. They scorch the earth so nothing can ever grow again.

But they have no idea how tough I am, or how strong Antonio and I are together. No matter what happens, if we're alive at the end, we will rise, and we will flourish.

"Are we ready for a meal?" Abel asks, cheerily.

My mind begins to pull away. *I'm going someplace safe*, it whispers, *where they can't hurt you.*

"Daniela, did you tell Antonio how his father pushed me off you in the meadow before I had my turn?"

I'm not afraid of you. You can soil my body, but you will never touch my soul.

Every muscle in Antonio's body is furled tight. *It's okay*, I want to assure him. *I've been through this before. I know how to deal with it this time. It's going to be harder for you. Don't look at them. Just watch my face, and I'll help you through it.*

It's how my mother got me through it last time. She stayed calm, and she held my gaze, stoically, as Hugo violated her, and then as I was violated. Now that I have a child, I understand. She was dying inside, but she remained outwardly calm to save me from some of the terror I knew nothing about.

Antonio's jaw twitches as Abel talks.

"I wanted you so much that day. But it wasn't meant to be. And now, it's too late." He's angry.

What a sick bastard.

"These men have been loyal to me throughout the years," he continues. "Since I can't have you, I've decided to give you to them as a reward."

I lift my chin and hold my head high. *My body isn't who I am. I'm not yours to give.*

Antonio's tugging wildly at his restraints. "You fucking son of a bitch."

"Don't worry. You and I are going to watch."

Before the words are fully out of Abel's mouth, Antonio propels himself forward and off the floor. Still tied to the chair, he lands on his uncle and knocks them both to the ground.

Antonio is on top, almost bouncing on the old man, trying to inflict as much damage as possible.

The guards yank him off, and they help a shaking Abel back into his wheelchair.

One of the guards reaches for his gun. He raises it and points it at Antonio.

I scream.

Pop! Pop!

"*Fuck*," he shouts. "*Fuck!*"

Seconds later, both doors fly open and the windows shatter, raining glass all over the room. Men swoop in, and before I even recognize Cristiano and Rafael, Abel's two guards are dead.

It's mayhem. I'm not sure if all the men are Antonio's, or if we're in the middle of a battle.

"Keep Costa alive," Antonio growls as he's uncuffed.

His shirt is soaked in blood. *So much blood.* I whimper as

they lay him on the ground, away from the glass. People are hovering over him.

Cristiano frees me. "It's going to be okay. You're safe," he assures me. "Are you hurt?"

I shake my head and rush to Antonio as soon as I'm loose. His eyes are closed. I kneel beside him and reach for his hand. "I love you," I murmur. "I'm right here."

He doesn't open his eyes, but one side of his mouth curls. "*Princesa*," he mouths.

Cristiano puts his hands on my arms and pulls me up. "We need to stay back so the medical personnel can stabilize him," he explains, leading me to a corner out of the way.

I grab Cristiano by the shirt. "I want to stay with him."

"The best thing you can do for Antonio is to let them work on him. They need room to do that. You can be with him the minute they're done."

"Cristiano," someone calls from the doorway.

He squeezes my shoulder before he goes to them. "Just give them a few minutes."

Everything's happening in a slow, hazy motion when I stand on a chair to see better. But even from a higher perch, I can't see Antonio anymore, because the medics are blocking him from view as they work.

Rafael is screaming at his father. *Screaming.* "Where is she? Where's my mother?"

A swathe of metal winks at me from under the desk. When I don't move, the gun beckons me closer. I can't resist the pull.

I climb down from the chair.

Rafael's still shouting at the top of his lungs—the echoes sorrowful and desperate. *The mournful wails of grief.*

I stagger to the desk and pick up the gun. It's heavy. Yet it feels right in my hand.

Something propels me toward Abel. One foot in front of the other until I'm inches from him.

"Get out of the way," I warn Rafael, who stumbles back.

I lift my arm and hold the gun to Abel's forehead. *I won't miss from here.*

With the barrel against his skull, my hands tremble.

His beady eyes are soulless, but not fearful.

He doesn't believe I'll do it. *Or maybe he wants to die.*

I bend my elbows slightly, to help absorb the recoil, like Santi taught me.

"I fed your whore mother to the dogs," he sneers at his son.

I squeeze the trigger.

Again. And again. And again.

Pop! Pop! Pop! Pop!

Blood spurts all over me, along with tissue, bone, and whatever else that holds a body together. Revenge is a messy red shower. It's cleansing and filthy all at the same time.

"That was for my mother," I snarl in a voice filled with so much hate I don't recognize it. Cristiano takes the gun out of my hand, but I don't move until I'm done. "And for Vera, and Lydia, and Isabel."

And for me.

79

DANIELA

It's been a grueling five weeks, but we're healing—all of us. Even Antonio, who was shot twice, at close range. One of the bullets nicked an artery, and he lost a lot of blood. Fortunately, he's young and healthy.

During the delicate surgery to repair the artery, I prayed, and prayed, and prayed. For him. For me. For all of us. *He couldn't die. We needed him. I needed him.*

My most desperate prayers have never been answered. But that day, God granted my plea, despite what I'd done hours earlier.

I killed a man.

And I felt no remorse. Not then. Not now. Nor any day between. *None.*

That part is more unsettling than the fact that a man died by my hand. But the most chilling aspect is that I'd do it again —in a heartbeat.

I shed no tears over this revelation. Abel deserved to die.

Does that make me evil, destined for an eternity in hell? I'll leave it in God's hands to decide.

For now, my family is safe, and I'm packing for Gray and

Delilah's wedding. Although I highly doubt I'll need everything I've laid out on the bed.

Antonio saunters into the bedroom with a manila envelope he tosses on the nightstand. Aside from a scar, his injuries have healed. No thanks to him. The doctor told me he's the most non-compliant patient she's ever met.

"I just spoke to Duarte," he says, casually.

"And?"

"The doctor cleared him to come back to work after the first of the year."

I smile until my cheeks hurt. We're still not exactly sure how Duarte survived. The experts believe that Lara didn't use enough of the toxin to kill him—perhaps because she was nervous about coming into contact with it herself. But it was enough to make him very ill, and it's been unclear, until now, if there would be lasting damage that would prevent him from working.

"We're not moving to Charleston," Antonio quips, surveying the piles of clothes on the bed. "It's just a vacation."

"One more word about how much I'm taking, and you'll have two injured shoulders."

He laughs. It's not forced or heavy. My whole heart smiles.

His mood is lighter these days, even with all that's happened.

It wouldn't have gone as well for him—for us—if he hadn't been wearing a listening device. His men were close, but they entered the house when they did because they heard the commotion.

I pray the luck continues, and the new year brings a fresh start for all of us.

"I'm not here to discuss your penchant for overpacking. I have something for you."

"An early Christmas present?"

"No. Although, maybe for me." He pulls me close and

sweeps my hair behind my ear like he does when he has something important to say.

"If this is bad news, save it for later. Like after the holidays—if it can wait."

"Marry me," he says, without preamble.

I cock my head, my pulse racing. *Marry me?*

Antonio swallows the knot in his throat. "Will you marry me?"

I smile at the inflection at the end of the request. "You're getting good at that."

"It's like learning a new language—a hell of a lot of work. But that's not an answer."

"Maybe I need a minute to mull it over. It's an important decision."

"You need time?" he asks, uncertainty weaving into his voice.

My heart melts. *I don't think I've ever heard uncertainty from him before.*

I shake my head. "I would marry you any day, anytime, anywhere. I don't need to think about it. But unless that thing we did earlier this year was fake, we're already married."

"I want you to choose." He reaches for the manila envelope and pulls out a laminated piece of paper, holding it up for me to see.

It's the betrothal contract he signed with my father. After he's sure I know what it is, he takes it over to the fireplace and tosses it into the fire.

The significance grips me, as I watch the flames eat away at the vestiges of the past.

"I'm releasing you from the betrothal contract," he announces, while my eyes are riveted on the flames. "I want the marriage to be on our terms. Partners."

Partners. The tears well, as the emotion twirls inside—broad satin ribbons in joyous colors, dancing to a jubilant tune. All I've ever wanted from him is to be his partner in life.

"I choose you," I say without hesitation, "and your love. Over everything else, always."

Before the words are out, he drags me to him and claims my mouth until my knees are so weak, I cling to him to stay upright.

His hand is still splayed at my nape, with his fingers in my hair. He tugs my head back gently, to capture my gaze.

He's achingly beautiful. Not just when he smiles, but in those raw, intense moments, like now.

"I don't have a ring for you."

"I have one." I smile, lifting my right hand.

"Let's find something that doesn't remind you—"

I put my fingers to his lips. "I want to be reminded of where we began, and where we are now. The journey is uniquely ours. The rocky stretches and the rolling plains. All of it." I hold out my hand and gaze at the ring, the diamonds sparkling in the light. "I love this ring. It helped you find me."

He kisses the bridge of my nose and pulls away. "While I didn't bring a ring, I brought you this." He hands me the envelope that held the betrothal contract.

"There's more?"

"Open it."

I pull out some documents. The top one is a deed, conveying Quinta Rosa do Vale *to me*. My hands shake uncontrollably as I read, and reread the document.

"It's yours," he says unequivocally. "Back in your family, where it belongs. You can do whatever you want with it."

I smile, thinking about those precious grapes that I doubt he's walking away from completely. *Even in this charming, generous moment, he's still Antonio, after all.*

"Whatever I want?"

He nods. "Whatever you want. I considered putting in a

clause that gave me the right of first refusal if you decide to sell the property. But then it really wouldn't be a gift. At least not the kind of gift my soul wanted to convey."

I wrap my arms around his neck, and he holds me against his pounding heart while I reflect on the magnitude of his gift.

"What would you have done, if I said I didn't want to marry you?"

"I was pretty confident."

I tip my head back, and he smirks—that arrogant, panty-melting smirk that makes me want to climb all over him.

"But when the idea came to me, I was in Morocco. I'd burned a lot of your goodwill before I left. I wasn't sure you'd ever forgive me. But I decided then, that I would abide by your decision, even if I hated it."

I search his face for evidence of the contrary. A gleam in his eye. Another smirk. *Something.* But all I find is love and a rare humility. *He means it.*

I've never loved this man more.

"Although," he teases, tossing me over his shoulder, like he didn't have life-saving surgery five weeks ago, "I would have forever stalked my dirty *princesa* and killed any man who dared speak her name." *He might not be teasing.*

Antonio drops me on the bed, his eyes flaring with the kind of darkness I ache for. No matter how intimate and tender a moment might be, my dark prince is never far away.

EPILOGUE I

Daniela
9 months later

Valentina, my maid of honor, is having her hair styled, in the newly rebuilt bride's parlor at St. Ana's church. I might be the bride, but as far as I'm concerned, she's the real star. I can't help myself from stealing peeks at my smart, gorgeous teenage daughter in the mirror.

Our relationship is on solid footing, now, but seven months ago, when I broke the news that I was her mother, I never thought we'd see this day. The fallout was swift and ugly, and it felt as though the damage was irreparable.

I rehearsed every word I planned to say. Read books about how to break difficult news to teenagers. Talked through every detail with Dr. Lima a hundred times, ran some of it by Antonio, and even Rafael. Still, I couldn't do it.

But it ate at me. *What if she found out from someone else?*

Some nights I tossed and turned, until the first light seeped through the shutters. I was terrified our relationship would never be the same once she knew. I was afraid she'd never forgive me, or worse, that she would somehow think less of herself because of the circumstances surrounding her conception.

I couldn't summon the courage—until one day, at the worst possible moment, in perhaps the worst possible way, while I was exhausted and at my outer limit with teenage moodiness, I broke the news.

I was so ashamed of myself about how it unfolded. I'm still ashamed.

"You're not my mother," Valentina announced for the umpteenth time that day. It was her favorite comeback when she didn't like some rule or restriction.

It never rolled smoothly off my back, but normally I ignored it. Not that day.

"I am your mother."

I panicked when the words came flying out, a wave of fear pulling me under while I stood frozen.

"Not my real mother," she hissed, fists clenched at her side. "My real mother is dead. You'll never be my *real* mother."

The words twirled round and round inside my head, but all my focus was on controlling my shaky voice. There was no turning back now. At least, I couldn't see a viable retreat.

"I'm your birth mother."

There must have been something in my tone or in my expression that made her stop and take notice. "What are you talking about?" she stammered.

I don't know, I wanted to say, or *April Fools!* Anything to make it all go away.

The confusion was scrawled all over her—in her eyes, her

expression, her posture. I knew it would soon turn to anger, again, and maybe to hatred, before there was any hope of things getting better. *They might never get better.*

"Isabel was your mother. But I'm your mother, too," I explained, the way Dr. Lima and I had discussed. "You grew in my belly. I gave birth to you." Despite my efforts to stay calm, the emotion seeped into my voice. "I've loved you with all my heart, from the moment you took your first breath."

Valentina paled as I spoke. "Liar!" she screamed.

The anguish in her voice echoed in my head for weeks. If I close my eyes, I can still hear it.

"I'm sorry. We wanted you to be safe and happy. It might not seem like it, but we did what we believed was best for you. Always." It seemed little more than a hollow excuse.

"You believed lying was best for me?"

I took a deep breath. "From the moment you were born, you were the light of everyone's life, especially mine. But I was too young to raise a child, and I didn't have my mother. Isabel agreed to raise you as her daughter, so that I wouldn't have to give you to strangers."

She didn't say anything right away, but the wheels were turning.

"How old were you? Twelve?" she eventually asked, in a tone that screamed *You're a liar.* "Girls don't have babies at twelve."

By that point, my soul was flayed wide open. "Not usually."

"Who's my father?" she asked so softly, I could barely hear anything but the pain in her voice. The pain of betrayal. *My betrayal.*

As much as I wanted to say something different, I couldn't lie—not about that. But I would use the distancing language, that Dr. Lima helped me with, to describe what happened in a way that would shield her a bit—at least for now.

"I got pregnant by Tomas Huntsman. Rafael's brother."

"He's dead," she said flatly.

I couldn't tell if it was a relief, or not.

"Did you love him?"

I imagined this as a dagger aimed at her chest, and I took a long breath to tamp down the sob. I shook my head. "No."

"He was your boyfriend?"

"No."

The silence wailed as she tried to put the pieces together. It would be a lot for anyone to process, but especially for a budding adolescent who didn't fully grasp relationships, or sex, or how babies develop. I wanted to go to her. I wanted to tell her that I was sorry, again. *I'll never be able to say it enough.* I desperately wanted to do or say *something* that would ease her pain.

But I remained quiet, and as calm as possible, like Dr. Lima instructed. At least on the outside. Inside, a tempest roared while I waited for her cue.

But it never came.

"I hate you with all my heart," she cried, before storming out. "You're a liar, and I'll always hate you for it."

I had been prepared for this. I knew full well this could be her reaction. But nothing could have prepared me for the agony of my heart being torn to pieces. *Nothing.*

"I love you," I called after her as I clung to the doorjamb. "I always have. And I always will."

She never turned around.

I ached to go after her, to wrap her in my arms and beg for forgiveness. But I didn't, because we could only move forward on her terms—at least that's what the expert advised. Valentina was the child and I had to be the adult, even though I was dying inside.

She didn't come down to dinner that night, or the next. I had Antonio check on her, and Rafael, and Victor, and even

Paula, who I'd rehired. *I'm not feeling well,* she told them. *I'm not hungry.*

When I knocked on her door, she pretended to be asleep.

The first night, I let it go. The second night, I went in when she didn't respond and fussed with her covers before placing a small kiss on her head. "I love you," I whispered into her hair, before leaving.

She didn't come out of her room for more than a week. She didn't shower. I'm not sure she brushed her teeth. We brought trays of food up, and Dr. Lima visited her twice. "You need to have patience," she explained, with great empathy. "It's all new for her. She needs time to process it, before she can even begin to deal with the emotions."

I went to Valentina's room every night. Every night I kissed her and told her that I loved her. Every night she pretended to be asleep, even the night the lone tear snuck out from the corner of her eye. My heart ached as I watched it trickle down her cheek.

It was ten days before she rejoined the family, but even then, my sweet girl remained on the periphery. She didn't spare me a glance. Although several times, Antonio caught her studying me when I wasn't paying attention.

I was hurting, but my agony was nothing compared to hers. Every night, I kept going back to her room. I wanted her to know that even if she never uttered another word to me, I would never stop loving her.

After two weeks, I pulled up a chair beside the bed and told her a story. Not the kind of bedtime story mothers read from a book, but the kind they carry in their hearts.

I talked about the first time I felt her move inside me. I described the magic of her kicking, and how I would lay still for hours, waiting for it to happen again.

The next night, I told her how I often fantasized about her

calling me *Mãe*. Not just when I was a girl, but even when I became a woman.

The night after that, I told her how grateful I was that Isabel agreed to raise her, so I could see her every day. I was there for everything. Every cough and sniffle. Every joyous moment. Her first word. The first time she pulled herself up. Her first wobbly step. Her first haircut. And when she lost her first tooth. *Every precious moment was etched into my heart.*

It was more than three weeks, when after I kissed her cheek and turned to leave, she asked, "Did it hurt to have a baby?"

My heart clenched tight, as I lowered myself to the edge of a nearby chair.

"Yes. But Isabel was with me, and that made it easier." I answered her question, but didn't give her more information than she asked for. That's what Dr. Lima, and everything I read, advised.

It was a yeoman's task to talk about harrowing events, *that happened to me*, using a detached clinical approach. But I wanted to protect my baby as much as possible, and I did my very best, even when it felt like I was feeling my way through the dark.

"Did I come out of your vagina or did they have to cut me out?" she asked the following night.

"My vagina. You came early, and you were very small. I didn't have to push for long. You wanted to come out."

I was sure she was thinking about herself, having a baby. It had to be frightening. That's all she asked that night, but I sat there until she fell asleep.

"Did he rape you, Lala?" Valentina whispered into the softly lit room, the following night.

Another dagger aimed at my little girl. I clung to the arms of the chair as I spoke. "He forced me to have sex with him," I explained, trying to keep as much of the emotion as I could out of my voice. One day, when she was older, we could have a different conversation, but right then, I didn't want to burden her with my pain.

"Were you scared?"

"Yes. I was scared."

"Did it hurt?"

"Yes. It hurt."

I didn't tell her the rest. About my mother. Or Antonio's father. None of it. Maybe one day I would tell her. But it wasn't germane to anything she worried about now.

"Did he know about me?" she asked the following evening.

"Not at first. I was afraid he'd try to take you away if he knew. And I didn't think he would be a good father for you. That's why we left Porto after my father died."

"Why didn't you tell Antonio? He would have protected you."

He would have protected both of us, and Isabel too. In hindsight, I should have told him. But at the time, there was no way to know.

"I could have told Antonio. But I didn't know him very well, and Tomas was his cousin. I couldn't take the risk."

It was more than a month before she said a single word to me outside our evening chats, where we would talk while she was in bed with her back toward me.

Antonio was a rock during the entire time. For me, and for her. As was Rafael.

Although Antonio was great with her, he struggled with his own emotions, not only about the rape and his family's culpability, but about me. I tried to shield most of my despair from him, but he knew. *He always knows.*

While I didn't know Rafael's inner struggles, he was there for her one hundred percent, and once she came out of her room, she sought him out regularly. I was so grateful she had him.

Even though Valentina felt we'd all lied to her, I was the one held accountable—as I should have been. Dr. Lima told me that she compartmentalized each of us in our roles. Antonio was the knight in shining armor, who would do battle with the monsters in the outside world. Rafael was her hip friend and closest confidant, who would do anything for her. I was the scapegoat. The place where she unloaded all her anger and fear.

"It's a place of honor," Dr. Lima explained, "and it's also what gives me great confidence that, in time, you'll have your little girl back. She feels safe enough to dump all over you, anytime, anywhere, knowing that no matter how badly she behaves, she won't push you away. You'll always love her."

When things got really bad, I would pacify myself with that knowledge, praying that the good doctor was right.

One afternoon when I went to the kitchen, Antonio and Valentina were already there.

"Sometimes we lie to protect people we love," Antonio explained—while I stood outside the kitchen, with my back braced against the wall, eavesdropping. "Sometimes they lie to protect us."

"You hate lying," she replied.

"I do. But this wasn't a lie anyone told to protect themselves, or to curry favor. This was a lie to protect a little girl they loved. I'm sure you're hurt and confused. And many other things that I can't pretend to know. But this is complicated."

"I feel like my whole life has been a lie. Everyone I loved lied to me."

I had taken lots of blows by then, and a part of me was numb, but the vulnerability in her voice sliced open a new wound.

"You can choose to believe that," Antonio replied. "And you can choose to never forgive Daniela for being part of that lie. Or you can believe, as I believe, that for your whole life, you've been surrounded by people who loved you dearly. You had two mothers. Both who made sacrifices. Both who gave everything they had to protect you. Not many people are so lucky."

She didn't respond.

"The choice is yours, Valentina. One choice might feel too hard right now, but ultimately it will lead to happiness. The other leads to bitterness, and while it seems easier, I bet inside, it doesn't really feel good. And in the long run, it will lead to more loneliness. I'm sure you're already feeling it. You're a smart girl. I have every confidence you'll choose wisely."

I prayed, every day, that she would choose me.

On Mother's Day, almost three months after I told Valentina the truth, my husband gave me a bracelet with a heart-shaped gold locket. On one side, there was a picture of Valentina, Lydia, and me taken from the harvest celebration before Lydia died. On the other, there was a copy of the photograph from my father's desk. The one of my mother and me, wearing a purple tutu.

"You are a wonderful mother," he assured me as I sobbed in his arms. "Selfless and giving. There's no child on this earth who has a better mother. Valentina knows it. That's why it's becoming so hard for her to stay angry with you."

Antonio and Rafael spent the day pampering me, but Valentina avoided me like the plague.

That night when I went up to bed, there was a beautifully wrapped gift and a handmade card on my pillow.

Dear Mom Lala,

I know this gift is babyish, but I didn't get you a Mother's Day present. I've been thinking about the presents I made for my Mom Isabel for Mother's Day. I always gave her the gift I made at school, and all the Mother's Day kisses. It must have hurt your feelings. It makes me sad to think about. I'm sorry. I don't remember all the presents, but I remember making a handprint in kindergarten. I want you to have one, too.

Love,

Valentina
PS. Next year I'll get you a real present.

I cried and cried, before I made my way to her room. She pretended to be asleep, but I knew we'd turned a corner.

———

Paula, along with a few other women, are still fussing over me in the bride's parlor. Hair, makeup, and now the *princesa* dress, with yards and yards of silk tulle fit for royalty. The veil, embroidered with tiny silk roses, will come later.

I'm not sure any bride needs this kind of extravagance, especially me, but I've reveled in every moment of the fairy tale. *Every single one.* My only regret is that my parents, Isabel, and Lydia aren't here to celebrate with us.

There's a knock that startles me. As Paula goes to the door, my eyes are glued there. It's hard not to think about what happened the last time we got married.

I'm sure there are those who wonder why I chose to be married here, again, in a place that holds so many bad memories, and perhaps danger. I'm not a coward, but I'm not a fool, either.

Duarte is stationed just outside the door, and security is tight, even by Antonio's tough standards, and with Abel and Tomas dead, and the Russians no longer a threat, our world is much safer.

Of course, there are the run-of-the-mill troublemakers to be mindful of, those who envy us and are always looking to stir trouble, and other more serious enemies too. But the most dangerous, with their deep-rooted grievances, are somewhere in hell from where there is no escape.

"Wow." Rafael whistles from the doorway. "Wait until Antonio sees you. Even an old man like him—"

He glances at Valentina.

"Will need a foot rub," I tease.

He throws his head back and laughs. Although he still has the heart of a teenage boy, he's filling out in ways that make him look very much like a man. Rafael is smart, and he understands human nature better than anyone I've ever met. Without his quick thinking, Antonio and I might not have survived Abel's devious plan.

"Valentina, when you're done, I need your help in the sanctuary. Nothing major," he assures me with an easy smile.

I don't even ask what he's up to. I'm sure it involves some young woman, and he needs a wingman, or in this case, a wingwoman.

"Don't worry, *Mãe*," my daughter quips, placing her bouquet on the dressing table near mine. "I'm sure it's nothing important."

"Really?" Rafael says to his niece, who's grinning from ear to ear. "That's how it's going to be?"

"We still have plenty of time before the ceremony starts," I tell her. "Keep him out of trouble, please."

As they leave with their heads together, I'm swamped with emotion. *Don't worry, Mãe.* I'll never tire of hearing her call me *Mãe*.

The last few weeks have been a whirlwind of epic proportion, and it's just the beginning. As excited as I am about marrying—*remarrying*—Antonio, I'm also reeling from everything that needs to be done for the harvest.

I convinced the groom we should wait to get married until right before the harvest, when the grapes are almost, *almost*, at peak. *What was I thinking?*

It's not only impossible to gauge when the fruit will be ripe and fragrant, but it's insanely busy at this time of year for him —for all of us, really. But Antonio wanted *this* to be the wedding of my dreams, and he agreed, without batting an eyelash.

Following the ceremony, we're hosting a luncheon for all our guests, under a tent in our backyard. But this evening, under the stars, in my mother's vineyards at Quinta Rosa do Vale, with the scent of ripe grapes perfuming the air, we're celebrating with our family, and our friends, who are like family. It will be a small celebration, the kind my parents would have planned for their only daughter. I miss them, always, but today, especially.

Our wedding will usher in the harvest, and all that follows. Relationships are like the vines, nurtured and fed over the long winter, so that they can root deep, and produce luscious fruit not just for a season, but for a lifetime.

Today is our harvest, when we reap the hard work we've put into cultivating a relationship that works for us. But just as the story isn't over when the grapes are cut from the vine, ours too, is just beginning.

"You look stunning," Paula gushes.

With lots of encouragement, she's emerging from her shell and becoming a fabulous personal assistant. "I loved the dress you wore the first time," she continues, "but this one is even more beautiful on you. You're radiating happiness."

Paula has the good graces not to say, *Unlike last time*. She was in the church on that fateful day eighteen months ago. Like me, she was blessed to be out of the room when the deadly explosion leveled the bride's parlor and nearly destroyed the adjacent chapel. It hurts my heart to think about the senseless death and destruction.

This morning when we arrived, she and I went into the sanctuary and lit a candle for each of the lives lost. I think of them often, especially Nelia and Pinto.

But even before the explosion, there was no joy in the bride's parlor that day. I was a pawn, forced to fulfill the betrothal contract my father and Antonio sealed in blood. Did he drag me kicking and screaming to the altar for all to witness? *No.* But not all chains used to bind a young bride are visible.

This time I'm here of my own accord. My heart is free to love who I choose. The difference is staggering.

"Let me adjust the bustle so that you can move around a little more easily," Beatriz, the young woman who designed my wedding dress, explains. "We'll lower the train when you get to the sanctuary so it doesn't drag all over the floor and get dirty before the ceremony."

I'm wearing a white dress today—not cream, or ivory, or any of the other colors that Clara, the first dress designer I consulted, deigned appropriate for a second marriage, or in this case, a second wedding.

Clara is very talented and much sought after. She designs wedding dresses for all sorts of celebrities and political types. She's also very traditional.

Although tradition is important, especially here in Porto, it's equally as important to know the difference between traditions that move us forward and those that hold us back.

"White is a symbol of purity," Clara told me when I met with her. "Even though we know that few brides are chaste, unless there's a baby bump," she raised her brow, "or a baby, we can look the other way. But a white dress is not appropriate for a second marriage. The bride is no longer pure, and everyone knows it. You don't want to give the gossips any reason to talk."

There was something about the way she talked about purity that made me feel unclean. My insides began to tremble, and for a fleeting moment, I was nothing more than a woman who had been raped as a child. *Dirty. Damaged.*

Clara didn't actually say it, and of course she didn't know, but she made me feel like less, and I'm sure I wasn't the first.

As I composed myself, I remembered something Lydia said to me while we had tea at Samantha's. *"I'm counting on you, my dear, to help Antonio grow into the good man that I know is inside.*

He has the ability to put an end to some of the old ways that are harmful. A lot rides on your success. I have great faith in you."

I glanced at Clara. Antonio wasn't the only one who needed to grow, and he wasn't the only person with the power to put an end to the old harmful ways. *I have a voice, too.*

"If someone like me, who's virtually untouchable, can't wear what she likes, where does that leave other women?"

"It's a wedding," she chided. "Not a political statement. You want your guests to feel comfortable."

It might seem like such a small hill to die on, but progress has to begin somewhere. And even more, I wouldn't make myself small so others felt comfortable with their archaic beliefs.

I sat up tall and flashed her a small forced smile. "It's my responsibility to provide my guests good food and drink, lively music, and a safe venue. It's not my responsibility to make them comfortable with the status of my *purity*. It's none of their concern, and shame on them for even thinking about it."

Clara swallowed hard. It was probably another lesson she'd like to teach me. "Of course," she replied with a brittle smile.

In the end, I chose Beatriz, a lesser known designer, to create my wedding dress. I'm thrilled that it's already given her business a boost.

There's a rap on the door, and Antonio strolls in without waiting to be invited.

"Ladies," the groom, who shouldn't be here, says to Paula, Beatriz, and the stylist, with their jaws on the floor, "I need a moment with the bride. Someone will let you know when I'm finished." In other words, *Don't come back until I give you permission.*

He's handsome, devilishly handsome, but insufferable.

―――

"You're not supposed to see the bride until she walks up the aisle," I warn, after Paula closes the door behind them.

"I'm too impatient for that. I wanted us to be alone, when I first saw you in your dress. It was a good decision," he adds, his voice like coarse gravel.

"Do you like it?" I know from his reaction he does, but I'm a little nervous, and I want to hear him say it.

"It's beautiful. You make it beautiful."

He prowls closer and kisses me roughly. I know exactly where this is going, and we really shouldn't—although the longer we kiss, the more tempted I become.

"Antonio, we can't do this here."

"We're already married," he replies, running his tongue along the shell of my ear.

"We're in a church."

He lifts his head. "Technically, this isn't the church. So don't act like I'm going to lay you over the altar and fuck you until you scream. That's for another time," he murmurs.

Good Lord.

"I'm pretty sure God considers this part of the church. Having sex in a church is blasphemous."

"We're married. God wants us to fuck. It's our duty to make more Catholics. I remember that from catechism."

I laugh. "Catechism? You remember catechism?"

"Only the part about God wanting people to fuck. That left a lasting impression on me."

I smooth the lapels of his tux, to distract him. "You look so handsome."

"Don't deny me. I want you. You want me, too. I'll be careful not to ruin your dress. Let's take it off," he adds, turning me around.

I'll be careful not to ruin your dress. Right. Famous last words.

I have a quick decision to make. Do I give in to the irresistible temptation that is my husband, or use common sense?

When his mouth finds my throat, I whimper, and my decision is made. *Not that it was ever really in doubt.*

"Taking off the dress was supposed to be foreplay for tonight."

"I'm practicing," he mutters, fumbling with the tiny pearl buttons.

"What if someone comes in?" *Or more importantly, how am I ever going to get back in this dress without having to explain to Beatriz that we were...making Catholics.*

"Duarte would never let that happen. Fuck this," he mumbles, impatiently. "Too many damn buttons. I want to tear them off."

"Don't you dare!"

He presses his lips to my forehead. "Don't worry," he assures me, as he lifts the layers of tulle and silk until they're bunched around my thighs.

"Stockings and a lace garter," he mutters, stepping back to admire the lacy white lingerie and silk stockings.

The outline of his hard cock pressed against his trouser zipper makes my mouth water.

"You are a sight to behold, *Princesa*. My dick aches for you," he murmurs, turning me so we're both facing the dressing table mirror.

His eyes are black, and my cheeks flushed as we gaze at each other in the mirror. "I need to taste you. More than I've ever needed anything."

Unbridled lust, woven through the fierce love in his face, is my undoing. As nervous as I am about him tearing my dress, I need him to taste me, too.

"Is your pretty pussy tingling with anticipation?"

My dark prince has a dirty, dirty mouth, and if my pussy wasn't already aflutter, it would be now.

Antonio lowers himself to his haunches, taking my panties

with him, while I gather the silk and tulle billows and hike them higher, trying not to wrinkle the delicate fabric.

He spreads my cheeks, and I shiver as his tongue glides down my crack, to my pussy. His strong hands hold my legs steady, and he licks my clit, until I'm bucking into his face. I whimper as his whiskers rasp against the sensitive flesh.

"You're divine. I think we'll skip the ceremony, so I can spend the day right here, with my mouth on your cunt." He slides two fingers inside me and groans.

I can't take any more. "Antonio," I beg shamelessly, teetering in my wedding heels and trying not to make too much noise. "Let me come."

"It's your day," he murmurs, rising behind me, his long fingers twisting inside my pussy. "Anything for the lovely bride."

I hear the purr of his zipper, as he inches me toward the dressing table, for extra support. He cups a hand over my mouth, and fills me with his thick cock.

I whimper and moan, biting into his fingers to strangle the cries.

"You feel so goddamn good," he grunts, as he fucks me with long, delicious strokes, each powerful thrust filling my grateful pussy, until I'm writhing against him, my thighs quivering.

"Are you going to scream when you come for me, *Princesa*? Are you going to squirt all over your white lace panties? Did you bring an extra pair, or are our guests going to be treated to the scent of your pleasure all day?"

I'm panting, seconds away from orgasm. I clutch the edge of the dressing table and tip my head up.

He's watching me in the mirror. His eyes are heavy and glazed.

My belly tightens, and I gasp and shudder, as his fingers swirl over my clit, faster and harder, until my walls clench around his cock, squeezing the steely shaft as I come apart.

"Good girl. Such a good girl," he mutters, his thrusts deep and erratic, until his body jerks, and he comes with a low, savage grunt.

Antonio rests his forehead on the back of my head for a long moment while we catch our breath.

"Don't move," he whispers, grabbing a handful of tissues from the box on the dressing table before he slides out of me. After he cleans me, and then himself, he tosses the tissues into the trash.

I'm still too sticky and wet to walk up the aisle, *in a church, no less.* I reach for more tissues, but before I can dab off the residue, he swats my hand away and wipes the remaining evidence from my pussy with a pressed, monogrammed handkerchief. *Not that different from the one he offered Valentina when she cried at the funeral. The handkerchief he carries for emergencies.*

When he's done, he folds it neatly and brings it to his nose, before slipping it into his back pocket.

"That's disgusting."

"We'll have to agree to disagree. Besides, I like disgusting," my groom murmurs, with a wicked leer. "The dirtier, the better."

I WATCH from just outside the ornate sanctuary, as Valentina walks up the aisle. Head high, shoulders back. She's growing into the young woman I hoped she'd become. Isabel, my mother, Lydia—and Vera—would be proud of her, too.

Isabel and I tried our best to make sure Valentina had a real childhood. The kind every girl deserves, although she's had to grow up fast in the last eighteen months.

"It's not healthy to miss too many milestones, or to be isolated from friends for long periods," Dr. Lima once explained. *"It's hard to be a well-adjusted adult, if you don't fully experience childhood."*

She might have been talking about me.

I'm supposed to be broken. Or at the very least, my pieces, the ones we could find, should be glued together with some type of adhesive that doesn't adhere all that well. It's been studied extensively by experts, and given the highest stamp of approval: Survivors of sexual assault are irreparably broken, with jagged edges and unsightly crevices. Damaged. *You could cut yourself,* polite society whispers, *if you get too close.*

It's funny, though. I only feel broken when someone remarks that women like me *should* be broken. The rest of the time, I just go on with my life, like everyone else. Yes, being raped at twelve and forced to have a child is—beyond traumatic. I still have nightmares about it. Nightmares that feel incredibly real. Once or twice a month, I wake up gasping, in a cold sweat. And the smell of wildflowers in a meadow can send me into a panic that takes days to fully recover from.

But why do I have to be the one who's broken? Why can't I just be considered a whole, well-functioning human who has an occasional blip? It's the monsters who assaulted me—and my mother—who are broken. They're the ones who are less than human. Disfigured. Damaged. Despicable. *Not me.*

The wedding march begins, and I step into the storied sanctuary, like so many brides have before me. My groom is at the altar with Lucas, Cristiano, and Rafael.

The moment he spots me, he steps into the aisle and waits for me, like a beacon. It's not the timing we rehearsed, but Antonio marches to his own drummer. *Always.*

As I continue up the long aisle, the church could be brimming with congregants or it could be empty. I don't know, because I have eyes only for him.

When I reach the halfway point, Antonio pulls out the handkerchief from his back pocket and brings it to his nose for a long moment, before putting it away. A deep flush warms my skin, as I meet his burning gaze.

My dark prince, handsome and brave, and filthy to the core. The leader the valley requires to thrive. The man our family needs to flourish. My love, who, every day, reinforces my belief that I'm not broken. That I'm a strong, capable woman. Not a victim, but a survivor.

EPILOGUE II

Antonio
10 years later

I nod at Santi and Mia, who are flanking the entrance to the bride's parlor at Santa Ana's, protecting the young woman they've watched grow up, for the final time. After the ceremony, Valentina will be guarded by her husband's men.

"Is it safe to go in?" I ask in jest.

"Do so at your own peril," Santi replies, with a broad grin, as I knock and push open the door.

The room is buzzing with activity, much of it from the little girls who have been eagerly awaiting this day. Catarina Isabel, Anabela Vera, and Viviana Lydia—eight, seven, and five—have larger-than-life personalities, like their namesakes—especially the youngest.

Daniela works hard to make them less demanding and sassy, but I let a lot go. I'm hoping they become obnoxious enough to turn off the boys. *It's a pity I didn't think of it when Valentina was younger.*

While the little girls primp and bicker, Daniela fusses over her oldest daughter's veil.

Valentina makes a beautiful bride, but her mother is hot as sin. *My favorite kind of sin.* We still fight like dogs and fuck like demons, and not a day goes by when I don't feel like the luckiest bastard walking the earth.

There's so much commotion in the room that they don't notice me come in, except for Gabriel Manuel, who never misses a thing where I'm concerned.

"*Papai*," my three-year-old son cries, as he leaps into my arms.

I press a kiss to his chubby cheek and inhale the sweet innocence.

"I have a tie like you, *Papai*." He tips his head back so I can admire the red bow tie.

While the girls are sponges who soak up *everything* around them—good and bad—it's this little boy in my arms who I worry most about. The child who looks to me for clues as he finds his own identity. It's the most humbling responsibility I've ever known.

This is the boy who will one day wear the crown. It's his legacy, just as it was mine. But it makes my heart pound to think about.

I want my son to wear it, just as I want his sisters to wear it, and Rafael, too. But when Gabriel was born, when I held him in my arms for the first time—so tiny, so vulnerable, so innocent—I ached for something better for him. A life that wouldn't keep him awake at night, flirting with the devil.

I knew then that things had to change.

After much deliberation, I broke the crown into pieces, and forged those pieces into something powerful, but manageable, so that by the time my son wears it, the responsibilities won't be quite so heavy.

It's not a perfect solution, but I sleep better at night.

My sexy wife smiles at me from across the room. She's wearing a sleeveless beige dress that dips in the back. Anyone who thinks beige is boring has never seen it on her.

The last time we were in this room together, I fucked her against that dressing table, and watched her come apart in the mirror. *No chance of that happening today.*

But I do need a moment with her. Maybe Rafael can help with this brood. We employ guards, and assistants, and all kinds of help, but aside from Victor and Alma, Daniela rarely allows anyone outside the family to watch the children alone. Some might say it's hypervigilance from her childhood trauma. I say, *Fuck them.* She's an amazing mother, and she can raise her children however the hell she wants.

I turn to Paula, who no longer jumps every time I open my mouth. "Have you seen Rafael?"

"Rafael is kissing a girl near the bathroom," Anabela, the middle terror, blabs.

Of course he is. I guess I should be grateful that they were just kissing. "What girl?"

"It's not your business," Viviana Lydia D'Sousa Huntsman tells me with a hand on her hip.

"Did you see the kissing?" I ask, pointedly.

She nods.

"If it involves you and kissing, it's my business."

In response, I'm treated to an exaggerated eye roll from a child who just turned five.

My wife's fingers are covering her mouth, hiding an impertinent smile. *It's not your business* is one of my lines.

I kiss Gabriel's little fist and put him on the floor, before I get down on my haunches in front of Vivi, as we call her. Unlike her two oldest sisters, she doesn't understand that I can't have that kind of disrespect in public.

"It's not polite for little girls to roll their eyes at adults."

"Or little boys," Anabela pipes in.

I glance at her.

"It's not polite for girls or boys to roll their eyes," she clarifies in case I missed the point.

"It's not polite for girls *or boys* to roll their eyes," I tell Vivi. "And I know you're a polite girl."

She nods, with a smile. "Yes, *Papai*."

This is my life now. Bossy know-it-all females everywhere I turn. *The sparkle in my day.*

Daniela comes over and presses her palms to my chest. "Are you here for the charm offensive, or do you need something?"

There's a touch of sass in her voice that makes my dick twitch.

"*Princesa*, you're raising mouthy daughters," I tease. "What are we going to do about it?"

Her lips are pressed together, eyes glittering. Any lesson she can't teach me, her daughters surely will. *Lydia Huntsman is cheering them on from heaven.*

We converted my mother's house into a shelter for survivors of domestic violence. Sonia chairs the board, and Daniela is heavily involved, although her work is strictly behind the scenes and anonymous. That's the most I was willing to compromise. I've been taught some new tricks, but I haven't learned to roll over—even for my sexy wife.

"I came for you." I take her hand. "I need a private word."

"Is everything okay?"

"More than okay."

She studies my face for any sign of trouble. "We need to take the children to the bathroom one more time before the ceremony starts."

"This will only take a few minutes. We'll be just across the hall. Someone else can take them, or they can wait. They'll be fine until we get back."

Out of the corner of my eye, I notice Catarina, who is

almost nine, pursing her painted lips in the mirror. *Jesus Christ.* "What is that shiny shit on Catarina's mouth?"

"Shhh!" Daniela hisses. "It's just a little pink-tinted gloss."

"I don't like it."

She rolls her eyes. *No secret where Vivi gets it from.* "It makes her feel special. By the time the ceremony starts, it'll be gone. If you make a big deal about it, she'll start sneaking makeup out of the house when we're not watching."

"I'm always watching."

Daniela glares at me.

"I still don't like it."

"I only have a few minutes," she says, warily, redirecting my attention like she does with the kids.

"Let me just say hello to Valentina."

The bride is having her makeup done, which I'm not crazy about, either. But she's a grown woman and it's her wedding day, so I keep my mouth shut, as I intrude for a moment.

"You're a gorgeous bride, *menina*." I squeeze her hand, and the girl who I adopted when she was thirteen—*the young woman*—gifts me a brilliant smile. "I'm borrowing your mother for ten minutes. We'll be in the bride's chapel if you need us."

"Saying a prayer for world peace, or trying to hide from the children?" she asks, her eyes dancing with mischief.

"They're not mutually exclusive," I reply dryly, taking Daniela's hand, again, and dragging her out before one of the kids needs something. Because someone always needs something from her. *Usually me.*

"The chapel?" my wife asks, when Mia and Santi are out of hearing range. "I'm not having sex with you in the chapel."

I laugh. "Don't put ideas in my head, *Princesa*. You know how much I love a challenge."

Several of my guards are outside the chapel when we arrive. "Is our guest inside?"

"Yes, *senhor*," the most senior replies.

"Antonio," Daniela sighs, as I open the heavy doors. "Valentina's getting married today. What's this all about?"

It's a surprise that I promised not to ruin, and I won't. "You'll see."

When we walk in, an old man is sitting on a bench, with a nurse beside him. He stands with the help of a walker as we approach.

He's had a lot of plastic surgery, and even his eye color is different now. Daniela doesn't seem to recognize him. It's been more than ten years since they last spoke.

It was a time when our life was hell. Oligarchs, and traitors, and Abel Huntsman who masterminded most of the terror, pulling the strings from what we believed was his deathbed. My uncle was a psychopath, who had everyone fooled. In the end, he was a worse human being than my father.

"It's been a long time, but I couldn't resist Rosa's granddaughter's wedding," the man says, through misty eyes. His body might be weak, but his voice is still strong.

"Dimitri," Daniela gushes, taking his hands and placing a kiss on each sunken cheek. "I think about you often. Each time I visit my parents' grave, there are roses. I prayed you were still alive, but—I assumed you had an arrangement with the florist."

Dimitri Fedorov, former *Pakhan*, smiles at her, with great affection. "I was touched each time you left roses at my grave, and heartbroken that I couldn't tell you I wasn't in the car when it exploded."

She turns to me, brow raised. "Did you know?"

"Not immediately. Although I've known for years. The stakes were high, and it wasn't my secret to share."

"I am forever in your debt, Huntsman. I've watched your career from afar. You've aged well. Earned your arrogance." He turns to my wife, who is still holding his hands. "And you, my dear, are even more lovely than I remember."

"Will you join us this evening at Quinta Rosa do Vale?"

My wife just invited the former leader of the European Bratva to a family party, without checking with me. She's lucky it's our daughter's wedding day.

"It's a small, private celebration."

He shakes his head. "I'm too old for parties. Soon I'll be seeing your mother. I wanted to be here, so I could tell her about the wedding, and what a wonderful woman you are, and that you're raising beautiful children. And how you were strong enough to make a good man out of Huntsman. So much more of a man than he would have been without you."

He's right, on all accounts, especially the latter.

She embraces him. "May I come visit you?"

"As much as I'd love that, it would put us both in grave danger, and my family as well. I've kept my identity hidden for them, more than anyone."

"If you change your mind, or if you need anything, promise you'll get in touch."

"Take care of each other," he tells us, before the nurse helps him out of the chapel.

"Thank you," Daniela murmurs, with her soft hand on my face.

When Fedorov first got in touch with me about the wedding, I was reluctant to allow him to come. But I knew it would make her so happy to see him, and there's little I won't do to make her happy.

"I wish I could bring back everyone you miss. I love you, *Princesa*. If I had my way, you would never want for a single thing or shed a single tear over anything, but some things are beyond even my capabilities."

"You've given me everything I could ever want." She stands on tiptoe and presses her lips to mine. It's gentle and sweet, with the promise of forever—at least that's how it begins. By the time I pull away, she's panting, and my balls ache.

"I'd love to christen the chapel, but I have a daughter to

walk up the aisle. You're far too tempting, and I won't be satisfied with a quickie. Not today. But tonight, *meu amor*, after the guests have gone home and the children are asleep, you're mine. And I'm going to defile every inch of that gorgeous body."

"Your dirty *princesa* will be waiting for you at the end of the night," she says, with a sultry gleam in her eyes that makes my chest rumble. "What should she wear for the occasion?"

Before I can reply, *Not a goddamn thing*, there's a knock.

"It's time," Paula says, from behind the door, piercing our bubble.

———

While the last of the guests are seated, I steal a few minutes alone with Valentina in the bride's parlor. She's an amazing young woman, so much like her mother. I'm honored to be her father.

"You're beautiful, inside and out, *menina*. I'm so proud of you."

She beams at me.

When Valentina asked me to give her away, the first thing that popped into my head was, *Fuck no. I'm not giving you to anyone. I'll escort you up the aisle, but I'm not giving you away.*

Old dog. New tricks.

I wasn't surprised when she came to me. Marco was smart enough to seek my permission *before* he asked her to marry him. He's a good kid, and I've been able to be more magnanimous about him than one might expect, mostly because Rafael has been like a hound with a bone from the moment he started coming around. Rafa checked him out so thoroughly, I wouldn't be surprised if he knows the exact length of Marco's large bowel.

"Sometimes brides plan grand weddings," I tell my daughter, "with all the trimmings, and at some point, even if they realize it's a mistake, they're afraid to turn back. They're afraid of the embarrassment, or of disappointing their families. Your mother and I would only be disappointed if you went through with a marriage you had misgivings about because you were concerned about us."

She touches my arm. "I love Marco. We love each other. He's a good man, and he's good to me."

You wouldn't be marrying him today if I thought otherwise.

"We love you. I hope you know that you'll always have a room in our house. Married couples have struggles and disagreements, as they build a life on the terms that suit them. But at no point in that life should you ever be afraid for your safety." I tip her chin, until our eyes meet. "That cannot be part of any equation, *menina*. Any problems, even if you're not sure if it's a problem, you come to me, or to your mother, or to Rafael, and we'll help you."

She nods, before getting her bouquet. "I'm sure Rafael will be a big help," she snickers. "Bury Marco first, ask questions later."

I open the door to the hall. "If I were you, I'd be more concerned about your mother."

Valentina chuckles, but as soon as she steps out of the room and spots her guards, a different kind of emotion swamps her.

She throws her arms around Mia, then Santi. There are a few tears, and then a quick makeup check before we take the short walk to the sanctuary.

We wait as the bridesmaids, and Alexis, the maid of honor, march up the aisle. And while several women smooth the train of Valentina's dress, I watch my three princesses, the flower girls, toss rose petals from white wicker baskets, as though it was the most important thing they've ever done. I chuckle at their serious demeanor. The little drama queens have been practicing for weeks.

Finally, the wedding music changes, cuing us it's time. I

force down the lump in my throat, as my oldest daughter stands on tiptoe, pressing a kiss to my cheek, before linking her arm through mine.

"You'll always be my hero, *Papai*," she whispers. "Always."

An imperfect hero, who struggles every day to be a better man, and leave a better world for her, and Rafael, and her sisters, and brother. But mostly I strive to be the man deserving of my *Princesa*, who owns me, heart and soul.

Thank you for reading **ENVY!** If you loved Rafael Huntsman, you can read his story, **PRIDE, HERE**

To read more about Gray and Delilah, begin with Depraved, **HERE**

JOIN me in my FB group, JD'S CLOSET, for all sorts of shenanigans **HERE**

If you enjoyed ENVY, I would be so grateful if you left a review so that others can find it too!

A FINAL NOTE FROM EVA

A prequel novella, three novels, and two extended epilogues... congratulations, you made it to the end of A Sinful Empire Trilogy! Your, *ahem*, prize is a rambling author's note, along with all my love, and endless gratitude for sticking with the series, and with me.

As a side note, for everyone who's asked: I'm going to Bourbon country, but first, Rafael Huntsman is getting his own book!

Back to Envy, I'll begin with the light topic, first.

Why Porto?

Porto is one of Europe's oldest cities, a jewel box, nestled along the banks of the Douro River, and the Atlantic Ocean. It has a rich history that comes alive as you stroll along the water, or through the old neighborhoods, admiring the *azulejo* facades and Romanesque architecture. The series was conceived several years ago while on a trip to the region. I was seduced by the cobblestone streets, steep hills, historic churches, lush vineyards, and of course, the Port, with its storied traditions. It was during a tour of a Port cave, in a two-hundred-year-old port lodge, that the characters first came alive. They appeared as I explored the tasting rooms and the dark caves, meandering down dimly lit aisles flanked with casks of aging Port, all while soaking up the vibe and letting my imagination run wild. Right from the start, the characters were larger than life, and chatting non-stop—except for Antonio who was always growling about something.

Some of the traditions and locations I mention in the books, like the Majestic Café, are real, and others, like Santa Ana's Church, are figments of my imagination, or a collage of places and events stitched together. The Portuguese are warm and friendly people. They will feed you well, and offer you their best wine and Port. If it's not already, put Porto on your bucket list!

Who are the three amigas? (Not to be confused with the Three Maria's, who deserve much gratitude as well)
Many years ago, I met a young Portuguese woman, "Z", who became a colleague and a friend. She grew up in Northern Portugal, where Porto and the Douro Valley are located. Z is the youngest of five sisters, and her mother was a mid-wife who practiced at a time when Portugal was led by a ruthless dictator, and the Catholic Church informed much of what happened in families and communities around the country. Women's rights were essentially non-existent during that time. (It's important to note that while Portugal was slow to evolve, they have made monumental strides with regard to women's rights, and in many ways, they've now surpassed other Western countries. This is especially true of Porto. But those changes didn't begin to happen until the 1970s).

Z told stories of playing with her sisters in strangers' yards while her mother delivered babies inside, or disseminated birth control, which was illegal at the time, or provided other health care services to women. In addition, Z's mother had a small group of like-minded friends, who together, arranged to have women in abusive relationships shuttled, and sometimes smuggled, to safe locations in, and out of the country.

The government had "spies" everywhere, sometimes pitting neighbor against neighbor. These courageous women shunned the law, and took enormous risks to ensure that other women were not only physically, but emotionally safe. Z's mother was lucky. She was never caught, but others were not so fortunate.

Outside of a small corner of academia, or the stories that their daughters and granddaughters keep alive, little is known about the women who formed the quiet, but mighty resistance. Through Lydia, Maria Rosa, Vera, and even Sonia, this series pays homage to those women who risked everything to make life better for their sisters, at a time when women had so few rights. Now you know about their heroic efforts, too.

How did childhood sexual assault find its way into a romance novel?

I have a lot to say on the subject, but I'll begin with this: Survivors of sexual assault deserve a happily-ever-after as much as anyone else.

I endeavored to tell Daniela's story in an honest way, one that not only did her justice, but respected the stories of all survivors. What made this especially difficult, is that despite what many believe, survivors are not a monolithic group. Each has her own life story, her own struggles, and a unique path that, hopefully, leads to a safe place.

Since the Lust release, I have received more correspondence than I ever have after publishing a book. Some of it from readers who are enjoying the series, (or not), but many of the messages and emails are from survivors of sexual assault. I'm humbled, and overwhelmed with emotion by each contact, by every survivor who shared her story, or thanked me for making my heroine a survivor (although I'm certainly not the first to do so), and for normalizing Daniela's adult sexual needs and fantasies. In a few sentences, I'll try to capture some of the sentiment for you. There are common themes, and we can all benefit from hearing them:

Society wants her victims/survivors to be chaste, with petite, vanilla sexual appetites. If you enjoy kink, or have a large appetite, or multiple partners, you're a tarnished victim—or maybe you don't deserve to be called a victim/survivor at all. Blaming and shaming weigh heavily on almost everyone who's reached out. We should be cautious about using language that shifts blame, always, but perhaps, even more when discussing childhood sexual assault. Beware of words like parentified, precocious, oversexualized, and hypersexualized. They are the equivalent of asking, about an adult survivor, *What was she wearing?* Sexual assault happens *to someone*. It isn't the sum of who they are. This isn't everything readers have shared, but it's a good representation.

I'm also a survivor of childhood sexual assault. I've kept it a closely guarded secret throughout my life. Before this, only a handful of people knew. Other than in a rare, fleeting moment, I'm not ashamed of what someone did to me—that's on them. Overall, I'm tough and resilient. But there's a piece of me that's fragile and vulnerable, and under certain circumstances, I can be made to feel like less, without much effort.

Mostly I've kept the secret because I hate to be viewed as broken or damaged, and the best way to prevent that, has been to keep my mouth shut. But as I unearthed Daniela's story, and read your messages, I realized it's time, maybe long past time, for me to find the courage to speak, too.

When we share our experiences, we make others feel less alone, less anxious, less ashamed. If a woman, like me, white, well-educated, straight, financially secure, and in a supportive, loving relationship—virtually untouchable—can't stand up and be counted, then no one can.

Maybe you've experienced sexual assault, or maybe you've had another kind of trauma, or maybe you've been spared, but still, you question your value. This is for you, for everyone who has ever felt like they're not pretty enough, smart enough, good enough, or worthy. For anyone who has ever felt tarnished or dirty: **You are not broken. You are not damaged. You are beautiful. And special. Your light can shine brightly, if you let it. You deserve a happily-ever-after of your very own.**

Don't just gloss over the words. Read them again. Internalize them. Let them seep into every fiber of your being. You deserve a full, happy life, and you can have one. No one will ever convince me otherwise.

If you don't know where to begin, start here. I've included the domestic violence hotline too, because sexual assault often plays a role in domestic violence.

The National Sexual Assault Hotline (RAINN): 1-800-656-4673

The National Domestic Violence Hotline: 1-800-799-7233

Childhelp National Child Abuse Hotline: 1-800-422-4453

ACKNOWLEDGMENTS

Writing a trilogy is a huge undertaking with lots of highs and lows. There was hand-wringing, some tears, and a lot of uncertainty, but I loved these characters with all my heart and soul, and I wanted to do right by them, and by you. Fortunately, I had boatloads of love and support along the way, much more than I deserve.

I am blessed, and I don't say that lightly, to have so many wonderful people in my corner. I will be forever grateful for your kindness, generosity, wisdom, and support. Thank you to everyone who helped breathe life into Daniela and Antonio's story!

A big thank you and a big hug to Veronica Adams, for your encouragement, support, and most of all, for your friendship. You can step in, without batting an eyelash, and make anything better. You have helped me grow in ways that are immeasurable, and I will always be grateful to you.

A BIG Thank you to Sarah Ferguson who mailed HUNDREDS of wedding invitations and swag, and kept the trains moving while I was writing. You are amazing! You are highly organized, and your guidance throughout this project has been invaluable.

An enormous, super colossal thank you to Dawn Alexander for guiding me through the process with the utmost patience and good humor. You kept me on track, and honest, even when I really wanted to make those timelines fuzzy. This series benefited immeasurably from your ability to see the forest through the trees. Envy would have NEVER been completed on the short timeline without your feedback and support. Thank you from the bottom of my heart!

A very big thank you to Nancy Smay who edited the prequel, Lust and Envy. Your willingness to be flexible was a God-send, and your attention to detail, big and small, made the books so much better. I included a dark church, but I kept smirks to a minimum, and bossy instructions to shower out of this series. Aren't you proud of me?

A big thank you to James Gallagher who edited Greed, and who didn't blink an eye at my bossy, dirty talking characters. I learned so much from your careful edits and comments!

Thank you to Becca Hensley Mysoor, who supported the series from the beginning, and gave me the boost I needed to write on. The bible you made for me is truly a work of art! I SO appreciate your kindness, generosity, your positivity, and your gorgeous smile. The world needs more people like you!

Faith Williams, your thoroughness and attention to detail is incomparable. You are the polish that makes the story shine. I'm always amazed not only by what you find that no one else did, but how you can give an off-the-cuff answer, anytime, anywhere, as to why something is grammatically correct, or not. It's impressive.

A heartfelt thank you to Virginia Carey who I trust to be the very last set of eyes on my books before release. Your eagle eye during the final proofread always catches the little things that were missed along the way. When you say a manuscript is ready for publication, it is. More, I cherish your support and friendship.

A giant thank you to Murphy Rae! You are an extraordinarily talented designer, professional, easy to work with, and just plain lovely. Thank you for taking my primitive idea and turning it into something spectacular! I hope my stories do your covers justice. Also, can you look at figs, yet, without getting a migraine? I can't...

An enormous thank you to the sensitivity readers who pushed through the pain, held their breaths, and read Lust—every difficult word, from the first page to the last. You are angels, and it's impossible to thank you enough for the peace of mind you gave me.

Thank you, thank you, thank you to Danielle Rairigh and Tami Thomason, who Beta read all three books, and the prequel novella. Your insight made each of the books infinitely better, and your unwavering support during the process is something I'll never forget.

A very big thank you to Skye Warren, an outstanding writer, entrepreneur, mentor, and human being, who never hesitates to put out her hand and lift someone up. Somehow it doesn't seem like anywhere near enough, but thank you for all your guidance and support, and for everything you do for the author community.

I don't even know how to begin to thank the Bloggers, Bookstagramers, and Booktokers who have given the series so much love. I SO appreciate your generosity and kindness, and I will always be grateful for everything you did to help launch A Sinful Empire. You make the book world turn, not just for me, but for an entire genre. Thank you for your tireless energy and generosity of spirit!

To the AMAZING members of JD's Closet and Bad Boys in Books, I've said this before, and I'll say it again: I love, love, love you all so hard! When my confidence is shaky, or my day has been long and prickly, you lift me up and nudge me forward. You're the very best thing that's happened in my writing career. It also bears repeating that, in a world filled with drama and intolerance, the empathy, support, and kindness you show not only me, but each other is awe-inspiring.

A heartfelt thank you to the readers—to everyone who read

the series, reviewed, and told your friends about it! Your ongoing love and support is humbling. I am truly grateful for all the love you've shown my characters, and me. You fill my heart with endless joy, and inspire me to keep writing even on the days when the words don't come easily.

Andy, there really are no words to thank you for loving me the way you do. You are my rock—the love of my life. *I only wish that I had met you sooner, so I could have loved you longer. Te amo, meu amor.*

ABOUT THE AUTHOR

After being a confirmed city-girl for most of her life, Eva moved to beautiful Western Massachusetts in 2014. She found herself living in the woods, with no job, no friends (unless you count the turkey, deer, and coyote roaming the backyard), and no children underfoot, wondering what on earth she'd been thinking. But as it turned out, it was the perfect setting to take all those yarns spinning in her head and weave them into sexy stories.

When she's not writing, trying to squeeze information out of her tight-lipped sons, or playing with the two cutest dogs you've ever seen, Eva's creating chapters in her own love story.

Sign-up for my monthly newsletter for special treats and all the Eva news!
Eva's VIP Reader Newsletter

I'd love to hear from you!
eva@evacharles.com

MORE SEXY ROMANTIC SUSPENSE BY EVA CHARLES

A SINFUL EMPIRE (TRILOGY COMPLETE)

Greed

Lust

Envy

Pride

THE DEVIL'S DUE (SERIES COMPLETE)

Depraved

Delivered

Bound

Decadent

CONTEMPORARY ROMANCE

NEW AMERICAN ROYALS

Sheltered Heart

Noble Pursuit

Double Play

Unforgettable

Loyal Subjects

Sexy Sinner

Printed in Great Britain
by Amazon

20123306R10226